The nice thing about being a modern-day undead in general and werewolf in particular was that the whole clothes issue had been solved by brighter minds generations earlier. So while I went more wolfy, my clothes didn't rip and shred so that I wouldn't be naked when I went back to human form. The Spandex-poly blend was a shape-shifting undead's best friend and it was spelled to let our fur through, so when we were in wolf form we didn't look like we were wearing stupid dog coats.

I shoved my so far useless special gun back into its rear holster, did my best to guess where this thing's vulnerable spot was, and gave it the old werewolf leap. I landed on what you could generously call its head and started clawing and biting.

"Go, Vicki, go!" Maurice was all over the cheering.

"This thing tastes worse than whatever's in the trashcans. And a little aerial support wouldn't be considered an insult."

Amanda flew up and landed on what I was going to insist, until told otherwise, was the thing's back. Vamps can do the whole extend the claws thing, too, and when they're really pissed, frightened or fighting something a lot stronger, they go all Nosferatu. It wasn't Amanda's best look, but then again, I wasn't going to win Best in Show, either.

GINI KOCH

THE NIGHT BEAT
From the Necropolis Enforcement Files

The Night Beat, From the Necropolis Enforcement Files
Published by Gini Koch at CreateSpace

Editors: Mary Fiore and Veronica Cook
Cover Artist: Lisa Dovichi

First Edition
ISBN: 978-1-47763-1386

Gini Koch
http://www.ginikoch.com

🐾 Dedication 🐾

To all those who wear a badge, uphold the law, and fight the good fight -- thank you.

🐾 Chapter 1 🐾

We pulled up to the scene of the crime. Such as it was. An alleyway in downtown, filled with trashcans and darkness.

"What do you think?" Jack asked as we got out of the ugly sedan that was supposed to fool the criminal class into thinking we weren't undercover cops. So far as I could tell, it had never worked in the history of law enforcement, but we kept on perpetrating the illusion.

I looked around. There was an amazing lack of activity. There was also a lack of anything that looked even slightly crime-like. Not that this meant anything. "See, that's what I love about you. We haven't even taken a look at the crime scene, and you're already asking me what I think about it."

He shrugged. "You have good instincts."

Yeah, if he only knew. Then again, I didn't want him to know.

I sniffed. "Something smells awful."

Jack pointed. "Well, those overflowing trashcans might be the stench culprit. Can your tender senses take it? Don't want you fainting on me again."

"Like you didn't love it."

He grinned. "Yeah, well, I'll admit getting to act all heroic was kind of fun. But, damn, you come out of a faint nasty."

Jack had been lucky I'd come out of the faint feeling sick, not hungry. Then again, I was lucky, too. Good partners are hard to come by. Good-looking ones who are also single and might, possibly, one day be interested in a high-excitement relationship were as rare as virgin groupies. Which, per some of my friends, meant very rare to potentially extinct.

I shook myself to get my mind back on the matter at hand. What I'd smelled wasn't trash. "Why are we alone here?"

"No idea." Jack pulled his gun as he reached into the car to grab the radio. "Darlene, this is Detective Wagner. Weren't we supposed to have a couple black and whites here?"

The radio crackled. "Yes. Two cars, four uniformed officers." Darlene sounded mildly worried. I was already past that.

I sniffed again. I didn't smell anything living, though the trash could be interfering. But the stench I was picking up wasn't trash, and the odds of anyone alive being in this alley were slim moving to none. I moved into the alley slowly, all senses on the alert.

"Victoria, get your damn gun at the ready!" Jack didn't make it sound like a suggestion.

He was right, and I knew it. But I took out the special gun I kept at the small of my back. It was smaller, but the projectiles were more effective. I sniffed the trash bins as I went by. I also activated my wrist-com. I was far enough away from Jack that he wouldn't hear. "This is W-W-One-Eight-One-Niner."

"Good evening, Agent Wolfe." The Count's voice was silky as always. He had unperturbed down to an art form. In all the years I'd known and worked for him, he'd never once lost his cool. "Status?"

"Four uniforms and two squad cars missing. Downtown alley, loaded with trashcans and stink. Special stink."

"We have so many varieties of special stink, Agent Wolfe. Truly, make a selection and advise."

"Snacked on the uniforms as appetizers and ate the cars for roughage kind of stink."

"Ah. Do you require backup?"

"Ya think? It's just me and my partner here. My *human* partner."

"Yes, the human partner you pant after."

"Funny. The human partner I want to both keep alive and keep in the dark. I'd like to see the sunrise, too."

The Count sighed. "It's overrated. Fine. Aerial support on the way. Underground support already activated by Agent Goode."

Good old Monty. I thanked the Gods and Monsters for his rebel attitude. He didn't like to follow orders but he was all over following me. He said I always landed the best cases. If his parts didn't fall off on a regular basis, we might be an item.

"Great news." I was at the end of the alley. No more trashcans, no sign of anything. Murky darkness in front of me. I pointed my gun into the center of it. "This is Prosaic City Police, drop your weapons, put your hands up, and come out slowly."

No movement, no noise. No surprise. I sighed. I couldn't risk a look over my shoulder. I hoped Jack was still at the other end of the alley, covering me. "Fine, have it your way. This is Necropolis Enforcement. Drop any non-organic weapons, put your arms, flippers, claws, tentacles, or any other extremities up, and walk, slither, stomp, crawl, et cetera, out of the darkness or be exterminated with extreme prejudice."

The murky darkness started boiling up and moving. It was still murky and dark, but it was forming into a shape. I stared at it as the hair on the back of my neck started to rise. My nails extended and so did my teeth. Some things you can't stop, even if you want to. Fight or flight is in every living being that's got mobility. And even beings like me have a fear of the dark, the *old* dark, built into us.

"Count?"

"Yes?"

"We are in *so* much trouble."

Chapter 2

"Jack, stay back and take cover!"

I heard him shouting for backup. Great idea, but not under these circumstances. I tried to figure out how to tell him to belay that without explaining why, while at the same time backing slowly to keep out of reach of the monster in front of me.

The sound of large wings floated on the wind and I wasn't alone any more. "Vic, what's up?"

"Um, Amanda, I thought vamps had the best night vision and all that."

"I was just being casual and human-like in my form of greeting." Amanda Darling was both a vampire and my best friend. She was older than me and sometimes had trouble letting go of the old-speak. "I can see what's in front of us. Unfortunately."

Someone behind me snorted. "She's so cute, isn't she? Pathetic, but cute." Maurice swished into view. He didn't have to swish, but he really enjoyed it. Unlike his sister, Maurice adapted to whatever age and mores he was in without a blink or a twitch. We all envied and hated him for that ability. "What have we here? A big, manly slime monster from the bowels of the earth? I'm all a-flutter."

"You know, Maurice, a gay vampire is so clichéd."

"But, Vicki, I do it so well." Maurice and Amanda looked alike. That was it in terms of proof of real blood ties. Then again, for our kind, blood ties were made as easily as born.

The slime monster was undulating. I didn't think that boded well for us. "Someone needs to distract Jack."

"Ooooh, I will!" Maurice said. "He's so tall, dark

and handsome."

Amanda and I risked it and exchanged the "he's such a jerk" look. "Maurice, Jack's straight," she said. "And he's Vic's."

"Not yet," another male voice said. Ken Colt was one of the younger vamps, but he was a natural. He did the whole turning to mist and hover invisibly thing as easily as breathing. Easier, all things considered. "But I agree, the human needs to be distracted. Who do you want to do it, Vic?"

"You." Ken wasn't gay, wasn't female, and Jack knew him. He knew him as my ex-boyfriend, but that wasn't important now.

Ken sighed. "Figures. Jealous to get you back or just chat sports?"

"Whatever, Ken. Kind of busy here."

"Doing nothing. Fine, fine, going off to distract and protect the human. I think I'm going with mind-control, though. We want all those human snacks sent back to police headquarters."

"Good, good. Carry on." The slime monster was forming tentacles. "Count, we're going from bad to worse."

"Slime monsters are difficult, Agent Wolfe, but hardly worth the panic in your voice."

"How about something that looks like a slime monster, but isn't. You know, something with tentacles and no face and that sort of fun thing?"

"Ah. How big?"

"Pretty damned." Amanda and I said that together. Because it was growing.

"I think we need to call in H.P.," Maurice said in a small voice. Maurice didn't scare easily.

The Count sighed. "The professor is resting."

"This is his area and we're not equipped for this," I snapped. "Slimy here has eaten four of Prosaic City's finest, eaten two of our snazzy squad cars and, most likely, several bums, hookers, and drug dealers. For all I know he has some pigeons in there, too."

"Rousing the professor now. He'll be to you shortly."

"What about Edgar?" Amanda asked.

"Not his forte," Maurice said dismissively. "He's better with the human side of things." This was true.

The slime monster that was more than a mere slime monster continued to form. I continued to shift into full attack form. Nails an inch long and razor sharp? Check. Fangs ready to rip and tear? Double-check. Eyes and ears altered to see and hear better? You got it. Damned fur all over my body, doubling as camouflage and protection? Sure. Problem was, in this day and age, fur wasn't camouflage any more. Fur was a sign you were odd at best, and a werewolf at worst.

I was both. I was also out of options. The monster finished forming. It was twelve feet tall if it was an inch, and almost as broad as the alley. I aimed for what was likely either its head or its main organ area and fired.

Chapter 3

"Impressive lack of something happening," Maurice said nervously.

I continued to fire. I spread the shots around -- up, down, interesting patterns -- to keep the monster guessing. Guessing about where it was going to get tickled next, as far as I could tell. Despite their reputation and my previous experiences with them, the projectiles weren't working. At all.

The monster raised a limb. A limb covered with about a thousand tentacles that all had awful suckers and pincers on them, but a limb, nonetheless. "Any ideas?"

"Turn to mist, fly away?" Amanda didn't sound like she was joking.

"Cry like a baby?" Maurice didn't sound like he was trying to be funny, either.

There was a rumbling noise, and the monster lost a few feet. Now it was only about six feet tall. And dark. Not handsome, however. Neither was what came out of the hole in the ground the monster had fallen into, but I was sure happy to see it.

A thick, long, and altogether huge white worm wrapped itself around the monster, effectively preventing it from attacking. Not from struggling, but you couldn't have everything.

"Good boy, Rover," a deep, rumbling voice said. Monty's head peeked out from the hole. "Vic, only you would find an ancient Sumerian demon while on routine patrol." He looked around. "Rover, tighter, boy, tighter." The worm constricted and the monster struggled a little less.

"H.P.'s on his way," I offered.

"Good. We'll need his help." Monty slowly crawled out of the hole. All his parts stayed put, which was pretty impressive. He'd been a lich for so many centuries it was sort of amazing he didn't disintegrate, though he insisted turning into stone was a bigger risk. Hard to prove it by my experience.

Rover had the monster well-wrapped, but he was only a giant white worm, after all, and his power wasn't going to hold an ancient demon forever. "Monty, is anyone helping Rover control our monster?"

"Dirt Corps is on it," he said, rather huffily.

"Oh, good." I tried to keep the concern out of my voice. Dirt Corps consisted of undeads who weren't exactly up to Enforcement standards. Most of them weren't whole bodies, even. Though, you had to give them a lot of credit for willing. Not a lot of credit for success, but sometimes they got lucky.

I looked over my shoulder. Jack leaned against the sedan with the dazed, confused and happy look on his face most humans got when a vamp was exerting serious influence. Ken, ever the multitasker, was on the radio, imitating Jack's voice and ordering all police units elsewhere.

Maurice drew in his breath sharply, always fun when it was a vamp doing it, and I turned around. To see the monster stepping out of his hole, a variety of Dirt Corps grunts clinging to his, for want of a better word, legs, and Rover draped over Monty's shoulders, looking tired. White worms were able to adjust their size, and Rover was back to his usual five feet, though he looked a little flabby around the middle, likely from his efforts to contain Slimy.

"Why is it never easy?" I asked no one in particular. Until H.P. showed up and told us, exactly, what to do to stop this thing, we only had one option.

It was time to kick icky butt and take unpronounceable names.

Chapter 4

The nice thing about being a modern-day undead in general and werewolf in particular was that the whole clothes issue had been solved by brighter minds generations earlier. So while I went more wolfy, my clothes didn't rip and shred so that I wouldn't be naked when I went back to human form. The Spandex-poly blend was a shape-shifting undead's best friend and it was spelled to let our fur through, so when we were in wolf form we didn't look like we were wearing stupid dog coats.

I shoved my so far useless special gun back into its rear holster, did my best to guess where this thing's vulnerable spot was, and gave it the old werewolf leap. I landed on what you could generously call its head and started clawing and biting.

"Go, Vicki, go!" Maurice was all over the cheering.

"This thing tastes worse than whatever's in the trashcans. And a little aerial support wouldn't be considered an insult."

Amanda flew up and landed on what I was going to insist, until told otherwise, was the thing's back. Vamps can do the whole extend the claws thing, too, and when they're really pissed, frightened or fighting something a lot stronger, they go all Nosferatu. It wasn't Amanda's best look, but then again, I wasn't going to win Best in Show, either.

However, six inch claws that looked like sling blades were impressive weapons. She slashed, I clawed, we both bit. We weren't doing anything other than ensuring we'd need the biggest bottles of Listerine in the universe later.

Maurice got into the act. He hated going into what

was politely called the Ancient Vampire Form, but he wasn't an idiot. If we didn't stop this thing, we were going to be dinner or minions. We were at the top of the food chain and refused to leave that spot without a fight, and if we'd wanted to be minions we would have already committed our souls to the Prince.

From the little I could see as I chomped on a big face tentacle and got flipped around, Maurice was attacking the stomach area, normally considered somewhat vulnerable. This thing had three top level, professionally trained, Enforcement personnel on it and all we were doing was causing it to stagger a little. I got flipped around even more and realized we weren't causing the stagger -- the thing's foot was sort of caught on the lip of the hole the Dirt Corps had created.

Slimy tried to shake me off, big time, but I clamped my jaws harder. Supposedly pit bulls have locking jaws, but they're Chihuahuas by comparison to a werewolf. If I didn't want off, I wasn't going off.

Of course, after being slammed against all three walls of the alley a few times, I was considering the benefits of letting go. The thing was, Slimy was moving towards the street. And a loose slime monster was bad enough, but a loose ancient Sumerian demon crossed with a slime monster was the definition of Foreshadow of the Apocalypse.

My particular tentacle flipped low and I caught that there were at least twenty Dirt Corps members clinging to this thing's lower half. As I was whipped around, I saw Monty slamming his hands into whatever parts of Slimy he could hit. Considering the fact that liches are stronger than vampires, this should have done something. But Slimy just did his version of a Santa Claus impersonation and shook like a bowlful of jelly.

Ken noticed we were having a little trouble and joined the fray. This was good in that he was the most powerful vamp on the scene, so he could probably do the most damage. It was bad, however, because Ken lost concentration for some reason, and Jack came out of that happy "it's all good" vamp stupor and took a good look around.

I moved out of werewolf form and into wolf, in the hopes I'd look more normal, so to speak. I also managed to catch hold and dig my claws in so I wasn't flailing around like Slimy was using me for fly-fishing bait. So I had a good view of Jack.

He was a cop on Prosaic City's Night Beat. They only took the best, and the ones who could handle the more-than-weird. Even so, he was a human and one of the things those of us in Necropolis Enforcement swore to -- aside from the standard protect and serve stuff -- was that we'd do our best to never let the humans know this wasn't really their city.

Now Jack was staring at pretty much every undead known to man and a couple man didn't really know about. All we were missing was a zombie to cover every trope -- the mummies were already there, being dragged along by Slimy -- and the minute H.P. arrived, that was going to be covered, too.

As I tried to figure out which was going to be worse -- Slimy stomping around using my city as a midnight buffet or Jack having to have a serious memory wipe -- he reached into the sedan. And pulled out our riot gun, which was a lot more like a bazooka, and aimed.

"All of you, let go on three!" I knew that tone of voice. It was the one Jack used that told all listeners he was the man in charge.

"Is he serious?" Amanda asked me.

"One...."

"He seems serious," Maurice offered.

"Two...."

"He means it!" I shouted. "Everybody, do it!"

"Three."

🐾 Chapter 5 🐾

We went flying -- in the vamps' cases under their own control -- as Jack fired. The riot gun held a lot of shots and it looked like he planned to use them all.

I hit the wall over the trashcans and fell onto the top of one. Mercifully, the lid was down and the thing was packed so full I didn't crash through. I was between Jack and Slimy, so I had a great view. Which was nice, because I'd spent a lot of time being the tetherball and I couldn't really move.

Jack was firing, calmly and consistently, laying down a steady stream that hit Slimy all over the place. He was also advancing while firing. Slimy, meanwhile, seemed somewhat rocked but not stopped, and he was advancing, too. At current rate and speed, they were going to slam into each other in front of me.

Jack knew it, too. He maneuvered himself in front of me, so he was between me and the monster.

I, as the Count put it, panted after Jack because he was literally the most manly man I'd ever met, seen or smelled. And he was in full-on manly mode at the moment. I was lucky the moon wasn't full -- I'd have been crawling on the ground in front of him, whining, with my tail up, in between rolling on my back and offering the full on "I'm your puppy mamma" routine. Hey, there are some things a weregirl can't control.

"Can you move?" he asked me, still watching Slimy and firing steadily.

"Sort of."

One of the undead benefits is an ability to concentrate on more than one thing at a time. As a werewolf, I had enhanced senses under normal situations, let alone during battles. So I'd counted the number of shots because I could and you learned to do things like that because they helped you stay unalive. And I knew Jack was out of ammo.

He did, too. He tossed the gun back towards the car, turned, grabbed me, flung me over his shoulder, and ran. It would've been more comfortable if I'd been in human or werewolf form, but I didn't complain. Slimy stomped the trashcan I'd been on about two seconds after Jack grabbed me.

We reached the car and he tossed me in it. I got the impression he was going to attempt to drive away, but he went to the trunk. I remembered what we had in the trunk. "I don't think an urban assault rifle is going to help," I called to him.

"Can't hurt." He leaned against the car and fired. This seemed to affect Slimy, but it was still coming towards us. "Any suggestions?"

"Oh, goodness. Good effort, young man, and you've certainly hurt it more than anyone else. However, it would help if you aimed for its vulnerable spots." The voice was old and quavered, with excitement.

I crawled closer to Jack. "H.P., if we knew where its vulnerable spots were, it'd be dead already. Jack, if he deigns to tell you, shoot wherever H.P. says."

H.P. wasn't the biggest man in the world. Well, he wasn't a man any more, technically. He also hadn't been that old when he'd died, less than fifty. He looked, sounded and acted old because he said he *felt* old. He was a zombie. But there hadn't been any choice, really. Once a human dies of natural causes -- well, natural human causes -- there's only so many ways to bring them back. And we'd needed H.P.'s expertise.

He smiled at Jack. "May I, young man?"

Jack sighed. "Sure, why the hell not?" He handed H.P. the gun.

H.P. shook his head. "Children, everyone needs to get clear please." Even though most of us were technically older than him, he called us all children -- he meant it lovingly so none of us minded. He was also unfailingly polite, due, according to the Count, to the era he'd been raised in. It never bothered me unless we were in pressure situations. Then I kind of wanted him to get a little testy. But he never did. He wasn't at the Count's level, but H.P. was pretty unflappable.

He was also shooting. At what I and, I was sure, the others, considered Slimy's feet. And it was working.

"You see, children, its power comes from below," H.P. said merrily as he laid down a steady stream of bullets and Slimy started shrinking. "Hence, you have to cut it off from the source."

"Does he always lecture?" Jack asked me.

Maurice and Amanda landed next to him. "Constantly," Maurice said.

I waited for Jack to react. He didn't. He was still watching H.P. take down Slimy. "Why?"

"He's a professor," Amanda offered.

"Professor of what?" Jack's calm and interest were starting to freak me out far more than Slimy.

"Ancient monsters," Ken answered as he landed, carrying Monty and Rover. He set Monty down carefully, but an arm fell off anyway. "Ancient gods and monsters," he amended. "And current ones, too, but his specialty is the ancient. Sorry, Monty."

Monty sighed. "It happens."

Jack bent down, picked the arm up, and handed it to Monty. "Need a hand?"

"Hilarious." Monty gave him a dirty look. "I'm used to it, thanks." He shoved the arm on and Rover did his wrap and squeeze thing that helped Monty reattach.

Jack looked back at H.P. Slimy was down to human sized and shrinking. "Good thing he showed up. What's his name?"

"Professor Emeritus Howard Phillips Lovecraft," H.P. called over his shoulder. "Tenured at Necropolis University. At your service."

Chapter 6

H.P. continued to take care of Slimy and I contemplated my next move. I could go human, but I was hurt and healing was better in wolf form and a lot faster in werewolf form. I wondered if Jack would notice if I slipped into the half-human, half-wolf look. I could ask Jack what he thought he was seeing, but I got the impression he was seeing exactly what was here. I could run away and hide, but that went against both my better nature and the oaths I'd taken for both of my jobs.

I was saved from making a decision by the radio. "Officers Wolfe and Wagner. Are you all right? Come in." Darlene sounded beyond worried. I couldn't blame her.

I also couldn't work the radio with paws. Jack reached in. "Yeah, Darlene, we're okay. Situation," he looked back at H.P., "seemingly under control."

"Detective Wagner, Chief wants to know how you knew to send other police support to stadium?"

"Pardon me?" Jack gave me a confused look. I shrugged as best I could.

"The Chief isn't upset -- they got there in time to stop a huge riot. But he does want to know how you knew."

"Perps gave us a clue," I managed to get out. The movie idea that werewolves can't talk when in non-human form is a lie. When you're younger, you sound like you're talking with a rolled up cloth in your mouth, but practice does make perfect. Now I just sounded out of breath.

"Yeah," Jack said quickly.

"I'll relay to the Chief. Do you need assistance with

the suspects?"

Jack and I looked at each other. We had nothing and no one to bring in, back, or even talk about.

Ken leaned in the passenger's window. "We need at least six ambulances, Darlene." He was talking in Jack's voice again. "Officers down."

When you're a cop, there's no worse phrase you can hear. When you're with Necropolis Enforcement, we have and hate that one, but there are worse phrases. Officer engulfed. Officer ingested. Officer staked. Officer doused. Officer dusted. Officer turned. That was the worst one, really. Because that meant one of your friends had given up and given his or her soul to the Prince. And that meant you had to dust them, as fast as possible and with the most extreme prejudice known to undead or human kind.

Jack hung up our radio, but I could hear Darlene in the background, calling for medical. "Ken, I'm not really down."

"I didn't call them for you," he said as he pointed towards H.P.

I got out of the car on all fours and stayed that way. Still hurt too much to go for upright, let alone human. We all walked closer to the carnage.

Apparently Slimy had swallowed without chewing. Guess they didn't teach proper eating etiquette in whatever level of Hell he was from. He'd ripped apart the squad cars, but the humans were each in one piece. I trotted over and started sniffing. Amanda and Maurice came with me -- she moved the living ones to H.P. and Maurice moved the dead ones to Ken.

We were lucky -- the four uniforms were all alive, though just barely. H.P. started doing our form of

C.P.R., which consisted of a lot more than chest pounding and the kiss of life. A couple of the hookers were still with us, and, sadly, the one dealer who'd been in the alley was clearly going to recover.

On the deader side, all the bums were gone. This wasn't a surprise. By the time someone was living on the streets, their natural resistance to the occult was lowered, let alone their natural resilience. We'd lost three hookers and a couple of junkies as well.

The mess was unreal, but one area Dirt Corps handled better than anything was toxic cleanup. I chose not to look -- their ways were effective, but unbelievably gross. I don't care who you are, watching a bunch of mummies, skeletons, liches and worms gobble up gross ick is more than any stomach can handle.

I went over to watch Ken work and Jack came with me. Ken had one hand on a dead hooker's head, thumb and forefinger on the temples, with the other on the heart. He was concentrating.

"What's he doing?" Jack whispered to me.

"Seeing if they're worth reviving." Ken had a perfect track record so far -- he'd never brought back a potential minion.

"But they're dead."

"Yeah, well, there are ways. I mean, they won't come back as human, but being a zombie's not as bad as it's cracked up to be. And there are other options. Hookers usually come back as succubae. It's typecasting, but it works."

"What do the junkies and bums come back as?"

"Bums usually opt for zombie. Junkies...well, junkies rarely come back."

"Why so?"

"They're already too close to the Prince." This was true. There were so many sins out there, and everyone indulged in at least one of them, even if they thought they didn't. But junkies were among the most willful, more so than alcoholics, adulterers, or murderers. Pedophiles, rapists and junkies rarely got a second shot at life from us. We had standards and we also had history to back up our decisions.

"Who's the Prince?" Jack asked as Ken shook his head and moved on to the next body.

"The Prince of Darkness."

"Oh. The Devil. Or is that Count Dracula?"

"Neither." I struggled to put the right words around what the Prince really was.

"Count Dracula gets a bad rap for no good reason," Ken offered. "He's one of the main reasons the Prince hasn't taken over."

"And the Devil's really Yahweh's servant," Maurice added as he joined us.

"Yahweh?" Jack sounded confused.

"The entity most humans call God's real name." I was very fond of Yahweh, some because he was strong and righteous, mostly because he was the strongest god fighting against the Prince and it paid to support your boss.

"God has a lot of names, but --"

Ken interrupted Jack. "Yes, he does. But there are also more gods out there than you can count. And they *all* have a variety of names. But each prefers the name he or she feels is truly theirs. The one you're talking about is named Yahweh. He likes his name used, by the way, though not in vain."

"So, what does he do when someone says 'God damn it'?" Jack sounded ready to sign up for H.P.'s

Gods and Monsters for Beginners class at Necropolis U. I was getting worried.

"He laughs," Maurice replied. "If he even hears it. 'God' is a general term. Now, if you cursed using his real name, then he'd be taking an interest. But when someone goes, 'Oh God, oh God' and then orgasms, it's just a general statement, sort of like 'the sky is blue' or 'demon kind are scary'."

"So, the Prince isn't Count Dracula and he isn't the Devil," Jack said. "So, what is he?"

My wrist-com came to life as the Count calmly answered. "Evil incarnate."

Chapter 7

Jack looked around. "You know, supposedly, all of you are evil." He didn't sound accusatory or even fazed.

"Those are stories," the Count explained. "Started by the Prince."

"But you're undeads."

"Yes? What's your point?" The Count sounded polite and mildly offended.

I decided to rejoin the conversation. After all, Jack was my partner. "We have souls. Unless we give our souls to the Prince, we're like humans, and we have free will. And, yes, we're undead. But we're also alive -- we call it being unalive. What we don't want to become is dusted. Dusted means unlikely to come back." We didn't want to become turned, either, to come back as a minion, but some things I didn't like to talk about, ever.

"But I thought you lost your soul when you became a vampire or a werewolf."

"No. You lose your soul when you give it to the Prince. Otherwise, it's yours. Well, yours and your god's."

"Which god is yours?"

"I'm a Yahweh girl, but there are plenty of other gods out there just as worthy."

"So, like, Zeus is still around?"

"Around and kicking. And still on the side of good, so to speak. The Greek and Roman gods were all about partying like it was the end of the universe. One of the reasons Yahweh could get stronger -- it's hard to keep your faith in a god who's more interested in screwing your wife, sister and daughter, all at the same time.

Especially when you had a god right nearby who was doing his best to kick evil in the butt on a daily basis."

I felt a little better and went to werewolf form and onto my hind legs. Jack didn't even blink, but he did catch me when I started to topple over. "You're not doing too great. I think we should put you into one of the ambulances."

Maurice snorted. "That would be a fun trip to vivisection hell. No, we'll take Vicki back to Headquarters. We have full medical there. Our kind of medical."

"I'm going with you," Jack said calmly.

I was going to protest but Ken said, "Okay."

"What?" Ken normally wasn't big on bringing humans over without major security clearances. "He's a human."

Ken shot me a look that said I was acting like an idiot. "He's a human partnered with a werewolf. He's a human who took in three vampires, a werewolf, a lich, a white worm, and a variety of Dirt Corps undeads fighting with an ancient Sumerian demon. And instead of running, wetting himself, or screaming like a little girl, he pulled out a gun and started shooting at the true enemy in front of him. I think he's passed the tests, Vic."

"But...but...." I couldn't bring myself to say what my real objection was. That the human guy I was sort of in love with was going to not only know I was a werewolf, but see all the undead side of me. I wasn't ashamed. I was afraid. Not afraid he'd try to kill me, but that he wouldn't like me any more, not even as a friend.

Jack cleared his throat. "I've known you were a werewolf for a while."

"Come again?" I swiveled my head so fast I cracked my neck. Which was a good thing, so I didn't complain.

Jack grinned. "I'm on the Night Beat, Vic. The Chief considers me one of his best detectives, and you're his favorite. I didn't get partnered with you by random chance. I got partnered with you because the Chief knows we need to work with Necropolis Enforcement to survive."

"You knew? How long? And, wait a minute. The Chief knows? Who else knows?" I was supposed to be undercover inside Prosaic City P.D. Not to spy on them, but to protect them. Kind of hard to be undercover if everyone knows your secret identity.

"Yes, the Chief knows. A select few others know. I think Darlene's figured it out, but if so, she's very discreet. Probably because she likes you. Everyone likes you, Vic. You're a great officer and a nice person. I've known since I took you on as a partner. A little bitchy around the full moon, but a lot of people are. The Chief wanted to be sure your partner was able to protect you, and you can't protect someone if you don't know what her strengths and weaknesses are." Jack sounded like he was trying to be soothing and reassuring. I didn't want to let it work.

But it did. I thanked the Gods and Monsters again for there being no full moon tonight. And decided to let that bitchy comment pass for now. "Well, okay. I guess. But you never said anything." And we'd been partnered for well over a year.

He shrugged. "I knew you were scared to tell me. Besides, it didn't matter."

"This is so touching." Maurice made a gagging noise. "When we get back to Headquarters, I think I'm going to barf up blood, I'm so nauseated by the love in the alleyway."

I was glad I was still fur-covered because that way Jack couldn't see me blush. He just grinned again, though.

I was going to say something when my ears picked up a noise. A high-pitched, urgent noise. "The ambulances are almost here. I think we have ten coming, maybe a dozen." I figured Jack was right and Darlene had a good idea of what was going on, because that was a lot of emergency vehicles for four police officers.

Amanda came over. "They'll be here shortly. We need to go back to human forms or we need to disappear."

Chapter 8

"There's no way Vic can go back to human right now," Ken said briskly. "She can barely stand upright."

"But I'm supposed to be one of the detectives on the scene."

"I'll handle it," Jack said. "I'd like one of the vampires to stay with me, though, just in case."

"I will," Ken offered. "Maurice, you take Vic back to Headquarters and get her taken care of. Amanda, can you carry the others?"

"Monty's done with cleanup and he's taking Dirt Corps back the way they came," Amanda said. "So I'll only have to worry about H.P."

Ken shook his head. "Nope. We have a new succubus and zombie that need to go with you."

Amanda sighed. "No problem." Vamps were strong and Amanda worked out. Not that she was the vampire equivalent of a body builder or something, but she was stronger than the average vamp. She was at least as strong as Monty.

"I'd take one, but Vicki squirms," Maurice said. Sadly, he was right. Werewolves don't like to fly all that much. And Maurice loved to fly fast and wild. It was all I could do to not claw him and jump for the illusion of safety when I wasn't hurt. When I was it took all my concentration and his to keep me from freaking out, even if he flew slowly.

"You need to get moving," Ken said.

"I'll see you later, partner," Jack said as he handed me to Maurice. "Behave and don't bite someone's head off."

"Funny. See you later."

Maurice snorted, Amanda picked up H.P., our new

zombie and our new succubus, and we all took off.

"Slow down!"

"Vicki, Vic, Vicster, Vicarino...you freak at granddaddy speeds, you freak at NASCAR speeds. I'm a formula vehicle and since it makes no difference, I'm going to get us there faster so I get clawed less."

Maurice had a point. I shut up, closed my eyes, and tried to relax.

Didn't help. I could feel the air moving past us, smell everything we whizzed by, hear the noises that showed me our speed.

"What happened?" This question came from the succubus.

"Well, an ancient Sumerian demon manifested and they always come out hungry," H.P. began. I could recognize a lecture starting. I opened my eyes, did my best to drown out the lecture by humming "Werewolves of London", and tried to enjoy the view.

All things considered, Prosaic City looked pretty good from the air. Like all big American cities it had a variety of business and high-rise sections, older stately buildings surrounded by newer, sleeker ones, scattered suburban sections filled with every kind of tract home from simple to McMansion, a lot of streets and highways, an old downtown nice people didn't want to be in after dark, a newer downtown where they did, and a variety of uptown and other higher class, hot spot, and trendy areas. Unlike many cities, it had a variety of rivers running through it and an impressive bridge system.

And unlike every other city in this hemisphere, it had an underground like you wouldn't believe.

Prosaic City was one of the country's older inhabited burgs. In the course of its existence it's been rebuilt several times. Because it was built on top of Necropolis. Which was a bad move by the old-time Prosaic City Planning Council, but everyone makes mistakes, right? Just because no one else had settled on the pretty spot next to the water didn't mean anything, they reasoned, they'd just gotten there first.

Actually, they'd gotten there last.

There are points in the world where the occult pull is particularly strong. Where the ley lines, longitude, latitude, winds, weather, and general forces of both nature and the occult combine with placement in the cosmos and an entity is formed that shouldn't be able to exist in reality. I've heard them called hell mouths, portals, doorways, entryways, and a variety of other terms. But those aren't really accurate.

What forms isn't a door. What forms is a city. A city that exists both in this plane of reality and all the others at the same time. A place that wasn't built but can never be removed, a power created by everything and nothing at the same time, something that wasn't born but can never die. What my kind call an Undead City.

In the American hemisphere, that city is Necropolis.

Necropolis was here first, but most of its residents immigrated over time. The pull from an Undead City is strong. The power in one is even stronger.

Prosaic City was built right on top of Necropolis. This made things hard for the Necropolites and weird for the Prosaics. Due to the way an Undead City worked, the humans could and did put their buildings and roads and such on top of things of ours that were already there. So, City Hall and the city courthouse was right on top of what was considered Necropolis' Red

Light District, which, as the Count said, made poetic sense.

All the undead can see into at least two planes of existence, and most can see into more. Vampires and liches can see almost as many planes as a god. Werewolves aren't quite as powerful magically, so we have limits. Which was okay with me. I had enough fun keeping Necropolis separated from Prosaic City on a nightly basis.

Not that I wasn't good at it. I was considered one of the best, if not the best, at cross-existence. But it had taken me years to hone the skill to perfection, and that much focus on one skill meant others weren't quite as sharp. Then again, I never found not being able to look into one of the levels of Hell without trying to be a hardship. I didn't care for Hell and never wanted to go there. That I had reasons *to* go there made it worse.

We call moving back and forth between the human and undead planes sliding. Everyone has to learn it, it's not natural to any being. Some humans did it as easily as undeads. They were usually mentally unstable -- not before the slide, but after. It's hard for a human to see myths and legends and worse in real life and know it's real. Most minds can't take it if they aren't prepared.

However, the younger, the better. That's the main reason changelings exist. Not to steal babies but to save them. Children who can see the undead normally have a lifetime of pain and torment ahead of them, unless we get them first.

Undeads, by our nature, don't have the same issues. We know the human plane exists -- at least two-thirds of us were human before we undied. But seeing the human world superimposed over the undead one was always good for a headache if your concentration faltered.

"Now, this is one of the greater ironies of this particular age," H.P. said, as I lost said concentration and "Werewolves of London" left my personal airwaves. "Necropolis Enforcement Headquarters shares existence space with the largest church in Prosaic City, Our Lady of Compassion, which has been compared favorably to Saint Patrick's Cathedral and Notre Dame."

"Not if you have to fly through it," Maurice muttered.

"And the University," H.P. went on, "sits on the same grounds as the Prosaic Country Club and Estates."

"You mean I'm gonna go to school where all the rich johns live?" The succubus wasn't totally adapted to the undead way of life yet, that was clear.

"Yes," H.P. said cheerfully as we landed in front of Our Lady of Compassion, or the OLOC as we Necropolites called it.

"But they won't be able to see you," I mentioned. The succubus looked disappointed. And familiar. "Sexy Cindy?"

"Yeah, that's me. Was me," she corrected. "Who are you, bitch?"

"I'll choose to take that as an attempt to be home-girly with me, and not stupid. It's Detective Wolfe. In, ah, wolf form." I looked down. "Sorry. In werewolf form."

Sexy Cindy's eyes widened. "Whoa. No wonder you were always busting me."

"We were busting you because you were a prostitute working the worst parts of town." Police work. It was truly all glamour and excitement.

"You just didn't like me propositioning your partner."

"True enough. You might have been the only one in Prosaic City's criminal class who fell for the unmarked police car."

"It looked like a regular car," she mumbled. "Not like I got a lot of time to go cruise the car lots or something."

I yawned. "Heard it before. Didn't impress me then, doesn't impress me now." This was an old argument. You bust a perp, right after they realize you're not buying that they're innocent they explain that they have no opportunity to better themselves. Sadly true more often than not. But most of them never tried, either. Sexy Cindy was firmly in the never tried category. I wondered what being undead was going to do to her.

"What am I in for now?" Sexy Cindy asked truculently.

I told her the truth. "The rest of your unlife."

🐾 Chapter 9 🐾

Necropolis Enforcement Headquarters followed standard Necropolis architectural design. I loved it, but it was always fun to see a newbie's reaction.

Our new zombie, who H.P. introduced as Freddy, and Sexy Cindy both looked around and gaped. "But...it's all...modern," Freddy said.

"The city of the future," Maurice said gaily. "We know, we know...where's all the gothic crap, right? What, no gargoyles? No creepy statues? No horrifying images or evil words? What kind of self-respecting city of the damned is this?"

"I think it looks cooler than cool," Sexy Cindy said softly. "If I'd known something like this existed, I'd have asked you to kill me a long time ago."

The buildings were impressive, even to someone who'd lived here a couple hundred years. We had our share of beings who could see the future. For whatever reason, they all worked in the artistic pursuits. So, every time Prosaic City encroached on us to the point where it had a collapse and we had our version of a bad infestation of vermin, we redid the place.

Current standard was wide at the bottom going quickly to various levels, but all slim and spiky after about the fifth floor. I called it a sort of Futuristic Eiffel Tower effect, which always made Maurice wince. Tons of shiny metal and windows that went dark when the sun was out, lots of light, no matter what. Grass where humans had streets -- we didn't have the same transportation issues they did, after all, and grass is so much nicer to pad on. And roll on. I started to whine and realized I really needed to get back into human form or I was at risk of going wild for a while. Nothing wrong with going wild, of course, but there was too much going on to indulge in that right now.

"Be a good girl and relax," Maurice said soothingly. Sadly, it helped. I'd been friends with Amanda and Maurice for my entire undead existence, and no one knows what you really need and want to hear like a vampire.

The doors slid open and Maurice and Amanda stepped on the moving sidewalk. Because we'd now entered Necropolis, but weren't in what was called Necropolis Proper, we could still easily see the human plane. We sailed past a ton of pews, through several statues of the Virgin Mary and over the altar. At the priests' room we went downward and into the Proper and the human parts faded away.

What we called the Proper and a human would call ground level for Necropolis was about a hundred feet under what Prosaic City called the ground. We still had sunlight and moonlight and all that, we just sat a little lower on our astral plane. No Necropolite complained about this -- walking through humans was freaky and most didn't like it. Those who did tended to be those who really thought they had definite human leanings and were just misunderstood. Yeah, even the undead have their version of modern day Goth kids. Not that a real Goth was a problem, but a wannabe is a wannabe, no matter what plane you call home.

The sidewalk took us into the main part of Headquarters. Personnel were waiting to take Freddy and Sexy Cindy to Indoctrination and there were a host of medical personnel waiting for yours truly. I tried not to cringe and didn't succeed, if Maurice's mutterings were any indication.

In addition to the med staff, there was another

being waiting for me. "Oh, no. Maurice, do something."

"Not a thing I can do to dislodge him, but I'll stay with you into the hospital," Maurice said in a low voice.

He was in full wolf form for no reason other than that he was a fanatic about it. I'd actually never seen him in human form and almost never in werewolf form, he was that committed to the rather ancient belief that werewolves were strongest in "natural animal form". He bounded over, tail wagging, eyes serious, ears alert for any danger. "Vic, what happened? Are you going to be okay? Do you need a transfusion?"

"Just got banged up, Ralph."

"I'd better stick with you. Werewolves need to pack together." He was serious. Ralph Rogers, Werewolf With a Cause. He was a big, good-looking wolf, but a weregirl could only take so much dork in her life and Ralph threatened to exceed my limit on a nightly basis.

"I think we can handle it, Ralphie," Maurice said, as he pointedly swished by. Ralph and Maurice didn't get along. At all.

The med personnel got their paws, claws and talons on me, and I got hustled into a medical bay. They tried to keep Ralph and Maurice out, but Ralph was loud and insistent and Maurice was willing to be nasty and they knew it, so ultimately, it was a intimate group of ten by the time I got onto a bed.

Ralph tried to get next to me. Maurice blocked him every time and made it look accidental. Really, a werewolf doesn't stand a chance against a vampire, especially a smart and sneaky vampire, and there weren't a lot of earnest and apple-cheeked ones out there.

"Ralph, I really think I'm okay. I didn't lose any blood, all my limbs are attached, and I can feel my bones setting themselves. Shouldn't you be out on patrol or something?"

"It's my night off." Ralph gave Maurice a dirty look. "Though I see I shouldn't have taken it."

"Ralph, it was an ancient Sumerian demon crossed with some sort of slime monster. Maurice gave it his all, just like the rest of us."

"I note he's not the one injured." Ralph made this sound like Maurice had tossed me to Slimy and then run off screaming.

"I wasn't the one who went on Mister Monster's Wild Ride," Maurice said haughtily. "I also wasn't the one listening to the Enforcement Band Radio to be able to intercept the object of my unrequited affections the moment she returned on premises."

Ralph growled, always impressive in a werewolf. The doctor in charge had enough. "All personnel who aren't medically trained and part of my med team, out. Now. That particularly means you, Agent Rogers."

Ralph bared his teeth, shot me an expectant look that turned to doggy-disappointment when I didn't demand he stay so we could hold paws, heaved the big sigh, then turned tail and left. The tension in the room dropped.

Maurice winked at me. "I'll ride herd on Mister Lovestruck. I can see why you want the human when this is your most likely alternate."

"I have options!"

"Uh huh. Let's talk about why you and Ken didn't work out, shall we?"

"Later," the doctor snapped. "After she's healed later."

Maurice blew kisses to all and swished out after Ralph. The tension in the room went back to normal.

"How do you deal with them?" one of the nurses asked as they started the various tortures we called medical treatment.

"I tell myself it could always be worse."

"How?"

"I could be living and working with my parents."

Chapter 10

I was through with the torture that was medical care and ready to go back on duty. The only downside was that I knew without asking that Ralph was waiting for me. I prayed Maurice was, too.

I normally didn't waste prayer on something minor, but it had been a long night and Ralph always jumped up and down on my last nerve. Besides, if things went according to how they'd seemed, Jack was going to be here soon, and I didn't really want to have to introduce him to Ralph.

Of course, what I wanted and what was going to happen were rarely the same thing. Yahweh didn't waste help on the minor stuff, which was why it never paid to bother him with it. This was one reason why plenty of other gods had a lot of Necropolite followers. Zeus and his gang were all over the little stuff, for example. But experience had taught me that when it was you against the Prince, it really paid to have the god willing to get down, dirty, and personally involved on your side.

However, I wasn't facing the Prince, I was facing the werewolf version of the entire cast of *Revenge of the Nerds* rolled into one. And sure enough, he was in the waiting room, at full alert. And, also sure enough, so were Ken and Jack. My ex, my hoped for, and my never gonna happen, all together in one small space. Sometimes my unlife was too good to be true.

Maurice and Amanda were there, too, and Monty and Rover. They all looked worried.

"I wasn't hurt all that badly," I said as Rover undulated over for pets and scritchies. As beings with no limbs, white worms unlived for the gentle scratching. I had Rover rolling around in wormy ecstasy in no time.

"Yes, we know," Ken said briskly. "We have a new problem."

I picked Rover up and let him drape over me. This earned me a happy smile from Monty and a glare from Ralph. Jack, thankfully, didn't look grossed out. He looked like Ken -- worried.

"Human, undead or otherworldly?" I asked while I scratched Rover under his chin and he gave me the white worm version of a love hug. Fortunately, Monty had him well trained, so no ribs cracked and I didn't have trouble breathing.

"We don't know," Ken said.

"We got things squared away at the scene of the crime," Jack added. "But...."

"But?"

Monty sighed. "But despite our cleanup efforts, there's a residue that shouldn't be there."

"Aura, deposit, signature, impression, what?"

"Aura, as best we could tell," Ken said.

"I couldn't see it," Jack said. "But I could feel it. It felt evil," he added.

"That makes sense." I wasn't looking directly at Ralph, but I could see him out of the corner of my eye. His tail was practically wagging itself off his body. I heaved a sigh. "This sounds like a job for us werewolves."

I knew I didn't sound enthusiastic, but you'd never have been able to tell from Ralph's reaction. He was practically bounding around the room with joy. "Vic and I will go check out the scene and report back."

Maurice snorted, big time. "As if."

"This is a werewolf job," Ralph snarled.

"And under chapter three, section twenty-two, paragraph fifteen of the Enforcement Codebook, no agent will go to investigate any source likely to be attached to the Prince without at least two other agents of different species." Ken could quote the Codebook verbatim and from memory. The reason none of us hated him for it was because he only did it in cases like this.

"That means you need a vampire and a lich along," Maurice translated snidely. "Or a zombie, but, since we don't have one handy, you're stuck with us. And, since we're *so* dedicated to the cause and there are two of you, you luck out and get *three* vampires, an extremely experienced lich, a white worm and, if I'm any judge, a human along for the ride. Aren't you *lucky*?"

Ralph growled. "We don't need any of you along. A werewolf pack together can never be defeated."

"Um, right, Ralph." I did not want to get into this subject with him here and now. Never, really. Ralph and I didn't see nose-to-nose on this one, and I doubted we ever would. "However, since I'm the agent in charge of this case, I say who goes along. And considering what came out of there almost kicked all of our butts and then some, I want everyone named already with us. And, if we cross any zombies, succubae, witches, warlocks, altar-demons, fairies, mummies, skellies, hellhounds, daemon cats, or any other undead species on active duty, I want them along, too."

"As far as anyone's ever heard," Maurice added, "two does not a pack make."

Ralph grumbled and growled, but I ignored him and strode out of the waiting room. Happily Amanda caught up to me before I had to stop and ask which way was out. Overachieving sense of smell or not, hospitals messed with me big time.

"Jack's taking this really well," she murmured to me as we walked briskly to the moving sidewalk that would take us from the hospital wing and into Central HQ.

"Yeah, I hope he's not faking it."

"He's not. We all scanned him. He's interested, but not freaked out. Probably why your police chief partnered him with you."

"We'll see, I guess." I tried not to be hopeful -- interested in the whole undead thing and interested in a relationship with an undead were two different things.

We reached Central HQ, hopped off the moving sidewalk, and went to the dispatch desk. The Count wasn't there, of course. He ran dispatch, but he ran it from higher up. He left the mundane portions of dispatch to those Enforcement personnel trained for it. Tonight we had three succubae, two banshees, and a couple of skeletons on duty. However, I wanted the being in charge.

"Is Clyde around?"

One of the banshees nodded and shrieked his name. Ralph and I just managed to cover our ears in time, and thankfully, Maurice covered Jack's. Vampires could mute a banshee's scream and liches and white worms were immune to it. But it was beyond painful for werewolves and humans.

"A little warning next time would be nice," Ralph growled. I didn't contradict him.

Clyde lumbered around from the back. He was an older mummy originally from Egypt. Amazingly, not all mummies were -- they were dotted all over the

Eastern Hemisphere. But we got a steady migration --
Necropolis was considered newer and more vibrant,
the place to go if you really wanted to make it as an
undead and set yourself apart from the rest of the
deaders. If you could make it here, you could make it
anywhere, kind of thing.

Clyde had come out before it was cool, though.
When Necropolis formed, centuries before, he'd
volunteered to come and help get things set up, and
he'd never left. He and the Count were close friends,
which helped. Between the two of them, they knew
everything that had gone on in and around Necropolis.
H.P. had them guest lecture a lot.

"Hello, Victoria," Clyde said slowly. Mummies
spoke faster than golem, but neither were speed
demons verbally. "Glad to see you back to normal."

"Me, too." I ignored Ralph's grumbling about how
human form wasn't really normal for a werewolf and
forged on. "Has H.P. briefed you or the Count about
what we encountered tonight?"

He nodded. "Yes. Very unusual."

"Getting more unusual. Ken and Jack found what
we think is residual aura left after some heavy-duty
cleanup. We're heading back to check it out, but do you
have anything for us before we go?"

Clyde was quiet for a few moments. "Take along a
hellhound. And a daemon cat."

Ralph's growling got louder. I continued to ignore.
"Who's on duty?"

Clyde brought one of the banshees over. I covered
my ears instinctively. I noted that Jack did the same. He
was a fast learner.

The banshee did her shriek of the dead thing. After
the sounds stopped reverberating in my head I heard

the sound of toenails clicking on the marble floors. So it wasn't a surprise to see a big cat and dog skid around the corner and come to an impressive, screeching halt right in front of me. They each put up a paw and saluted, too.

"Hansel, Gretel, good to see you, and glad you're here."

Jack sidled up to me. "Um, Hansel and Gretel?"

"Code names," Hansel's middle head said. The right and left heads usually let the middle head do the talking -- it stressed other beings out a little less.

"We were really siblings, in the old days," Gretel said in the half-snarl, half-purr that was daemon cat speech. She stood up on her hind legs and put her paw on Hansel's middle head. "What's the situation, Major?"

Jack looked around and then stared at me. "Major?

I shrugged. "Down here, yeah. I'll try not be insulted by the shocked look on your face."

"We use military titles," Maurice said. "It makes it less confusing when we chat with humans. For example, Amanda and I are both Captains. Ken's also a Major, because he's an overachiever."

"Heading fast for Lieutenant Colonel," I added. Hey, Ken and I weren't an item any more, but we were still friends and I was proud of him.

Jack gaped, then looked around. "Monty? And, uh, him?" he pointed to Ralph.

"I'm the Major General of Dirt Corps. I'm dotted line into Necropolis Enforcement, in that sense."

"And Ralphie's a Second Lieutenant," Maurice said. "Though he acts like he's the being in charge."

"Werewolves don't need ranks," Ralph snarled. "We have a pack leader and we follow his lead."

"Her lead," Amanda said sweetly. "Since Vic's the leader of this team."

Ralph started to argue but I gave him a long look and he shut up. "Let's get moving. We can brief Hansel and Gretel on the way."

Chapter 11

"You know, we should get H.P.," Amanda said. "Or at least Edgar."

"Why Edgar?" Maurice asked. "This isn't his specialty."

I thought about it. "Yeah, but something's wrong. What we did should have left no trace. But there's a strong one if Jack can feel it."

"Thanks a lot," Jack said.

"Not an insult," Ken replied. "But human senses are weaker than undead senses. If you can feel it, it's strong."

"Nice to know I'm the team mine canary." At least he said it with a grin.

I activated my wrist com. "Count?"

"Yes, Agent Wolfe? Is there a reason we're chatting or do you just feel lonely and unloved?"

"I'd like to have Edgar with us."

There was a significant pause. "Not H.P.?"

"Well, H.P. did his thing earlier and I know he's having fun helping indoctrinate the new recruits we bagged. Besides, something's off, and that usually means human intervention in some way."

"You're the field agent in charge." The Count didn't make this sound like a stirring endorsement.

I pulled out the big gun. "Ken agrees with me."

"Oh, fine."

I hated having to do it, or admit it, but Ken was the best agent we had. He was probably the best undead in centuries. I knew the Count was grooming him to be his replacement. Even eternal undeads can crave retirement, after all.

Ken had the whole package -- handsome, brilliant,

fastest learner around, photographic memory, natural leader. One of the few newer undeads who could interact naturally with the ones who'd been undead for millennia as easily as one formed the day before. Compassionate and caring without being sappy, gentle and kind while never being weak, never made someone else feel like they were less than he was unless it was necessary for his team's survival. And yet, somehow, I'd dumped him. And didn't regret the choice. Maurice felt there was something seriously wrong with me, and he was probably right.

"Edgar will meet you outside the OLOC," the Count informed me.

"What's he doing in Prosaic City?" There was a significant lack of an answer. I did the math. "H.P. was already worried and he asked Edgar to take a look, right?" The academics always stuck together.

"And this is why you're considered our best field agent. Yes. Please proceed." The Count actually sounded pleased. It was always nice to impress the boss. I didn't feel like I ever did it often enough.

"Will do, over and out." I thanked Clyde and his staff for their help, jerked my head at my team, and headed off.

"I'm getting confused," Jack said to me as we rode the moving sidewalk back through the OLOC.

"That's natural."

"No. I mean, I wouldn't have thought the three-headed dog and the cat that looks half-human would have *been* humans originally."

"Oh, that. Well, it's kind of complicated, but I'll try to do a fast overview of Edgar's 'The Undead World' class. Undeads can be made or born. The original ones were born, or hatched, or whatever." I had no idea how white worms actually reproduced and had less interest in finding out.

"Where did they come from?"

"Depends on whose theory you agree with. Some say the Prince created them. Some say it was one or more of the gods. Some say it was an accident, sort of like life forming here in the first place."

"So Earth's the only planet with life on it?"

I snorted. "Hardly. But life is still rare, percentage-wise. I mean, when you consider all the universes."

"There's more than one universe?" Jack was starting to sound like he was getting a headache.

"Yeah. You know, let's just focus on Hansel and Gretel for the moment. They were never human siblings. Humans don't turn into hellhounds or daemon cats. Demons do."

"So they're evil?" Jack didn't sound like he believed it, which either showed his insight or naiveté. I went for insight.

"No. Demons aren't born evil. They're just born in the nether realms. They have souls and so have the same choices the rest of us do -- serve the Prince or refuse and fight him. If you want to get technical, an altar-demon's soul is pledged to a god and hell-demon's soul is pledged to the Prince. If an altar-demon runs into a werewolf and gets bitten, then they don't change into a wolf, because only a human base gives you a werewolf. They turn into a daemon cat or a hellhound, depending."

"Depending on the sex?"

"No, natural proclivity. Hansel and Gretel could have both been one or the other, or switched, but this was what was 'right' for each of them. Good for us, by the way, because many times hellhounds and daemon cats fight like, uh, cats and dogs, but having a team of them is really helpful."

Jack seemed to consider this. "You know, here's something else. You call yourselves undeads. But you're alive. I mean, you breathe, you eat, you sleep. I can understand why many of the others are undeads, but not you, or them," he indicated Hansel and Gretel.

"Well, they stopped being otherworldly and I stopped being human. Essentially, those parts of us died. Demons, like humans, have average lifespans. Once you're a werewolf, hellhound, daemon cat, or any of the other species we call part of the greater undead, you can unlive forever. You can be destroyed, of course -- dusted or so damaged you're unable to function -- but it's much harder. So, we're part of the undead, no longer a part of the living worlds we came from."

"That must be hard," he said softly.

I shrugged. "It's not too bad. There are a lot of benefits. And the undead community is pretty welcoming. Besides, the alternatives for some of us made becoming an undead very appealing."

"Like what?"

I was saved from avoiding an answer by our arrival outside of the OLOC and the appearance of a thin, sad-looking man with a receding hairline. His face wreathed in smiles when he saw us, though.

"Victoria, my dear, I'm so relieved you weren't badly injured." Edgar gave me a hug, then shook hands or paws with the males, depending, hugged the females, and patted Rover. He turned and looked expectantly at Jack.

"Edgar, please meet Detective Jack Wagner, Prosaic City P.D. Jack, this is Doctor of Demonology Edgar Allen Poe."

Jack's mouth dropped. Edgar twinkled and gave him a sweeping bow. "At your service."

Chapter 12

I wrapped my arm through Edgar's and Amanda did the same. Gretel adjusted her size and jumped up onto his shoulder. H.P. was fun and polite and fatherly; Edgar was charming, he loved the ladies, and we loved him right back.

Even though he was actually a lich, I always thought of him as a man, mostly because he was so young, as liches go, that he was at no risk of turning stone-like and none of his parts ever wobbled, let alone fell off. Monty assured me that in a few hundred years Edgar was going to stop being the ladies' man of the lich set, but I didn't worry about it and I knew Edgar didn't, either.

It was always fun to see the other males' reactions to Edgar's effect on the females. It was nice to see that Jack seemed just as annoyed and jealous as the others. Maurice was the only one not bothered by it one way or the other.

"So, my dears," Edgar said to me, Amanda and Gretel. "What is our plan?"

"Well, first off, what did you find at the scene?" That Edgar had already been to the scene was a given.

He shook his head. "Human intervention for certain. However, I have nothing more than that. Those with the enhanced senses of sight and smell need to weigh in."

"Pretty much what we figured." I looked around. "How do we want to get there?" I hoped someone else would suggest not flying.

"Well, I left our car the next street over," Jack said. "I think the Chief would like it returned, so some of us can go in that."

"I think everyone but the vamps can fit." It would be cozy, but I was willing to sit right up next to Jack. Anything for the cause, me.

Ken nodded. "Sounds about right. We'll stay with you overhead, though, just in case."

We found the car and piled in. I made sure I was in the front seat next to Jack. Thankfully, I was joined by Edgar. Hansel "accidentally" shoved Ralph into the backseat and the others piled in. Gretel stayed small and sat on Edgar's lap. No one other than Jack bothered with seatbelts -- a car crash wasn't going to kill any of us unless we crashed into a silver and garlic factory made out of wooden spikes and filled with unholy water. And even then, our chances were better than average of not having any problems.

Jack drove quickly, but even so, downtown was far away from the OLOC. "This is cozy," he said quietly. "You and the other girls all part of Edgar's harem?"

"Gee, you sound jealous. I'll be flattered later. He's charming. More males could try that as a technique. Besides, he's happily married." This was true. The first thing he'd done when he'd been turned into a lich was find his late wife and see if she could become undead. She'd turned into a zombie and they had a very happy, though quiet, family life. She didn't get involved in Enforcement work, but she did handle a lot of "wife of the dean" chores at the University. She covered those for H.P.'s side of things, too, since he wasn't married.

"If you say so." Jack didn't sound convinced. I wasn't sure if I should go for hopeful and flattered or businesslike and educational. I was saved from a decision by the radio.

"Detectives Wagner and Wolfe, please come in." Darlene sounded stressed again. Probably not a good sign.

I grabbed the radio since Jack was driving. "Here, Darlene. What's up?"

She sighed. We were supposed to use the official police call numbers and codes, but I almost never bothered. I had enough Enforcement info rattling around in my head; the human stuff was more confusion than I felt I needed to deal with. Besides, it wasn't like it affected my performance. "Chief would like to know where the two of you have been. You did not respond to radio or cellular."

That made sense. My cell phone was still in the car, on the dash -- I was staring at it. It was blinking merrily. I took a look. Oh yeah, a lot of missed calls. Jack's was there, too, blinking just as much.

"We, ah, were in pursuit."

"Of what?" Darlene didn't sound amused.

"Perpetrators of the crime we investigated earlier." I mean, technically, we were in pursuit now, so that counted, right? "How are the four officers who were down?"

"They're all going to recover, at least so far as we've heard."

Jack and I both relaxed a little. "That's great news. What about the others?"

"The drug dealer's already back on the streets," Darlene said. "Figures, doesn't it? The ladies of the evening are likely to pull through, though they're still in the hospital."

A thought struck me. "Where was the dealer released? And what's his name?"

"Angelo Tomio was released from City Hospital twenty minutes ago. Do you want officers looking for him?"

"No, we'll find him. Thanks, Darlene."

"Chief wants to see you both before you go off duty," she said by way of signing off.

I hung up the radio. "Can't wait."

We reached our special alley of fun and everyone poured out of the car. Jack stopped me. "What are you thinking, that Tomio had something to do with the attack?"

"Possibly. Edgar says a human's involved. The only human not dead or still hospitalized just strolled out, apparently fit as a fiddle. It seems suspicious to me."

He nodded. "How are we going to find him?"

I got out of the car and Jack followed. "Amanda, we need the drug dealer from this whole incident found. He was released from City Hospital about twenty minutes ago. Think you can remember his signature?"

"Of course. You want me to tail him or pick him up?"

"Depends on what he's doing."

"Take someone with you," Jack said.

"What?" Amanda looked shocked. "It's a human."

"It's a human potentially involved in this," Jack pointed to the end of the alley. "Take your partner."

Maurice sighed. "I'd whine about it, but the human has a point. We'll contact you if there's anything interesting going on." They flipped out their wings and took off.

"How do they get them to sort of disappear?" Jack asked.

"Illusion. They don't disappear, they just sort of envelop them so no one sees. Standard vampire stuff."

"Unreal." Jack led the way back to the scene of the

manifestation.

We got close and I started to growl. So did Ralph, Hansel and Gretel. Gretel jumped off Edgar's shoulder and went normal-sized. I switched to full werewolf form. Whatever it was, we didn't like it.

"Ken, keep Jack at hand. Monty, Edgar, full alert. Rover, c'mere, boy."

Rover undulated over. White worms can't growl, they don't make much noise as a rule, and they aren't the kings of expressions, either. But what they lack in vocal and facial expression they make up for in body language. And Rover's body said we had bigger problems than an ancient Sumerian demon.

I had to say it, some because it was true, some because I was the leader. Mostly because I was scared and wanted to share the fear.

"I think the Prince passed through here."

Chapter 13

I heard Ken speaking softly. He'd contacted the Count and was advising Amanda and Maurice to treat their quarry as the most dangerous man on the planet. Tomio might be an ordinary drug dealer, but he'd walked away from Slimy's attack and no one else had. So we were going to have to find out if he'd walked under his own steam or the Prince's.

Meanwhile, I and the rest of the animal squad did our sniff and freak out thing. "I've got a trail," Ralph said. Even he got subdued when we were faced with the biggest bad in the universes.

"Me, too," Hansel said. "And, of course, it's not the same as Ralphie's trail."

"Same here," Gretel said.

"I've got an airborne trail, and," I looked at Rover, "Rover's got an underground one. Fabulous. Either the Prince manifested through five different beings, or four of these are decoys."

"Maybe all of them," Jack said. "If what I'm guessing you all think -- that our drug dealer du jour is alive and kicking because he's the vessel or whatever for the Prince -- then these could all be false leads to keep us away from Tomio."

"Amanda and Maurice have Tomio in sight," Ken advised. "They're staying well back. Neither one is picking up any signs of the Prince, but they may not be close enough."

"And if the Prince has a plan, he's sure not going to go waltzing around being all obvious with his psychic signature." I tried to figure out what to do and came up with the idea I liked least. "We have to split up."

I expected to hear a lot of protests and "are you

kidding me's" , but all I got were heads nodding in agreement, even Rover's.

"I hate it when you guys are reasonable. Okay, how're we going to do this? We go against every code in the book if we separate."

Monty coughed. "I've called Dirt Corps in."

"Oh. Ah. Good."

"I know regular Enforcement doesn't think much of them," Monty said testily. "But they're brave, dedicated, and fit the code requirements."

As he spoke a variety of the Corps arrived. Monty had apparently requested top of the line -- all of the ones before me were full bodied, which was a refreshing change. We had two mummies, three skeletons, two ghouls and a wraith. Not bad.

"Okay, I want a mummy and a skeleton each with Hansel and Gretel. Our third skeleton and a ghoul with Ralph. Second ghoul and wraith with Ken. Monty, I assume you and Rover can get more support than I can contemplate for the underground trail, right?"

"Right."

"Great. I want regular reports, in to me if possible, but the Count for certain. Edgar, are you okay staying here to man the portal?"

He nodded. "Absolutely, and I'll be fine alone. However, if it would make you feel more secure and if we have some other Dirt Corps personnel who wouldn't mind playing some whist while guarding and waiting, I'd be amenable."

I shrugged. "Sure, why not? And, yes, I'd feel safer if you had someone around to back you up." Even a young lich wasn't easy to hurt or kill, but Edgar, like H.P., was special and I'd never forgive myself if either one of them got hurt due to my lack of vigilance or preparedness.

No sooner agreed to than two eager-looking ghouls and one clearly excited ghost arrived, table, chairs and deck of cards in ectoplasmic hands.

Monty gave some orders while I helped Ken recognize the aerial trail. This took some time -- vamps smell blood like nobody's business, but otherwise their sense of smell isn't anything to get excited about. However, they can see a psychic trail almost as well as a werewolf. Once Ken could spot what I smelled, he was able to confirm it had absolutely flown away, and that it wasn't a trail from any vampire who'd been here earlier. There were other flying undeads, of course, but neither one of us could be certain of the species the trail belonged to.

The aerial team took off and the ground teams left right after. Edgar and his group were already into their game. Monty draped Rover around his shoulders then gave me a long look. "What trail are you going to be following?"

I shrugged. "My partner and I are going to follow the human ones."

"There's more than one?" Monty asked.

"I think we're going to find there are a lot."

Chapter 14

I went back to human form and Jack and I got back into the sedan and started off. "Police headquarters first?" he asked me.

"Yeah. We need to check in and, since I now find out the Chief knows all about me and Necropolis Enforcement, we need to let him know what's going on."

"What *is* going on?"

"Takeover bid. Standard, really. The Prince wants to control all the planes of existence. When he can do that, he'll have enough power to destroy any and every god. Without a god, even if it's one puny weak one, every living soul is in jeopardy."

"Why is that?"

"Souls need a...higher source...to tap into. It's how they work."

"Sounds like souls are kind of useless, all things considered."

I shook my head. "Souls are what powers the universes. All of them. There's no power greater than that of a soul, let alone a combination of souls."

Jack was quiet for a minute or so. "So, an entity that controlled a lot of souls would be powerful?"

"That's the basis for gods, yeah. A god is a concentration of multi-universal energy with the focused power of belief from the souls it controls."

"Ugh."

I laughed. "It sounds gross, yeah, but it's not. It's kind of beautiful, really."

"So, the worshipper creates the god?"

"Sort of. And the god creates the worshipper. Kind of a cosmic, metaphysical chicken and egg scenario."

"What about the Prince?"

"Same idea, turned to complete evil."

"Okay, but there's, what, hundreds of good gods and only one bad one? How does that work?"

We pulled into the Prosaic City P.D. parking lot. "The good gods don't force the other gods to join them."

Jack snorted. "The Greek and Roman ones did."

"No, they have an almost military hierarchy, but the lowest Greek god still has free will. Zeus can't stop them from doing whatever they want. He can punish them, but he can't control them."

"And the Prince controls the evil gods?" We parked and got out of the car.

"No. He absorbs them. There are no evil gods, not any more. The Prince joined them into himself centuries ago."

Dawn was coming. Probably less than an hour away. That was going to cause problems for Ken, Amanda and Maurice. I activated my wrist-com. "Count?"

"Here, as always."

"I need our top daytime aerial teams to hook up with Ken and Amanda. Ken's following a trail, Amanda and Maurice are trailing a human who could be the Prince's current vessel. Or could just be a lucky drug dealer. We're not sure yet."

"Understood. Sending Black Angel Teams One and Two to support."

"Thanks." I turned off the com.

"Black angels?"

"Literally. The best day fliers around."

"Real angels? You're serious?"

I rolled my eyes. "You've seen everything else, or

heard about it, and yet the existence of angels seems hard for you to fathom?"

"I guess I didn't associate them with --"

He stopped himself, but I knew what he was thinking. "With 'my kind'? Yeah, I know. They're pure and holy and we're the evil undead." I tried to keep the hurt out of my voice. Figured I didn't succeed.

Jack stopped, grabbed my arm, and pulled me against the side of the building. "That's not how I meant it."

"Yes, it is." I tried to get away. "Look, we need to see the Chief."

"No. We need to get this straightened out, right now." Jack was a lot taller than me and bigger all around. He was using his body to keep me in place and struggling meant I was rubbing up against him. I tried not to like it and failed completely. Of course, I had werewolf strength, but I didn't really want to send him flying into the parking lot. Besides, feelings hurt or not, being this close to him made my senses go haywire. He was in a form of supreme manly-mode and it was all I could do not to start that doggy begging whine he seemed to be bringing out in me more and more.

"There's nothing to straighten out." I tried to look away but he had big brown eyes and they were hard to avoid. They were also flashing.

"I don't think you're evil," he said through gritted teeth. "Or weird or frightening. I don't even think you're all that strange."

"What do you think I am?" This didn't come out in the strong, authoritative voice I was shooting for. It came out like a little girl whisper. Sadly, I wasn't covered with fur, so as I felt my cheeks get hot, I knew Jack could see me blushing like an idiot.

He gave me a slow smile. "I think you're one of the best cops I've even known. You're smart, gutsy, funny and loyal, and you have the best instincts going. I also think you're the hottest woman on two or four legs."

Then he bent and kissed me and I started blushing all over. At least, my whole body felt like it was on fire.

Jack kissed me for a good, long while, until I wasn't trying to do anything but hump his leg. Hey, there are some things you can't help if you have a drop of canine in you. He pulled away slowly. "Now, are we past that?"

"Ah, past kissing?" I was okay with moving fast, but even I had speed limits.

Jack rolled his eyes. "No. Are we past you thinking I don't like you because you're a werewolf?"

"Um, dunno."

He kissed me again. "How about now?"

I really wanted to tell him I wasn't sure again, because if his method of convincing me was to kiss me, I wanted to stay unconvinced forever. But we were in the middle of a case with horrifying ramifications and I'd been in law enforcement for several human lifetimes. "I guess so."

He stroked my face. "I think it's kind of sexy."

"What is?"

"You turning into a hot-looking wolf."

"I had no idea you were into bestiality."

"I'm not. Ken explained, it's not the same thing at all."

As ex-boyfriends went, you couldn't get better than Ken. "Um, what else did he explain?"

Jack grinned. "That if I wanted to make a move, I had a good chance of not having my throat ripped out." He let me go but took my hand. "Think we need to pretend that we're still just professional partners, at least as far as the rank and file here are concerned."

"We're an item?" I wasn't arguing, but we were back to moving faster than I'd been prepared for.

He pulled me to him and kissed me again. Okay, yeah, we were an item. My butt wagging was a clear sign.

🐾 Chapter 15 🐾

Jack and I finally stopped making out and went into headquarters. I was glad I didn't bother with makeup, because if I'd had any on it would have been all over my face and his.

We supposedly looked the same as we always did. I mean, we'd straightened our clothes and fixed the hair and all before we went into the building. And I didn't think we got a lot of looks from our fellow officers.

However, the moment we were alone with the Chief, we got the superior glare of disapproval. "You know you're not supposed to become involved with your partner."

I did my best "innocent puppy has not piddled on the rug" look. "What do you mean, Chief?"

The Chief was short and stocky, pretty much all muscle and coiled energy. I'd never been able to figure out how anyone had managed to convince him to take the highest desk job available on the force. He always seemed like he was ready to trot over to the holding cells and beat a confession out of the perps, probably all at once.

He glared at me. "I mean you two have crossed the line."

"How do you figure?" Jack asked calmly.

The Chief rolled his eyes. "I'd say it was the fact you both look guilty, but really, how stupid are you?" He pointed to the video monitor screens to the left of his desk. To the one trained on the parking lot, in particular.

"Oh." Well, I felt stupid. And forgetful. Hey, a lot was going on.

"It's not a normal situation, and you know it," Jack said.

"Fine, whatever. What's actually going on, now that we can, I assume, all stop acting?"

"You could have told me you knew a long time ago."

The Chief shrugged. "I didn't want you getting sloppy. If you had to fool me and Wagner, then you were going to fool anyone else you came across. As this morning has just proven, the moment you got to stop pretending you also got stupid and careless."

I tried to apologize and yawned instead. Widely.

"Vic got hurt tonight," Jack said. "She had to go the hospital in Necropolis Enforcement."

"I'm fine. My kind heals fast." Under most circumstances, anyway. However, much as I didn't want to admit it, while stifling another yawn, I was dog-tired.

And not hiding it well, if the Chief's reaction was any indication. "Go home and get some sleep."

I considered our options. There were a lot of options, of course. But all the vamps were out now that the sun was up. The Black Angels were top-notch, so were Hansel and Gretel. Monty and Edgar, too. So if something were going down with them, I'd know soon enough. Ralph I wasn't so sure about -- he had a tendency to make high-level decisions without asking first -- but he had Dirt Corps with him, and they knew better than to keep Monty in the dark about anything. So, all trails covered. But we had four cops and two hookers in the hospital and they needed to be sniffed, at least.

I shook my head. "Can't. Need to question the survivors and make sure they're not carrying something…extra with them."

"Is there anyone else you can trust with it?" The Chief didn't look like he was going to take no for an answer.

I gave it a shot anyway. "No. How about this? Jack and I go take a look at City Hospital. If everything seems secure, we're fine and heading home. If we're not sure we have a possession, I'll have Enforcement assign a tail. If things are bad, I have a feeling that'll wake us both right up. Okay?"

"No, but I'll take it. I want you two extra-vigilant and I want you, Wolfe, to stop relaxing. You're still undercover, and I expect you to stay that way. As for you," he glared at Jack. "You watch yourself. You've already overstepped your assignment and put yourself and your partner in danger."

"I know the rules," Jack said. He sounded tired, too. "There are always reasons to break them."

The Chief snorted. "Oh yes. Of course there are."

"We don't have the 'no partnering with your significant other' rule in Necropolis Enforcement." We didn't. We also didn't have the "no partnering with your sibling, parent, family member, ex, or wannabe lover" rule, either. Point of fact, we didn't have the "no partnering with your unlifelong enemy" rule, either. In Necropolis Enforcement, the main rule was "whatever works". In some cases that was great. I'd have done a lot to get a rule that allowed me to never work with Ralph, though. But no such luck. My wrist-com beeped, and sure enough, it was my least favorite werewolf on the line.

"Vic, trail's gone dead." Ralph sounded tense and disappointed.

"For real or because it was time to go dead?"

"I think the latter. But we've got nothing." There was something in Ralph's tone that made the hair on the back of my neck rise.

"Where, exactly, did the trail die?"

"Right in the middle of the Prosaic City National Cemetery."

"Fabulous." We were going from bad to worse. "Okay, stay there. Contact Monty. It's not a cause for panic unless one of the other trails ends there, too."

"You got it. Uh…what're your orders in case, ah, we run into difficulties?"

"If the Prince manifests, Ralph, I want you and the others to run like hounds out of Hell, you got that? You do not engage the Prince!"

"Okay." He sounded relieved. Ralph was annoying and overly into the whole pack thing, but he wasn't an utter moron. He had a tendency to grandstand, but only if I was there in the audience. And self-preservation was an animal instinct.

"Let me know if anything happens, even if it's a minor thing."

"Will do. Over and out."

My wrist-com went dead and I looked at Jack. "We need to get moving. No telling what's going on." We got up and I headed out the door.

"Wagner," the Chief called. "I want you, alone, for a minute."

Jack shrugged and I closed the door behind me. It took a lot of willpower, but I forced myself to move down the hall and hum, so I wouldn't hear whatever it was the Chief wanted to say to Jack. Some of this self-control came from the fact that it always seemed wrong to me to eavesdrop on people I liked. More was because I didn't want to hear the Chief warn Jack about the stupidity of this kind of inter-species dating.

I leaned against the wall and hummed good old "Werewolves of London" again. There was a concert coming up soon. I hadn't wanted to go without a date, and while Maurice and Ken had both offered to be my escort, and Ralph would have leaped at the chance, I wasn't into pity dates on either side of the fence. But now...maybe. Then again, as I watched Jack slam out of the Chief's office, maybe not.

He strode over to me, looking angry. "What's wrong?" I figured I knew, but why not pretend, right?

"Just how damn many surrogate fathers, brothers, and uncles, not to mention far-too-interested ex-boyfriends do you have, exactly?"

"Uh, no idea. Why?"

Jack took my arm and started moving us along. "Oh, I just got the 'you treat her right or I'll make your life a living hell and I have friends who know how to ensure that's meant literally' lecture. I got similar from Ken. And the Count, via Ken's wrist-com. I got it from Amanda, and Maurice. I got it from Monty and, from what I gathered, Rover. Lord, even the white worm's giving me lectures."

This wasn't exactly what I'd expected. I felt kind of warm and fuzzy that so many beings cared. "Sorry?"

"Not your fault. You know, I'm not that much of a jerk, or that much of a womanizer. Am I?"

"I don't think so. Then again, you know us werewolves. We're loyal to a fault."

He managed a snort of laughter. "Thank god. I'm okay to say that, right? No smiting, per the lectures?"

"Right. Though a lot of them like to take the thanks. But, nothing to worry about."

"At least that's one worry I can write off." He

looked at me out of the corner of his eye. "I guess it's flattering."

"How so?" I was going for cool. Cool isn't a canine trait, however. I was pleased I wasn't panting at him and my butt was only moving normally for walking.

"That everyone thinks you're so into me that I could break your heart without trying."

"Oh." I wondered how to respond to this. "I so totally am" was the truth, but I'd always understood you weren't supposed to say that before you'd even had a first date. "Oh, not at all" was both a lie and probably not destined to start any relationship well. "We'll see" seemed bitchy. "I don't know" was stupid, since I absolutely did. "Doesn't matter" was a lie.

Jack slid his arm around my waist. "I don't plan to break your heart."

"No one ever plans that." The words slipped out before I could stop them.

He hugged me. "Yeah, I know. How about, I'll do my best not to break your heart if you do your best not to break mine."

"That seems fair to me. Not that I don't like it, but didn't the Chief want us pretending for the rest of the squad?"

Jack sighed. "Yeah." He stopped, pulled us into a supply closet, and kissed me. "You know, I've wanted to kiss you since the first time I saw you."

"Really?" My butt was doing its thing. Sometimes it was easier to be in wolf or werewolf form.

"Yeah. Figured I didn't have a chance, considering who you were dating at the time." I'd been dating Ken, point of fact, and I could see how a human would look at him and figure any girl who was with a guy that suave, sophisticated, handsome and charming wouldn't be looking to trade in any way. "Then I got you as my partner and knew I didn't have any chance at all."

"Because you knew I was a werewolf?"

"Because I knew you were a good cop and good cops don't get romantically involved with their partners."

"I guess we're both bad cops, now." I tried to feel guilty about it and didn't manage it. Probably because Jack was nuzzling my hair.

"No. Per the Chief, these things happen." He hugged me tightly. "It's going to get ugly fast, isn't it?"

"Yeah, it is."

"I just want you to know that I can handle it. I'm sure there are going to be things I've never imagined coming at us, but you're still my partner, no matter what. And partners back each other up."

"You're the best partner I've ever had, Jack. And I've had a lot. Our Enforcement team is great. We'll all manage." I hoped.

Of course, I'd been wrong before. But even the Count said I needed to let that one go. I still hadn't, but maybe someday.

My wrist-com went live. "Vic, it's Monty. Guess where I am?"

"At the cemetery with Ralph?"

"You're so good with guessing games."

"Yeah, it's one of my gifts. Jack and I are headed to City Hospital. Keep me posted."

"Will do."

Jack opened the closet door. "I know. Romantic moment over. Time to roll."

Chapter 16

We drove to City Hospital like good human cops -- seatbelted and not snuggled. I reminded myself that Jack could be killed by a car crash and snuggling was best left for the privacy of one of our apartments.

My virtue was flying high by the time we got into ICU. I wondered about Darlene's concept of the term "pull through", though, because none of our six injured looked good. I wasn't a medical professional, but unless they converted to an undead way of life, they weren't leaving the hospital any time soon.

I dutifully sniffed each one of them. Well, I sniffed one of them, gagged and barfed into a nearby wastebasket, and then tried again. Supposedly they'd been cleaned off, but you couldn't prove it by my nose. The cop we were with was covered with Slimy innard goo, blood -- his own and the others' -- and something else.

"Sulfur." I sniffed again and managed to control the gag reflex. "Dung."

"Dung makes you barf?" Jack sounded worried.

"This dung, yeah. It's Depths of Hell Dung. Special designer scent."

"Can't wait."

"You can't really smell it. Thank Yahweh, or whoever you're into, for that one."

"From what you said, I've been with Yahweh, so I'll give him the thanks, in a big way. You're green."

"Bet I get greener."

We moved on, but it was the same in each room. By the time I got to the sixth one there was nothing in my stomach so my gagging under a semblance of control. I knew I'd be hungry, but not as long as I was near any of these people.

Jack rubbed the back of his neck. "What does it mean?"

"Well, I'm not sure yet." I sighed. "We need an exorcist."

"They're possessed?" Jack's gun was out of his shoulder holster faster than I could blink. I controlled the impulse to crawl to him on my belly.

"I'm not sure. I don't think they are now. But I think they were." There was nothing for it. When it came to this kind of stuff, you really did have to call in the best. I called the Count. "I need Martin."

"You're sure? You know how he hates to be called out for nothing."

I snorted. "In my experience he likes to be called out for a routine blessing, let alone to verify demonic possession."

"I think he pretends."

"I think you're stalling. Where is Martin that you don't want to send him here?"

"At the Prosaic City National Cemetery."

So not good. "So, who called you that didn't call me?"

"None of your team. Routine daytime patrols spotted some oddities. They investigated, called in, and Martin and H.P. agreed it should be investigated."

"Can he leave? I really think we need an expert here." I gave the patient we were with another look. She didn't look like an evil demon was about to burst forth from her being, but then again, I wasn't an exorcist.

"I'll request it." The Count hung up. I got the feeling he was tired of hearing from me. I was instantly sorry I'd thought the word "tired", because I was already and getting more so every minute.

"Do you need to stay here if you're calling in someone else?" Jack asked.

"No idea. Depends on whether or not Martin thinks they're clean or not."

There was a chair in the room. Jack pulled it over, sat in it, and pulled me into his lap. He still had his gun out. I would have protested that this didn't look professional, but I was too tired and snuggling was so much nicer than standing around waiting.

I leaned my head against his shoulder. He rocked gently. "How long do werewolves live?" he asked softly.

"Until we're dusted or destroyed. Just like any other undead."

"How long have you been alive?"

I thought about it. It wasn't something any but the newer undeads really worried about. "I'm too tired to do the math."

"What year were you born?"

"As a human, seventeen-ninety-nine. As an undead, eighteen-nineteen."

"You were twenty when you were, what, bitten?"

"Yeah."

"So, you've been an undead for around two hundred years."

"Sounds right."

He kept on rocking. "You don't look twenty. You don't look two hundred, either."

"Yeah, I look late twenties or early thirties, I know. But we age, all undeads age. We just do it at such a slower rate than humans that we seem young forever. But we don't actually stay that way over the long course of time. Monty's been alive for over fifteen-hundred years. He's an old lich. And he looks older than Edgar, for example, who's a much younger lich."

"Is that why Monty's arm fell off?"

"Yeah. And he's seen a lot of action, too."

Jack was quiet for a moment. "How can you age, even slowly, and yet still live forever?"

"How do the Gods and Monsters do it? I'm not sure. Maybe we do die, but so far as I know, no undead has ever died from old age. Maybe one will someday, but seeing into the future isn't a werewolf trait."

"Do undead ever get tired of living?"

"We call it unliving, and I suppose some do. But in my experience, just like humans, most undeads would like to stay unalive forever. We just have a better shot at it than humans do."

"Why don't you make all humans undeads?"

I shrugged, which happily snuggled me closer. "Not everyone can handle it. Not everyone should. Some people would turn minion, and that's the last thing we need."

"Minion?"

"Willing servant of the Prince."

"Ah. Yeah, from what everyone's said, we don't want that."

"Ever."

"You know anyone who…what, turned?"

I tried to figure out how to answer that without lying, telling the truth, or sounding like I didn't want to tell him. Even though I didn't. But I was saved by a group of beings walking in.

Three were tall, black-skinned, and almost too beautiful to behold. Best wings in any plane of existence. Angels, you'd hate them if they weren't so amazingly perfect. The three here were all male, which was nice for me. I dreaded Jack meeting a female angel. Angels gave vampires a run for the suave, sexy and devastatingly attractive money, and usually won.

The fourth was also an angel, but he'd been angelicized once he'd died. He was shorter, fair-skinned, with piercing eyes. His wings were white, but that was because angels really didn't go in for the two-toned look.

Jack and I stood up hurriedly. I tried not to look guilty and failed. Martin excelled at reminding you of your sins, even when he wasn't trying.

But he gave me a warm smile and a hug. "I'm glad you insisted," he said as he let me out of his embrace. "We could tell there was something wrong just walking into the building."

It was kind of a relief to be right. But, manners first. "Martin, this is my human police partner, Jack Wagner."

Martin put out his hand and shook Jack's vigorously. "Martin Luther. Very pleased to meet you, young man."

Jack shot me a look. "*The* Martin Luther?"

Martin twinkled. "If you mean the founder of the Reformation, yes."

Jack gaped. "*You're* an undead?"

"He's an angel. Yes, they're undeads, but as you know, they're the ones everyone likes." I shrugged. "What can I say? Yahweh really liked him."

Martin chuckled. "So I'm told." He rubbed his hands together. "Now, let's get down to business, shall we? We've got something nasty to banish."

Chapter 17

"We think the Prince came through a portal," I told Martin.

He nodded. "I'm not surprised to hear it."

I gave Martin the high-level version of our night. He was a great listener, all angels were, really. Another reason everyone liked them. The three escort angels listened as attentively as Martin. It was flattering, unless you knew it was just how they were. And then it was still flattering because, well, they were *angels*.

I finished up and Martin nodded. "What happened to the dead bodies?"

Jack answered. "Ken had Dirt Corps deal with them. He'd checked them all, only two were able to become undeads."

"Freddy and Sexy Cindy, yeah." I got a bad feeling. "I need to call Monty." Did the wrist-com thing. "Where did Dirt Corps dispose of the dead bodies from the fracas?"

"Fracas, nice word. Good to see you expanding your vocabulary."

"Monty, I'm here with Martin, about to help with an exorcism. A little less levity."

"You need to learn to relax."

"Right. Where?"

"They were humans, so Prosaic City National Cemetery. And, to anticipate your next question, the trails led right to where we put them. Oh, the gang's all here, by the way."

"All five trails led there?"

"Yes. I checked on Black Angel One. They're still trailing our drug dealer. He's still not doing anything suspicious. I mean, for us. He's out dealing drugs, of course, but that's not suspicious, in that sense."

Martin leaned over. "Montague, please ensure no one remotely suspicious comes near the bodies, either over or underground. We'll need to exhume the bodies when I get back to you, and also perform a cleansing ritual wherever they were. We have traces."

"Got it." Monty signed off.

"Traces?" Jack asked.

"Yes." Martin was back to examining the body.

"Traces of what?" Jack wasn't going to let this one go.

"Traces of Hell," Martin said absently. His eyes narrowed. "But...interesting." He motioned the other angels over. "Thoughts?"

The four angels went into a huddle. Angels have the strongest psychic abilities, so I knew they were talking in their minds only. Which was fine with me. I wasn't nearly as interested in this as Jack was. For him it was all new. For me it was routine. Scary routine, but still, routine.

"Why wouldn't Ken be able to spot what you did and Martin has?" Jack asked me quietly.

"He was reading their souls, looking for those who wouldn't become minions and who'd be able to adapt to the undead lifestyle. Every one of the bodies, dead or alive, reeked at the scene. But our senses of smell were numbed from fighting Slimy, the Ancient Icky One. The problem I have with our living victims here in the hospital is that they still smell like they just came out of Slimy's tummy, with some extra added stink that wasn't there in the alley. They've been cleaned, worked on, given fluids, everything. They should smell of antiseptic, if nothing else. And they don't."

"No," Martin agreed, coming out of the holy

huddle. "They smell of the Prince. But...."

"But?" I hated it when one of the big guys did that whole drag it out thing. It always boded, and never well.

"But I don't think the Prince is in them," Martin said. "I'm not convinced he ever was."

"So, no exorcism?" Not a disappointment. I wanted to go to bed and exorcisms tended to be long and showy, though supposedly Martin could do it fast if he had to. He just didn't like to, and you didn't argue with an angel in his position unless you really felt you had to. And I currently didn't feel I'd be able to work up the energy necessary to get him to go for an Exorcism Lite.

Martin sighed. "No, we have to exorcise, just in case. But the odds are it's a waste of time."

"Why go to the trouble?" Jack asked. "I mean, what's the point? You can't be the only exorcist."

"I'm not," Martin agreed. "And while it would be a good guess that Victoria would call me in on this, I find it hard to come up with a reason for why."

"Diversion." Everyone looked at me. Interesting. I wasn't used to angels looking surprised. "What? We had five trails that led on a wild ghoul chase that all ended at the same spot in the cemetery. We have six people who we have to exorcise, just in case. Potentially an entire cemetery to cleanse, just to be safe. And while we're dealing with all of this, one person's wandering free, dealing in his own way."

"You think the Prince is in Tomio?" Jack asked.

"No idea. But he's the one who sauntered out of here without a real problem."

Martin gave a start. "I missed that before. That's right, one was here." He nodded to the three escort angels and they sauntered out of the room. "They're looking for evidence."

"Evidence of what?" Jack asked.

Martin opened his mouth, but I answered faster. "Proof that Tomio visited each of the other victims before he left the hospital. Evidence that he planted the Prince's trace in them. Or proof that he didn't."

Martin closed his mouth and beamed at me. "You really are an excellent agent, Victoria. And, yes, that's exactly what they're looking for."

"Black Angel One is watching Tomio," Jack protested. "Wouldn't they be able to, I don't know, *tell* if he was really the Prince?"

A thought slunk up and nuzzled the back of my mind. "Yeah, but not if what Amanda honed in on wasn't actually the real Tomio."

Martin looked at me. "Oh dear."

"Oh dear?" Jack looked back and forth between me and Martin. "Oh dear *what*?"

I figured I'd beat Martin to this one, too. "Oh dear, we have a doppelgänger on the loose."

Chapter 18

We all looked at each other. Martin and I exchanged the "we're so screwed" look. Jack just looked confused. "So, Tomio has a twin?"

Martin shook his head. "A doppelgänger isn't a twin. It's a facsimile."

"Always evil," I added. "They're also called a fetch. As in, they fetch whatever their master wants, which is usually the soul of the person being duplicated."

"But why would the Prince need to fetch Tomio's soul?" Jack asked. "I mean, the guy's a drug dealer. If there's anyone who's probably already sold his soul to the first bidder, it'd be him."

"Maybe," Martin said mildly. "But men can do much evil before they lose their souls. Many do evil in Yahweh's name, or the name of another god. And yet, they still remain on our side of the great battle."

I let this one run in my mind. "So, let's say Tomio was like everyone else in that alley -- either a cop or a petty criminal. I mean, it's not like someone dealing in an Old Downtown alley is exactly livin' the dream."

Jack nodded. "Too true. I ran his file while you were in the hospital -- typical dealer. Rap sheet longer than your tail but nothing anyone outside of the Vice Squad would be interested in."

"You're adapting to this so well." I tried to keep the sarcasm at bay, but didn't succeed if Jack's grin was an indication. "Okay, so let's assume he still had his soul. Why would he be the one picked?"

"Perhaps his was the strongest soul," Martin offered.

"Maybe he was the easiest mark," Jack countered.

I thought about this. Not like a cop, not like an

Enforcer. Not even like an undead. I thought about it like a woman. Slimy or the Prince or whatever had made this decision had specific types to pick from -- cops, hookers, bums, junkies, and one dealer. None of these would automatically be considered a pure soul.

"In my experience," I said slowly, "strength of soul is something you can never judge from outward appearances."

Martin nodded, reached out, took my hand and gave it a gentle squeeze. I could see that Jack noted this, but happily he didn't ask about it. "Yes, Victoria, you're correct. What are you thinking?"

It was a polite thing angels did -- they could read your mind if they were close enough to you physically, but they didn't unless they felt they had to, for your protection or the protection of others. So, even though he could just take a look-see, Martin didn't. If you wanted to meet the epitome of self-control, you wanted to meet an angel. Yet another reason everyone loved them.

"Well, I'm thinking that we can't bet either way that Tomio was either the strongest or the weakest soul. In fact, I'd guess he wasn't better or worse than at least half of the victims. So the question is, why him, over anyone else?"

"He was healthier?" Martin didn't sound like he thought this was a good guess.

"Better wardrobe?" Jack didn't sound like he was trying.

I thought about the types of people in the alley. It was a good bet they knew each other. The cops probably knew them, they were street cops working that section of town on the Night Beat. They knew all their denizens. So, why Anthony Tomio as the doppelgänger of choice, over anyone else?

"What does Tomio have that none of the others have?" I asked.

"More money?" Jack shrugged. "I mean, it's not like any dealer doesn't probably make more than the police."

"And poor hookers don't exactly meet the better johns." I thought about Sexy Cindy's comment -- that she'd get to go to school where the rich johns lived. It was a safe bet neither she nor Freddy had ever been there before. A good bet no one in that alley had ever been uptown, other than the junkies, possibly, before they went into full addiction.

I thought about what I'd seen of Tomio. He was mixed race, normal looking, one of those people who could blend in easily as long as he was wearing the right clothes. Unlike the others, he didn't look like anything much good or bad. He looked average.

It clicked. "He was two things the others weren't."

"And that would be?" Jack sounded impatient. He wasn't normally impatient. I took a close look. He looked as tired as I felt. I forgave the snap.

"He's the one who was the most normal, so the most likely to be able to go anywhere and blend in, and he's also the one who has the biggest network of people he knows or know of him."

"How is a drug dealer normal? And what would his network of drug addicts matter? Couldn't evil find them without a problem?"

Martin nodded slowly. "That makes sense, Victoria."

I could tell Jack wasn't convinced, angelic approval or no. "Cops radiate authority, no matter how they're dressed or where they are. Hookers radiate whatever it is hookers radiate, and the cheaper ones pretty much stand out the moment they leave the crap parts of town. Bums and junkies, same thing, and people see them and radiate away from them. In fact, people tend to try to get away from all four types unless they're a john looking for a quickie, and that doesn't make up the majority of the population."

Realization dawned on Jack's face. "But people search a dealer out. And if you don't know he's a dealer or a criminal, if he's just walking down the street, he looks like a regular guy, no one to avoid."

"And dealers don't always work just one part of town. For all we know, last night was just Tomio's day to do his Old Downtown route. And dealers have a large network of people they deal through and with, let alone meet. After all, you can't sell the drugs unless you have a buyer, and the more buyers the better."

"Tomio's file indicated he wasn't a user," Jack added.

"So, not as close to the Prince." Martin looked thoughtful. "That also makes sense."

"How so?"

"If, as you suggested, this is all being done to distract us and allow Mister Tomio's doppelgänger free run in Prosaic City and Necropolis both, choosing a vessel none of us would have had our eyes on makes sense."

"True that." I thought some more. "There were five trails, six victims who are supposed to recover, and three bums, two hookers, and two junkies who didn't make it and also didn't make the leap over to the undead world."

"That's eighteen," Martin said. He sounded worried. Because he was a wise being.

Jack looked at Martin's expression then back to me. "Am I guessing right? You both think there are eighteen doppelgängers out there, wandering around?"

I nodded as I activated my wrist-com. "Count?"

"Agent Wolfe. We're not using standard procedure why?"

"Because you know who it is and I don't have time for my call letters. I need two things. First, an All Being Alert -- we have, potentially, nineteen Anthony Tomio's wandering around, and all of them need to be apprehended with extreme prejudice and more care."

The Count sighed. "May I run this by H.P. and Edgar before I panic the entire community?"

Martin leaned in. "I'm sorry, Vladimir, but no."

"Ah, Martin, didn't realize you were still with Agent Wolfe. Your will and all that. What was the other issue, Agent Wolfe?"

"I need H.P. and the newest recruits assigned to me as soon as possible. I'd like to keep Edgar along as well."

"May I ask why?"

"H.P. and Edgar because of what we're dealing with. Freddy and Sexy Cindy because they were in the alley, in Slimy's stomach, and around for the entire ordeal, and yet they were clean enough to be changed. Either Ken's lost it, which I doubt, or the two strongest souls in that alley are now on our side. I want them with me so I can use them to spot the Prince or his minions or whatever it is that's wandering around my cities right now."

"Not to sound argumentative, but why do you think they'll be able to help?"

I sighed. I hated having to give this answer, but it was the truth. "I just feel that they will be."

"Ah, fine. Never let us argue with werewolf instincts or feminine intuition. I'd like to suggest you and Detective Wagner get some sleep first, however."

"No argument. Have them ready to go at dusk. Call if you need us sooner."

I switched off the wrist-com to see Jack gaping at me. "You want the bum and the hooker? Sorry, the new zombie and succubus? And you also think we have time to nap?"

"Just because all Hell's trying to break loose doesn't mean you shouldn't take care of yourself."

"Words to live by," Jack muttered.

"Well, let's hope."

Chapter 19

We waited until Martin's angelic escorts returned and confirmed that, sure enough, Tomio had wandered in to see how the others were doing. He'd been allowed to, without much fuss. Martin called in some additional angels for support and Jack and I left them to do their exorcisms.

"Can't be standard operating procedure for the hospital to let Tomio go in to visit every room," Jack said as we headed back to the car.

"Be happy he only visited the six who were involved. But, yeah, I'm sure he used influence."

"I'm betting you don't mean that word the way I'd think."

"Right. Influence in this sense would be like, oh, similar to what Ken used on you to keep you from realizing what was going on at the start of all this excitement. Only, the Prince and his minions use it differently. It's just a nudge, usually."

"A nudge to do what?"

"To do what they want."

"Didn't Ken make me do what he wanted?"

"Yes, but it took more effort than influence." I tried to think about how to explain it. "It's like…you're the nurse on the floor. A patient comes out of his room. He's recovered, he's nice and friendly, he seems genuinely concerned about these other patients. He wants to see them to reassure himself they're going to be okay, give them the old encouraging words, and so on. The nurse knows she isn't supposed to let him. Influence shoves just a little bit, so the nurse says, sure, okay, go ahead, what can it hurt? In her mind, she never felt the influence and she's made the decision herself."

"Okay." Jack was quiet while we got in and he started the car up. "But, couldn't vampires do that, too? I mean, isn't that really what Ken did with me?"

"Well, let's think about that. We were in the middle of a danger situation. Would a gentle nudge have worked? How much shoving would someone have had to do in order to convince you that you didn't want to get involved?"

"Where are we headed? And, yeah, okay, a lot. So influence is used when it can be more, what, subtle?"

"Yeah, that's a good word for it." I thought about it. Well, no time like the present. "Um, your place or mine?"

Jack grinned. "I thought you'd never ask." He shrugged. "Where will you feel the most comfortable?"

I thanked the Gods and Monsters for the seatbelt. He made me want to roll and whine without even trying. I really hoped this wasn't going to end disastrously. "Well, my place has the convenience of an easy slide in and out of Necropolis."

"Let's go there, then. By the way, Ken warned me about sliding, but it wasn't hard at all. But I can't see Necropolis now, even though I've been trying to."

"Be thankful. It's hard to see both at once. I tend to focus on wherever I'm really supposed to be at any given time, it's easier."

"But if you wanted to, you could see Necropolis now?"

"Yeah." I knew what request was coming.

"Where are we, in Necropolis?"

Happily, by now we were near my apartment. "We're in Enforcement Housing. Dammit!" I slammed my eyes shut.

"What? What's wrong?"

"Nothing. We just drove through a phalanx of beings. But not really."

"Huh? There's no one here."

"In Prosaic City, it's still early morning and only the trash guys are out, yes. In Necropolis, the Day Shifters are coming on duty. There are tons of beings out and about."

"Did we hurt anyone?" He sounded tense. I could understand -- it was hard to comprehend.

"No. Two different planes of existence, intersecting here. On our side of things, we choose to see the human side as, oh, holographic images, I guess. Almost as moving background. Undeads are used to living in more than one plane. The unborn -- those born as an undead of some kind -- they have no learning curve. They see all the planes their species can with ease and without issue. Those of us who become undead, well, it's a little harder, but you adjust fast."

"What about humans?" He pulled into my underground parking garage. Conveniently, we had visitor parking underground, too. I lived in a good building, one of the perks of an Enforcement job.

"It's very hard for humans. Makes most of them go crazy."

Jack was quiet as he found a parking place. "Artists, human artists. Do they see the other planes?"

And yet another reason I panted after this guy -- he was smart and intuitive. "Yes, most of them. Some don't realize it, some think they dream it, some *know*, and that knowledge puts them over the edge."

"All artists?"

"Most. All the creative types, yeah. Their gift and their curse, I suppose."

"Why don't the undeads help them?"

We got out and headed up into my building. Because we were talking about it, my ability to focus on one plane or the other wasn't functioning well. Fortunately for me, I'd been purposely housed in this location because it was one of the few areas where Prosaic City's layout coincided with Necropolis'. High-rise apartment in Prosaic City on top of and next to high-rise Necropolis Enforcement Housing. I wasn't the only undercover agent, and all of us housed here.

I was on the top floor of the Prosaic City building. As we rode the elevator -- and I watched a group of banshees and succubae flying up the side of the other building on their ways home -- I answered Jack's question. "It's cruel to let someone sit in a sort of madness, yes. At least, in a way. But it's crueler to take away their gift, the thing that sparks their creativity. It's like killing them but leaving them alive, and not in the undead way of being alive."

"Why don't you make all the humans undeads? You all seem so much...I don't know, better than we are."

"We have our foibles and failings, just like humans do. Some more than humans do. Besides, we can't make everyone an undead. The universes need humans, too. The gods need them. Heck, even the monsters need them, and I mean the monsters like Slimy, not the monsters like me."

"You're not a monster," he said softly. "None of the people I've met last night and today are monsters. You're just...different."

"Yeah. With some serious dietary challenges. But...thanks."

He smiled. "No need to thank me." We got out of

the elevator and Jack looked around. He'd been here before, to pick me up for shift, usually. But now he looked like he was seeing it for the first time. "How do you afford to live in a penthouse suite on a cop's salary?" he asked as we went inside.

"I can't. Necropolis Enforcement pays for it as needs of the assignment."

"Why didn't I ever ask that before?"

I grinned. "Well, because you were influenced not to notice."

"You can influence?"

I snorted. "Hardly. Not a werewolf gift. But one of our stronger warlocks cast an influence spell on my building and my apartment in particular. Any human comes up or in, they don't notice that it's more pricey than I should be able to afford."

"But, I'm a human."

"You're also a human in the know, now. The spell can't work on you any more."

Jack looked around. "Nice place. Always been nice, but I feel like I've never really looked at it before."

"You probably haven't." I took his hand. "This is the human side. I'd rather sleep on the Necropolis side." I walked us through the outer wall of the human building, stepped through the outer wall of the Necropolis building, and into what I considered the other half of my home.

Jack gaped. "That was amazing!" His head swiveled like he was an owl. "I can still see the human side."

I was shocked but kept that to myself. "Don't try to slide over without my help, at least not until you get good at it, okay?"

He nodded, still looking around like a tourist. "You

know, put together, you have an incredible layout here." He looked out the window and whistled. "And what a view!" He went to the outer wall side and looked. "You know, I can see the Prosaic City view from here, too. This place, well, these places are great." He sounded ready to move in.

I was just this side of suggesting it, but my vision started to blur. Jack was enthusiastically in my home and adapting to my life with rapid ease, but all I wanted was to get undressed and go to bed. I wasn't even sure if I had the energy to be amorous, which almost worried me, considering I'd fantasized about being in this situation with him for over a year. I wondered if I was getting a fever or something.

Jack stopped examining my dwelling and looked at me. "You look beyond exhausted. I know I am. Will this sound like a total letdown if I suggest that we go to bed but worry about seeing how compatible we are *in* bed after we wake up?"

I couldn't help it. I rubbed up against him. "Not a letdown at all."

He grinned and put his arm around me. "Then why are you rubbing up against me with a come-hither look?"

We headed into the bedroom. I wanted to lie, but I was too tired. "It's a wolf or canine thing."

"A good thing?"

"Yeah." I managed to keep from sharing that it indicated he was either my mate, my pack leader, or both. One more manly, thoughtful, or sexy statement or action out of him and I'd end up deciding I wasn't too tired to go for the gusto right now. After all, we'd be lying down, so resting. In a way.

Jack nuzzled my hair. "Well, as long as it's good."

I held onto my resolve by a claw. We separated and got undressed. I let my clothes drop. He folded his neatly and put them on the chair in the room. Well, neatness was a good trait. I hoped he wasn't looking for it in his girlfriend, of course.

I managed not to drool when he took his underwear off but only by focusing on being tired. He had a great body and was clearly going to be the alpha male in any pack. I reminded myself that he was tired, too, and what we needed more than anything was to sleep so we could get back on the case, refreshed and energized.

We slid into bed and, in an effort not to seem either like I was about to hump his leg or like I was frigid, I snuggled my back up against him. He wrapped his arms around me and kissed my ear. "Just out of curiosity," he whispered, "what do you want me to make you for breakfast, since we're skipping dinner?"

That last claw holding onto restraint slipped off the side of lust mountain. I rolled onto my back. Thankfully, before I went into the full-on whining, rolling and undulating thing I couldn't stop when I was this tired and around this appealing a male, Jack rolled on top of me and kissed me.

Really, tired or not, it was a lot better than sleeping.

Chapter 20

I woke up alone in bed, brain fuzzy and nose going crazy. Someone was cooking and the smell made my stomach growl and my mouth water. It was still daylight, but I could tell it was late afternoon.

I crawled out of bed, tossed a long t-shirt on, and trotted to the kitchen. Jack was there in his underwear, cooking up a storm. He grinned as I came in. "I woke up starving. You were out, but I figured the sooner we ate, the better."

I sat at the little table I had in the kitchen. The Prosaic City side of my home had a dining room area, but I only used it if I had to. I ate the majority of my meals here. I noted he'd already set the table.

"So, you're like the perfect man?"

He laughed. "Don't know about that. But I'm a bachelor and I don't like to eat out every meal. Glad you have a well-stocked fridge. Impressive deep freeze, too."

"Werewolves have to have food available for whenever the hunger hits." At least those of us who didn't want to go create more werewolves via unwilling participants or perpetrate the bad stereotypes had well-stocked freezers and pantries. It was just good sense.

"I guess so. You said sausages were good, right?"

I had to wipe the drool. "Yeah. Are they ready yet?"

Jack chuckled. "Almost."

There was coffee percolated and he already had the orange juice on the table. I wondered if it would mark me as ridiculously eager if I proposed marriage right now. Probably.

He dished up and presented my plate with a flourish. "The kitchen hopes this is to the lady's liking." There were three kinds of sausages, breakfast potatoes, scrambled eggs, toast with butter and jam, and sliced fruit. It was like I'd gone out to one of the nicer breakfast eateries -- I'd certainly never seen food this lovely in my own home before.

I managed to wait until he seated himself, forced myself to say grace, which caused a raised eyebrow but no questions from Jack, and then waited until he picked up his stainless steel flatware. Silver, even silver-plate, isn't good for werewolves.

As soon as he started, I dove in. I'd spent years being sure I was still able to eat like a human, but I hadn't had food for going on twenty-four hours, and hunger is a dangerous thing with my kind. I wolfed my food, literally. I tried not to, but I was starving,

I finished well before Jack did. He smiled, got up, took my plate, went to the stove, and returned with a new plateful of food. "I like a girl with a healthy appetite."

"Thank the Gods and Monsters." This serving I could eat a little more slowly. The third plateful I could eat like a human. I finished plate three when he finished plate one. I managed not to burp, but only just. "You're a great cook."

He grinned. "Glad to hear it. You always pack away that much food?"

"Yeah, pretty much." Not in front of him before now, though. He'd only seen me eat like a human girl before. I wondered if I'd blown it.

"I'm amazed you stay so tiny. Is it because you burn it off?"

"I guess. And I'm not that small, I'm just a lot

smaller than you." This was true. I wasn't going to be mistaken for either a skeleton or a slime monster -- I was an average-sized female, at least as far as I'd ever seen. "It takes a lot to get a fat werewolf. Our metabolisms run high, and we have to eat well and frequently, or we start to go...a little on the bad side."

"I can imagine. You need more?" He sounded ready to cook again.

"Nope, that was great. I'm full and ready for a nap. Not that we have the time."

Jack reached across the table and took my hand. "Wish we did, but I know you're right." He took a deep breath. "Last night, well, I guess, this morning...."

I tried not to tense up. Tired or not, being with Jack had been fabulous. I'd felt relaxed and happy as well as aroused beyond belief. I wanted to pray on this one, but held it. If it hadn't been that way for him, there wasn't anything Yahweh or any other god could or should do about it.

He stroked my hand with his thumb. "It was...really special for me. I...I know it's kind of fast, and it's going to sound kind of high school-ish, but...you want to go steady?"

I let out the breath I'd been holding. "I never went to high school." Whoops. Not exactly the smooth response I'd been shooting for. Found myself wishing I was in werewolf form as I felt my cheeks get hot.

Jack just smiled. "Not sure if I can take that as a yes or if that was a nice way of saying a human just can't stack up to the undead guys."

"You more than stacked." Wow, perhaps, somewhere, I could get a coherent, non-stupid sentence out about this. Not right now, perhaps, but was someday too much to hope for?

He grinned. Either he thought this was cute or he liked idiots. Maybe both. I hoped for cute. I cleared my throat and tried again. "I'd really like to be in a monogamous relationship with you." Hmmm, not better, really. Now I sounded like I was trying for the Stuffiest Girlfriend award.

Jack started to laugh. "Is there a way that undeads do this that I could learn, just to make it easier?"

"No, not really."

He stood up, helped me up, and pulled me into his arms. "You're mine, I'm yours, no one else in between. Yes or no?"

"Yes."

I was rewarded for brevity and coherence by him kissing me. I was then further rewarded by another round of truly amazing mating. All in all, it was a cheerful way to start the night.

Chapter 21

Fortified with food and sex, we showered and I dressed.

"I should have washed these or something," Jack said as he stared at his clothes. Still folded neatly? Yes. Ready to wear? Not so much, really. They'd been through a lot the night before. "I'd put them on, but, uh...."

"They reek, yeah. Fortunately for you, we undead have our ways." I called Maurice. "You up and about?"

"Yes, and don't you sound all relaxed and satisfied. The human came around? Pun completely intended."

"Funny you ask. I need a set of men's clothes, pronto."

"What, you ripped them to shreds or something? I mean, I know werewolves can get into it but --"

"We were too tired to do laundry," I interjected quickly. "And we need to get out there on the Beat. I know you either know where Jack's apartment is or where you can get him another set of clothes without issue. Do the mist thing, or whatever, and help me out."

"My sister's your best friend. Why doesn't she get these kinds of calls?"

"Because you're far more adept at this kind of thing and you know it."

He sighed. "Too true, too true. Be there shortly. Please have Mister Yummy greet me at the door. I'll take that as payment." He hung up, snickering.

"You sure it's okay to ask someone to get clothes for me?" Jack looked uncomfortable.

"Yeah. Breaking and entering is old hat for vamps. They do it when they're learning how to turn into mist.

You'll have clothes in no time."

I considered what we were likely heading into, and pulled out some serious weaponry. If the Prince was out of Hell, we were in real trouble. If it was just one of his stronger minions, well, we were still in real trouble. I figured it was better to be prepared, and besides, we had that nice, unmarked yet oh so obvious police car. Plenty of room in the trunk for what I wanted along.

Jack gaped. "What the hell is that thing?"

"Multi-round crossbow."

"And that?"

"Holy water shooter. Works like a Super Soaker. In principle."

There was a knock at the door. I went to open it while Jack trotted to the bathroom to get a towel. He still managed to shout a question while doing so. "Holy water, isn't that supposed to be deadly to undeads?"

I opened the door to find Maurice standing there with a set of men's clothes. He grimaced. "You are not upholding your end of the bargain."

"I never said yes."

"Huh." Maurice shoved in and handed the clothes to Jack, who was clutching the towel around him. "Really, sweet cheeks, I'm sure I've seen something equally as magnificent as what you're hiding."

I took the clothes. "Don't count on it."

Maurice grinned while Jack blushed for the first time I'd ever seen. "Oh, and as for holy water, if your soul isn't given to the Prince, holy water can't hurt you. But unholy water can," Maurice added as he picked up one of the shooters. "You really think we need these, Vicki?"

"Yeah, I do. I think you and Amanda need to go armed for warlock."

"Warlock?" Jack asked.

"Well, in your case, armed for bear."

"Okay. But...I thought you said warlocks were good."

"Some warlocks, and witches, yeah. Like demons."

"No," Maurice corrected. "Demons are like humans -- they get a choice."

"Warlocks and witches get a choice," I argued.

Maurice rolled his eyes at Jack. "This nuance was never her strong suit. Did she tell you about Changelings?" Jack nodded. "Wonderful. Human children, see into all the planes, taken for their own good. Because of the nature of their existence, they become witches or warlocks under most circumstances. Of course there are some who want to be just like their adoptive families, so they might choose to turn vampire or werewolf or something, but most of them remain on the spell-casting side of the house."

"I thought you said they were undead," Jack said to me. "How does that work?"

"Call them differently undead. Rituals and things that turn them into what we are more than what you are." I sighed. "I'm going to get more weapons while Maurice finishes his lecture. I had no idea you were bucking for a University job," I tossed over my shoulder.

"You wish," Maurice replied. "So, that's how you get a good witch or warlock."

"Wait," Jack said. "A lich is a spell-caster, from all I've ever heard, which wasn't a lot. How does that work?"

"Similarly." Maurice sighed. "It's nuances, really. A lich is a being who in their pre-undead life was able to become a witch or warlock, but never made the transition for whatever reason. So, they cast spells when they were living, but unknowingly. The bent of their souls determines where they end up. Their interests determine what they do."

"Monty, for example, is far more interested in running Dirt Corps than casting spells." Hey, Maurice wasn't the only one who knew stuff. "It's one of the reasons we consider witches and warlocks more powerful -- a lich has the skills, but rarely the inclination."

Jack nodded. "I guess I can see that. But some liches cast?"

"Sure. Most of them, at least for fun, just to keep their hands in. But, overall, nothing like witches and warlocks, who are casting magic every day, at minimum."

"What about the bad ones?" Jack asked.

Maurice shrugged. "The bad ones, well, they're always humans who have given themselves to the Prince for occult power. Liches as well as witches and warlocks. Some of them are very strong and always scary."

"Devil worshippers?" I heard Jack ask as I went back to my weapons room and rummaged around. So everything wasn't perfectly hung or organized or cataloged, or whatever. Werewolves didn't need a card catalog to find what we wanted, that's what our noses were for.

"Yes," Maurice said with a sigh. "But again, Satan's Yahweh's servant. He appears to everyone who calls on him, and then explains how things are."

"Really?" Jack was back to sounding fascinated.

"Yeah." I came back laden with weapons. "Some, like Martin, catch on."

"Martin Luther didn't call on the Devil!"

Maurice and I exchanged a look. "No," I said slowly. "He didn't. He did, however, try to banish Satan, and so, essentially, called on him. It was complicated, but I'm sure Martin will be glad to explain once we've handled this latest takeover bid by the Supreme Evil One. And all that."

"I'm just curious," Jack muttered.

"Anyway," Maurice went on hurriedly. "The ones who chat with Satan and still want to commit their souls to evil send said souls right to the Prince."

"Okay." Jack sounded doubtful. "I don't get it with demons."

"Demons, like humans, come from a different plane of existence. If they're good demons, they support a god and that's who their soul belongs to, in addition to themselves. If they're bad demons, their souls go to the Prince." Maurice looked at me. "Beautiful but dumb?"

"Tired and overwhelmed." I shook my head. "You're just so old you've forgotten what it was like."

"Darling," Maurice said as he swished to the door. "I was so happy to discover I didn't have to continue to fight in the war and hide from the British, I had no transitional problems whatsoever."

"Which war?" Jack asked as Maurice opened the door and headed out.

"Revolutionary. Ghastly times, just ghastly. I'll say this -- nothing trumps indoor plumbing and central heat and air, nothing." With that, the door closed and he was gone.

🐾 Chapter 22 🐾

I had the weaponry out, but getting it to the car was going to prove a little exciting, since we had to slide back to Prosaic City.

"Seriously, we can both barely carry all this stuff," Jack protested as I put another crossbow on the stack he was holding. "How're we going to explain it if we see someone? And do we really need it all or are you just a typical woman and you over-pack for all occasions?"

"Yes, we need it." Well, we might need it. And better to be prepared. What if the one thing that would stop the Prince was my Evil Fairy Repellent and we didn't have it with us? I grabbed another can and shoved it under Jack's arm.

Laden for ancient gods, bear, warlock and potentially the Supreme Evil, I slid us across. Jack impressively didn't drop anything. He didn't stop muttering, either, but I let it pass.

The only beings on the top floors of the Prosaic City building were other undercover agents. So waiting for the elevator was no issue. However, we all could and did get human visitors, so being sure the coast was clear was still a necessity. Werewolf senses being what they were, it was easy for me to wait until I knew we had a clear elevator.

We loaded in and I pushed the special button that only those with top floor access had -- the Express button. We headed down to the parking garage with no stopping. Once there, however, I had to do the intent sniff and listen thing. There were a lot of human tenants going out and a few coming in. Fortunately there were several elevators and there was another special button for top floor folk -- the Door Sealed button.

After holding the elevator for a long ten minutes, the garage was clear and we headed to the car. Jack dumped the stuff in the trunk and moaned. "I don't think I can move my arms. Hopefully nothing attacks us until I get the feeling back in my fingers."

"Give me the keys, I'll drive."

He snorted. "No way."

"I drive well."

"You drive recklessly."

"Do not." Well, not always.

Jack opened the passenger door and waited for me to get in. He wasn't normally this gentlemanly and I had to figure it wasn't because we were now an official couple -- he just didn't want me thinking I had a shot at the steering wheel. I gave him a dirty look as I seated myself.

He grinned, closed the door, and got in on the driver's side. "I'm relieved our working relationship isn't going to change now that we're a couple," he said with a laugh. "Where to?"

As Night Beat detectives, we didn't have to check in at headquarters if we were in the middle of a case. The Chief would contact us if he needed to, but if we were following something, we had a lot of autonomy.

I activated my wrist-com and decided to throw the Count a bone. "This is W-W-One-Eight-One-Niner."

"Agent Wolfe, how kind of you to follow procedures. I trust the daylight hours were good to you?"

"Fantastic. What's our status?"

"Black Angel One has changed shifts with Vs-Seventeen-Seventy-Five and -Six."

"What did Black Angel One have to say?"

"They shared that their quarry did nothing suspicious, but since they were following orders, they didn't engage."

"Fair enough. What else?"

The Count sighed. "A-Fifteen-Forty-Six has conferred and briefed Z-Nineteen-Thirty-Seven and L-Eighteen-Forty-Nine, and they are with V-Nineteen-Sixty."

"Martin's staying active on the team?" This didn't bode well.

The Count sighed. "And here, I thought we were following procedure."

"Fine, fine, carry on. Who else is with V-One-Nine-Six-Zero?" The Count got to use the shorter number codes, we agents didn't. I was sure it was because the Count thought the whole numbering thing was ridiculous in the first place, but so far had never gotten him to admit it.

"Also with the group are L-Seven-Ten and HH and DC Sixteen-Oh-Six."

"No one else?"

"Should there be?"

"I don't know. I lost count a while back."

"That remains your problem, not mine, Agent Wolfe."

"And you wonder why I hate the call letters." I gave up on the formality. "What about the doppelgängers? Anyone find any or all of them during the day and eliminate our problem?"

"If it were that easy, Agent Wolfe, why would we need you on the case?"

"Fine, where're Ken and the others actually at, the cemetery?"

"If you already knew, why did you ask?" The

Count disconnected. Sometimes he could be a royal pain in the tail.

Jack cleared his throat as he headed us on the fastest path to National Cemetery. "So, first question. Your agent codename -- does that stand for werewolf and the year you, ah, undied?"

"Yes." I was glad we'd done the roll in the sheets thing a couple more times after breakfast. It muted my desire to do the roll and whine thing every time he said something intelligent or did something manly. I hoped it would last through the night.

"So, by that code, and knowing what Maurice said, he's either V-Seventeen-Seventy-Five or -Six, right?"

"Right. He's Seventeen-Seventy-Six, Amanda's Seventy-Five."

"L is lich, Z is zombie, and HH and DC are, what, hellhound and daemon cat?"

"Yep."

He was quiet for a few long moments. "Wow. Monty *is* old."

"Old, experienced, cagey."

"I thought he ran his own thing, was dotted line to Necropolis Enforcement."

"Yes, but he still has a call codename."

"Rover doesn't?"

"Rover's assumed to be with Monty unless otherwise stated. Most white worms are within Dirt Corps. Monty has them assigned whatever codes he wants, I'd assume. Doesn't matter."

"Because Dirt Corps isn't as good as Necropolis Enforcement?"

"No. They do their best. And they come through when you really need them." Why I felt the need to defend Dirt Corps, I couldn't say.

Jack smiled. "I'm not dissing them, Vic. It's just obvious they're not the elite."

"True. But Rover doesn't have a call code and it doesn't matter because most white worms aren't going to see a lot of active duty. Monty's been training Rover for over a thousand years. He's like Kato." Prosaic City's top police dog. Retired now, but still held as the K-9 standard against whom all others would never measure up. "But most white worms are pets."

Jack mercifully didn't make a joke. "I guess when you're an undead you don't have a lot of pet options."

"True. For some reason, werewolves and hellhounds find others having dogs as pets somewhat demeaning. Daemon cats and feline familiars feel the same way. Undeads aren't big on horses -- most of us can move faster on our own, and those who can't usually prefer a smoother form of transportation. And so on. So, yeah, white worms are popular pets." So were spiders, snakes and bugs, but only with Dirt Corps and their ilk.

"Is it true that animals are afraid of werewolves?"

"When faced with a hungry werewolf? Yeah, they should be afraid. But it's like zebras and lions. If the lion's full, the zebras are wary but not panicked. Same concept."

We reached the cemetery and drove through slowly. It was quite large -- Prosaic City wasn't small, housing several million souls, and the National Cemetery was the main cemetery for the city. It was placed on top of Necropolis' Evangelical Quarter. I was pretty sure someone on the undead side had influenced that decision. It made the cemetery a much safer place to be than it would have been normally. It also made undead transitions for those interred there easier. Not all humans who died became undeads, but Monty was always looking for talent and really, ghosts created themselves.

Jack's questions were causing my migraine-inducing double-vision. So I saw a solemn, lovely, well-kept cemetery sitting on top of the roofs of every kind of religious shrine known to human-, undead-, and all otherworldly-kind. If they were a good god still unalive and kicking, they had a shrine in the Evangelical Quarter.

I squeezed my eyes shut. "Jack, you need to slow down on the questions. I have to concentrate on our problem at paw. Hand. Whatever."

"Okay. Is that you concentrating or are you seeing both worlds at the same time again?"

"The latter."

"Sorry."

I opened my eyes. Good. I could only see the spires from some of the larger shrines, temples and churches sticking out of the ground. I could also see Ken and the others gathered around the largest tomb in the place.

"It'll pass. Let's really focus on the human stuff for right now. Because potentially the Prince and/or a wide variety of his stronger minions are wandering around in the human plane with intent to destroy and conquer."

Chapter 23

We reached the group and I did a quick nose count. In addition to everyone I was expecting, Black Angel Two was with us as well. I got the impression they'd replaced Martin's escorts because they gave the impression they were more than willing to exterminate with extreme prejudice should anyone look at him cross-eyed.

"Who're the chicks?" Jack asked in a low voice.

Great. I knew I didn't want female angels around him. "Black Angel Two." I bit the silver bullet, gave them a smile, and made the introductions. "Miriam, Magdalena, this is my partner, Jack."

They both eyed him. "Externally…I approve," Miriam said, right before she turned away, presumably to watch Martin's back.

Magdalena gave him a longer look. Then she smiled at me. "I think he's a keeper. If you can keep him alive, that is."

"Ah, nice to meet you both," Jack said. Then he sidled away to stand next to Monty and pet Rover.

I followed. "What's up with you?" I didn't really want to hear about how hot and awesome Miriam and Magdalena were, but I figured it was better to get it over with now.

"Are all female angels Amazons?" He didn't make it sound like a good thing.

"Well, no, but when humans become angelic they alter. Not just the wings and all, but there are other changes."

"Those two were humans? Ever?"

"Yeah. From what I've been told, they weren't quite that hot when they were alive."

He shook his head. "Define 'hot'. If you mean scary and emasculating, they're smokin'. If you mean someone a guy would want to go to bed with, ah, not really."

I tried to sniff surreptitiously. If someone was telling a whopper of a lie, there were usually telltale signs, and their body odor was one of them. I didn't smell lying on Jack -- I smelled fear. He was afraid of Black Angel Two? I was both pleased and concerned. "Angels are normally considered the most attractive undead species in existence."

"Really? Well, I'll be sure to keep an eye on you around Martin and any other male angels."

"Martin remained pretty much himself. He had the choice."

"And the two scary chicks didn't?"

"Um, I think it was more, at the time, when they died, that they wanted to fit in." I was reaching. I had no idea what Black Angel Two's mindset had been at the time. They'd died centuries apart and more centuries before me, but over time had worked hard to become one of the two top Angelic Enforcer teams. Considering that Black Angel One had been together far longer, and had died closer together, all things being equal, Two's rise was very impressive.

"Fit in where?" Jack shuddered.

"With the other angels. And, what's wrong with you?"

He shook his head. "I grew up thinking angels watched over us. I never want something like that watching over me."

Miriam was next to us. Angelic thing. One moment there, the next, here. They moved fast, that was all, but it was freaky the first few hundred times it happened.

She looked Jack right in the eyes. "You must tread carefully."

"Sorry, didn't mean to insult you," Jack said.

She shook her head. "I don't care what you think of me. But your soul is in jeopardy."

"Because I'm a human?"

"No," Miriam said slowly. "Because you no longer want to be."

And then she was gone, back next to Martin and Magdalena, her back to us.

Jack looked at me. "Really? The most attractive undead species? Compared to what, Dirt Corps?"

"No, really. More than vampires, even."

"Um, I'm not really attracted to Amanda, but I'd take her in a heartbeat over Black Angels Charm and Charmer." He looked around. "They're going to be working with us for the rest of this case?"

"I think so. Don't worry, maybe Black Angel One will drop in, too."

"More 'hot chicks'?"

"No, they're male. Brothers." Considered the hottest things with two wings, too, but I decided not to mention it.

"I can't wait."

"You'll have to," Monty said. He'd played dead while this was going on, but I knew he'd taken it all in. "Black Angel One spent all day trailing Tomio for, as near as we can tell, no reason. They're resting, but I believe they plan to join us in a few hours."

"Good, I'm sure we're going to need them." I decided to let Miriam's comment about Jack's soul wait. We had to plan our course of action. I'd have time to find out what she meant -- about his soul as well as him not wanting to be human -- later. "Ken, what've we got?"

Ken came over to us and the others followed. "Nothing much. Amanda and Maurice are as bored on their trailing detail as they were last night and Black Angel One was all day."

"No one's found any of the doppelgängers? Not one?"

Gretel shook her head. "We put out an ABA. Nothing."

"ABA?" Jack asked.

"All Being Alert." I heaved a sigh. "So, all the false trails led here. What happened with the people who died at the scene last night?"

"They're still interred," Monty answered. "Nothing different about them."

"The living victims are exorcised," Martin offered. "But, as I'd suspected, it was a waste of effort. The traces were all external, only. Left to confuse and delay."

"But why? The Prince's side hasn't done anything now for going on twenty-four hours. And with doppelgängers wandering loose, you'd think something would have gone down by now."

"Are we sure we have doppelgängers at all?" Jack asked.

I shrugged. "No. We're not sure the Prince or his stronger minions are on the human plane, either. But if they're not, what's with all the divide, conquer and confuse tactics? It's not like doing that would cause us to take monitoring off the normal entryways or stop watching the usual suspects."

"Everything seems normal, on all the planes," Magdalena said. "Even in Hell."

Martin nodded. "Undercover agents report no

unusual activity, other than the incident from last night, which appeared to be an attempt to impress the boss that went wrong."

"Our agents think Slimy acted alone and there was no one else on the grassy knoll or, in this case, in the creepy alley?"

"As far as they can tell," Magdalena said. "As far as anyone can tell, we shouldn't be gathered here, trying to find doppelgängers. Or anything else, for that matter."

The group started discussing the situation, options, theories. I let it wash over me and didn't add in. Neither, I noted, did Miriam. She still had her back to the rest of us, watching. She was still alert for danger. And I knew I needed to be. Werewolf senses work on many levels, and all of mine were saying we were in not just trouble, but real, potential Apocalyptic trouble. The trouble was, I had no idea of what it was, where it was coming from, or what to do to defend against it.

I realized we were missing two beings I'd requested. "Hey, where are Freddy and Sexy Cindy?"

"Finishing indoctrination," H.P. advised. "They'll be along shortly."

"Good."

"Why?" Jack asked, sounding tired already. "What are a former bum and hooker going to have that everyone else doesn't?"

I shrugged. "Whatever they have, the Prince couldn't get them. Besides, maybe they know where Tomio normally hangs out. We need to know if the person Maurice and Amanda are tailing is the real Tomio or not, for starters."

"How would they know more than anyone here?" Jack shook his head. "If this were a human-only situation, I'd tell you to round up the usual suspects and find out what's going on."

Miriam stalked off. She went to what I knew were fresh graves.

"What's she doing?" Interestingly, this question didn't come from Jack, but from Ken.

I watched her. "I think she's going to do what Jack suggested. She's gathering the usual suspects, at least the ones from our favorite alley."

"How is she doing that?" Jack asked.

"By raising the dead."

Chapter 24

Despite what many religions would have you believe, raising the dead isn't all that hard, shocking or unusual. Angels and gods can do it any time they want. They just don't usually want to, for a variety of reasons.

There are also a variety of ways to raise the dead. Resurrection is a rarity -- most who die really don't want to come back as humans or whatever they were before. The ones who die and are undead material are usually already out of their graves before an angel or god would be coming by.

I let Monty handle Jack's new, myriad questions, while I went over to Miriam. Raising takes concentration, but she was so strong I figured she could talk and raise at the same time. I watched her movements -- she was going for a limited raising, which I considered good sense. The problem was, a limited raising was just that -- limited. You got a short time to ask whatever you needed of the dead and then they were back to dead.

"What are we going to ask them?"

"You're the detective." Miriam had supposedly had a way with people when she'd been alive. You couldn't prove it by anyone these days, but she didn't bother me all that much. In a little way, I sort of idolized her and Magdalena -- they were at a level I was never likely to achieve and they'd worked harder than anyone else to get there. I wanted to be like Black Angel Two when I grew up.

"True." I considered what we really needed to know. What was going on, for starters. But the questions had to be posed in a way to get the right answers. The dead weren't any smarter or with it in the grave than they'd been in life. And we had a lot of life's losers raising up.

"You've achieved much in your unlife," Miriam said apropos of nothing other than, I suspected, reading my mind.

"Thanks." The freshly turned earth was starting to move, in a way that looked like it was boiling.

"Your drive is understandable, your conviction stronger than most. You'll need to be stronger than you've ever had to be, sooner than any would like."

"I didn't know you were a prophet." Now the earth was moving like liquid in a blender within the confines of each grave.

"Magdalena and I both spent our human lives around the most influential prophets the human world has known. Some of it rubs off."

"I know you think Jack's in danger, but we'll all protect him." The earth in each grave moved to the sides now, so there were openings. The air above the openings shimmered.

"The danger is more than physical." She looked away from the graves and right at me. "I want you to know -- if you fail, it will not be your fault, it will be his. You have the responsibility only for your own soul, no one else's. None who have come before, exist now, or will come in the future are your responsibility. Every being can only do what is right for their own soul, no one else's."

"I don't believe that. I think we all help or hinder each other."

She shook her head. "Right now, two new undeads are coming to join us, to fight the eternal fight alongside all our other warriors. You had no control over their souls. Neither did the Prince. That they were the only two worthy of an unlife was neither your loss nor your victory." She looked back at the graves. "Remember this -- when it comes down to it, it's always you alone against the Prince. No matter if there are thousands standing with you, each of you fights him alone."

The others joined us now, so I wasn't able to question Miriam further. Seven bodies floated in the air above their graves. They didn't look good, but they hadn't looked good prior to Slimy's attack, either.

I examined them. I didn't really know them. They were vaguely familiar faces, people I'd looked at to make sure they weren't committing crimes in front of me. Then I'd looked away from them. Like everyone else had.

Jack was next to me. "Monty said we had limited time. What do you want to ask them?"

All seven were staring at us, their expressions a mixture of fear, truculence and insolence. Just like we'd brought them into the station for questioning. This was truly a routine round-up.

Things being what they were, I decided to go for broke. "What did you all see, right before, and most importantly, right after you died?"

There was the dead version of foot shuffling and averted eyes. The hookers stuck their chests out and tried to distract that way. The bums muttered. The junkies laughed. I decided to focus on them. They were, as we'd all told Jack, much closer to the Prince.

"You," I pointed to the nearest junkie. "Why didn't the Prince take you with him?"

He was young, no more than twenty-two. He just grinned at me. "That's Jerry," someone said in a quiet voice from behind me. I looked over my shoulder to see

Freddy the new zombie standing there. "He don't like authority. His daddy's a preacher."

"Who's the other junkie?"

"Bobby. Used to be on the corporate ladder, wife, kids." Freddy sounded sad.

I looked back at the resurrected. "Bobby, why didn't the Prince take you?" Bobby looked away. "You know, if the Prince is here, he'll take your family. Even if you're no good to him, I'll bet your wife and kids will be just what he's after."

Bobby's head swiveled back. "I don't have a family any more."

"You may have deserted them for addiction, but you're still connected to them. Forever. But...maybe you don't care about them now any more than you did when you started using."

"You know nothing about me," Bobby said angrily.

"Your wife came to try to get you into rehab last year," Sexy Cindy said derisively. "You shoved her away and she fell. I had to help her up and get her back to her car. She cried the whole way."

One of the bums nodded. "You showed me pictures of your kids, when you first come to live with us."

The others added in. Clearly, Bobby had clung to the idea of his family, even if he'd gone to living death on the streets. But he still wouldn't give us anything. I tried Jerry again. "What if the Prince goes after your father?"

Jerry grinned. "Him? He says he's protected from the devil. My mom, too."

"You have any sisters or brothers?" Jack asked, sounding bored.

"Nope." Jerry laughed. "Just me. Just me to put all

their damned hopes and dreams on. Like I wanted to be what they wanted."

"What was that?" I kept my voice mild.

"Respectable." Jerry snorted. "Be good, grow up right, serve the Lord, don't have any fun, don't ever get into trouble. Or you'll embarrass us."

Sexy Cindy sighed. "Your mamma came to see you every damn week, you whiney little weakling. Only reason you're still alive, 'cause she brought you food and water."

Jerry laughed. "And money. Money for Tony Tomio. I miss him. He was good people."

"He's still alive," I mentioned with a touch of sarcasm.

Jerry looked right at me. This was a rarity in a junkie, and I didn't get the feeling he was doing it accidentally. "So you say...bitch." His eyes widened then quickly narrowed. He smiled slyly. "I bet you like to do it doggy-style, get the back of your neck bit. How many cops do you do a night, huh? All of 'em, or just a few?"

I could smell everyone's anger. Jack's, in particular. But he didn't react. We'd been cops too long -- we both recognized when a perp had slipped up and was trying to cover by making us angry.

I smiled slowly. "Where's Tomio, Jerry?"

"You wanna try me doggie-style?"

"What plane of existence is Tomio on, Jerry?"

"What's it like, to get it from a real bitch?"

"I'm going to dust you, Jerry."

That got him. Alive he might not have known what that meant. Dead, he knew. His eyes widened again. "No way."

"Yes way. I have two powerful liches with me.

They'll dust you and spread you. No hope then for a rescue, is there, Jerry?"

Hard as it was to believe, him being dead and all, he got even more pale. "You wouldn't."

"Why not?" I let my smile go wide and feral. "Because we're the good guys? Yeah, we are. But we're the *scary* good guys. And you're dead and you weren't good enough to join us. So you know what that makes you?"

I waited. I could see the other resurrected looking confused and frightened, Bobby included. So, they didn't know. They'd been left behind because they weren't useful right now. Left to be resurrected when the time came, to serve as foot soldiers in the Army of the Damned.

"What does that make you, Jerry?" Jack asked. "You answer the lady, like a good boy."

"I'm not a good boy!"

"True enough." Jack grinned. "Not good enough to live up to your parents' hopes, not good enough to live anywhere but on the streets, not good enough for the Prince to take with him. Good enough to use. But not good enough to save."

"He'll come for me!" Jerry started to shake. I wasn't sure if it was him or if Miriam's resurrection was about to end. "He's coming and he'll put me where I belong!"

"No, Jerry," I said softly. "He already did that. He put you where you belong -- in the ground."

Jerry started to cry. "No. He promised. He promised."

"Jerry." I waited until he looked at me. "Jerry...he lied."

Jerry closed his eyes, threw his head back, and howled. Pity he'd been too close to the Prince -- with a howl like that, he was real werewolf material.

Magdalena moved up next to Miriam and put her hands out. I could tell she was taking over the resurrection, to keep them going longer.

Bobby looked shaken. "The Prince, he didn't say anything about our families."

"What did he say?" Jack asked.

Bobby was shaking now, too, just like Jerry. The others weren't. I got a bad feeling at the base of my tail. "Ask fast," I murmured to Jack.

"The Prince, he said it was what we had to do." Bobby started to cry. "Just let the monster in. That was all."

"You and Jerry created the portal?" I found that almost impossible to believe. They had no psychic talent, Ken would have spotted it. Heck, I would have spotted it.

Edgar whispered in my ear. "It's possible. If they were given the right incantations. As I told you, it was human-created."

"Who gave you the words?" They didn't answer. I tried again. "Did Tomio give you the words?" The junkies didn't answer, but one of the bums raised his hand. "Yes?"

"Tony, he give us all words. Everyone had some words to say. He said it was like…like a prayer."

"A prayer for the dying," one of the hookers said.

Sexy Cindy gasped. "He did. Freddy used to be a professor, 'way back when. I saw what Tony gave us and made Freddy take a look. And you said those words were wrong, didn't you, Freddy?"

"Yeah." Freddy sounded angry. "The words were evil. I told 'em not to do it, but Tony said we needed to, to help him out." He shook his head. "I'm sorry, I didn't make the connection. Tony gave us those words to read months ago."

"Months?" This was asked by every living and undead being, other than Black Angel Two, who were concentrating.

Freddy nodded. "Months easy."

I did some fast math. "Nine dead, seven hurt. That's sixteen."

"Doesn't add up," Jack said quietly.

"It does if you subtract," H.P. offered. "Of the nine dead, two were able to become undead, and of the seven hurt, one walked away healthy. That leaves thirteen."

"Evil number?" Jack asked.

"The Prince likes to ensure humanity continues to think so," H.P. replied. "So, it's always a good bet."

"There's another option." I looked at Freddy and Sexy Cindy. "Who made it out of the alley alive and on their own steam?"

Freddy shook his head. "No one. We nine, like you said. And then the others at the hospital. All accounted for."

Sexy Cindy's eyes narrowed. I realized they were narrowing in thought. "No," she said slowly. "There were two more, really."

"Who?" Freddy asked, rather huffily.

Sexy Cindy gulped, then pointed. At me and Jack. "Them."

Chapter 25

We all let that settle for a moment. "Okay, that's eighteen." There was another option, though, at least according to the base of my tail. "How many of the dead have family still living in Prosaic City?"

Amazingly, Jerry and Bobby both raised their hands. I figured they were *just* smart enough to have figured out we already knew. The hookers looked uncertain and looked at each other. "They got no family here," Sexy Cindy said. "But, I dunno...does your pimp count? 'Cause if he does, they got a real possessive one."

"He counts. You sure there's no one else? Trust me when I say it's important."

One of the hookers looked at me. "I got family I don't talk about." I could see everyone's expressions -- she really hadn't talked about them, no one else knew.

"Who, where, how many?"

"My parents, my two younger sisters and my little brother. They live in Prosaic Country Club and Estates." She said it defensively. It was an easy guess why she'd never told anyone. It was a sad statement, though, that, unlike Jerry and Bobby, no one in her family had tried to help her.

"What about the others?" I asked Freddy.

"My family's gone," Freddy said. "All dead. However, the others might have someone close still living." He spoke to the bums. "Fellas, really, you need to answer. You have any family here still?"

One shook his head but the other two raised their hands. "Got a daughter," the one who'd mentioned Bobby had kids said. "She's married. May have kids now, too." He looked down. "Don't know. She and I didn't...talk." And now they'd never get the chance. I didn't let it affect me -- cops have to keep the emotional side protected, otherwise we'd spend our days and nights crying or falling for sob stories.

"What about you?" I asked the last one.

"Got two sisters, younger than me. Not married."

"How old are they?"

He shrugged. "Guess they're about seventy now."

I managed not to react. It was hard to tell how old a street person might really be, for a variety of reasons, but this was older than I'd been expecting.

"How'd you survive so well?" Jack asked.

The bum shrugged. "Don't see how you call it 'well'. Come from hearty stock. Still, dead now, right?"

"Right." I could see they weren't going to stay resurrected for much longer. "Did all of you say the words Tomio gave you?" They all nodded. "What about the ones in the hospital, the ones who aren't dead -- did they say them?" More nods. I heard Martin speaking softly, into his wrist-com, I presumed.

"Did the cops on beat say them, too?" Jack asked. To my stomach's horror and my tail's expectations, their heads nodded again.

"They were trying to humor them," Freddy said quietly. "You know how it is, they worked our area, knew all us regulars. They didn't see no harm in it, and some bum telling them otherwise? Well, it was read the words and appease the majority or not read them and appease me and Cindy."

I noted Freddy's speech was starting to go back to what I figured it had been before he'd become a bum. The undead lifestyle was good for a great number of those who'd failed at being successful humans.

"Does an ex-husband count?" Sexy Cindy asked.

"I'm sure."

She grimaced. "Then I got one of those. Well, had, I guess. No other family, Jerk Face moved us here, used up all our money, then dumped me for some gal who grew her own pot."

"I'm going to guess she counts, too. Why didn't you go back where you were from?"

She shrugged. "He'd put me onto the streets to make money already. Not like I wanted to go back to my grandmamma's house like that." She glared at me. "They'd have taken me back, sure. But I can survive on my own."

I refrained from mentioning that she hadn't survived and wasn't on her own. I had nothing against moxie, and a new succubus with drive was always a helpful addition to any team. "So, that's seventeen. If we guess that there's at least one child or other family member not accounted for, we get to eighteen easily."

"So, that's three options, right?" Sexy Cindy's brain appeared to be chugging along, too. I wondered what she'd been before she'd become a hooker. Besides a girl from what I guessed was a pretty strict family.

"Yes." I directed one last question to the resurrected. "Again, I want to know -- what did you see and hear right before and right after you died?"

I didn't expect a lot and wasn't surprised. The bums and hookers all looked confused. The bum with a daughter answered, seemingly for all of them. "A big, horrible monster came outta nowhere and ate us all before we could run. Then, the pain stopped and it went all black. I thought we got to see some kinda light when we died," he added in the tone every sinner uses when they find out they really did have responsibility for their souls.

"The light is for those ascending," Martin said gently. "The choice is for those like Frederick and Cynthia, who are in a moral and mental state to make it. The darkness is for those who have not yet...been called." He looked right at Jerry and Bobby. "And the hellfire is for those who know their choices -- and choose incorrectly."

Jerry seemed to have recovered his junkie decorum. "You don't scare me, weirdo."

"You *should* be scared," Miriam said. "When the time comes and you are called, I promise you -- I will destroy you myself."

"Scared me," Jack whispered to me.

Bobby looked away from Martin and back at me. "I saw the monster, but I also saw something else. It was smaller than the monster and it shimmered. I thought it was the drugs, they do stuff like that."

"Shut up," Jerry snarled.

Bobby shook his head and went on, talking faster. "There was a sound, like millions of buzzing flies or insects or something. And it...it was like the sound went into the shimmering. And all that went into Tomio, after we all died -- that was the last thing I saw, that shimmering thing go into him. He opened his mouth and it sort of flowed in."

"He'll kill you when he comes back," Jerry said almost gleefully.

Bobby gave him a look that said what we were all thinking. "We're already dead, you moron." He looked back to me. "I don't care what happens to me, but if you're right, I don't want anything to hurt my wife and kids. I never thought this would touch them. Please...do whatever you need to do to me, but keep them safe. Keep everyone's families safe."

The resurrection was fading. The bodies moved back to their graves. I had only seconds. "We'll do everything we can to protect the people close to you -- I promise."

There was a collective sigh, and then the bodies went back to very clearly dead. Black Angel Two worked fast, and soon there were seven neatly filled graves in front of us. Martin said some prayers over the graves, then we were done.

"What now?" Jack asked quietly.

I looked to Martin, Edgar and H.P. "It's exactly what I think it is, right?" They all nodded.

Jack coughed. "What do you, and apparently everyone else but me, Freddy and Cindy, think it is?"

"Well, on the good side, it's probably not the Prince."

"Oh, good. So, what's the bad side?" Jack asked.

"I'm pretty sure that Abaddon is already here, since they did the incantation a while ago. So this would be Apollyon."

"Those are the same name for the Devil," Freddy said. "Book of Revelations."

"Scribes can get confused," Miriam said. "They're actually two different beings, and have nothing to do with the Devil. Yahweh is not their master."

"No, the Prince is." I heaved a sigh. "I think it's time to go back to the alleyway and take another look at the portal from Hell."

Chapter 26

There was a little discussion about who was traveling how. I stood firm and insisted Jack and I had to remain with the car, so we got to drive over. Sadly, Ralph insisted on coming with us. Happily, the moment he so insisted, Hansel and Gretel also insisted. So we had the three of them in the backseat. Ralph and Hansel were panting and Gretel was grooming. I felt like we'd either joined Animal Control or were running our own mobile pet grooming business.

"I'm sure Freddy and Cindy are asking the same thing," Jack said as we drove out of the cemetery. "What's with the number eighteen and what's also with the idea of three different schemes?"

"The number is only significant because it's a common number we're placing again and again at the scene of the crime."

"Yes," Gretel chimed in. "It could be seven, it could be thirty-three, hundreds, one. It's the fact that we can easily slot to that number that indicates the problem."

"But we got to eighteen because there were five trails that led off from the alley," Jack said. "Maybe we're just reaching."

"But we're not," Hansel said. "If we were reaching, we couldn't have matched that number so well and so often."

"Eighteen minus five is thirteen," Ralph added. "Easy to match to the Prince's favorite 'bad' number, too."

"So, no matter what, we have a big problem and a lot of people involved in it, right?" Jack asked. There was unanimous agreement from the rest of us. "So, what's up with Abaddon and Apollyon? Who are they?"

"Angels who went to the Prince. Any turned undead is powerful, but angels, by their nature, are worse."

Jack nodded. "I can see that. I don't want to be around Black Angel Two right now. I don't want to try to imagine what they'd be like completely evil."

"They'd be like Abaddon and Apollyon," Gretel said, softly.

"God deliver me," Jack said only half-jokingly.

"Gods help. When they can." I thought about what Miriam had said to me. "But, when it comes down to it, it's you and your soul against the Prince."

We drove the rest of the way in silence. Well, other than the panting and other animal-related noises our backseat passengers were indulging in. I chose not to look.

I spent the time instead running through the three options we'd identified. They all led back to the idea that we had, if not the Prince, then some of his strongest minions running around free on the human plane.

We didn't have enough data yet to be certain of what the play might be, though. And there was always the possibility that we didn't have three plans, we had one big, nasty one. Eighteen doppelgängers was still a strong possibility -- once the pattern was imprinted, you could make as many as you wanted to, within reason, that reason being there had to be the right number of corresponding souls to connect with.

Eighteen fake Tomios wandering around was a bad enough idea. The essence of evil put into eighteen separate beings, myself and Jack included, was also not anybody's idea of good. Eighteen souls connected to the infected souls -- also badness. But if what Jerry had insinuated was accurate, it wasn't Tomio who'd been in the alley last night.

We poured out of the car and met the others at the end of the alleyway, at the dead-end. Examination of the physical revealed nothing new.

I knew what was on the right -- a small grocer who closed before dusk every night. There was a bridal shop on the left, also closed at night. Even the Prosaic City poor liked to look nice when they got married, after all. "What's in the building that makes up the back side here?" I asked our newest recruits.

Freddy and Sexy Cindy both shrugged. "Didn't get to that side much," Freddy said.

I gave Sexy Cindy a look that said I wasn't going to buy that from her. "We're talking the fate of the known planes of existence here. What's on the other side?"

"I'll go look," Ralph offered eagerly.

"Sit, stay, good boy. I asked Cindy a question and I want an answer."

She made a face. "I didn't go there, not my kind of place."

Jack nudged me. "The Pleasure Palace, it's a skin club."

I chose not to ask how he knew. "You're telling me you didn't cruise outside a skin club, looking for business? Seriously, we're on the same side now, and just how naïve do you think any of us are?"

She shrugged and looked down. "Didn't like the clientele, okay?"

The base of my tail did its thing. Sexy Cindy had known instinctively that the incantation Tomio handed out was evil. "What about them made you uncomfortable?" I used my "questioning a frightened witness voice". It was normally considered soothing.

Her head shot up and she glared at me. "I ain't a baby."

I gave up. "No. You're an undead, a succubus, to be exact. One of exactly two who were swallowed by Slimy, Creature from the Hell Lagoon, who survived relatively unscathed."

"We died," Freddy said dryly.

"Cry me a river. You're standing there, unliving. You just talked to seven of your brethren who aren't going to open eyes or mouths again until the Prince can arrange his Final Solution Attack and then they'll be raised up for cannon fodder for the side of evil."

"You can't know that," Freddy argued.

H.P. cleared his throat. "Actually, we can. There's ample proof, in a variety of tomes. When we have a spare minute, Frederick, I'll be happy to show you. Until then, you'll have to trust that Victoria does know of what she speaks. The dead who do not ascend, who do not join the unliving, and who do not automatically go to the Prince's Hell remain interred in the earth, in blackness, until such time as they are called to fight. Those who died more on the side of the Prince than on the side of goodness will fight as part of the Army of the Damned."

Sexy Cindy processed this. "That's going to be most of them, isn't it?"

I couldn't help it, I had to ask. "What did you do, before your ex forced you into hooking?" She mumbled something. "What? Didn't catch that." She mumbled again. "Really, speak up. Time's wasting here."

"I was studying to be a preschool teacher." Sexy Cindy had the combo of defiance and embarrassment down perfectly.

"Oh, I think you should aim for higher education," H.P. said, with complete sincerity. I couldn't blame him. The streets were burning off of Sexy Cindy and Freddy at the speed of Zeus' lightning bolts. "We always need good instructors."

"Recruit for the University later," Monty said. "We need to plan our next moves."

"No, actually, we need Cindy to tell us exactly why she didn't like the clientele at The Pleasure Palace."

"I agree," Edgar said. "Because I believe there's a good chance the monster originated on the other side of the wall."

Chapter 27

We all stared at Sexy Cindy. She glared back.

I gave it another shot. "Look, we're not asking because we think you're stupid or not good enough or whatever inferiority thing you've got going is telling you. We're asking because you're spotting evil naturally, and you're repelled by it. Ergo, if you were repelled by The Pleasure Palace's clientele, we really want to know why, in that cop way of ours."

She deflated. "Okay, fine. They all seemed...wrong to me. I don't know any girl who ever picked a john up from there, either. Well, except one. But she's dead now."

Jack and I exchanged the cop "oh really?" look. "What did she die from?" he asked.

"Got real sick, sort of wasted away."

"How soon after she picked up that john from The Pleasure Palace?"

Sexy Cindy's brow crinkled in thought. "Maybe a week, maybe a little more."

"How long ago was this?" The base of my tail mentioned that it knew exactly what Sexy Cindy was going to say.

"Right about the time when Tomio had everybody read those evil words." Her expression said she had a direct line to my tail. "Oh, crap, it killed her, didn't it?"

"No. Well, yes, but not in the way you probably think. And," I added to the glare that was starting to radiate out of her eyes, "not because I think you're stupid. Because you've been undead about a day and I just doubt Indoctrination taught you about what possession by a major evil minion does to a human."

Ken put his hand against the wall and

concentrated. "It's not giving off any evil resonance."

"And yet, it should," Edgar said. "A manifestation of the size you dealt with should leave resonance for days. Which means it's got a spell on it."

"So, what do you figure?" Ralph asked me.

"The incantation provided Abaddon with a portal. He came through into The Pleasure Palace. For whatever reason, he didn't take a possession there. Isn't that odd?"

Edgar shook his head. "It makes sense. The clientele are the Prince's servants. They want a strong army. Better to take an innocent, ensure one less for our side."

"Okay, so he picks up the poor girl unlucky enough to score a john from our little den of iniquity. He drains her life source and drops her back on her street corner." A thought occurred. "Cindy, did you know her well enough to know who her pimp was?"

"Yeah. Same pimp as the other two girls we just, ah, talked to. She worked that side of the block, though, so I didn't see her much."

"How well connected to Tomio is this pimp?" Jack asked.

Sexy Cindy shrugged. "I dunno. Tomio knew everyone."

"Which was why he was the perfect choice for infiltration," Martin said. Black Angel Two nodded. Not that I felt we needed angelic confirmation because it seemed obvious Tomio had been hand-selected for evil quality.

"I go back to the question of what our plan is," Monty said. "Figuring things out is nice. Doing something about it is better."

"Thank you, oh fount of wisdom and experience." I

considered our options. Splitting up seemed like it was going to be in order. We clearly needed to investigate The Pleasure Palace, we needed to track down all the potential relatives of the dead, keeping an eye on the folks in the hospital was going to be a given, and finding out what was up with Tomio had to be a good idea.

It dawned on me that it was probably past time to check on Amanda and Maurice. I dialed up Amanda on my wrist-com. No answer. Okay, no reason to panic. Called Maurice. No answer. Called the Count. "Have you heard from Amanda or Maurice? Recently, I mean?"

There must have been something in my tone of voice that told the Count that now wasn't the time to chide or complain. "No. I'll try now." It was quiet for a few long seconds. "No answer from either one. Black Angel One just came back on duty, sending them to intercept."

"Good. Please tell them to be careful and fast."

"Just out of curiosity, what do you think has befallen them?"

"I think they're fighting Abaddon and Apollyon." Or they were dead. I decided not to mention that possibility, because it was all too possible and I didn't want to think about it.

"I see. Black Angel One advised. May I suggest that Black Angel Two be ready to assist?"

My conversation with the Count had everyone's attention. Well, it would save time. "You may." Miriam and Magdalena both nodded, but made no move to leave. "However, until Black Angel One either doesn't respond or calls for backup, Black Angel Two plans to stay with our teams."

"Teams?" the Count asked politely.

I brought him up to speed quickly. "So we're going to have to split up into several teams to tackle everything." I refrained from adding "unless we have to go save Amanda and Maurice" because that would mean Black Angels One and Two were in need of assistance, and that was never a sign of good times ahead.

"I see." The Count was quiet for a few moments. "Carry on."

Somehow, I'd expected something more from him than that. "Uh, okay. Will do." My wrist-com went dead.

Ralph was the first one to speak. Well, first he did the canine throat-clear, but right after that, he spoke. "Did that seem…odd to anyone else?"

"Very much," Monty said. As the being with us who'd known the Count the longest, this held a lot of stressful weight.

I looked around. Everyone was nodding in agreement, even Jack, Freddy and Sexy Cindy. "So, what're we thinking? The Count's got a lot on his mind or we've got an infiltration and he's trying to give us a hint?"

"Oh, I'd go with infiltration," Monty replied. "It's always a favorite."

"Who could infiltrate that place?" Jack asked.

I thought about it. Sexy Cindy had made the point that Jack and I could be considered part of the group who were part of Slimy's attack. And the stronger minions had serious skills. We probably did have eighteen doppelgängers walking about. They just were now unlikely to all be Tomio copies.

"I have a sinking suspicion, Jack, that you and I not

only could infiltrate, but did."

"Great." At least he didn't sound freaked out. "How do you fight a doppelgänger?"

"You don't touch yours, for starters," Edgar said. "Touching your own duplicate is dangerous at best and normally permanently fatal."

"Oh. Good." Jack shook his head. "What kills them?"

"Same things that kill us. That's the one positive."

"Yeah, I'm feeling the positive in the situation." Jack sighed. "So, you and I have to engage the doppelgängers, right?"

"How do you figure that?" Ken asked him.

I answered. "We're the only ones who can be sure we're really us."

"Good point. What'll the rest of us be doing?" Ken looked ready to fly off and fight something.

"You'll be dividing up into teams to handle all the other issues we've got."

"You know, they're doing a very good job of dividing us," Martin said.

"And potentially conquering, yeah, I know." The base of my tail wanted a word. "However, what they may be doing is trying to get us away from here, right here. Meaning we want to stay here and continue investigating The Pleasure Palace."

"Shouldn't you and Jack be the ones to do that?" Ken asked. "You're the only two who we could laughingly say have a reason to go in that isn't related to the undead world."

As always, Ken had a point. A good point.

H.P., Monty and Edgar were all nodding, as were the angels. "So, Ken's right, as per usual. So, how do we stop the likely doppelgängers at Enforcement?"

Gretel raised her paw. "Send me, Hansel and Ralph. No matter what they look like, the dupes don't smell right. Close, but not close enough."

This was true. "Okay, let's make that happen." The three of them did an intense scratch and sniff on me and Jack, minimal scratch, maximum sniff. Then they took off.

"Think they'll be okay?" Jack asked me.

"Probably better than we'll be."

"Comforting. Remind me to make sure that, should we have kids, you leave the nurturing parts to me."

Chapter 28

I left Ken in charge of group divisions. He could do it as well as me, and I wanted to get into The Pleasure Palace and out again as soon as possible. However, Jack and I didn't go alone. I insisted on taking Freddy and Sexy Cindy with us.

They weren't thrilled, at least if their grumbling as we walked out of the alley was any indication. "Okay," I snapped once we were in front of the bridal shop. "Want to tell me why you don't want this assignment?"

"I told you, I don't like that place," Sexy Cindy whined.

"Hell's no fun, either, but some of us have to venture there on assignment. I'll wager there's not a lot of fun being had at Enforcement HQ right now, but you didn't hear that team whining about it."

"We're dead," Freddy snapped. "And you want to take us in with you to someplace we never went anyway."

"You're undead. It's different and, by now, you both know it. Besides, I don't care if you never went there before -- you're going in there now to give me and Jack a believable reason to follow you."

"How are we going to be believable?" Sexy Cindy asked. "We're undead."

"You don't look it," Jack said. "I can't tell the difference between what you looked like alive and now. Your brain's working better, but if no one in there knows you, Cindy, they won't notice you're not acting like a moron all the time. Same with Freddy. You haven't been undead long enough to have that gray-around-the-edges look H.P. has. You look better than you have in years, but you still look like a bum."

"Uh, Jack? Maybe we'll leave the nurturing of potential young to me after all."

Freddy sighed. "No, he's got a point. The Indoctrination people --"

"Beings. We're beings. Of everyone with us now, Jack is the only person."

"Got it. You teach at the University on your off days?" Freddy asked with far more sarcasm than I thought necessary.

"No. It's just a big deal, okay? At least half of us were people, at one time, and we're not any more. We're beings. Only living humans get to be called people." It bothered me that it still bothered me, after all these years, but it did. I'd been a person, and I wasn't any more. I moved my mind off the past quickly. "So, anyway, you two need to wander in and look like you're trying to get away from the cops. We'll be pretty much right behind you."

"What have we done to get you interested in us?" Sexy Cindy asked, sounding a little less sulky.

"We're asking questions about Anthony Tomio," Jack replied. "You don't know anything, but you don't want to be questioned, either."

They both nodded, looking unhappy. "Those expressions are good. Add in some fear, too. You know, just figure that if you can't manage to do this one little assignment you'll probably get to work with us a lot...and we're both really hard on rookies."

"Wow, this unlife's so great," Freddy said. "We both feel really lucky."

"We should," Sexy Cindy said in a low voice. "You saw the others."

He sighed and took her arm. "You're right. We'll head off and do our act, such as it is. Just don't wait too long to come after us. Cindy's not the only one who never wanted to go into that place."

Jack and I watched them hustle off. "What's our plan once we get in there?" he asked when they were far enough away they couldn't hear.

"I think this falls under the 'wing it' line of attack. We know this is Evil Headquarters, for this part of town, at least. That something's going on is a given. What or who we're going to find in there is the issue. I just have no guess."

We started off after our "quarries". "You think Abaddon and Apollyon are in there?"

"Yahweh protect us if they are." I meant that, and ensured I said it in a way Yahweh would recognize as prayerful, not flippant.

"I second that. So, do bullets actually work on the undead?"

"Some of us, yeah. I'd bring in our real weaponry, but I think it'll be spotted the moment we cross the threshold. Gotta assume Evil HQ has some serious weapons detectors on their entryways."

"So we packed the trunk full for no reason?"

"Oh, I'm sure we'll end up using it. Just not at this exact moment."

"Okay, so you want us acting like we would have two days ago, right?"

"Right. Human cops, hunting a perp, following clues."

"Think they'll fall for it?"

"Well, I'm sure some of them know who I am or will be able to tell I'm a werewolf. But who knows? Most of life and unlife's a crapshoot, when you get down to it."

"The undead gamble?"

"You have no idea. Unlife is long, and even the most dedicated like to take a night off. Gambling with undeads is a little different, though. If we ever catch a break in this case, I'll take you to one of my favorites, The Crypt."

"Looking forward to it." He stopped us before the corner, pulled me into a doorway, and kissed me. He was a great kisser, and my butt was doing its thing in a matter of seconds. He stroked my face as he pulled slowly away. "I never thought I'd have a chance with you."

"I felt the same way." I had to admit, Slimy had been a precursor to the major evil, but he'd certainly given my love life a huge assist.

He sighed and stepped away. "Back to work."

I nodded and we headed off. Turned the corner, walked briskly up the street, making sure to look very undercover cop-like. Rounded the next corner. No sign of Freddy or Sexy Cindy. This street was almost like an alley. The street our favorite alley led off of was a main street, well traveled in the day. This one, however, while running parallel to the bigger one, was infrequently used. I wondered now if the humans were being affected by The Pleasure Palace in some way, sort of psychically driven away. Maybe. We'd probably know soon enough.

There weren't a lot of people on the street, either. There was a large parking lot across the street from The Pleasure Palace, well filled with a variety of cars there from the standard lowlife POS to sleek BMWs and Mercedes. Whoever was doing business here covered all the walks of life. There were also a lot of dingy buildings that had clearly seen better days, perhaps when Prosaic City had first been founded. Most of them looked closed, not at night, but in general.

Our side of the block was the same, and I noticed the storefronts around The Pleasure Palace -- most of them had "out of business" signs in the windows. I checked the other side of the street. Yep, I could spot the little signs if I squinted. Aside from The Pleasure Palace, only two businesses on the entire block were still active -- one was Killjoy's Pawnshop, and the other was, against all the odds, The Salvation Center.

"We need to check those two out, the moment we have a chance."

Jack nodded. "I worked this beat when I was a uniform. Never really went into any of these much, if at all, but they've all been here for years."

"How about the other businesses? Here or out of business when you worked a beat?"

He looked around. "The block hasn't changed. At all."

"Bad sign." We reached the front door of The Pleasure Palace. I felt absolutely nothing from it. It smelled almost like it wasn't there, and it gave off no sense of anything. "Definitely under a spell," I murmured. "I get nothing."

"Huh. I...want to go in. It's like it's...welcoming me."

"Worse sign." I made him look at me. "You need to be very careful in here. It repelled Cindy and Freddy, it's giving nothing to me, but it's attracting you. Whatever that means in the long or short run, your soul's in danger the moment we step in." I wanted to tell him to wait on the street, but I knew what he'd say.

"No." He grinned. "I can tell you want me to stay here. I'm not letting you go in alone. Two days ago, we wouldn't have had this conversation, we'd have just walked through the door. So that's what we're doing to do now."

With that, he turned the knob. Interestingly, the door opened in, not out. Jack stepped through and, praying to Yahweh and suggesting that, if he had pals around they keep an eye on us, too, I followed.

Chapter 29

Like every dive bar or club in every city or town, The Pleasure Palace had no windows. It was dark and murky, and smelled of tobacco, booze and a variety of other scents, most of them indicating squalor and decadence.

Unlike most other dives, it was huge. I thought about the rest of the block and realized it had taken over the buildings on the side that didn't have the pawnshop. It easily stretched to the end of the city block. The walls were dark red, the lighting leaned towards the red side, and the furniture was all black. They had a theme, all right.

Music was playing, loudly. This wasn't unusual in a dance club, but most dive bar denizens liked lower volumes. I didn't recognize the song but I did recognize that it wasn't recorded by any act a normal human would have heard of. The lyrics were in Latin, and they weren't nice lyrics, either. Humans who wanted to accuse heavy metal rockers of being Satanists should have taken a listen to this -- this was truly evil music, and it bore the same resemblance to heavy metal as I did to a Pekinese.

Also unlike most dives, it was packed. There were people everywhere, mostly men but more than enough women, and they didn't all look like they were in the Sexy Cindy Sisterhood. Some of them were in suits and had clearly come with men in suits, and probably in the Beemers and Benzes.

I sniffed deeply. Every drug known to mankind was in evidence. Every liquor and burning substance, too, other than sage and cedar. No cleansing scents were allowed in here, that was clear.

Jack and I shoved through the patrons. I couldn't see Freddy or Sexy Cindy, but I could smell them. Because they were afraid and they were the only ones in here who were. No one looking at me and Jack gave off the smell of fear, which was proof, as if we needed it, that this place was bad to the bone. No one, no matter how cool or deadly, doesn't feel a twinge of fear when a cop shows up, at least no normal human. But these weren't normal humans, not by a long tail.

I grabbed Jack and headed for the other half of our team. They were huddled in a booth in the back, in the corner and in the dark. Before Jack had been born there had been a song with those lyrics. It had no relationship to our current situation, but it did remind me that I had a couple of hundred years on him. It didn't feel like it when we were together, though. He'd been a cop longer, and he was so incredibly male that it didn't matter.

I dragged my mind back to the situation. I could get moony about Jack later. We needed to ensure we all *had* a later.

We reached the booth and both Freddy and Sexy Cindy looked relieved. "Took you long enough," Freddy said quietly.

I put my back against the wall and took another long look around. No one, literally no one, was paying any attention to us. "You getting what I'm getting?" I asked Jack.

"Total lack of interest in the police? Yeah. By the way, to ease your troubled mind, now that we're in here, I don't feel anything."

"Nothing at all?"

"Normal revulsion, desire to burn the place down, strong wish to make arrests. Standard cop feelings. But nothing else. Other than a longing for nose plugs. This place reeks."

"Tell me about it," Sexy Cindy muttered. "Can we go?"

Before I could answer that, someone slithered over. Sure, he walked, but it was slithery walking, the kind of walking that only certain beings can do -- and none of them are human. He was slender, had slitted eyes that slanted up, very little nose, and a wide, smiling mouth. However, I didn't need more than his walk to know what he was.

I moved in front of Jack and the others. Not because I was trying to make Jack think I was as tough as Black Angel Two, but because the chances of any of them knowing what to do when a lesser snake-demon attacked were slim to none.

But the snake-demon in front of me just smiled even wider. "No reason to fear," he said, the "s" in "reason" slightly elongated. "We welcome all here."

"I'll bet." I decided to just go for it. "We're looking for a drug dealer named Anthony Tomio. Seen him lately?"

"I am Ishtrallum, the owner of this establishment, here to help you. However, I prefer to know who I'm speaking with." Every "s" elongated. He sure wasn't trying to hide what he was.

"Again, I'll bet. Shockingly, I don't plan to tell you. Tomio, you seen him lately?"

The fake smile disappeared. "No. Look, I don't like cops in here unless they're here for a good reason. You're not." He waved at Freddy and Sexy Cindy. "Take your flunkies and get out. Unless you're all on your night off and here for a good time. In which case, happy to assist."

"Where's Tomio?

"Don't know, don't care. His tab's paid up, and that's all I care about in regard to a human." Against what I would have thought possible, Ishtrallum's eyes narrowed. "What's this really about? Our taxes are paid up, I own the building, and there's nothing illegal going on here."

I managed not to bark a laugh. "There's nothing legal going on in here, and you know it."

Ishtrallum shrugged. "True. However, the cops leave us alone. You looking for a payoff?"

This wasn't going exactly how I'd figured. "Uh, no. We're looking for Anthony Tomio. And...some other beings."

He shrugged again. "Tomio's not here. Feel free to search the place. If you don't want a bribe, a drink, or anything else we offer, why don't you search fast and leave faster?"

"When did you see Tomio last?"

Watching a lesser snake-demon roll its eyes is always fun. "Look, bitch -- and I mean that being-to-being -- I'm just trying to make a living here. I do well, keep myself out of trouble, and provide what the patrons want. The cops on this beat never bothered me. Why are you?"

"Did the uniforms come in here?" Jack asked.

Ishtrallum shrugged again. "Once in a while. Usual cop stuff. They were clean if you're on some sort of internal affairs thing. Took free drinks but no money."

I was getting the horrible feeling Ishtrallum was telling the truth. "Why does the building have an avoidance spell on it?"

"It's got an ignorance spell on it, actually," he said with a touch of derision. "And, I can't imagine why I'd want that with Necropolis Enforcement wandering around. Look, I can't make money in the Levels."

"Levels?" Jack asked.

"Levels of Hell. Why not?"

The snake-demon sighed. "Too damned much competition. What resident of the Levels or turned anything thinks a joint like this is decadent? I'll tell you -- none. But here on the human plane? I've got the hottest spot around. I make a fortune."

"Is that why you helped Abaddon and Apollyon enter this plane?"

It was more interesting to see a snake-demon's eyes open wide. Ishtrallum's were the size of golf balls. "What the hell are you saying?" He looked horrified and sounded terrified.

"I'm saying they're here and they came through your business to get here. Separately, I might add."

He shook his head. "Impossible. I'd know. I'm always here --" He stopped himself and narrowed his eyes. "You said they came through separately. Was one time a few months ago?"

"Yes, as far as we know."

"And the other, night before this one?"

"Yes. Why?"

He hissed. Literally. "That slime bag. I don't take a lot of time off, but even I need a break from success and wild living. I was off yesterday, and the last time I took time was a few months ago. Betting it coincides with the arrivals."

"Why are you telling us this?" Jack asked.

Another hiss. "I'm happy here! I'm making money tail over fang, I have a nice house in the Estates, I'm respected as a successful businessman by the humans and as a being who flies quietly and legally under the

Necropolis radar. Why would I want to muck that up by helping bring about Armageddon?" His eyes narrowed again. "But him? Oh yeah, I can see him thinking that would be a great idea."

"Who, exactly, is this 'him' you're referring to?"

"My assistant manager and junior partner, and, if you're right, still the biggest Roman bastard there ever was."

"Does said bastard have a name?" Jack asked.

The base of my tail did some fast calculations, and Ishtrallum and I answered together. "Nero."

Chapter 30

"Nero?" Jack asked. "As in 'fiddled while Rome burned' Emperor Nero?"

"One and the same," Ishtrallum hissed, with heavy emphasis on the hissing. Either he was a great actor or he was seriously pissed. I hated to vote that way, but I went with the seriously pissed option. I got a lot of things from him, but not lying.

"He around for us to talk to?" I asked without much hope of hearing a yes.

"No. Said he had family stuff to take care of. Took the rest of the week off." Ishtrallum looked around. "You want to tell me what's going on that I've been set up to take the fall for?"

"Can't say if you're set to take the fall. However, in addition to Abaddon and Apollyon, we probably have some doppelgängers wandering around."

"Does it get any better than this?" he asked of nobody in particular.

"Probably, but we don't know yet. Where does Nero go, in his off hours?"

"He wanders. Has a place in the high-rise district, usual pit in the Levels. No idea if he goes into Necropolis Proper, however."

He didn't. Nero was on our Watch List. There were certain beings who it always paid to keep several eyes on, and he was one of them. However, we'd failed, big time, since we were supposed to be keeping eyes peeled for him in Prosaic City, too. "Is he using some sort of disguise?"

Ishtrallum shook his head. "Not that I know of. But he's good buddies with the warlock who spelled this place. Why?"

"I work this beat and had no idea he was around." Hey, I could admit when I screwed up or didn't know something.

"You didn't know I was around, either," Ishtrallum mentioned.

"Yeah, but you keep your nose clean from all you've said. Nero? Let's be real."

"True." He swiveled around slowly, looking at his patrons. "You know, not that I'm desperate to get you out of my business, but you might want to talk to the folks next door and down the street."

"At the pawnshop and the Salvation Center?"

"Yeah. They may have something for you." Ishtrallum gave me the wide, snake-smile. "Might make you feel better about missing all this, too. Then again, maybe not."

Jack gave Ishtrallum his card. "If you remember anything, spot anything, or Nero shows up, call."

"Oh, will do. I live to stay on the side of right and justice."

"Sarcasm is such a lovely trait in a lesser snake-demon." I motioned to Sexy Cindy and Freddy that it was time to go. They got up quickly and sidled next to Jack.

"Just one of the many services we offer here. Don't let the door hit you and all that. However, should you want a relaxing time when you're not on a case or trying to stop the end of all the worlds, feel free to come back. Free drinks and reduced price food for our fine folks in uniform." With that, Ishtrallum slithered off.

"Interesting, ah, being," Jack said.

"Yeah. Well, I don't smell or see Nero here, so we might as well try the pawnshop."

"You sure we'd see him?" Jack asked. "If he has a spell on him, maybe we wouldn't."

"Good point. In which case, this place reeks, I'm fighting to stay in human form and not go into 'eat them all and let Yahweh sort it out' mode, and we have a lead, however weak, from our beloved proprietor."

"Let's get out of here," Sexy Cindy said. "I wanna toss my cookies and I ain't got no cookies to toss."

I noted her vocabulary was shifting back into street-hooker. Association was powerful, and she was too newly undead to fight it without help. I didn't wait for consensus. I strode to the exit and onto the street. Happily, the others were right behind me.

This part of town was dingy and dirty and so was everyone in it, but I took a deep breath once I was on the sidewalk. It stank, yeah, but not like The Pleasure Palace stank. I didn't doubt Ishtrallum was raking it in -- I just didn't want to have to go back there, for any reason. Sadly, I figured my luck wasn't going to run that well, so settled for not going back in right now.

I took a quick look up and down the block. A whole lot of nothing going on. A couple of cars pulled into the parking lot, one cruddy, one in good shape. Their drivers and passengers got out and wandered into The Pleasure Palace. They didn't act like they knew each other and they also didn't act furtive going in.

"I want to crack down on this place so badly I can taste it," Jack said. "You know, I'll bet there's some spell on the doorway, though. Because when we left, I wanted to go right back in. But now that we're a few feet away? Nothing. Well, revulsion, but nothing you wouldn't expect."

"Once we get this settled, we can see about making

it a little harder for The Pleasure Palace. But if we don't find out what the real plan is and stop it, Ishtrallum's little hot spot's going to look extremely appealing, at least by comparison to what the rest of the planes will be going through."

"That snake-man said Armageddon," Freddy said. "Was he serious?"

"And accurate, yeah. And he's not a man. He's a lesser snake-demon, so, a being."

"She's touchy about that, remember?" Jack muttered to the other two.

I rolled my eyes. "I'm not the only one. Now, come on, we have a pawnshop to shake down."

I strode off the whole five feet or so it took to reach Killjoy's doorway. It didn't look unusual for a pawnshop, though the windows were smaller than most. But they were as heavily barred as any other I'd seen. I sniffed. Nothing other than the standard street stench.

"Any odd feelings from the three of you?"

"Nope," Jack said.

"Me, either," Freddy added.

"I don't wanna go in," Sexy Cindy said.

"Any real reason or you just being a pain in the tail?"

"I don't like the guy who runs it," she muttered. Apparently Sexy Cindy had gotten around.

"Because he's evil?"

"Because he's a jerk."

"The way things are going, that's an improvement." I opened the door and walked in. There was a cheerful, jangling bell that rang every time the door opened wide enough to let a normal-sized being through. As I entered, it was cheerful, I mean. By the time all four of us were inside, I was ready to rip the bell off the wall.

The pawnshop wasn't as large as The Pleasure Palace by half, but it was still good-sized, all things considered. It bore more of a resemblance to an antique shop, though, at least if the dust and randomness of the displays were anything to go by.

"From the stink of depravity to the stink of the ancient and discarded." Jack chuckled without a lot of mirth. "We hit the best places."

"What kind of pawnshop has old *National Geographic* magazines?" Freddy asked. "I mean, I suppose they're worth something to collectors, but who collects from a place like this?"

"Jerk-face probably took 'em 'cause someone was late on a payment," Sexy Cindy said under her breath.

"You dealt with the proprietor frequently?"

"Yeah. For some reason, my life wasn't going in that up direction." Sexy Cindy was trying to give Ishtrallum a run for the sarcasm money.

"That," a man's deep voice boomed from the back, "is because you gave yourself over to sin instead of to goodness."

My ears pricked up. I knew that voice. I *hated* that voice. "Uh, Cindy, don't tell me, let me guess. The proprietor's a self-righteous, hypocritical, hyper-judgmental type, looks middle sixties in human age terms, and loves, just *loves* to preach."

She nodded as he came around a corner. There he was, in all his so-called glory. Most ghosts were subdued, but not him. He glowed -- with ectoplasmic smugness.

He gave me and Sexy Cindy condescending smiles and bowed to the men. "Welcome to my establishment."

"And, boy, is it aptly named."

"I assume your manners are as atrocious as ever, Victoria?" he asked me in that way of his where it didn't matter what you said or did, he'd already passed judgment and you'd failed.

"Oh, heavens no." I ensured I was in a dead heat with Sexy Cindy and Ishtrallum in the Sarcasm Olympics. "Detective Jack Wagner, human, and Freddy, brand new zombie, please enjoy the rare thrill of meeting the Right Reverend and all around swell guy -- as long as you're not a female, anyone considered inferior at any time in the history of the world, or, all the Gods and Monsters help you, a *witch* -- and my personal favorite undead of all time...Cotton Mather."

Chapter 31

Cotton put his hand out. "Pleased to meet you, gentlemen. Please excuse Victoria -- she's never pleasant this time of the moon cycle."

It took all my self-control not to go into wolf form and try to rip his throat out. Of course, as a ghost, there really wasn't any throat, or any other substance, to rip. But that hadn't stopped me when I was a younger undead and it wasn't stopping me now.

Jack standing there was stopping me. I didn't want to do anything that would make him think that Cotton had a real line on me or how I thought or acted.

Freddy took Cotton's hand, insomuch as you can take a ghost's hand. "Pleased to meet you." He didn't sound like he meant it all that much. He also looked slightly grossed out. Touching ectoplasm could do that until you were used to it.

Jack cleared his throat. "We're here on an investigation, and we'd like your cooperation. This involves Prosaic City Police as well as Necropolis Enforcement. I trust we can rely on your assistance?" He didn't take Cotton's hand or offer his. Instead he pulled his notebook and pen out of his jacket pocket, flipped the notebook open, clicked the pen, and gave every impression of being about to take a statement.

Cotton gaped for a moment, then slammed his mouth shut. "Of course. I have always served the laws of man and Gods my entire life and unlife."

I managed not to make the gagging sound, but only because Sexy Cindy was doing it for me, albeit quietly.

"Yeah, he was so dedicated to the cause he turned ghost for no reason other than to keep on hunting witches. What a *pity* none of the people he helped condemn to death actually *were* witches or warlocks. Nor has he ever once apologized to any of them for the torment and horror he helped put them through."

Cotton gave a supercilious sigh. "They were convicted of their crimes on the human plane. Their guilt was proven there. I have no need to apologize for doing God's work."

"You weren't doing Yahweh's work during the trials. You were doing the Prince's."

"So you love to insist. I note that I dwell in Necropolis Proper, not in the Levels. Clearly those in power agree with my eternal life's work."

I wanted to argue this misconception of his, but I'd learned a century and a half ago that it was useless. His mind was firmly closed -- to new ideas, to the truth of what he'd done, to the concept of his true place in both human and undead history. And yet, as much as I hated him, Cotton managed to fly under the radar, just like Ishtrallum. He wasn't on the Watch List like Nero. He was just an unpleasant being who had no idea that he actually *was* unpleasant. Amanda suggested pity when dealing with Cotton. Maurice suggested banishment. I always sided with Maurice on this one.

Jack, thankfully, continued to take the police lead. "We're looking for a variety of beings. Let's start with Nero. Have you seen him recently?"

Cotton shrugged. "Well, recently, no. He came in a few months ago, looking for a book. Took me a tremendous amount of effort to find it, but, unlike some, he was grateful for the effort."

I clamped my jaw shut as Jack asked, "Name of the book?"

"*Bringing it On*, by Timothy Leery...and that's with

two e's, not the same as the hippie from a few decades ago."

I resisted the urge to call H.P. or Edgar. The base of my tail told me that what this book was teaching wasn't either how to get high, get your cheer squad to nationals, or get happy. It was going to end up the how-to book for Armageddon.

"What year was it written, do you know?" I managed to get out in a fairly civil tone.

"Oh, sixteen-sixty-six, I believe." Cotton smiled benevolently. "I was only three, but I recall it as being a good year."

"No connection made to the number of the beast and all that?" Freddy asked. I was impressed. He really had been a professor of some kind.

"I doubt it." Cotton waved his hand as if to dismiss the idea. If he'd taken it as merchandise and sold it, in his mind, it was on the side of good.

"Seen Nero since?" Jack asked, reclaiming the lead.

"No. We're not close."

"How about two, ah, fallen angels, Abaddon or Apollyon?" Jack was still all business. He almost sounded bored. I knew he wasn't, but he'd clearly read Cotton right -- sound like it was important and he'd spend his time lecturing and avoiding. Sound uninterested and you'd get what you wanted.

"Hardly. And, despite the insinuations of some, I do know to alert the authorities should I spot high minions of the Prince."

"What about a human, named Anthony Tomio?" Jack was just managing not to yawn. I was impressed down to my claws.

"Young man?" Cotton seemed to be thinking.

"Yeah, late twenties, early thirties. Spent a lot of

time down in this area."

"His profession?"

"Drug dealer mostly." Jack looked at Freddy and Sexy Cindy. "Right?" They both nodded.

Cotton still seemed to be in thought. "He might not have used his real name," I suggested. "Might have been afraid to let you know he was a bad guy."

Cotton nodded. "Yes, you may be correct. I never dealt with anyone identifying as Anthony Tomio, but in recent months, there was a Tony, called himself Tony T. He was also looking for the book that Nero wanted, but Nero had claimed it first. However, he was satisfied with an ancient scroll."

"Sounds like our man," Jack said. "Title on that scroll?"

"*The Calling of the Many.* Quite old, Sumerian, I believe."

"I see." Jack nodded. "Mind if we take a look around?"

"I'm not harboring criminals, young man."

"Oh, nothing of the sort insinuated." Jack gave Cotton his "humoring the unknowing witness" smile. It was a good one, and worked nine times out of ten. "You just have some fascinating merchandise. I'd like to take a fast look."

Cotton seemed about to argue. I knew what to do. "Oh, come on, Jack. We need to find Tomio and Nero. We don't have time to lollygag."

Cotton shot me a look of pure disdain. "Young man, by all means, feel free to look at anything and everything. Take your time. Call me if you spot anything you want to take a closer look at or even purchase. I offer a ten percent discount for all Necropolis Enforcement personnel, and I'd be happy to extend the same to the Prosaic City Police as well."

"Speaking of which, did any human uniforms ever come in here?" I did my best to keep my tone reasonably uninterested. It was a shot in the dark, but most of this investigation was based so far on wild guesses that were turning out horribly right.

Cotton nodded. "They came in, to check on things."

"Don't take this the wrong way, but, how in the world didn't they notice you were a ghost?" I'd known this being for my entire undead existence and he'd never once *not* looked like a ghost to me.

Cotton didn't look like he wanted to answer, but Jack backed me. "Honestly, Mister Mather, that's a good question. And it could be important to our investigation."

Cotton sighed. "Well, it's a simple thing, really." He pulled a small device out of his pocket. It looked like a cigarette lighter, one of the nicer kind. He flicked it, and suddenly he looked human and solid.

"That's how he always looked to me," Sexy Cindy said quietly. "Didn't know he was a ghost until tonight."

I managed to hold on to my temper. I also managed to speak calmly. "So, Cotton, you're using an Enhancer, right?"

"Of course." He said it like it was of no consequence.

"You realize that a powerful witch or warlock created that, right?"

He shrugged. "Yes, again, of course."

"And you have no problem using it?"

"None whatsoever. Victoria, do you have a point?"

Jack nudged me as he turned and started wandering the shop. I shook my head. "Nope, no point.

Just mentioning it for Cindy and Freddy's sake. They're new. Learning and all." I figured mentioning his massive hypocrisy wouldn't do anything other than earn some choice comments from Cotton and make me even angrier. He was supposedly just fine with "good" witches and warlocks now, and somehow, that was supposed to make what he'd done as a human all okay. Maybe it did for some beings, but not for me.

Cotton looked pleased. "Excellent. Good to see you focused on helping others for a change. Now, if you'll excuse me, I have paperwork to attend to. Call if you need any assistance with the merchandise." He turned and floated away.

Once he was out of sight, Sexy Cindy let go of the back of my pants. "Girl, I hate him, too, but I don't think you killing him would help us find Tomio."

I took a deep breath and let it out slowly. "Thanks. But, I thought I was pretty restrained."

"I figured I was gonna have to tackle you if Cindy couldn't hold you back," Freddy said. "Not that I can blame you."

"Yeah. Well, let's figure out why Jack wants to look around."

"Rather hang here than go to the Salvation Center," Sexy Cindy said.

"Why?"

She shrugged. "I never been in there before, but after this place and The Pleasure Palace, I'm figuring whoever runs it's gonna be the worst kind of bad news."

While we wandered off to find Jack, I wondered if Sexy Cindy was going to prove prophetic. I hoped not, but the base of my tail said it was going to be a bumpy ride and we should all fasten our seatbelts.

Chapter 32

Jack was working his way through the pawnshop quickly. We caught up to him. "What are you looking for?"

He shook his head. "No idea. But Mather clearly doesn't pay attention to what he gets or who he gets it from. I don't buy that Abaddon or Apollyon didn't come in here. If they were able to disguise themselves even a little bit, they probably fooled him."

"That I could believe," Sexy Cindy said. "He always called me 'like unto the Whore of Babylon' even if I was in here with folks who were really doing bad things. And it's not like hooking hurts anyone."

"Other than the hooker." Those words were out of my mouth before my mind could stop them.

She didn't seem upset or offended. "Yeah, well, there are worse things, okay? He never gave the rapists or murderers or drug dealers in here any crap. Besides, no one cares about the hookers, just the johns."

"Now isn't the time for a discussion of questionable vice practices," Freddy said. "Jack, I echo Victoria. What are you looking for? If we know, we could split up and perhaps spot it faster."

I noted that, in here, both Freddy and Sexy Cindy were starting to sound more like I'd assumed they had before they'd hit the streets. Interesting. Much as I despised him, Cotton was running what could be considered a legitimate business, not a den of evil. Pity. I would have loved a good reason to force him out of business.

A thought occurred. "You guys search for whatever it is we're searching for. I need to talk to Cotton again."

"I'm looking for anything that gives off an evil feeling or seems like it could relate to Armageddon," Jack said quickly. "Look when you're with him. For all we know, he keeps that stuff in his office under the idea they're interesting bits of history."

"Wow, you got him down in one short interview?"

Jack shrugged. "Studied the Salem Witch Trials in school. You get an idea of someone when you've learned what they did as a human and why."

I didn't trust myself to say anything, so I just nodded and trotted off to find Cotton. His office was buried in the back of the pawnshop but ectoplasm has a distinct odor -- like old, wet socks -- so it was easy to find him.

He was humming while doing some filing. He was clearly happy here. Which made no sense. "Hey, Cotton, sorry, but I thought of some questions I wanted to ask. In private."

He looked over from his filing. "Oh? Something insulting, as usual?"

"I don't think so, though, as always, you'll be the judge, jury and executioner. I'm wondering a couple of things. First off, how long have you owned this place? This is part of my beat for Prosaic City P.D. and no one told me you were here." Or that The Pleasure Palace was here, or the Salvation Center. Which was odd. I could understand the Count expecting me to notice -- not that I had -- but not for over a year with no mention.

"I've owned this business for several years. It was human-owned and run for decades. However, the last owner wanted to leave town, so was selling on the cheap. I saw an opportunity to run this for both Prosaic City and Necropolis citizens. After all, even the best people can fall on hard times."

"Okay, but why here, why this business in particular?"

He stared at me for a few long moments, then realization dawn on his face. "Oh, that's right. In your position, you have to function as human more than undead. If you're able, look around with undead eyes."

I was embarrassed that I hadn't thought of this on my own. But, fine, I'd throw one to Cotton. I shifted my mind and opened my eyes. And managed not to scream.

"Why didn't anyone mention this?"

Cotton sighed. "I assume they thought you knew, or would pay attention."

"You know, it's hard to pretend to be human if you can see Necropolis. Or this."

"No need to get defensive." He was quiet for another few moments. "Do you think it's significant to your case?"

"Yeah, I do. How long has this been here?"

"It appeared just before I took over the business. I'm sure it's why I was encouraged to do so. Someone must guard the portal, so to speak."

I dragged the words out. "Thank you, this is a great help, Cotton."

"You're very welcome." He sounded incredibly pleased. "You know, I've been thinking about the young man, Tony T. The last time I saw him was several months ago, right after he'd come in for the scroll. He came back and gave me a great number of items for pawn. He insinuated I shouldn't worry if he didn't come back for them and also suggested I sell a few for profit."

The hairs on the back of my neck stood up.

"Cotton, do you know where you put those things? All of them?"

"Yes. I'll show you." He glided out of his office and I followed. We wandered in what seemed like random directions while I spent my time trying not to look down or towards the street. We reached a display marked "Specialty Items". "Here we are."

I looked at what Cotton was showing me. Nothing screamed out that it was from the Prince, but that didn't mean anything. The Prince and his minions were all over the idea of disguising evil items to look innocuous.

"Cotton, doesn't it...bother you? I mean where your business is located?"

"Not so much. Convergence points aren't an issue if you're not heading down into the Levels."

"But we're standing on the edge of a convergence chasm, not a point."

He shrugged. "Same thing. I don't understand why you didn't notice, however."

"You know, I've never come onto this side of the block, possibly in the entire time I've been with the Prosaic City Police. Doesn't that seem odd?"

"Yes. You do the job you do because of your skills, not just appearing human, but because of your powers of investigation." Cotton looked thoughtful. "You know...it seems odd to the point of unlikely that, in a year or more you've never come in here."

"The Pleasure Palace next door has a spell on it. It extends to the back of the building. I wonder if the whole block was spelled."

Cotton nodded. "Could be. I don't know how to check for that, however."

"The former owner was a human? You're sure?"

"Fairly positive. However, he was aware there were undeads about, though I don't think he was a human in the know. The patrons considered him crazy. Crazy Ed was his name -- even he called himself that. He told me business was good and steady, but that the clientele weren't always what they looked like. I got the impression he was getting out of Prosaic City because he was frightened."

"His pawnshop was sitting here and you think he *might* have been frightened?"

"No need to take that tone. *You* didn't notice. Why would he?"

"I didn't notice because when I'm on Prosaic City P.D. business, I make it a point not to look into the planes. But if Crazy Ed was a human who could see us, then he wouldn't know how to block it out." No wonder the poor guy was crazy and wanted to leave. "You sure he left and wasn't killed or something?"

"I received a letter from him a few months after he'd sold me the business. Told me he was in New York City and happy. It seemed legitimate."

I hoped it was. "Okay. So, how well do you know the owners of the other businesses here, The Pleasure Palace and the Salvation Center?"

Cotton's lip curled. "The Pleasure Palace is not a place I enter. And I have no need of the Salvation Center."

I refrained from comment and focused on the specialty items. "Which ones did Tony T give you?"

Cotton pointed out several things -- an old book, a large knife with an intricately carved ivory handle, what looked like an ancient phonograph and a set of vinyl records, a bag of marbles, and a small statue of something that gave me chills to look at.

"Were there any other items Tony T sold to you that you've resold already?"

"No. These six were it, well, if we count the records as one item, which Tony insinuated I should. All worth a good deal, honestly. I had them appraised before I gave him any money."

"Who did the appraisals?"

"Benny the Fence."

"Best choice. Cotton, I need to take these as police evidence." And to prevent him from selling them to another unsavory being. "I'll give you a receipt so you can reclaim them once our investigation's over."

He sighed. "I assumed as much. Anything else you want to keep?"

"Yeah," Jack said from behind us. "I found a couple of things." I turned. He was holding something that looked like a small guitar made by someone who didn't know how a guitar actually worked, and several scrolls.

Cotton sighed again, but didn't protest. He zipped off, got a receipt book, marked down what we were taking and their estimated values, gave us a copy, then put everything into a large bag. I had to hand it to him, he did seem to have the whole customer service thing down.

Jack took the bag, we said our goodbyes, and left. The jangling bell was just as cheerful the first time and just as annoying by time four as when we'd entered. I wondered if Cotton liked it or if it drove him crazy, too. Decided I didn't care.

"Salvation Center next?" Jack asked.

"Yeah. But first, I need to tell you guys what a convergence point is, and explain why being on, in or around one can be bad."

Chapter 33

The three of them gaped at me. "A what?" Sexy Cindy asked.

"A convergence point. They tend to be small, usually about the size of a quarter. They're points where time and space and the various planes of existence all meet."

"Are they rare?" Jack looked around. "And can humans see them?"

"Not so much and generally no. Being as small as they normally are, most beings won't spend a lot of time around them. Since they're also part of the space-time continuum, they tend to shift. So, just because there was a convergence point on, say, Sixth and Main last year, it doesn't mean it's still there this year."

"Okay, so what's the big deal?" Sexy Cindy sounded bored.

"Well, if a being stays on a convergence point too long, then it can affect them -- psychologically and emotionally, as well as physically. A lot of missing humans locked onto a convergence point at the wrong time and were shifted to another plane of existence. Some make it back, some don't."

"Are the ones who make it back those who insist they were abducted by aliens?" Freddy asked thoughtfully.

"Frequently, yeah."

"Huh. Figures, I suppose." He shook his head. "So, is there a convergence point around here?"

"No." They all looked relieved and like they thought I was a weirdo for making a fuss. "There's what I'd call a convergence chasm here." I pointed to the street as they all went from relieved to worried, fast. "Freddy and Cindy, you two may be able to make it out. Jack, don't even bother to try. Convergence points glow golden -- when people are dying and think they're going into the light, there's a convergence point in or on them somewhere."

"But a lot of those people come back," Jack protested.

"Yes. Because they were being moved to a positive plane of existence, usually the angels' realm, and the beings there helped send them home. Anyway, metaphysics and such later."

"That's not metaphysics --" Freddy started.

"Not for humans, no. For us? Yes, it is. You can discuss it with H.P. and Edgar, okay? Right now, we're standing on what looks to me like the biggest convergence point ever. Cotton said it appeared just before he took over Killjoy's. From what he said about the former owner, he was a human who could see into the planes, meaning he was going crazy."

"Crazy Ed, yeah," Sexy Cindy offered. "I liked him a lot better than Cotton."

"Shocking. Anyway, from what Cotton insinuated, someone suggested he take over this pawnshop. He thinks his presence is guarding, so to speak."

"Is it?" Jack asked.

"I doubt it. Cotton's not a really powerful undead, most ghosts aren't."

"Ishtrallum's not guarding anything," Jack snarled.

"No, in fact, I'd assume he's doing better being on a convergence point of this size. They're attractive, in their way, even if you don't get shifted by one. But the issue is -- no one at Enforcement Headquarters has mentioned this to me. Cotton thought they'd figured I'd find it -- but no one, not even the Count, has that much patience. They didn't tell me about it, even though it's in the heart of my Night Beat jurisdiction, because they didn't think I needed to worry about it. So...someone's actually doing the guarding, and whoever it is, they're a being of high aptitude and trust, or they wouldn't be here." I looked at the Salvation Center. "So, let's go find out who that is, shall we?"

"We in danger, being on the convergence chasm and all?" Sexy Cindy was heading back towards sarcastic.

"Yes. But we're somewhat protected."

"How?" All three of them asked that as one.

I shrugged. "Martin and Black Angel Two are watching over us."

Angels did really watch over beings they considered in their care. The more powerful the angel, the more likely they could keep their particular charges out of danger. I knew how Martin and Black Angels One and Two operated -- we were all working a case of epic ramifications together, so they were watching over our entire team. As powerful as they were, it should be enough to keep the four of us from being sucked into the convergence hole I could see under the asphalt.

I walked into the Salvation Center. No jangling bell, which was a relief. Compared to the other two establishments we'd just been in, it was small. And dowdy. Dull, quiet, hushed, really -- almost like a library without too many books.

We looked around. Not a lot of activity, and no sign of any being. I sniffed. There was something vaguely familiar about the scent in here, but it was faint.

I felt rather than heard the step behind me. I spun to see someone I knew very well standing there. As I stared at him, it occurred to me that no one had mentioned this block to me, or the convergence chasm, or anything else about this area, because they were hoping I would never have to come here.

He smiled, a crooked smile that I hated myself for still finding attractive. "Hello, Victoria. It's been a long time."

"Love the name of the place," was all I could come up with that wasn't going to sound stupid, pathetic, lovelorn or bitter.

"It's appropriate. You'd be amazed, despite the location, we actually get a lot of foot traffic."

"I'll bet."

The others clustered around me. "Who's this?" The way Jack asked, I figured my expression was telling him not necessarily who but definitely what was standing in front of us.

"You can call me Jude." He put his hand out.

Unlike with Cotton, Jack took it. "So, how long ago did you two break up?" Yeah, he was a *good* cop.

Jude's smile went a little wider. "Oh, a long time ago." He let go of Jack's hand and shook Freddy's and Sexy Cindy's. "Nice to meet you all."

"We haven't been introduced," Jack almost growled.

Sexy Cindy coughed. "Dude's an angel. Think he's already done that whole fast read of the mind thing."

Jude nodded. "You're very bright. I'd always hoped you'd come in here...while you were alive, I mean. I'm certain you'll make an excellent undead, both of you," he added with another nod for Freddy.

"You dated an angel?" Jack muttered at me.

"Long story." Very long. Did not want to go into it here, either. "Jude, you're guarding the convergence point?"

"Yes. And yes, you're right. They didn't tell you because you were doing so well, they didn't want me to mess you up in any way."

"Stop doing the mind reading thing."

He shrugged. "I can't. Rules. Whoever's guarding has to be reading at all times. It's too dangerous otherwise."

He was right and I knew it. It didn't make it any easier to deal with.

Jude gave Jack a friendly smile. "You really don't need to be jealous. I still love her, but we haven't been an item for more than three of your lifetimes. Oh," he added with a grin, "you don't have to be jealous of Ken, either. They're more done than she and I are."

"You're not helping," I hissed.

Jude grinned. "Nice to see no one's taught you to sit or stay." I wanted to lunge at him, but a part of me asked if I wanted to so lunge to touch him again. I held myself in check. His smile widened. "Proud of you. Your self-restraint is much improved."

"Thanks, I think. What's going on?"

"As far as I know, exactly what you think. There's a powerful witch or warlock involved, maybe more than one, because I didn't feel any arrivals of the magnitude we're talking about, and I have to assume Cotton didn't, either, or he'd have alerted all of Necropolis Enforcement."

Sexy Cindy was staring at Jude thoughtfully. "You know...you look familiar. I don't know why...you ever been one of my johns?"

"Hardly," Jude replied with a chuckle. "There aren't a lot of pictures of me around, so maybe I just look like someone else you know." He looked back at me. "I'm sure the convergence point helped. It might be why they did this now."

"Cotton said it's been here as long as he's run Killjoy's, and that's been a lot longer than this plan's been active, at least on these planes."

"True. I've been here longer than you've been on undercover duty."

"Nice of you or anyone else to mention it."

He shook his head. "Wasn't relevant. Still isn't, really. The overlap between our assignments is the only reason you're here. And when your case is done or this particular convergence point shifts, you'll move on or I will. We're both mature undeads. This isn't any different than the rest of the time since we broke up has been."

It was different, however, for a variety of reasons. Most of my reasons started and ended with Jack, but Jude and I had a lot of unresolved issues of our own and the middle of a case of end-of-all-the-worlds' proportions wasn't the best place to work through them. Not that, apparently, I was going to have a choice.

"So, Abaddon, Apollyon and an ancient Sumerian demon-thing all make it into the human plane and you, of all beings, don't notice? Even though you're here specifically *to* so notice?"

Jude shrugged. "Looks that way. Figure you're looking for the witch or warlock, or however many of them are working on this, on the human plane as well."

"What about the doppelgängers? As in do we have any, a bunch, an army's worth?"

"No idea." Jude looked thoughtful. "I know your team's divided up all over the place, following a variety of leads. I'm just wondering...."

I waited for a few seconds, but he didn't say anything else. "You're wondering what, exactly?"

"If all those leads are there to prevent you from finding whoever's masterminding on this plane."

"Um, wouldn't that be either Abaddon or Apollyon or, more likely and how fun for us, both of them?"

Jude shook his head. "I've spent time down in the Depths, remember. Those two are excellent at following a complex plan and ensuring maximum mayhem. But they aren't the brains of any operation. And this seems like a complex plan that's got a variety of offensives, foot soldiers, generals, feints and mythic misdirection."

The base of my tail got a really bad feeling going. I could tell by Jude's expression his wings were tingling. Interestingly, however, the person who spoke up next wasn't him or me, it was Sexy Cindy.

"You know, I do know you." She was staring hard at Jude. "Only...you're nothing like I was taught, are you?"

He smiled. "Well, that's open to debate."

"No, it's not." I looked at Sexy Cindy's expression. I had a feeling she'd truly figured out who Jude was. "He's one of the best undercover agents Yahweh's ever had."

She nodded. "Yeah, guess so. Doesn't it bother you, to be considered the most evil man in history?"

Jude shook his head. "The beings whose opinions matter to me know the truth. Besides, there have been plenty of people more evil than even my worst detractors could say I was."

Sexy Cindy snorted. "Yeah, too true. Start with Hitler and work up or down, right?"

The bad feeling at the base of my tail slammed into my stomach as Jude and I looked at each other. "Oh, please, tell me you know where he is."

Jude shut his eyes and spread his wings. I knew this meant he was accessing the angel collective. He didn't open his eyes for a good long while, but when he finally did I knew for certain we'd moved from bad to beyond worse.

"No one knows where he is. Our agents in the Levels haven't seen him for the last few days. But he hasn't come through as far as anyone on any other plane has been able to tell."

"Because he traded places with Anthony Tomio." I tried to swallow the bile but couldn't.

Jack cleared his throat. "Am I hearing this right? You two mean Adolph Hitler, most evil man of the twentieth century? He's an undead?"

"Yes. Unsurprisingly, the moment he died, he went to the Prince. And because of his natural skills, he became a warlock of great power." I wanted to kick myself.

"It didn't occur to me, or Black Angel Two, or anyone else, either," Jude said quietly. "But it means we have the most strategically minded of the Prince's minions, along with his most rabid enforcers, on the human plane. And they're only here for one thing."

"What they're always here for. I know." I tried to think calmly. "How many of his generals do you think he brought with him?"

"You figured eighteen had the potential to pass, right?" Jude asked. I nodded. "Then figure all of them, and probably some others from history just as bad. They're focused on the human plane, they'll go with beings who were humans when they were alive, at least for the majority."

Jack cleared his throat. "One of those eighteen ideas

meant that the four of us were used. Is there any way to make sure we're not…infected?"

"Should be." Jude put his hands on the sides of my head. "Nothing unnatural." I tried not to look relieved, but failed if Jude's chuckle was any indication. "You're hard to infect, Victoria. One of the hardest."

"Good to know."

He moved on to Sexy Cindy. "Impressive. I foresee a good career." He looked at me. "Keep her with you."

"I was planning on it."

"Yeah, I know you can spot talent." Jude moved on to Freddy. "Hmmm, another good one. I know they'll want to keep him at the University, but like H.P. and Edgar, make sure you keep Frederick on call for active duty."

Freddy and Sexy Cindy both looked surprised and pleased by these assessments. I had to remind myself they hadn't been undead long. I could remember my first days and, like theirs, they were faster-paced than normal. Happily, they were holding up, like I had. I hoped they continued to do so -- we didn't have time to deal with either one of them cracking under pressure.

Jude went to Jack now. He didn't say anything for what seemed like a long time. When he did, he wasn't speaking to me. "You're the one at risk. You've been warned. The longer you ignore the warnings, the worse things are going to be."

Chapter 34

Jack pulled away from Jude. "Look, I'm getting tired of all the angelic warnings. You'd think you'd be happy I could handle all of this and instead all I hear is a lot of vague crap about my soul. My soul's just fine, thanks."

Jude turned away. "If you say so." He looked at me. "Remember -- you aren't responsible for any soul but your own."

This was getting to be an angelic litany, and it didn't make me feel any better that it was going along with the general angelic consensus that Jack's soul was in peril. A horrible thought occurred to me.

Jude shook his head. "No."

"No what?" Jack snapped.

Jude looked over his shoulder. Even though he was in profile to me now, I could see the look of disdain. "No, her becoming romantically involved with you isn't why your soul is in jeopardy." He sighed and turned back to me. "He needs time with Edgar, and soon."

"We're sort of in the middle of saving the worlds. Kind of hard to get that one-on-one time with anyone. Besides, Edgar's part of the team at this point."

Jude rubbed his forehead. "You never could find the easy way."

"You are such the one to talk."

He laughed. "Too true. The hard way *is* more...challenging. And lasting."

Jack looked ready to get into a fistfight with Jude. Sexy Cindy and Freddy were holding him back. Apparently Jack and I weren't handling anger very well tonight. A different thought occurred.

"Probably," Jude said with a wry grin.

"Stop it with the mind reading! I mean, you can do it, clearly you can't stop it due to your assignment, but could you pretend that you aren't?"

He chuckled. "Now, where's the fun in that?"

I remembered why I'd fallen in love with him. He was maddening and attractive, mysterious and wise, all rolled into one. But...like Ken after him, he hadn't been what I really wanted.

Jack relaxed, or Sexy Cindy and Freddy lost their hold on him, I wasn't sure. He walked over to us. "We're on a case. Tracking a variety of perps who are trying to pull the biggest job ever, right?" Jude nodded. "In which case, a little more cooperation and a whole lot less statements of doom would be appreciated. Unless you can pinpoint where all our quarries are so that we can just round them up and call it a night."

Jude's wry smile was back. "No, I can't do that. If I could, I already would have. That is why I'm here, after all." He sighed again. "And I've failed, in that sense. Of course, failure can become victory, in the long run."

"And if you can't say something nice, don't say anything at all," Jack snapped. "Got it. Thanks a million. The Prosaic City Police appreciate your assistance." He jerked his head. "Let's go."

Jack stormed out. Sexy Cindy shook her head. "Boy, he's steamed. Guess he's having some trouble in the measuring up department."

Freddy nodded. "We'll go stay with him. You won't be long?"

How they knew I was going to stay to talk to Jude I didn't know, but I had a feeling it was because they were looking at my face and body language. Meaning Jack had stormed out in part because he, too, had taken a look. Oh well, my life was all about the complexities. "Thanks. Shouldn't be too long, no."

They hustled out. The moment the door closed Jude pulled me into his arms. I would have resisted but I was in shock. He shook his head. "Not trying to rekindle the passions, though, I confess, if you were willing, I could be easily convinced. I need to protect you."

He extended his wings and wrapped them around us. We started to spin, and as we did, he spoke a prayer. It was in ancient Hebrew, but I could pick up a word here and there. The basic "Yahweh protect us from horrible evil" kind of thing is what it seemed like. After what seemed like a long ride on the Spin-Out, Jude stopped praying and we stopped spinning, then he let me go and took a step back.

"Uh, that was, ah, different." I didn't ask why he'd never done that before, like when we were an extremely hot and heavy item.

"I never did it before because you didn't need it."

"And now I do?"

"And now you do."

"Because of Jack?"

"Because of what's to come, some of which will involve Jack, yes."

I hugged myself and looked down. "Is he evil?" I tried not to dread the answer and couldn't.

Jude put his hand under my chin and moved my face up until I was looking right into his eyes. "No. He's human. And he no longer wants to be."

"Miriam said the same thing. Is…why is that bad?"

"In and of itself? It's not." Jude half-laughed and half-sighed. "It's almost similar to him wanting to convert to a different religion because it would make him closer to the one he loves."

"He really loves me?"

Jude kissed my forehead. "Yes, he does."

"Then I really don't understand why any of this is bad or puts Jack's soul in danger."

"You will. In time. Sooner than later, I fear." He walked me to the door. "I can't leave to help you. If I do, they'll be able to bring the armies through."

"How can you be sure? I mean, they're getting past us right and left."

"My presence here is the main deterrent. And, I'm not quite as alone as it seems."

The light dawned. "Oh. He's here?"

"Yes. Keeping his usual low profile, but yes."

"Does Magdalena know?"

Jude shook his head. "She needs her energies focused on fighting. We all do. He and I, we fight a little differently from everyone else."

"I don't want this to be the final battle."

"No one on our side does. You'd be amazed -- many on the other side don't, either."

"Really?" I found this difficult to buy. The Prince's minions were all about total domination. It was one of the main reasons they joined up at his myriad recruiting stations.

"I think our agent on the inside would know."

"He doing okay?" It wasn't wise to say his name aloud. As one of the few who knew what his real role in the grand scheme was, I also knew I was only safe thinking about Lucifer in this capacity because I was right next to an immensely powerful angel who could block my mind from others'.

"So far as the few messages through can confirm. However, we do know not all the minions want the great war. Some, like Ishtrallum down the block, are far happier with the status quo than they would ever be if the Prince were to achieve his goals."

"If he says so, okay."

"He does. He also says that, should any of us face him in battle, we have to treat him like an enemy."

I considered this. Abaddon and Apollyon I would have no trouble killing. Well, I'd have trouble in that they were frighteningly more powerful than me, but none whatsoever with guilt or indecision. With Lucifer -- with someone who, by a long tail of comparison, was doing the same kind of job I was, albeit in far more dangerous circumstances -- it wouldn't be so simple. I didn't know him, of course. He'd been in deep cover so long that he'd never come to the human plane, never visited Necropolis.

I'd met Satan. Martin had introduced us. I rather liked Satan. I couldn't kill him, but I wouldn't be asked to. I wouldn't be asked to take out any of those who actually worked for the gods.

But if the Prince was bringing out his biggest, baddest lieutenants, then Lucifer was going to be in the fray, some way, somehow. And I didn't know if I would be able to treat him like an enemy, even though I'd never met him. "Can you block my mind so that no one else, other than you two, can tell if I'm thinking about him?" I'd never felt the need for this before, but the base of my tail said this was a good idea and that if Jude said no I should hurt him in some way.

"I suppose so. Why?"

Lucky Jude, no hurting from me coming. "We have major minions in this realm and you have to ask?"

He grinned and put his hands on my head. "Okay, don't hurt me. I don't do this often, but you're probably right to take the precaution." He put his forehead to mine. I felt a flutter inside my head that lasted for a few long moments. "All done."

"Good. This way, if I do have to face him, no one else will realize I'm concerned about it." Or read any other thoughts about Lucifer I might have.

"No one but the two of us can access your thoughts about him now. Well, other than Yahweh." Jude patted my back. "When the time comes, if it comes, you'll do what's right, Victoria. That's why you're so important. You always make the right choice."

"I don't think so."

"I do." He nodded towards the back of the room. "And so does he."

"So it was the right choice to break up with you?"

Jude chuckled as he opened the door. "I meant in terms of the greater fight. In terms of your personal life, sorry, you screw up just like all the rest of us."

"Dang."

Chapter 35

I felt funny back on the sidewalk. A big chunk of my early undead life was tied to Jude and it was unsettling to realize my present undead life was now wrapped up with him again.

Happily, Jack looked a little calmer. "You get any other insights into my impending doom?"

"Don't buy long."

He laughed. "Good to know. Where to next?"

"No idea." I decided my wrist-com hadn't gotten enough work recently. I tried HQ, hoping I was going to hear good news. "Agent W-W-One-Eight-One-Niner reporting in."

Nothing.

I tried Hansel and Gretel. Nada. Tried Ralph. Got static.

"Things suck at Headquarters."

"Great." Jack rubbed the back of his neck. "Should we head over there?"

"Let's check in on everyone else." Just to give optimism a go, I tried to raise Amanda and Maurice. Then Ken. Then Monty. I quickly raced through the entire extended team. No one was answering. "Okay, before I totally freak out, we need to go back into the Salvation Center." I didn't wait to see if they were following, I ran through the door.

Jude was waiting for me. "I think it's intentional interference, not that everyone's dusted or worse."

"Great. Any way we can tell for certain?"

He coughed. "Yeah. They're all alive."

I didn't have to ask who was providing this reassurance. Of course, I was the only one.

"You mind expanding on that?" Jack asked.

"Yes, I do. Some things do require faith. Or the acceptance that the short answer is all you're going to get." Jude didn't seem too upset, but he didn't seem overly amused, either.

Jack and Freddy both started to argue, but Sexy Cindy cocked her head and stared at Jude. Then she looked around the Salvation Center. "Guys? I think we can take it at face value." She looked at me. "If it's good enough for you."

"It is." Interestingly, Jack and Freddy both quieted down. "Jude, any suggestions for our next steps? Any help would be appreciated."

He got a faraway look, which I knew meant he was listening to someone talking inside his head. I also knew full well who that someone was. Well, said someone did have a direct line to Yahweh, and that was good enough for me.

Jude came back to the rest of us. "Go to Necropolis Enforcement."

"Why? Just curious and all."

He shrugged. "I think everyone else is heading there."

"So, either things are wicked bad at HQ, or everyone's heading back to home base to report and regroup." I stared at Jude. He didn't indicate which answer was the right one. "Thanks, you're a great guy."

Jude grinned. "You used to think so, yeah." He shrugged. "You know the rules, you don't get a lot of freebies when you don't need them."

I made the exasperation sound. "Fine, great. Heading off. Hopefully to a happy team reunion, not to a pre-Armageddon party."

We left again, but this time we headed for the car. It was a relief to move away from the convergence chasm,

I had to admit. I didn't want to have to visit this block again for a long time, if ever. Pity the base of my tail said we'd be back, and a lot sooner than I wanted.

Jack handed me our bag of goodies and I tossed it into the trunk, Sexy Cindy and Freddy piled into the back, Jack took the wheel, and I grabbed the radio. "Darlene, Detectives Wolfe and Wagner checking in."

"How nice of you to remember us back at Headquarters, Detective."

I breathed a sigh of relief. Things were at least semi-normal somewhere. "We've been following leads. Anything going on we should know about?"

"It's very quiet. Chief feels it's too quiet."

"Oh. Good. Where in the silence would you like us to go?"

"Nowhere in particular. We'd just like it if you'd check in more than once every few days."

"Hilarious. We'll do our best to keep the regular cards and letters flowing. Over and out." I hung up and looked at Jack. "This is getting weirder by the minute."

"I agree. I mean, we've had quiet nights -- I think maybe a whole dozen in the time we've been partnered -- but quiet right now? Seems unlikely."

"Well, let's get to Enforcement Headquarters and see what fun awaits us there. I'm sure we'll have time later to rock the bad guys on the human plane."

Jack drove back to OLOC. This time we used the church's parking lot because I had the special parking tag and now wasn't afraid to use it.

"Really? Necropolis Enforcement can legally use a handicapped hanger and no one complains?" Jack sounded ready to give me a ticket.

"It says 'Differently Abled' and we pay a lot of money for these. I'd like to mention that we aren't using the real handicapped spots. We're using the Differently Abled spots. As in, the ones we've paid for."

"Huh." He sounded like he was going to run this by the Chief when we got back to Prosaic City P.D. I got the impression his fur was still ruffled over meeting Jude.

We poured out. Before we left the car, though, I had everyone take a small weapon of some kind, just in case. I didn't think it was a good idea for us to waltz into Our Lady of Compassion toting multi-round crossbows, but a can of Evil Fairy Repellent and a miniature single-shot crossbow were a lot easier to hide.

Cruised through OLOC and into the Proper. Jack didn't seem to have any trouble with the slide. I figured I'd let him go through the next time without my holding onto him, just to see how it went.

Moving sidewalks were working just fine, no one we passed seemed panicked or like they were trying to pass furtive signals. Nor did anyone look or act possessed. It was just a typical night in the Proper -- beings out, many working, some having a good time, some hustling about their business, some strolling. Normal.

I spotted what looked like some University students taking classes outdoors, as well as a group of younger undeads clearly on an outing to the hospital. That was considered a big deal for the young ones. Why, I could never figure out -- I wasn't wild about visiting hospitals, though I was a big fan of their work -- but apparently the little undeads had to pass tests and get perfect attendance and citizenship marks before they got to go. Strangely enough, there were always enough young ones who'd made the cut that groups ran at least weekly, sometimes more often.

"What are little kids -- ah, *beings* doing out this time of night?" Jack asked.

"Uh, they're little vampires and ghosts and such. They're night creatures."

"Oh." Jack looked embarrassed. "That was a stupid question."

"My teachers used to say there were no stupid questions," Sexy Cindy offered. "Of course, they also said there was no such thing as ghosts and vampires and werewolves. So I guess they didn't know much."

"Thanks." Jack shot her a dirty look. "I have another question."

"Go ahead."

"How do they handle being kids forever?"

"Oh. They don't. Naturally born undeads age, ah, naturally until adulthood for their particular race. After that, it's onto the slow but steady wins the eternity race thing."

He shrugged. "If you say so. So, what's the plan?"

"Go in, see what's going on." I shrugged. "If it's bad, we'll know."

"How so?" Freddy asked.

"Well, if it's not obvious so that we can all just see or hear the bad going on, then I sort of figure either Jack or Cindy will be affected by it."

"I love being the team mine canary. It's almost as emasculating as being around Black Angel Two."

Sexy Cindy snorted. "Yeah? Well, being Spot the Evil Girl ain't no great shakes, either."

"Boy, do you two always complain this much or are Freddy and I just getting the special treatment?"

Freddy chuckled. "Some people bicker when

they're nervous."

"I'm not nervous," Jack snapped. "I'm annoyed and a little tense."

"I'm with the big guy," Sexy Cindy said. "Annoyed and tense."

"I'm resisting the urge to spin and shout 'boo!' at the two of you. Relax. It's either very bad or it's going to be business as usual." I sounded very reassuring, calm and cool. I was glad we had to take courses in that in order to move up in Enforcement ranks. Because, in reality, I was as nervous as Jack and Sexy Cindy were, and I was pretty sure Freddy wasn't as calm as he was pretending, either.

So, in this great state of mind, snipping and snapping at each other's tails all the way, we reached the entrance to Necropolis Enforcement.

"Everyone, weapons at the ready. If I attack, follow me. If I run like a bat out of Hell, follow me. If we're attacked and they don't call off when they know it's us, shoot to kill. If I'm shot down, grab me and run for OLOC."

"Don't I feel all safe *now*?" Sexy Cindy muttered.

"Why don't you think they'll shoot one of the rest of us first?" Jack asked.

I took a deep breath and shifted into full werewolf form. I was still on two legs, gun in one paw, single-shot mini-bow in the other. The beauty of an undead life was years and years in which to practice things that were awkward or downright close to impossible. Claws and paws or no, I was going to shoot first, bite second, and ask questions whenever I got around to it.

"Because I'm the strongest and scariest of the four of us, and the hardest to dust. What would *you* aim for?"

Jack sighed. "Gotcha."

"Oh, and don't forget, I'm gonna be hiding behind her, and so is Freddy if he has any sense at all," Sexy Cindy tossed out. "So, they won't *have* us to aim for."

"I feel the love."

"Hey, I'm the evil spotter, not the evil sniffer."

"Hilarious. When this particular situation is over, remind me to lift my leg in your general direction."

Jack shook his head. "Shall I get the door, Cujo?"

I gave him as dirty a look as it was possible to give. "Oh, please, Prince Charming."

Jack grinned, gun at the ready. He stood to the side, grabbed the door handle, and pulled it open.

Chapter 36

"Bad night, Vic?" Clyde asked, as he slowly lowered the weapon he'd had trained on the door.

"You tell me, you're the one sporting the Duster."

Clyde didn't normally hang around the entrance to Necropolis Enforcement. He also rarely if ever carried a Duster -- not the long coat they wore in the Old West, and not something with feathers on it.

Dusters were the final solution for undeads, their shots containing a mix of everything known to destroy any and all unalive beings with some extras thrown in just in case. They were weapons of vast, scary power, and only a few were allowed to carry them in non-war situations. Clyde was one of those few -- age and experience had a lot of prerogatives in the undead world -- but I hadn't seen him wield a weapon of any kind for decades.

He did the slow mummy shrug. "True. However, under the circumstances, the Count felt it would be a good idea for me to watch the door."

"Everyone all right?" I didn't see or hear anything wrong, Sexy Cindy wasn't suggesting things were going evil dead, and hard as I sniffed, nothing smelled out of place. Though I did get a faint whiff of sulfur.

"We are now." Clyde pulled a wand out from his back. Mummies used their entire bodies as one big pocket. I was glad I couldn't see from where exactly he'd pulled. He waved the wand around all four of us. The air sparkled.

"Pretty. Are we late for a surprise party?"

Clyde chuckled. "No. You haven't had to deal with one of these much, I suppose. Easy way of proving you're who we think you are."

"How does it work?" Jack asked.

"If the air around you sparkles, you're not possessed, turned, a dupe, or similar."

"Dupe?" Jack sounded like he was back in class.

"Short for doppelgänger," Clyde explained. "Since we had some fun with them earlier, the Count and I decided to go for the easy confirmation. If you'd been more dupes, the air would have looked muddy, like dried blood."

"Gag me," Sexy Cindy said. "So, we good to get out of the doorway or what?"

Clyde nodded, turned and lumbered off. I followed him and the others followed me. "So, what happened?"

"Well, as we know you guessed, as the Count was concluding his last conversation with you, you and Mister Wagner appeared in his office. Miss Cindy and Mister Freddy appeared as well."

"We have...dupes?" Freddy asked. He sounded both worried and fascinated.

Clyde chuckled again. "Well, not any more. Because the Count was fairly confident he'd spoken to the real Victoria he was on guard. When Hansel, Gretel and Ralph appeared there was quite the brawl, but nothing too serious. We knew we could eliminate with extreme prejudice, and we did." He cracked his knuckles, or whatever the mummy equivalent was. "I must say, there are times I miss active field work."

"I don't think I want to know, but glad it was a fun time for you. Did you get anything out of them before you destroyed? Like how many doppelgängers we have wandering around, what the plan is, things of that useful nature?"

We went past Dispatch. The smell of sulfur was getting stronger the further into HQ we got. It was clear there'd been a ruckus -- the whole place was in disarray. Beings were straightening and cleaning up. Some looked a little shaken, but most just looked like it was nice to get a break in the routine.

Clyde went to the lift. Our elevators were different from human ones -- no enclosed sides, for starters. Plenty of beings didn't want to be boxed in, and most wanted easy escape. I made sure Jack was in the middle of the platform. For those of us who couldn't fly or turn into something that didn't go splat, lifts were a little nerve-wracking. For a human, it could be a thrill or it could mean total whacked out vertigo. We didn't have time to find out if Jack liked to live on the edge in every aspect of his life or not.

He stayed behind me, so I voted not. "Are we safe trusting this?" he whispered in my ear.

I nodded.

Clyde turned around and smiled. Always odd in a mummy. "If I was turned, young man, Victoria would know."

"How?" Jack asked bluntly.

Freddy sighed. "She's a werewolf. Remember, dupes smell different."

"Turned and doppelgänger aren't the same thing," Jack protested.

"I'd know, and so would Cindy." I hoped, anyway.

Jack made a gagging sound. "What's that smell?"

"Sulfur. I smelled it the moment we arrived. It was faint at the front door and is getting stronger the closer to the Count's office we get. However, it's not on Clyde."

"Meaning," Clyde added as the lift stopped, "that it's unlikely I'm hiding a minion under my wraps."

"Good to know," Jack muttered as we got off and

Clyde headed to the Count's office.

"We heading to see the top dude?" Sexy Cindy asked nervously.

"He's fine."

"He's a vampire, right?" Freddy asked.

"In that sense, *the* vampire, even though he wasn't really the first." I looked over my shoulder. "Guys, really. You've been around Ken, Amanda and Maurice and didn't bat an eyelash. Why are you worried now?"

Freddy shrugged. "The way everyone talks about him...."

"You mean the way human stories talk about him or the way the undead talk about him?"

"We mean we didn't dress to meet the head honcho," Sexy Cindy snapped.

"Just stick your chest out. He appreciates women." I turned back to watch where I was walking. The sulfur smell was bad and getting worse. "Clyde, seriously, why hasn't anyone cleared this out?"

"Agent Rogers wanted you to smell it." The Count's office was at the end of the hall, double doors, very impressive looking. He deserved it, but I always thought he had this set up because he found it funny, not natural or necessary. However, seeing Sexy Cindy's and Freddy's reactions, perhaps he also did it to intimidate. Maybe I'd ask him, one day, when we weren't in the middle of a huge altercation with the forces of evil. Or not. You know, on my whim. Not because he intimidated me in any way.

I almost couldn't breathe the smell was so bad. I figured Ralph must have realized Jack and I were an item and was upset about it. Why else keep the stench around for my sensory enjoyment? "And you're all letting Ralph run the show why?"

Clyde sighed as he opened the doors. "Well...you'll understand once you see everyone."

Chapter 37

The Count's office was a disaster. If I'd thought the lower levels looked bad, it was nothing compared to this. Whole walls were down, I wasn't sure if there was a piece of furniture still intact. It was too crowded in there to be sure.

Gagging from the smell, I did a fast nose count. Other than Martin and Black Angel One and Two, the full extended team was accounted for plus extras. I recognized the extras as the Dirt Corps beings who'd helped follow the scent trails the other day.

Everyone looked like they were still with us, but they all looked worse for wear, too. I was relieved down to my claws that Amanda and Maurice were ambulatory. The Count was doing the vampire hover thing, but even he looked like he'd seen some action.

As I looked around, I realized Ralph was the least injured. He was also growling, but not at anything in particular. I realized he was growling at the smell.

I concentrated and examined the scent with all my senses. I started to growl, too. I was surprised Hansel and Gretel weren't, but managed to take a better look at them -- they weren't looking too great. We were going to have a lot of beings heading to the hospital. Hot night for the little undeads tour group.

"You get it?" Ralph asked through bared fangs.

"Yes. Can we track it?"

"No. I just wanted you to know and to be sure that it wasn't me making it up."

"Ralph, there's a lot of things I know about you, and one is that you'd never make something like this up. But, I'm glad you let me smell it for myself." Well, glad was pushing it. But I didn't have time to find the correct word.

"What's Ralph talking about?" Jack asked.

"The stench, I'm sure," Sexy Cindy said, waving her hand in front of her face. "Damn. I thought the sulfur was bad. What *is* that?"

Every head, even the ones that were extremely banged up, turned and every set of eyes stared at her.

"What do you think it smells like?" I asked carefully.

"Shit, of the worst kind. Mixed up with, I don't know, skunk stink and, gag me, rotting parts." Sexy Cindy gagged for real. "How can you all stand it?"

Ralph and I exchanged a look. "Only Ralph, Hansel, Gretel and I actually *can* smell it."

"Girl, the place reeks. You telling me no one else is ready to toss it because of breathing?"

The Count floated down and landed next to her. "How did they miss you?" he asked softly. "How did they let you escape?"

The answer came to me. After all, I'd spent a lot of time with her now. "She'd shut her brain off, to survive. And she's like a chameleon in a lot of ways -- when she's around scum, she reflects them. When she's around good beings, she reflects that. They only saw the cheap hooker side of her."

"I didn't," Freddy said loyally.

"That's true," Sexy Cindy said. "Freddy always told me I was a lady. But then, he was a professor before he fell on hard times."

"Professor of what?" It had never occurred to me to ask.

"Theology," Freddy replied, as if it had no bearing on this entire situation.

I nodded and refrained from kicking myself. "Yeah,

they missed both of you. I mean, we did, too, but they had more time to sniff you out than we did. What did you two do when they did that incantation?"

"We booked it out of there," Sexy Cindy said in between gagging. "Went to the shelter for the night."

"So Abaddon never saw them, never felt them," Ken said quietly from behind me.

"Therefore, Apollyon wouldn't have known to dust them." I looked back to the Count. "They stay with me."

He nodded. "I agree. However, I believe I must insist that you have angelic support and protection as well."

Jack groaned quietly. "Before that, you mind telling the rest of us what's so special about Cindy and Freddy?"

Ken cleared his throat. "I didn't realize, or I would have given them more undead options."

"Not your fault," the Count said soothingly. "Not all the fallen are found, and all the Gods and Monsters work in mysterious ways, you know that."

"Fallen what?" Jack asked, cop voice back in place.

"Fallen angels."

"Oh, you have got to be kidding me," Sexy Cindy said. "I ain't no fallen angel."

"No, you're not. 'Not all the fallen are found' is an undead expression," H.P. explained. "It started with the true fallen angels, of course, but it's expanded in its usage to cover any time a mistake is made with resurrection or the creation of an undead."

"You saying we shouldn't have been turned into undeads?" Now Sexy Cindy sounded ready to cry. "You think we belong in the dirt and the dark?"

I was still in full werewolf form. Didn't matter. I

put my gun and mini-bow away, went to her and put my foreleg around her. "No." I put my other one around Freddy. I had a feeling they were both going to have some trouble with what I was going to say next. "We're saying that when Ken brought you to the undead side of existence, he gave you a limited range of options."

"Dude never stopped talking," Sexy Cindy said. "It was like this never-ending list."

"But in that list, only a few options stood out to me," Freddy said thoughtfully. "Zombie, lich...warlock. I picked zombie because it seemed the most...right."

Sexy Cindy nodded. "Yeah. I picked succubus because, well, it sounded like me."

I cleared my throat. "How about 'angel'?"

"H.P. just said they weren't fallen angels," Jack protested.

"They're not. A fallen angel originated from the angelic plane and fell from grace." I sighed. "They're like Martin. They could have, and probably should have, angelicized."

I'd been right -- they both started to shake. I held onto them and held them up.

Ken shook his head. "I should have realized --"

Edgar interrupted him. "How? How exactly would you have realized? It's only because of what's gone on and is in the process of unfolding that the realization has hit any of us. Stop blaming yourself." He grimaced. "It's too late to fix it, isn't it?"

"Far too late," the Count said. "They've settled into themselves."

"Don't take this the wrong way," Sexy Cindy said. "But I don't want to turn into some big fighting girl with badass wings."

"I'd rather teach," Freddy added.

"Well, that's good," I said as cheerfully as possible. "Because you're pretty much stuck as you are." I hugged them. "But don't worry -- we'd rather have you like this. Angels sort of make everyone feel inferior."

"Got that right," Jack muttered.

"Besides, they might not have chosen, even if given the option," Monty added. "Not all pick what we think they should. They pick what *they* think they should."

"Well, that's a comfort," Freddy said. He didn't sound all that comforted, but both he and Sexy Cindy seemed like they were relaxing a little.

"Every undead serves in their own way," H.P. said. "You're serving in yours. Splendidly, too, especially for your first days." Those heads that could nod without too much pain or trouble did so. We were Go Team central.

"Now what?" Sexy Cindy asked. "Do we clear out the damned smell?"

"Interesting choice of words. See, what Ralph, Hansel, Gretel and I can smell, and what you can smell, is the scent of Hell. That 'all the crap that's fit to make you sick' scent is the rarified dung from the Depths. But the skunk stink and rotting entrails addition lets us know, roughly, who came by to visit in our skins."

"Who would that be?" Jack asked.

Oh well. I couldn't dance around it any longer. Better they should know now, probably. So when the confrontation came it would be less of a shock.

I would have liked to take a deep breath, but the stench was too much. I settled for fur ruffling and the wave of my tail that said I was really unhappy, annoyed and angry. "My father."

Chapter 38

I wasn't watching anyone else's face, only Jack's. He took it in fast, did the mental calculations thing, and kept his expression extremely neutral. "I see. Does this complicate things?" He didn't sound freaked out, he sounded like he did when we were dealing with a domestic dispute.

"The only complication is that Victoria's father is, sadly, one of the Prince's most powerful minions," the Count answered for me.

"Want to clarify?" Jack asked, detective voice on full.

"Just lucky, I guess."

This earned me a dirty look. "I want answers, Vic." Jack didn't sound like he was going to put up with me stalling any more. I sort of couldn't blame him.

Oh well. I'd known it was coming. Sooner or later, you have to tell beings the truth about your family, even if you don't want to.

"There were these two cousins, but they called themselves brothers. They were well beyond crazy -- they were evil and vicious because they could be. They stole two women and made them their wives. The younger one actually legally married a third woman. In addition to the well over thirty people they murdered, they also killed all their own children. All but one."

Jack kept his expression very blank. "I see. What were their names?"

"They had a few first names, but went most commonly by Big and Little Harp. Big died first -- he was beheaded in seventeen-ninety-nine. Little died about five years later. The women went off. Two of them remarried and went to different parts of the

country. Susan Wood, the one with the only surviving Harp child, went to Tennessee. " I wasn't shaking. I was proud of myself.

"How did they survive?" Sexy Cindy asked softly. "The mother and...daughter?"

I nodded. "Eudora Harp was an infant when Big died and because Little had run off, she didn't really know him, either. Susan felt Eudora's life had been spared because the Harps thought she was special, that she would be their legacy. Susan told Eudora all about her father -- fathers, really -- about all they'd done. No one was ever sure which Harp fathered which child. Not that it mattered."

"Lineage does matter," Freddy said.

"Not in this case," the Count interjected. "In the case of the Harps, part of the reason they were so evil is that they shared one soul between them. They'd each sold half their soul to the Prince and then he mingled what was left between them. It gave them power and strength, in that sense, but it also made them what they were. Then again, they wanted to be what they were."

"They were the Prince's loyal and enthusiastic servants on the human plane," I continued. "And when they died, what was left of their souls went straight to him. He created one being from them -- the Adversary."

"Another name for the devil in the Bible," Freddy said. "And, I assume, like the others, incorrect?"

"Right. It's a title, really, for the Prince's top general in the war. Reporting wasn't all it could have been in the olden days and innumerable translations tend to mix things up a bit. In the course of time, the Prince has had many hold the position of Adversary. But none have been as successful as this one." I took a deep breath. "In the time since the Harps became the Adversary, murder, sin, depravity, evil in general has increased exponentially. The more evil done, the stronger the Adversary grows."

"Is it stoppable?" Jack asked.

"Yes," the Count answered. "All the Adversaries who have come before have been destroyed by our side."

"Usually at a great cost," Monty added. "It was bad enough with Abaddon and Apollyon here. With the Adversary on the plane, we've gone from bad to horrifyingly worse."

"Thanks for the booster speech," Sexy Cindy said. "So, what happened to Eudora? And her mother?"

My jaw clenched. "The Adversary came back and found them." Sexy Cindy and Freddy looked concerned, Jack looked angry. I shook my head. "You might have thought those three women would have hated the Harps, wouldn't you? But they went back to them any time they were separated. Even when the women were imprisoned for the men's crimes, once they were freed with provisions and a way out, they went back to them. Back to the men who had murdered their children and a slew of innocent people."

I was still in full werewolf form and it was all I could do to keep from baring my teeth. "The Adversary arrived on the doorstep and Eudora discovered that Susan had been pining for the Harp brothers. She gave herself to them, willingly."

"What about Eudora?" Sexy Cindy asked. "What did they do to her?"

I could barely get the words out. "They offered her immortality, to join them as the Prince's servant."

"What did Eudora do?" Jack asked softly.

I couldn't talk. Because all I could do was growl.

Monty cleared his throat. "She stood up to them, to her parents, to the Adversary." He chuckled. "She told them to go back to Hell, where they belonged."

"Then what happened?" Freddy asked.

I found my voice. "Then they brought Hell to her, right there."

Eudora watched the monster that was her father grow into something indescribable, but terrifying. Her mother gazed upon it lovingly, and Eudora's stomach clenched.

"You will join us, or we will obliterate you from existence," the thing said to her, voice booming. Horrifying things, things of nightmare, surrounded her. Eldritch flames surrounded them, and a pit appeared before her, filled with noxious smells and worse things.

Eudora was terrified, but she shook her head as defiantly as she could. "I won't. Go back to Hell, where you all belong. You're an abomination in the eyes of the Lord, and I won't ever join you."

"You will obey us! We are your father!"

"No, you're not. You're nothing but evil."

"They *are* your father," her mother said. "You should come with us, dear. We can be a real family." Her mother was so calm, so happy, it was more horrifying than the monster and everything else around her ever could be.

"If this is what my family can be, then I choose to be an orphan. And I choose God, not you." Eudora prayed silently, wondering if God was listening.

"No god is stronger than us! You pray to a god who cares nothing for you. You were created by sin, born in sin, and now, you will die from sin, and be cast to the great nothingness." The monster made some movements, the creatures closed in, and Eudora braced herself. She wanted to run but knew she couldn't escape this -- there was nowhere to go, no way out.

A bolt of lighting came from the clear skies and struck the pit, destroying it, returning the smooth ground between her and her parents. More lightning flashed and crackled, and the horrors around her screamed in agony as they were destroyed. Eudora heard a voice, in her mind more than through her ears. *She has chosen, and she is mine. And I will protect my child.*

Then lightning flashed around the monster that was her father, caging it. Eudora didn't question, she took the opportunity and fled. But even though the monster was hindered, as she looked over her shoulder, she saw it coming for her.

She heard a wolf's howl in the distance, and then another, closer. Soon the air was filled with the sound of a full pack in hunt. She was running right towards the howling, but if she stopped, worse horror awaited her.

Just before she reached the woods the pack appeared. But they didn't look like real wolves. They seemed like a cross between a wolf and a man. They stood on their hind legs, they were bigger than any wolf she'd seen, and they were talking. Not in a language she could understand, but not in animal growls or grunts, either.

The pack surrounded her and Eudora stopped running. One stepped closer to her and nodded his head. "You choose Yahweh or Usen?"

"Excuse me?" Being polite in this situation seemed more surreal than anything else had tonight, but despite the evidence, her mother had, apparently, raised her right.

"Choose your God." The wolf which, upon closer inspection truly looked more like a wolf-man, seemed impatient. Not that she could blame him. It was easy to hear the monster, since it was bellowing for her and her blood.

She blinked. "I choose whoever answered my prayer, whoever sent the lightning."

"Huh, that's Yahweh. Usen sent us," he added, somewhat reproachfully.

"Should I pick both? I ask because we're all about to die."

He shrugged. "Good friends, no problem." He cocked his head. "Okay, Usen says fine for you to go to Yahweh, more natural for you." He smiled, which wasn't all that comforting to look at. "Call me Black Wolf. Won't hurt. Much." Then he lunged, grabbed her arms, and bit her neck.

Eudora would have screamed, but Black Wolf had been too fast. She waited for the other wolves to attack and eat her alive, but they didn't. Instead they moved to stand between her and Black Wolf, who was still holding her, and the oncoming monster.

She realized she was still alive, though she felt like she was on fire. "What's going on?"

"Change coming. Have to wait."

"For what?"

"For you to undie."

Eudora heard snarling and turned to see the wolf pack attack the monster. They were doing a good job against it, but it was clear it was stronger. "Are they going to die?"

"Hope not. How you feel?"

"Strange." This was true. Her body now felt icy and leaden.

Black Wolf nodded. "Common. When you feel hunger, tell me."

"Hunger? We're fighting something from Hell. I'm not going to stop for supper." No sooner were these words out of her mouth than it hit -- she was ravenous, more hungry than she'd ever been.

Black Wolf could tell, possibly because she was growling. "Good. Change complete." He barked and growled, and the other wolves leapt off the monster and ran into the woods. "Follow me." He turned and ran.

Eudora did as she was told, the hunger told her she had to do what Black Wolf said. But she was running strangely. She looked down. She was on all fours, running on paws, not hands and feet. She didn't stop to ask how or why, she sped up. She was faster this way. As she followed the pack she heard the monster screaming obscenities, its voice getting farther and father away until she could hear it no more.

Chapter 39

"I changed my name as soon as our pack reached a larger group of undeads."

"I'd have gotten rid of Eudora as fast as I could, too, girl," Sexy Cindy said.

"I wanted to get rid of Harp more. Besides, Black Wolf named me Victoria." For victory, my victory over the Prince. My throat felt tight. Black Wolf had been more of a father to me than anyone else. He'd made me a werewolf, he'd taught me how to be a good one, and he'd loved me. While Wolfe was sort of obvious, I'd taken that as my last name to honor him, not so much to species-identify.

"Lucky for you his werewolf pack was nearby," Jack said.

"Black Wolf's pack was assigned to, in that sense, outpost duty. Their job was to find new undeads formed or created too far from Necropolis and bring them back safely."

"Was?" Freddy asked. "What do they do now?"

I looked away. "They're all...gone. The Adversary marked them and found them...one by one."

"They live on in memory," the Count said gently. "Now," he added more briskly, "since we're all up on history, we need to determine our next steps."

"Where are all our angels?" I hoped they were following leads, not at the hospital already. I chose not to think about any worse possibilities.

"They couldn't take the smell, literally," the Count said. "Once the Adversary was run off they had to move as well."

"So, what interfered with Vic's wrist-com?" Jack asked.

"The Adversary," Clyde answered. "He has much power."

"Power to disrupt isn't all that big a deal, either," I added. "Just mess up something here at headquarters and all of a sudden, we can't talk to each other any more." I tried not to growl but didn't manage all that well. "So, how many of us were 'here' as dupes?"

"You, Mister Wagner, Miss Cindy, and Frederick," H.P. answered. "We arrived as the altercation was dying down."

"It was good timing that you'd checked in when you did," the Count said to me. I didn't preen -- luck was great but it wasn't something to brag about. "Because I knew where you were and who you were with, I was quite clear that I was dealing with doppelgängers."

"How'd they get in?" Jack asked, back to full on cop. He even had his pad and pen out. "From what I've seen, there are a variety of beings who could've and should've smelled the Adversary."

"The minions don't give off much of an odor unless they want to or have been injured in some way," the Count explained. "Even a werewolf would have to be up close to one in order to spot the differences in smell."

"Which is why we look so great," Gretel said. "The three of us got here first. For some reason, the Adversary didn't focus a lot of attention on Ralph. Can't say the same for me and Hansel."

"That seems odd," Jack offered. "I would think the Adversary would view every werewolf as a reminder of...Eudora." He said the last word carefully.

"Me. You mean dear old Dad would want to kill all werewolves because I'm one. And, yes, you're right."

Ralph gave me a hurt look. "I fought as hard as the others. I'm not a turncoat, either."

"We know, Ralphie," Maurice said. He grimaced at me. "I'd assume your not-so-dearly suspects you and Ralph are an item. In which case, leave him alone until he can be destroyed or turned in front of you."

"Supreme punishment for disobedience or annoyance. Yep, sounds like my family." I examined Ralph. He was the best of the lot, but it didn't look like he'd been sitting it out, hiding in the doghouse somewhere. "Saying Ralph looks the least hurt is sort of damning with faint praise. If I didn't have the rest of you to compare him to, we'd be rushing him over to the hospital right now."

"Speaking of which," Edgar said, "let's get all of us over there now. The sooner the better."

Internal communications had been disrupted and was still offline, which was why no one had come up to help, as near as I could tell. The four of us who weren't injured took the worst hurt, so I had Gretel, Jack had Hansel, Freddy had Amanda, and Sexy Cindy had Maurice. The others did the mutually hurt lean and drag and in this attractive way, we managed to get to the lift and down levels, in shifts.

By the time the last load arrived we'd gotten some help, and one of the ghosts in attendance had flitted off to the hospital. The emergency personnel arrived as we reached the exit.

Much medical chaos ensued, but finally even Ralph was on a gurney and headed off to give the little undeads tour group a real wake up call in terms of choosing their adult careers carefully. If they were still there. I realized we were very close to dawn. This night had flown. I wondered what the day would bring and if we'd get to sleep or not. I didn't want to place a bet on it, per the base of my tail.

Sure enough, as the four of us stood in the Necropolis Enforcement doorway, wondering what to do next, the suns started their slow rise. The undead world had its own sun, moons and stars. Thankfully, they followed the Earth solar cycle, or at least they appeared to. It was always interesting to watch sunrise in Necropolis, though, because it was the clearest point in the day where you could tell for sure you were in one plane of existence and watching another at the same time. I made sure the others weren't in a position to look. Beautiful, yes. Potentially disconcerting, bigger yes. And we had enough disconcertion going on; we didn't need any help from the planetary elements.

"I got some information from the Count while we were waiting for his gurney," Jack said. "Big fight, but he didn't sound like he thought the Adversary was trying all that hard."

"Makes sense. They have a larger plan than just getting rid of us. But still, disabling Necropolis Enforcement permanently would have to be a good thing in the Prince's mind. So, why was the damage so minimal? In that sense?"

"They want you," Freddy suggested.

"Maybe." I thought about it. Didn't come up with enough. "Did the Count, or anyone else, mention if the dupes were destroyed?"

"Yeah," Sexy Cindy said. "I heard all the vampires talking. Ralph, Hansel and Gretel all wounded the dupes, and when the vamps arrived with all the angels, they destroyed the dupes completely. That's when the Adversary appeared. I think part of it was in each dupe."

"Yeah, they can do that. It's one of the reasons they're so strong. They were used to having divided souls, so doing it comes naturally and easily to them now."

"You think they're in more of the doppelgängers than just the four of ours?" Jack asked.

"Not sure. If so, it would explain why the Adversary wasn't able to kill everyone or destroy the building. It's a possibility, but there are others, too. Besides, I'm pretty sure Abaddon is walking around in Tomio's skin, and that means Apollyon is probably the Tomio doppelgänger. So, find a Tomio, find a major minion."

"Hitler could be in Tomio, too, you said," Sexy Cindy reminded me.

"Yeah, but he's vain. He'll look like himself as fast as possible. So even if he used Tomio's body to get through, he's in a dupe and it's altered to look like him now." One small blessing, because every being knew what Hitler looked like, alive or undead.

"But why didn't they show up to everyone who was tailing them?" Jack sounded as frustrated as I felt. "I mean, maybe they could have fooled Amanda and Maurice, but Black Angel Two?"

"And Black Angel One." It didn't make sense.

"Sure it makes sense," a smooth male voice said from behind me. "If you remember that angels have strong psychic powers." I turned around, knowing who I was going to see. Sure enough, I got the glittering grin as he went on. "Abaddon and Apollyon were as powerful as Lucifer when they fell."

"Not as powerful as us," his younger brother said with another dazzling grin. "You going to introduce us to your new friends, Vic?"

"Sure." I risked a look at Jack. He didn't look happy. For some reason, that made me feel good. "Jack, Cindy, Freddy, meet Black Angel One. Their friends and associates call them Cain and Abel."

Three jaws dropped. I turned back to Cain. "Look, that's peachy, but if you and Abel couldn't spot that you were following Abaddon or Apollyon, we're really screwed."

Cain shook his head. "Remember what our orders were? We were tailing and watching for odd activity."

"Yeah," Abel added. "And we had to hang back. I mean, I know we and Black Angel Two have the best range, but even we have limits."

"Do Abaddon and Apollyon have limits? Or the Adversary? Since all three are on the human plane now, wandering around, doing Gods and Monsters knows what."

Cain chucked me under my chin. "Vic, you worry too much."

"Excuse me." Jack's voice was like ice. "Am I understanding this right? You're *the* Cain and Abel? From the Old Testament?"

"That's us," Abel said with a wide grin. "We look pretty damned good for being this old, don't we?"

"I'll say," Sexy Cindy muttered. I got the impression she was ready to offer up the Corner Special for Two. Not that I could blame her. Sexiest things with two wings, that was Black Angel One.

Jack pressed on. "So, you," he pointed to Cain, "murdered him," pointing to Abel, "and yet you're an angel and happily working together? And this doesn't seem odd to anyone?"

Cain sighed and rubbed his forehead. "You make one smartass comment to your parents at what turns out to be the wrong time, and you're branded for life."

Abel put his arm around Cain's shoulders. "I knew. I was waiting for you, wasn't I? I tried to tell them, they didn't listen."

"Tell who what?" Jack asked.

Abel shrugged. "Cain didn't kill me. He always took care of me. But we'd had a fight and I ran off because I was upset. Ran into trouble, didn't have my big brother there to back me, I was murdered. Yahweh angelicized me, I tried to let the others know -- the scribes and the storytellers, let alone our parents, that Cain wasn't to blame."

"It got so bad I had to leave," Cain said with a sigh. "But, you know, in the long run, things worked out." He tousled Abel's hair. "Was nice to see my baby brother waiting for me, I must admit."

Jack caught my eye. "Seriously?"

"Yep. Haven't you picked up yet that the religious texts of the human world, while well meaning and doing their best and all, aren't necessarily the most reliable reference materials on the planet?"

"Most humans don't use them for reference, Vic."

"Yeah, Jack, I know. Most humans don't think I'm real, either. We're here to protect them, not make them love us."

He gave me a long look. "Cops stick with cops."

"Right. You're hanging with a bigger force than you're used to, that's all."

Jack managed a weak grin. "Well, I did always tell my parents I wanted to fly with the angels."

"Give it time," Cain said.

Abel nudged him. "Actually, I think right now is good."

"Why?" Cain asked, sounding slightly annoyed.

Abel shrugged. "Incoming." With that he grabbed Jack and Freddy, while Cain grabbed me and Sexy Cindy. They took off like the proverbial bats out of Hell.

"Not that this sucks," Sexy Cindy shouted. "But what's going on and what's coming in?"

"Black Angel Two are under attack and they'd like our help," Cain said as he went supersonic and I tried not to squirm, to no avail. "Vic, hold still!"

"Trying." Failing. I looked down, the suns were high enough that I could see the ground clearly, and it was too far away. Werewolf paws demanded ground, Cain lost his hold, and then I got to see what flying without wings felt like.

I wasn't a fan.

Chapter 40

There's no good way for a canine to fall from a great height. Cats have that land on their feet thing, but even Gretel would have been hard-pressed to land from this height without shattering all her bones. And I wasn't a daemon cat.

Normally panic meant I'd change into or stay in wolf or werewolf form. Apparently when I was plummeting to my death, my subconscious wanted to die human. I changed back into my human form. Great, just great.

I could see Black Angel One above me. Cain was doing his best to catch me, but he had Sexy Cindy and she was a hindrance. And Abel had his hands full, so to speak. I decided that, as far as deaths went, this one was going to go down as truly stupid. Not exactly the way to go. And this could indeed dust me -- because my mind believed it could.

That was one of the little secrets about being an undead that no human ever got to know. Sure there were plenty of real ways to dust us into oblivion. But our minds could do it in the right combination of bad circumstances. And I was in one of those. I knew that no one could survive falling from this height and my mind was prepared to die therefore. I tried to swing it back into positive city, but it wasn't having any. We were going splat and then we were going into the eternal blackness.

All of a sudden I wasn't falling any more. I wasn't splatted, either. I risked a look over my shoulder. There was a whirlwind under me. A whirlwind made up of Dirt Corps.

The half mummy who I was resting on grunted.

"You're heavier than you look."

"Thanks. Meant both sarcastically and extremely gratefully. I'd ask how you knew to show up and do this impressive save, but truth be told, I don't care."

There were a variety of ghosts who were on the outside of the whirlwind, essentially keeping it moving. They all chuckled. One who I was pretty sure was someone who Maurice had fought with during the Revolutionary War spoke up. "We're going to transport you to your next destination. Black Angel One feels that might be safer."

"Couldn't be less safe than any other form of flying." Frankly, it felt safer to me, which was ridiculous. But I didn't argue. I also didn't struggle or feel terrified. Dirt Corps Whirlwind was definitely the way to fly.

In this interesting fashion we went through Necropolis to the site of the disturbance. Interestingly enough, Black Angel Two and Martin were at the Prosaic City National Cemetery. I was sick of that place already.

We slid up to the cemetery through one of the temples to Yahweh. My personal Dirt Corps whirlwind handed me gently back to Cain. Then they spun off and the six of us shifted onto the human plane. I noted that Jack did it without any indication of confusion or problems. He was coming along fast. I was going to have to have Martin check his brainwaves -- this fast was possible without the risk of going crazy, but it was rare.

I looked around. Impressive lack of nothing going on. "I thought you said they were under attack and there was incoming or something."

"Will be," Miriam said. The others nodded. None

of the angels said anything else. Apparently we were either supposed to guess or shut up. I picked shutting up.

Jack pulled me aside. "What was that? Testing to see how easy it is to give someone a heart attack?"

"I hate flying. In an airplane it's okay, sort of. Any other way just plain sucks."

He hugged me tightly. "I thought I was going to see you die. I mean, I suppose you would have recovered, but it didn't feel like that was going to be an option when I was watching you. I thought angels were powerful. And after all that talking up about Black Angel One, I didn't think one of them would have butter-fingers."

"They are powerful, and Cain did his best. I don't work with Black Angel One a lot." Ever, really. "Maurice and Amanda would have known to have just one of them take me, Cain didn't. It's normally considered polite and a relief if they're not reading your mind, you know."

"Yeah, I wasn't enjoying that Jude guy reading me, I can say that."

I let this one pass. "We need to get ready for whatever's coming, you know, if we figure it out before we're attacked. And then we need to figure out a plan, because we've spent a lot of time running around and precious little thinking or running where we think we should be."

"I agree." Jack let me out of his arms. "I think we need to check on the families of those from the alley. Jerry the Junkie knew something. Bobby did, too, but not as much as Jerry."

"Jerry was clear that Tomio was dead. So he knew it was Abaddon a few months ago, and probably that

Apollyon came through the other night. I think we need to find Nero." A thought occurred. "I think we really need to find Nero, and I'll bet cash money that he's either with the Tomio dupes or he's with the families of the deceased."

"No argument, but why?"

"They wanted us away from that block, and that has to mean they wanted us away from The Pleasure Palace and possibly Cotton's pawnshop." Me seeing Jude would only work in the favor of the Prince, because of all the past relationship issues, so they probably didn't care about that one way or the other.

"Yeah, you seeing your ex-boyfriend you still have the hots for probably would be viewed as a benefit to the other side."

I felt myself flush. Either Jack had acquired mind-reading abilities from hanging with Black Angel One for ten minutes or I hadn't kept any emotion off my face when we were with Jude and probably wasn't doing too great a job right now, either. "I don't still have the hots for him. We just broke up kind of strangely. Besides, in case you've missed it, I have the hots for you now."

Jack grinned and I felt him relax. "Good to be sure."

"If you're feeling all better, we need to get addresses on all the recently dead's relatives and probably the relatives of the recently hospitalized as well."

Jack pulled out his cell phone. "Decided not to leave this in the car." He dialed and started talking to Darlene.

While he was occupied I sidled over to Black Angel Two. "What, exactly, are we waiting for?"

Miriam shook her head, Magdalena heaved a martyred sigh. Nothing coming from them. Did the same with Black Angel One. Got charming smiles, but in the "go away little girl" way.

Decided to give Martin a try. "Want to share? At all?"

"Psychic attack. Really, Victoria, we all need to concentrate." He didn't sound angry, just very, very focused.

I sidled away. Jack was off the phone and Sexy Cindy and Freddy were standing near him. Huddled near him, really. "You two picking something up?"

Sexy Cindy shook her head. "Just that the angels are really focused."

"They do seem intent," Freddy agreed. "But I don't understand. If there is an attack, why don't we see anyone or anything?"

"Martin said it was psychic. Which begs the 'why aren't there any other angels arriving' question."

"Begs another one," Jack said. "What's being attacked? As in, are our favorite big-winged buddies defending themselves or someone else?"

"And from what?" Sexy Cindy added.

"And why did they bring us here, if they're not going to tell us what's going on or ask us to help?" Freddy asked.

I considered all these questions. They were good questions. The beings with the answers weren't sharing, however. Therefore, it was time to act like a cop. I sniffed. Nothing smelled off. I looked carefully at where the angels were standing. Roughly where Black Angel Two had been when they'd resurrected the recently dead.

I looked at the graves. The earth was moving. Not

like it had when Miriam had done the raising. It looked more like the earth was heaving up and being shoved back down, but in a small way, which is why I figured none of us had noticed it.

The others saw where I was staring and stared there also. "I'm just betting that's not good," Sexy Cindy offered.

"Right you are." I took a deep breath. "Well, now I know why we're along for this ride."

"Why's that?" Jack asked.

"One or more of the minions is trying to raise these dead. Probably as a test run, but who knows, maybe for more nefarious purposes. Our side's working to keep that from happening."

"What happens if they fail?" Freddy asked quietly.

I shrugged. "To prevent the Prince's minions from forming the Army of the Damned, we dust them."

Chapter 41

My dusting comment was greeted with horrified stares from all three of them. "What?"

"You'd send them to nothingness?" Sexy Cindy asked, clearly appalled. I had to remind myself that the dead were, for all intents and purposes, the closest friends she and Freddy had probably had in the past few years.

"Look, they went into the ground and stayed there." I tried to speak as patiently and kindly as I could. "Ken checked them all before they were interred. None of them could become an undead. None of them ascended."

"We didn't ascend," Freddy interjected. "And according to all of you, we were angel material."

"Angel material and ascension aren't the same thing. In many cases, yes. Black Angels One and Two, Martin, Jude, and so forth. But in other cases, souls ascend and don't become undeads."

"What do they become?" Jack asked.

"Well, they're still them, but they reside with the Gods, so to speak. They don't fight in the War. I think some of them act as advisors. Others I think really get their version of heaven."

"You want to explain that?" Freddy sounded thoughtful.

"I can't. It's complicated and the only undeads who ever go up to visit with the Gods and those who have ascended are angels. They don't share much, as a rule." I tried to think of an example they'd understand. "Mother Theresa's up with the Gods and Monsters, in what she would consider heaven."

"She didn't turn into an angel?" Sexy Cindy

sounded shocked.

I coughed. "No. She'd done her angel work on Earth. I guess…look at ascension as retirement. You did everything the Gods and Monsters could have hoped for on your original plane of existence and unless you want to fight, you deserve your chance to relax. Martin wanted to fight. Mother Theresa didn't."

They all nodded. "Why the Gods and Monsters?" Jack asked. "Why not just the Gods?"

"Some of the monsters are good, too. In case you missed it."

Jack had the grace to look embarrassed. "Sorry. So, back to why you're okay with dusting the dead perps here?"

I sighed. "If they didn't ascend and weren't undead material, as explained before, they're here, waiting to be foot soldiers in the War. As Cindy pointed out the last time we visited, they're all set to be a part of the Army of the Damned. There are a lot of dead who just didn't have an undead nearby to help them change, and they could end up on the side of the Gods and Monsters. However, in Prosaic City, that's not really the case. You die here, we're on it. Ergo, if you die here and you stay in the ground…."

They all nodded. "Makes sense." Jack was back to full cop. "So, how do we dust them, if we have to?"

"Lucky for the three of you, I'm the only one with the right weapon."

"What about the little crossbow and the Evil Fairy Repellent?" Sexy Cindy asked.

"Not evil fairies, not undeads. Won't do a thing to them."

"What about that special gun of yours, the one you keep at your back?" Jack asked. "Why don't you have that out?"

"It's got special bullets, but they're for undeads and the like. Not for dead bodies."

"What are you going to use then?" Jack sounded concerned.

I shifted into wolf form. "Me."

I truly hoped I wasn't going to have to dust. There were a variety of ways to dust a dead body, but only a few undeads were any good for it.

"You mind explaining this?" Jack asked, back to cop voice on full.

"Yeah I do, but anything to pass the time. Because the dead whose souls remain in the dirt and the dark are tied to their bodies, it's easier to dust them than to kill an undead of any kind."

"They know they're in the dark?" Freddy sounded horrified.

"No. The soul is, oh, call it the sleep of the dead. No comprehension, no knowledge. Until they're awakened, and then, as you saw, knowledge of what's going on comes to them. But they can only comprehend what they could when they were alive. So, stupid in life means stupid in death."

"Makes sense," Jack said. "So, you destroy the bodies?"

"Yes. We turn them to dust, literally."

"You mean like cremation?" Sexy Cindy asked.

"In a way. It's one of the reasons Yahweh's sort of big on the no cremation thing. He doesn't want to lose potential good undeads. However, a cremated human could still turn undead, since cremation happens days after someone dies and undeads form pretty much immediately upon death, give or take a little wiggle room. Only humans cremate, by the way. Interesting trivia fact you should store away in case you end up playing *Undead Pursuit* with Edgar or H.P."

"So filing," Freddy said. I figured he had the best shot for that game, anyway. "So, how does it work?"

"Well, it's easiest with liches, witches or warlocks. They cast a 'dust and scatter' or 'dust and contain' spell and, as long as it has enough power and hits the target, it's all over. A Golem will take the body into a live kiln and do some sort of Golem thing to ensure the soul goes along with the rest of the dusting. Neat and tidy."

"No liches, witches, warlocks or Golem around," Jack mentioned.

"And, sadly, no fiery furnace either. For vampires, drain any blood left, suck out and spit out other fluids, body withers into dust, taking soul with it. Gross but effective."

"Also no vamps here just now," Sexy Cindy offered.

"Right. And if they were, they'd be more worried about getting some SPF one thousand to avoid being dusted than dusting someone else. Angels can do it, but it's complicated for them and normally angelic dusting is reserved for a major minion. While we have angels here, they're kind of busy. Which leaves werewolves. For us it's even grosser than for vamps. And after my freefalling experience, I'm not hungry at all."

This floated heavily on the air. The three of them looked a little green, though Jack also looked far too interested. I didn't really relish the idea of him watching me chow down in this way, but I wasn't in a position to ask him to look away.

"What'll we do while you do...whatever it is you're going to do?" Sexy Cindy asked finally.

"Back me, keep any of the deaders from getting

away, help the angels if they need it." I tried not to gag thinking about what might be coming. "Find me some seriously strong alcohol to wash my mouth out with. That sort of thing."

I heard quiet gagging from the others. They had no idea. A werewolf in full devour was terrifying as well as gross, and I'd have to work fast because there were a lot of deaders and only one me.

I managed to control myself from praying. Clearly the gods, Yahweh included, were already paying a lot of attention to what was going on, so if they were going to show up with an assist, it wasn't going to be to prevent my having to chow down on a bunch of icky dead bodies on the hoof.

The earth over one grave heaved and I almost reconsidered that prayer. Jerry the Junkie's body exited the earth, looking just as lovely as before. It figured that he'd rise first -- he wanted to help the Prince's side, after all.

Jerry lumbered towards the angels. Deaders don't move too well, as a rule. Worse than zombies or mummies, though a tad faster than Golem. Then again, almost everything was faster than Golem. Slow, ponderous and steady won the Golem race, that was their unlife motto.

I took a deep breath. Tossed in a howl for good measure. Hey, I had an audience. Then, I charged.

Chapter 42

Jerry made eye contact with me as I barreled towards him. "Here girl." He grinned like he was the first one to toss out that knee-slapper. "Wanna fetch my stick?"

Did the fast thinking thing. There was something wrong about all of this. Not that this was some sort of brilliant revelation. Three top level minions on the human plane hardly spelled out "all's right with the worlds". But Jerry looked too happy about the situation. And he'd had dusting explained to him.

I decided to go with my gut. I didn't bite him. I hit him with all four paws, claws out for full effect. One thing I'd neglected to mention to the others was that deaders could actually feel. So could undeads, of course. But we were unalive, so that made sense. I hoped the others wouldn't catch on, though Jerry shrieking when I raked his body up, down and sideways might have been a clue.

Jerry was flat on his back and I was off him, doing the impressive turn and skid maneuver. He flailed to his feet, looking much worse for wear. "What the hell are you doing?" he yelled.

"Having fun." I ran behind him, knocked him onto his face, and did the claw you up thing on his back. Then I jumped up and down. "What's going on, Jerry?"

"Aaah! Get off me!"

"Not an answer, Jerry. You're too happy about being raised and potentially dusted. What's the plan, Jerry?" Jump, claw, jump. I started to enjoy myself.

"Stop! Stop!"

Happily, Jack was a great cop. He trotted over. "Jerry, you know, she's in a bad mood," he said soothingly, working the good cop routine to the max. "Vic, please, the poor guy's just been raised. Again."

I jumped higher and slammed harder. "Pity for him. I want to know what's going on." I landed, clawed some more, then flipped him over, so I could jump on his stomach. "You know what, Jerry?" Jump, claw, jump. "If I don't actually eat you, you don't dust." Jump, claw, scratch face, jump. "You just get to be turned into scraps." Jump, rake claws down arms, jump. "So, what's going on?" Jump, jump, jump. Playing bad cop was so much fun, I almost forgot there were bigger issues at hand.

"Help me!" Jerry shouted to Jack.

Jack shrugged. "She's in that feral thing werewolves get. Where only mayhem will appease them. Or answers."

I sang quietly under my breath. "Jump up, turn around, claw a bit of deader. Jump up, turn around, scratch him on his face. Jump up, turn around, claw more of the deader. Jump up, jump around, bite him in that place." It was an interactive song, at least how I was doing it. Except for the last line. I hoped Jerry was going to crack before I had to follow through on that.

"Nice lyric change to Belafonte's 'Jump Down, Spin Around' song." Jack said. "Didn't know you liked oldies."

"I like to improvise, I consider anything by Belafonte to be a classic, not an oldie, thank you, and besides, werewolves are very musically inclined."

"Really? Interesting." Jack looked back at Jerry. "You want to answer the lady's questions now?"

Jerry whimpered. "They don't want me to."

I sang louder. "Bite him in *that place*." I even added a leer. I'd usually let Jack be bad cop, but not any more.

He was not allowed to have all the fun.

Jack coughed. "I think, Jerry, you need to consider who's going to cause you more pain and anguish, in both the short and long term."

Fangs bared, drool dripping, I gave a big growl and looked down at Jerry's very personal region. As a deader he really had no use for it, but males stayed attached to those parts, whether alive, undead, or in the ground. It was a guy thing, I didn't try to understand it. I just used it to my advantage when necessary.

"Okay! Okay! Call her off!"

"Give her the answers, maybe she'll stop."

"I don't know all the plan!"

"Share what you *do* know," I growled through bared fangs. "Start with why you were hoping I'd try to eat you."

He didn't want to answer, that was clear. I put a hind paw onto his personal parts and leaned. With all my weight and muscle. Jerry made a very animalistic sound. As a werewolf I'd heard it a lot -- a pathetic whine of pain and terror meant to make you feel sorry and stop.

But werewolves didn't feel sorry all that often, and never in a situation like this. And cops didn't feel bad about roughing up a perp to get information to save hundreds or more. I let up a little, then slammed down, even harder.

"Okay! Okay!" Jerry sounded like every other perp ready to crack, which was what I wanted. I let up a little, but the indication that I'd lean right back down again if necessary was clearly there in the way my claws were tapping. Yeah, werewolf claws are like digits, we can move them all we want. One of the many benefits.

"So, tell me what I want to know." Growled through the teeth with the extra drool, just 'cause I could. "Why were you okay with getting dusted by me?"

He gulped. "They...put something in my body. If you eat it, it'll kill you."

"What, exactly?" Jack didn't sound like good cop now. He sounded like angry boyfriend. I was good with that.

"Not sure. Something...heavy. It feels heavy."

"Silver, silver nitrate, something with silver, maybe liquid mercury, some sort of metallic combo that's deadly. Probably some unholy water, too." I nudged Jerry. "Okay, so you just get to be torn to shreds. Check. What's the plan? As much of it as you know, or else. Oh, and you may be a deader, but you're giving off more scent than death and decay, probably because of what they put in you, so I can smell when you're lying."

Jerry's eyes widened and he looked terrified. Good. Because I couldn't tell for sure from the smell, just a good guess. "I...I don't know much."

I leaned on my hind leg again. "Oh, I'm sure you're selling yourself short, Jerry."

"Tell us what we want to know," Jack said quietly. "Or I'll bring your parents to see you."

Interestingly enough, more than anything else, this worked. I saw the expression in Jerry's eyes change. Not to fear, though, or regret. To amusement tinged with mania. "They'll be here soon enough."

"Who's after your parents?" Jack asked.

"No one." Jerry giggled. I really loathed this guy. It was a pity only a Golem would be able to dust him now -- none of us could ingest him and I was going to ensure he was in myriad pieces which, sadly, made it almost impossible for a spell to work.

"Who's already with them?"

Jerry gaped at me. Apparently someone able to think still shocked him. "Ahhh...."

I leaned on his private parts and sunk my claws in. Squishy and icky, but oh so effective. "Who's with them, and who's with the families and associates of the others who were in the alleyway when Abaddon and Apollyon came through?"

"T-Tomio."

"But Tomio's in Hell already, isn't he, Jerry? I mean, that's what you told us."

"I didn't tell you anything!" His voice was raised and I didn't get the impression he was talking to me.

Instinct's a wonderful thing. According to some, instinct was nothing more than the sum total of all your experiences -- everything that had ever happened to you, that you'd ever read, seen, heard, felt or thought -- bundled together in a tiny part of your hindbrain. Others said instincts were passed down species by species, to help said species survive, and that most instinctive reactions have no real basis in thought or even the experience of the specific reactor, just that if you were a gazelle and you saw a lion, you were going to run, period.

My personal opinion was that both were true. I had instinctive reactions to things as a werewolf that I'd never have had as a human, and vice versa.

One thing about instinct -- I never, ever argued with it. And my instincts told me that Jerry was about to be dusted, but not by my side.

I leaped off him, grabbed Jack, and flung him and myself at Freddy and Sexy Cindy. Uninjured werewolves are strong and I threw the three of them as far as I could. I leaped after them, landed and turned, ready to go knock the angels out of the way.

But there wasn't time.

𝄜 Chapter 43 𝄜

Jerry exploded into dust. One moment I was staring at a ripped up junkie deader. The next there was a layer of rust-colored dust floating over his grave.

On the plus side, the ground stopped moving. On the negative side, the dust swirled up from the ground. The angels flipped their collective wings out and around themselves. They were protected, but the four of us weren't. Jerry's dust could infect us, based on who was likely controlling it.

I had to figure Abaddon and Apollyon were with Jerry's parents and the others, meaning we were likely dealing with the Adversary. I had to get the others out of here. Well, no time like the present for the learning of new skills.

"Cindy, grab Freddy and Jack and fly out of here."

"Excuse me?" She sounded like I'd asked her to grow another head.

"You can fly. You haven't been trained yet, but you can, it's a succubus trait." I watched the dust float around the angels. It wasn't sticking to them, but we weren't likely to be that lucky. "Grab them and fly away."

"I can't."

I turned and did a full on werewolf growl-snarl-howl combination that said I was going to eat her and anyone else nearby. "DO IT!"

Werewolves can be very scary, and I'd ensured that I'd looked and sounded as much like Queen Bitch as possible. Sexy Cindy gave a little shriek, grabbed the others, and leaped into the air away from me. Her flying left a lot to be desired -- she was about a foot off the ground, no more, and wobbling like it was her first time on rollerblades. However, she was carrying the other two and they were getting away, and that's what mattered.

I turned back to watch Jerry's dust. It circled the angels, gave up, and headed towards me. Normally when someone got dusted they went into the earth or sea or wherever. It didn't matter if their motes were floating around, they were rendered null and void. In this case, I knew better.

That the dust was animated meant it was under the Adversary's control. Due to what had been in Jerry's body, the dust would be deadly to me. I couldn't breathe or swallow it, and I had a good guess that letting it land on me wasn't going to be all fun and frolic either.

I readied myself to jump and dodge, but was interrupted by Freddy dropping down in front of me. "Come on, you dirty little bastard," he shouted at the dust. "Pathetic mamma's boy can't even die right!"

Apparently the dust still had some of Jerry in it, because it veered right towards Freddy. Before I could react he opened his mouth and the dust flew into him, every single mote. Then he pulled a flask out of his hip pocket, took a long drink, and burped.

He turned around, grinning, and winked at me. "A little dry."

"What did you do? We have to get you to medical right away."

He took another swig and wiped his mouth on the back of his sleeve. "Nope. Little zombie trick H.P. and Edgar filled me in on. Zombies can't do the dusting, but we can indeed do the clean up."

"Huh?" I had nothing better to offer. Two hundred years plus undead and this was a new one to me. Sexy

Cindy and Jack landed, to use the term loosely. After they picked themselves up from the ground, I tried again. "What are you talking about?"

"Only matters in times like these, when you have an infected deader. I hadn't understood what the others were talking about the other day, but once I saw what was happening, it became clear. Zombies are able to ingest carrier dust because we can ingest pretty much anything, other than certain kinds of salt, with no problem. Then we neutralize it with holy water." He waved the flask.

"What the hell is carrier dust?" Jack asked. I was glad he did, since I didn't have any idea. But I had a good guess.

"Jerry had something deadly to Victoria in him," Freddy explained. "Meaning his dust was deadly to her. So, he's infected, or a carrier of disease." He chuckled. "And I'm the vaccine." I was a good guesser. I was also happy I looked forward to learning new things daily, because this was a doozy. I wondered what else I didn't know, even after all this time.

"Thank the Gods and Monsters." Jack shrugged at my look. "Hey, not like you own the saying."

I shook my head. "True. Freddy, you sure you're okay?"

"Feel fine. If I start to feel evil, I'll let you know." He grinned again. "Nice to be useful to the team for once."

"You've been useful before." I hugged him. "Thank you."

"Any time, Zombie Fred's got your back."

We went to the angels, who had de-cloaked. "You guys okay?"

They nodded. "What about you?" Cain asked.

"You were the target."

"Yeah, she was." Jack sounded angry. "Why didn't you do anything to protect her?"

I put my paw on his arm. "I'm sure Jerry had unholy water in him. That's not exactly nectar to an angel. Besides, of the six of us, I'm more expendable than they are." Jack started to argue but I put my paw up. "This is a war. We have military titles, remember? For a reason."

Jack still looked like he was going to argue, but my wrist-com went off. "Vic, it's Ralph. Status?"

"All fine here, I think. How's the hospital gang?"

"Well, I'm released. I'm the only one, though."

I resisted the urge to growl and curse. "How long for the others?"

He heaved a sigh. "At best, at least a good part of the day. Clyde had more damage than he was showing. He needs full rewrapping. The Count needs a complete transfusion. Hansel and Gretel had to be knocked out to get treated. Those four won't be out until tonight, maybe tomorrow. You want me to go on?"

"Not really, but I think I'd better know. Amanda, Maurice and Ken?"

"Okay, but they all have to sleep in their coffins."

"Oh, that's not good."

"Why not?" Jack asked. "They're vampires. Don't they always sleep in coffins?"

Ralph's low growl came through my wrist-com. He was touchy about humans buying into all the negative undead myths. I answered quickly. "No, that's a myth, in a sense. They need to sleep in their coffins, in some dirt from the ground where they died, only when they're close to becoming dusted." My throat felt tight. "Ralph, are the others just as bad?"

"Yeah. The doctors told me they'd barely finished fixing up Black Angel Two and Martin when the rest of us hit the floor. They're worried about them, by the way."

There was nothing for it. "Ralph, we're at the cemetery. Get here as fast as you can."

"On it, W-W-One-Six-One-Two over and out!"

"Why are you bringing him back?" Jack asked. "He's recovering, too. And he drives you nuts."

"We need him. Most of our team's down." I looked at Martin. "How badly are the three of you still hurt?"

"We were released from the hospital, Victoria," Martin said reassuringly.

"Uh huh. Ralph may indeed drive me crazy but I know when he's trying to pass a message along. The hospital didn't want to release you, did they?"

Martin tried doing the shrug and twinkle thing, but I didn't buy it. I looked at Black Angel One. "And what Ralph was really trying to share was that you two didn't get treated at all."

Cain and Abel tried to look innocent, which, considering they were angels and all, they should've been able to do well. Only, angels have real issues in regard to lying -- one of the reasons they weren't a talkative group -- it's easier not to answer than to tell an untruth. Not that they couldn't lie, it just took a lot of effort and most of them considered that skill not worth the work.

"That's why you couldn't hold me and why neither one of you could catch me when I fell. You're both hurt." I looked at the graves. "It's why the five of you were having so much trouble keeping them in the ground, and why Jerry got free." I stared at the graves some more. "The Adversary knows he hurt you and he also knows you weren't fully or even partly healed. Jerry got out and he was dusted before he could tell us too much. But...why did the Adversary stop trying to raise the deaders?"

Miriam spun and did her raising spell. The ground moved and boiled, but nothing came up. Magdalena touched the moving earth of each grave. She shook her head. "There are no bodies in here any more."

I hit my wrist-com. "Monty, how're you doing?"

"Not really well. Put it this way, it's a good thing they have my arms stacked next to each other, or I couldn't have answered you."

"Ugh. I don't want to know. I need an All Dirt Corps Alert. We need to know if any of our favorite recently raised deaders are anywhere around, on any plane, but most likely Undead or Human. Jerry the Junkie was dusted by the Adversary, but the others have disappeared."

"Not good. Okay, I'll alert the troops. Where will you be?"

I considered. "What day is it?"

"Pardon?" Monty sounded as shocked as those around me looked.

"Day. What day is it? I haven't gotten a lot of sleep, or food, in the past I don't remember how many hours now, and I'm not sure. Day of the week. Surely someone over there knows."

"It's Sunday." Monty sounded confused. "Why does that matter?"

"You asked me where we were headed. And it matters because now I know."

"And," Monty said, like he was speaking to a crazy person with a loaded gun, "just where is that?"

"The Little Church of the Country."

🐾 Chapter 44 🐾

Ralph arrived as I announced our destination. He hit a full stop and a salute. "Ready, Major."

I tried not to sigh. "Ralph, we don't have time for the formality." Based on the glare he shot at Jack, I figured Ralph was going for the full on military bearing in an attempt to outshine Jack.

"Fine." Ralph put his paw down but his body language was Ready For Action. At least he was eager. "Why the Little Church of the Country as our destination?"

"Jerry the Junkie was a little too involved and in the know. His father's a preacher of some kind, and his family lives in the Estates. There are only a few men or women of the cloth who can afford to live that well."

"Television evangelists," Freddy supplied.

"Yep. And we have a couple who live in the Estates. One in particular."

"The Right Reverend Gerald Johnson," Jack said. "Called Jeremiah Johnson by most of his flock. Okay, I can see it, and I'll just bet our favorite dusted junkie was named for his father."

"I'd give it pretty even odds. Johnson controls a flock that consists of most of Prosaic City's wealthy and also lures the poor and lower middle class." The Little Church was also a total misnomer. It was huge and glorious -- lots of glass, gold and silver plate, and reflective paint, along with many more spires than one normally needed for a house of worship -- built on one of the hills in the Estates, so you could see it for miles.

"So, that would mean, since it's Sunday morning, they've got a packed house and all the bodies they need, right?" Sexy Cindy ventured.

"That's my current guess." The base of my tail felt that Sexy Cindy was a keeper. I checked out the angels. "Much as I'd love to have aerial backup, I want the five of you back to the hospital. Monty, if they don't show up within fifteen minutes, I want an All Being Alert on Black Angel One, Black Angel Two, and Martin. Brought in for extreme stubbornness."

He chuckled. "You got it. I'll alert the hospital staff that their errant patients will be returning." My wrist-com went dead.

Martin shook his head. "You need us."

"Yeah, I need you alive and well. Go get fixed up. If it's that bad, I'm sure you'll know."

"I'm sure." Martin sighed and nodded. "Let's do as Victoria asks. The sooner we go, the sooner we'll be released." They all nodded to us and flew off. Slowly.

I turned back to the others. "Okay, we need a car."

"Why not use your detective car?" Sexy Cindy asked.

"I have no idea where it is." This was true.

"At Our Lady of Compassion," Jack said. "Illegally parked."

Oh, right. "Legally parked, and get over it. Too far away, and besides, we need a nicer car."

"Why?" Freddy asked, as he looked around the cemetery. "I see no cars here."

I sniffed and saw Ralph's ears perk up. "There will be cars here shortly, and we need a decent one because we're about to infiltrate the church where all the money goes. We need to fit in."

"What's wrong with our car?" Jack asked.

"Other than it screaming 'undercover police'? Nothing."

"I'm not going to human," Ralph said flatly.

"Yes, yes, Ralph, I know. Werewolves Wear Their Pride. Got it." I shifted to human and rubbed my forehead. "Fine. You're a purebred wolfhound. Make sure you look all friendly and such, wolfhounds love people. But not for dinner."

He gave me a betrayed look. "You're going to put a leash on me?"

"If only I could. No. I'm going to brag about how you're so well trained you can follow my verbal commands and hand signals. Unless I decide to just lock you in the car with the window rolled down a tiny bit."

"Funny." Ralph ruffled his fur. "But, undercover work isn't always enjoyable."

"No kidding." I started walking towards the sounds and the smells. There was an early morning funeral going on. And happily, it was attended by several people with very nice cars.

There was a pretty decent-sized crowd for this time of day. They seemed to cover all walks of life, too, if the clothing was any indication. Not all the cars were nice -- some had decidedly seen better driving days. I took a closer look at the crowd. They were in front of a set of big flower displays but not by any graves.

We took care to amble and look reverent. No rushing about furtively -- that tells everyone you're trying not to be seen. Look like you don't mind being seen and no one pays any attention. I had to stop paying attention to the mourners and look for a suitable vehicle to "borrow".

One of the cars parked the farthest away was a Mercedes S-Class. I was good with that. No one in the good parts of town would question anyone's right to be there if they arrived in an S-Class.

The Gods and Monsters were on our side. The driver had left the keys in the ignition. Jack slid into the driver's seat, I took shotgun, and the others got into the back. "Ralph, try not to rip the upholstery."

"I only rip what I want to," he muttered.

"Good boy."

"You're not funny, Vic."

Jack chuckled. "Yeah, she is. However, I don't think we should be stealing cars."

"It's in the execution of our duties."

"It's grand theft auto."

"No problem, I'll drive."

Jack sighed. "No, let's not add manslaughter, being-slaughter, destruction of public property, and reckless endangerment to the list." He started the car and we backed away. No one seemed to notice we were stealing a hugely expensive car, though I figured that wouldn't last long. As soon as we were out of sight of the funeral, Jack sped up and out of the cemetery. "So, you think we're right about the Little Church?"

"Yeah. And the Prince and the minions love a good show. Plus, think about it -- worldwide, televised audience. Great way to influence the masses, and not just the masses in Prosaic City. I'd say the odds are just too good that Jerry's father is Johnson, and that the minions are with him in some way."

"I agree," Sexy Cindy offered. "His mom would come in a fancy car like this one. They make some real money at that church, I've heard." From what I'd heard they made so much money that the I.R.S. always took a personal interest. However, Johnson was found clean, year after year. The possibility that he was a truly good man with a loser son was at least as good as the option that he was a manipulative scumbag who used the idea of God to control the masses and steal their money in a legal way. It wouldn't matter to the minions -- on the Prince's side already, turned to the Side of Evil, or destroyed, that was their goal no matter what or who.

We wound our way through Prosaic City in some of the nicest luxury ever. "I could get used to this."

"I hope we don't get busted for grand theft auto," Jack muttered.

"We're cops. Taken in pursuit of a criminal."

"We stole the car, Vic."

"Details, details." I was ready to go to sleep and the car was comfy enough to do it. I heard Freddy snoring softly behind me. My eyes closed.

They opened because a wet nose was in my ear. "Wake up," Ralph whispered.

I was going to say something nasty but fortunately looked ahead before I glared at Ralph. We were at the Prosaic Country Club and Estates. But we weren't going to be able to get in.

There was a wall of flame around the entire perimeter. I could tell because Jack was slowly driving past it. "Can everyone see that?" I asked. I could just make out the Little Church in the distance -- the flames were obstructing my view extremely well.

"I see signs saying that entry's forbidden," Jack said. "But I think I see something else, like…fire?"

"Yes," Ralph said. "It's Hellfire." He was growling. Not that I could blame him.

"I see it, too," Sexy Cindy said.

"I as well," Freddy confirmed. "But, how and why?"

I thought about it while we drove around in a big, winding, sort of circle. "How is simple. Abaddon and Apollyon are together. Hellfire's the least of what they can bring to any party. Hitler's got to be with them -- the barriers Jack can see, and I can see if I focus, are warlock-created for sure. To keep humans out," I added before anyone could ask.

"Why would they want that?" Sexy Cindy asked. "I thought they wanted to take over."

"They do. But they don't need all the humans to do that." I was worried they already had all they needed in place and on the human plane. "Why is the real question."

"What's going on is the bigger question," Jack said.

"Creating more dupes, creating a living zombie army, gathering hostages, mind-controlling people via the televised feed, the usual evil minion ploys," Ralph said. "What's going on is simple -- something we don't want. Vic's right, why is the real question." His nose was still near my ear.

I shoved his muzzle away gently and got the sad puppy eyes. I did my best to ignore them. "I've got a reason for why, but I don't like it."

"Is there a possibility for a reason we'd actually like?" Jack asked. "Spill it, Vic."

I took a deep breath. "The Hellfire's there to keep us out, since we can't safely pass through it. You could," I said to Jack. "But only if you couldn't see the Hellfire. You can see that there's something else there, so it'll hurt or kill you to pass through. Same for us. Demons and Golem can pass through, but the rest of us need more equipment than we have with us." I remembered all our stuff back in the unmarked car. We needed to get back there.

"Is that the entire answer?" Jack asked shortly.

"No. Head for the OLOC. I want to dump this car and get our usual one."

He muttered something under his breath but did as asked. "So? Why the Hellfire and why are we leaving?"

"They knew we were coming. That's why the Hellfire's up. Whatever they're doing, they don't want us disturbing it."

"How could they know we were headed here?" Sexy Cindy asked. "We didn't know until you said it."

"I know." I sighed. "I think we have a mole."

Chapter 45

Ralph broke the silence first. "Who do you suspect?"

"Not sure."

"You're lying. You have a guess. I can tell."

I glared at his nose, which was back to being right near my ear. "How so?"

He moved so we were eye-to-eye and gave me a look that said I was a moron. "You, like every other being, smell different when you lie."

Duh. Couldn't argue with a werewolf nose. "Fine. I hate what I'm going to say." The words dragged out of my mouth. "Monty's the most obvious choice. He knew where we were going, he controls Dead Corps, he's been undead for centuries."

"You have no proof," Freddy said, sounding upset. I couldn't blame him. I didn't want to consider Monty an enemy. The mere idea hurt too much.

"True. Just supposition. But we need to be careful and hyper-aware of what we say to and around him."

"Could be someone else," Ralph said. "Anyone could have been in the room with Monty, after all."

"Yes, which is why it's supposition right now and we're not making an arrest."

"That's ridiculous," Ralph argued. "Monty's in a huge position of trust. Clyde and the Count would never have let him get to that position if he were a double-agent."

"See, the thing is -- if you're a good double-agent, that's the whole point. That you look just like you should to the side you're infiltrating." After all, I knew we had beings in deep cover -- why wouldn't the Prince have the same? Frankly, why wouldn't the

Prince have more agents infiltrating us, not less? Double-agents, like a good double-cross, were more the Prince's side of things than ours, after all.

"So, Monty's a suspect," Jack said shortly. "Who else?" He shot me a look I was familiar with -- he suspected someone near us of being about to try something.

I considered who in the car Jack didn't trust. The answer was easy. But I wasn't going to accuse Ralph of being a double-agent right here and now, for a variety of reasons, not the least of which being if he *was*, we'd tell him that we suspected him, and that would mean we wouldn't catch him, because he'd be on guard.

So, I considered other options, while adding Ralph to my turncoat suspects list. None of the options, Ralph included, made me happy. But then again, finding out one of your friends is actually your enemy is never fun. "Clyde."

"Why?" Ralph sounded shocked. "He had to be rewrapped! How's he a suspect?"

"He runs Necropolis Enforcement's day-to-day. And yet, the Adversary made it in without issue, did his thing, and escaped. I just think it's a possibility that he had inside help, and if he did, then Clyde's the best choice."

"The Count, too," Sexy Cindy said, her voice low. "I mean, if you're looking for who it would suck beyond belief to be on the wrong side. Martin and Black Angel One and Two, too. They were with us and angels can talk in their minds and all."

"Yeah." The downside of knowing we had a deep cover operative about as deep as you could go meant the other side could as well. I'd been happier back in The Pleasure Palace.

"All the angels, any angel, by those standards," Freddy said, sounding dejected. "Even Jude. He's supposed to be blocking the bad guys and yet all the minions are on the plane, right?"

"Right." I wanted to throw up. "Cotton." Suggesting him didn't give me any pleasure. "Though I think he's unlikely." But ghosts had the ability to follow you without your knowing it. Not for too long, but a short time could be enough.

"Ken," Jack offered. "He made the decisions about who to resurrect. And he screwed up Freddy and Cindy. Maybe he did that on purpose."

My stomach was in knots. "You have a point." My friends and my two ex-boyfriends were suspects. Throwing up wasn't an option, neither were tears, but it took a lot of work to prevent both. I couldn't even trust everyone in the car, since Ralph was a suspect, though thankfully Jack wasn't going to say it aloud right now, either. Freddy and Sexy Cindy, by benefit of being resurrected by Ken could also be considered suspect. I felt quite alone and surrounded.

Ralph sighed. "Honestly, it could be anyone. Vic's the daughter of the Adversary, Jack's a human who's adapting amazingly well...I could go on. I don't think we have enough to know."

Ralph had a point. "True. So, we work under the mole assumption and stay hyper-alert, but until we have something more, no friendships are destroyed by quick-trigger accusations. Agreed?"

The others all murmured their accord. We drove on, and I was sure the others felt like I did -- like the world had just shifted again into an even scarier and sadder place.

Chapter 46

We arrived at the OLOC parking lot. Sure enough, there was our unmarked car, looking very police-like. It was getting furtive glances from the few humans wandering around. They were also clearly looking for the cops. No one had paid any real attention to us in the S-Class.

"Let's load the weapons into our, ah, borrowed vehicle."

"Hell with that," Jack muttered. He went to the sedan's radio. "Darlene, Detective Wagner. Any interesting news?"

"Darlene is off shift, Detective. This is Susan." There was something odd about how she said her name, but I couldn't place what. I tried to remember what she looked like but couldn't. Blonde, maybe.

"Oh, right, sorry, losing track of time. How're you doing?" Jack sounded friendlier than normal. I figured he'd picked up that he'd annoyed her in some way.

"I'm good, thanks for asking. Are you still on shift?"

"Yes, Detective Wolfe and I are both going to have to keep on rolling."

"Bummer."

"So," I interjected, "what's going on today and what went on last night that we might not know about?"

"Last night was another quiet night. Nice change. Darlene told me the Chief is worried, though." Susan sounded bored.

"Nothing at all on the radar?" Jack was fishing for something, but I didn't know what.

"Minor stuff so far today. Someone stole a car from

the National Cemetery." Jack gave me the "I told you so" look. "Road work's blocked off most of the Estates area. Nothing for Night Beat to worry about, though."

"Most of the Estates, but not all?" I asked, since Susan had no idea what we actually were doing or needed to worry about.

"Apparently there's some big religious deal going on at the Little Church, big fundraiser," Susan said. "They've been advertising it for months. They have the streets blocked off -- you can't get in without a ticket and they're cross-checking against a list or something. Why is this of interest to you or the police department?"

"Just want to know how to get in or out if you don't have a ticket." I was used to Darlene's level of sarcastic help. Susan seemed a lot more difficult to work with. I didn't envy the day shift.

"Utility road, where city workers go in and out. Anything else, Detective Wagner?"

I ignored the snub. "Yeah. A couple of nights ago Darlene said there was a riot. Can you tell me about that?"

"You could come into the station and read the officers' reports." Susan definitely wasn't into the give and take I was used to.

"We could. Or, you know, you could give us the highlights and we could continue on, fighting crime, keeping Prosaic City safe for dispatchers with attitude."

"Vic," Jack hissed. "Sorry, Susan. We're both tired. Been a long night after a couple of longer nights. Can we have those highlights?"

Susan sighed the put-upon sigh of a woman forced to actually do something when she was going to paint her nails. I decided I didn't like her. "Fine. There was a riot at the stadium. Even with a lot of reports, we have no clear idea why or how it started."

"There wasn't a game this week," I mentioned.

"Right you are," Susan said snidely. "There was a revival."

"Revival?"

She sighed again. She was big on sighing. I moved to intense dislike. "Reverend Johnson brought in religious leaders from all over to do an old-fashioned tent revival. Big rally kind of thing. As the kickoff to the fundraiser starting today. Do you ever read the paper or listen to the news?"

"No. I like to remain unaware and get all my news from dispatch. Until this morning, never been a problem."

"Right. So anyway, some thugs, or kids, or criminals, no one was really sure, crashed it and thanks to *Detective Wagner's* tip, our officers were able to get there in time to get things back under control."

I knew the tip had come from Ken. Needed to ask him what he knew. If he wasn't the mole, of course. Well, I had to ask him whether or not he was the mole. The question was going to boil down to -- could I trust his answers? I hated the way this day was going.

But not as much as I currently hated Susan. I'd picked up the massive emphasis on "Detective Wagner" and I was getting the distinct feeling that Susan had the hots for my guy. This was not an acceptable thing. I considered going to headquarters and eating her, but decided going for demure and sweet might be better, particularly since Jack looked both embarrassed and frustrated.

"Yes, Detective Wagner's the best, isn't he?"

"You have no idea." Susan sounded just a little too

smug. And Ralph wasn't the only one with a werewolf nose. Jack was giving off guilt pheromones.

"I'll bet. Anyway, Susan, thanks so much for all your help. We'll be checking in later, I'm sure." I hung up the radio. I almost opened my mouth to discuss this little situation with Jack, but the presence of three other beings helped me stay quiet. He was allowed to have dated other people before we got together -- I certainly had. He'd met them. Lucky me. But the point was, if he'd had a relationship with Susan the Dispatcher from Hell, that was his business. Going forward it was my business, but retrospectively, not so much. So I went for cool. Not a canine trait, as mentioned before, but sometimes we can do it. "We need to ask Ken what tipped him off to that riot and what he picked up from it."

Jack looked relieved and nodded. "I agree. Hope we can trust his answers."

"Me too. Now, like I said before, let's move the equipment from this car into the nice car we've borrowed while in pursuit of dangerous criminals."

"Great spin," Jack muttered as Freddy and Sexy Cindy started to shift our stuff.

I considered what to do with our bag of pawned goodies from Cotton, and decided they didn't need to come along. I shoved the bag behind the spare tire and handed another set of crossbows to Freddy. As I did I noticed Ralph looking at Jack, eyes narrowed. I was about to say something about this when he gave the canine snort of dismissal and trotted back to the S-Class.

"What's wrong with our beloved wolfhound?" Jack asked, sarcasm dripping.

I had a few guesses, but I kept them to myself. "No

idea."

"So, your plan?"

"We're going to infiltrate via the only road that's apparently letting beings in and out."

"How? We drove by. We saw nothing but Hellfire."

"True. But we now have the means to go through Hellfire unscathed."

Jack raised his eyebrow. "Really. I carried a lot of crossbows and swords and Evil Fairy Repellent, but I didn't see any fire retardant suits."

I picked up the last thing in the unmarked sedan's trunk. "Nope, you didn't. And you didn't carry it to the car anyway. It was already here." I held up my prize.

Jack stared at it. "It's a fire extinguisher. Are you telling me that Hellfire is put out just like a campfire?"

"Nope. This didn't come with the car. I put it in months ago. Read the label."

Jack read aloud. "Spray widely in an up and down and back and forth manner." He gave me a look that said I'd lost it. "You mind explaining how this is going to help?"

Sexy Cindy came over and looked at the label. She grinned and shook her head. "Savior Spray for all your firefighting needs." She snorted. "You all have a sense of humor, I'll say that."

"I still don't get it," Jack said flatly.

Sexy Cindy shrugged. "Spray widely in an up," she pointed to her head, "down," pointed mid-chest, "back," left shoulder, "and forth," right shoulder, "manner. Or, for the marvelous detective, make the Sign of the Cross while spraying." She rolled her eyes at me. "Is he always that slow?"

"Some consider him the best detective on the force." Susan, for instance. Me, under most circumstances. The Chief occasionally.

Sexy Cindy apparently not. "Really?" She sniffed. "When an undead hooker's ahead of you, maybe you should rethink your career choices." She sashayed off to the S-Class while I tried not to snicker.

"I don't like her," Jack muttered.

I grinned. "I think she's great."

Chapter 47

Back in the S-Class and rolling. I found myself wondering if there was going to be any way we could keep the car for good. We'd achieved far more stealth in it than we'd ever had in the unmarked sedan. And it was comfort to die for. Well, not literally.

While Jack drove, I contacted Ken on my wrist-com. "How're you doing?"

"I'm in my coffin. I was trying to sleep."

"I know, and I'm sorry. I need info on the riot from the other night."

"What? Oh...yeah, that. Sorry, so much has been going on." Ken was quiet for a few moments. "You want to know what, exactly?"

"How'd you know, what did you get from it, the works."

"You know," he said slowly, "I can't remember too much."

I found this horribly suspicious in that mole way. "Try, if you can. I know you don't feel well." I hoped it was because he'd been bashed around by the Adversary, not that he was in league with the Adversary. Having someone who'd been that intimate with me and who I'd been that close to emotionally as well as physically turn out to be part of the Prince's loyal squad made me nauseous. Almost as nauseous as thinking about a mole in the first place.

"I didn't get what I would normally." Ken sounded like he was trying to remember. I hoped it wasn't an act. "I knew there were a lot of humans in one area, I felt fear and anger, all the signs of a riot. Really, that's about it. I was focused on getting the police over there and trying to stop the demon."

"Yeah, Slimy was the sort to rivet your attention."

"What are you doing? Where are you?" Ken sounded drowsy and out of it.

I chose to go with reassuring. "We're good. Following up some leads. You get some rest and feel better. I'm sure we'll need you back in action fast."

"Yeah. Vic...."

"What?"

He took a deep breath. "Vic, be careful."

"Always."

"No, I mean it. Be really careful. I feel like I should tell you to trust no one. Whatever's going on, I think it's bigger than anything we've ever dealt with. Not just me, but you, too. Maybe everyone. Watch your back."

"Will do."

"Promise me." Ken sounded stressed and a little freaked.

I decided to ensure relaxation. "I promise." I looked behind me. "I'll watch my back and trust no one." Ralph glared, Freddy shook his head, and Sexy Cindy grinned.

"Good. See you later, V-One-Nine-Six-Zero out." My wrist-com went dead.

"Ken's really hurt," Ralph said quietly.

"Why do you say so?"

He snorted. "That warning was for you alone, Vic. I don't think it occurred to Ken that you had anyone else around, or that anyone else could hear him, even though he was talking to you through the wrist-coms. He doesn't make stupid assumptions."

"True." Very true. Oh good. More things to worry about.

"Maybe he knew we were all here and is trying to create suspicion among the five of us," Jack offered.

Sadly, I knew that Ken didn't need to do that -- we were all undoubtedly suspicious enough of everyone else already. Of course, he wouldn't know that if he was the mole. But if he wasn't, that meant he was hurt badly enough not to be thinking clearly, and that meant very badly.

I took a deep breath and let it out slowly. Worrying about a mole was destined to drive me crazy. Maybe we weren't infiltrated. Maybe we were. I'd worked for Necropolis Enforcement for a long time and it had never been an issue before. Maybe the best thing I could do was stop trying to find the mole and go back to business as usual.

All this introspection had taken time and we were back at the outskirts of the Estates. Jack drove slowly and we looked for the servant's entrance.

"There it is," Ralph said, pointing with his nose, possibly to get it right back by my face.

But he was right. We'd missed it before because it was designed to be missed and we'd been looking at the Hellfire.

"You sure that's a road?" Sexy Cindy asked. "Looks more like a bike path."

"No, I see a road sign," Jack said. "Workmen's Access Road. Yeah, this is it." He stopped the car. "But I still see the Hellfire."

"Yep." I got out of the car. Ralph scrambled over the back of the front seat and came with me. I decided not to argue. "Good doggie, coming to protect Mommy-Dog while she puts out the nasty fire."

"Hilarious," he growled. "I just don't want you alone out here."

"Can't argue with your judgment." I lifted the trunk and got out the Savior Spray. We trotted over to the Hellfire and I looked for the right spot to spray.

Hellfire was interesting in a variety of ways. For one thing, and against all human expectations, it didn't burn hot. Until you were engulfed in it, you couldn't feel that it was there. Once engulfed, it burned like ice. Nothing dusted you faster than Hellfire, though.

Ralph and I stayed a respectful distance back from the burning. "How deep do you think it goes?"

He sniffed. "Looks about ten feet, smells like less."

"Huh." I couldn't argue, that's about what I'd come up with as well. I chose my spot and sprayed in the correct pattern. Nothing looked different.

"No change," Ralph noted.

"No kidding." Something wasn't right. Savior Spray was designed to douse Hellfire. So, why wasn't it working?

Ralph whined and nudged up against me. I looked around to see a jogger coming down the access road.

"Morning!" the man shouted cheerfully. "You folks having some trouble?"

"Ah…yes," I answered lamely, trying to come up with why I was holding a fire extinguisher and standing with what truly looked far more like wolf than hound.

The jogger trotted blithely through the Hellfire and came over to us. "Engine fire?" he asked, seeming fully ready to pop the hood and take a look.

"No. I…I saw a little fire here. From someone's cigarette. But we got it, didn't we, boy?" I ruffled Ralph's head in that dog owner way.

"Good thing you were looking," the jogger said seriously. "Last thing we want is this beautiful place engulfed in flames. Whereabouts are you in the Estates?"

"We don't live there...yet," I added to his look of disappointment and mild suspicion. "We're still sort of...house browsing."

"Ah." His eyes lit up. "I'm a realtor. I'd be happy to show you around if you're not already represented." He whipped a card out of the pocket of his jogging pants. It was only a little damp.

"Bill Bennett, Realtor for all seasons," I read aloud as Ralph sniffed him openly and I sniffed surreptitiously. "Great. We'll definitely give you a call."

"I'll look forward to it. Beautiful dog," he added, as he did the manly pet the dog thing. I got the distinct feeling Bill was hitting on me. "What breed is he?"

"Russian Wolfhound. Very highly trained. I paid a fortune for him, but he's worth it, aren't you, baby?" I said in that nauseating way pet owners talk to their animal friends.

Ralph got into the act, doing the happy doggy dance that begged for more attention. He got it from Bill. I was getting tired of the act. Besides, the canine part of me sort of wanted to go all wiggy, too -- Bill was clearly either a dog lover or pathologically lonely, because he seemed ready to take Ralph home.

"Well," I said as regretfully as I could manage, "we'd probably better get going."

Bill nodded and gave Ralph one last enthusiastic pet-rub combo. "Bring your dog along when you're ready to house hunt," he said as he started jogging off around the perimeter of the Estates. "You should be sure he likes it, too." Yep, definitely a dog lover. He waved to our cars' occupants as he trotted off, which reminded me that they were still there. Acting human took a lot out of me when I hadn't had food or sleep for a while.

We went to the car and got in. "Something's odd about the Hellfire."

"Your new boyfriend didn't seem to notice it," Jack said sourly.

"More to the point," Ralph said before I could work up a suitable comeback, "he didn't smell of it."

"Of what?" Jack asked.

"Of Hellfire, of sulfur, of anything other than laundry detergent, sweat, and a little more cologne than necessary to go jogging," I replied.

"He probably picks up girls all along his jogging route," Jack muttered.

"What's him not smelling of Hellfire mean?" Freddy asked.

Ralph beat me to this answer, too. "That it's not Hellfire we're seeing."

Chapter 48

"What do you mean?" Sexy Cindy asked. "You said it was Hellfire, we can see it. You said humans can go through it safely, so maybe that's why he didn't smell."

"He smelled. He just didn't smell like he should have. Humans can't feel Hellfire if they can't see it, so Bill was safe jogging through it."

"Bill?" Jack asked.

"Bill Bennett, Realtor for all seasons. I told him we were thinking of moving in. Anyway, even though most humans can't sense Hellfire, going through it should leave traces, one of the easiest to spot being smell. And there was none."

"There's a smell of Hellfire when you're close to the flames," Ralph added. "But there was none on Bill, and I got some good, intense sniffs in."

"Meaning?" Jack asked.

I thought about it. "They knew we were coming." I thought some more. "The Hellfire's an illusion. Designed to send us away, keep us out, make us waste time, effort and materials to get rid of it. But it's not really there."

"And if you're wrong and we go through it, then what?" Jack asked.

"We're dusted."

There was dead silence in the car. Ralph broke it. "I'll go through."

I resisted the urge to mention that he always grandstanded when I was nearby. One of us actually had to test it. But he wasn't the one in charge. "No, it should be me."

Ralph actually bared his fangs at me, which I was

pretty sure was the first time, ever. "No. If anyone's going to risk getting dusted, it'll be me, and not you. Ever."

"I agree," Jack said. He got out of the car and held his door for Ralph.

"Ralph, what if we're wrong?" I asked as he again scrambled over the front seat.

He looked at me. "Then the pack goes down by one."

"You sound awfully cavalier."

Ralph closed his eyes. When he opened them again he looked sad. "No. I just think we're right. And even if we're not and I get dusted, well...." He sighed. "I'm alone anyway. No one'll miss me, not really." He turned and quickly jumped out of the car.

I sat there with a variety of feelings running through me. Guilt was really high on the list. I knew Ralph liked me and I didn't like him back. But it wasn't just that. As I sat there and thought about it, the truth of the matter was that I couldn't come up with anyone Ralph "hung out" with. I had Amanda and Maurice for the off hours, and now Jack, too. And those were just for starters. Clearly Freddy and Sexy Cindy were going to stay together -- maybe not romantically, but they were sort of clinging to each other in an understandable way. Everyone had someone, but as I rolled back through the years, Ralph didn't. And for all his pack talk, it was an ideal. We had no pack. Werewolves hadn't run in packs for decades for a variety of reasons.

"Why don't you like him?" Sexy Cindy asked quietly.

"Ralph?" He was sniffing the Hellfire again. Jack had the Savior Spray. I had no idea what he thought he'd do with it should Ralph and I be wrong about this, but at least he was going to try.

"Yeah."

"He's...he's kind of a dork. And sometimes he's a real goof, too." And a werewolf solidarity fanatic, but now probably wasn't the time to list all his faults.

"I suppose." She sounded thoughtful. "Only, he's brave and loyal and it sure seems like he's got the major crush on you. And he's willing to risk his life to protect you. I don't know, I wish I had a guy who was like that interested in me, kind of goofy or dorky or not."

I almost mentioned that Ralph tended to grandstand any time he was around me, but it died before it could get off my tongue. Because if we were wrong, then Ralph was really offering to die to protect me, and Sexy Cindy was right -- that wasn't grandstanding, that was heroic.

"Yeah, I guess he is. Jack's brave, too," I added apropos of pointing out I was already with someone.

"I guess." She sounded a little doubtful. Then again, she'd already been dead when he'd grabbed the gun and taken on Slimy. "But...he's not the one who offered to go through the Hellfire."

I found myself wishing Amanda and Maurice were here. The need to discuss this with someone was almost overwhelming. But the only someones I could so discuss with were in the backseat.

"We should perhaps call him Cyrano," Freddy said.

"The guy with the big nose?" Sexy Cindy asked. I was impressed she knew.

"Yes." Freddy chuckled. "You do know your classics, don't you, my dear?"

We were spared any more literary comparisons by

the fact that Ralph moved into a springing stance. I guessed he'd chosen the find out and/or die fast option. Couldn't blame him. He sprang and I held my breath.

He sailed through, looking like he was practicing to get the blue ribbon in the dog show agility event. But he didn't burn and turn to dust. I let my breath out.

Ralph landed, spun and trotted back. Still no harm and no foul. He came over to my side of the car and I opened the door. "It's a good illusion. It felt hot when I went through it."

I sniffed him. "You smell wrong. Not of Hellfire, not of anything related to fire, really."

"Yeah. I'm not sure what base they used for the incantation, but this is warlock-created. I'd bet my tail on it."

"You feel okay?" He looked okay and he smelled reasonably normal, but it never hurt to check.

Ralph nodded. "I don't think it's supposed to do anything more than it did. Keep us out and make us waste time and effort." He crawled into the car and got into the backseat as Jack tossed the Savior Spray into the trunk.

Jack got back behind the wheel and we started off through the fake Hellfire. I still held my breath as we went through it. So did everyone else, if the collective sigh as we passed through it unscathed was any indication.

We wound up into the Estates through the narrowest road I'd been on in a long time. Any part of the Estates not covered with house or grandiose grounds was covered with nature -- trees, bushes, grass, flowers, anything and everything. I'd heard they imported deer and other benign wildlife, but I'd never hunted up here so couldn't confirm or deny. It was shady and lovely and all that, but there was no shoulder or turnout. "Why do you think they make this road so hard to use?"

"No idea," Jack said. "But if we meet another vehicle we're going to be in trouble."

"Maybe they restrict how many workmen can come in at a time," Sexy Cindy suggested.

"Maybe. But you know, one of the things they brag about is how this *isn't* a gated community. It's to let the people who live here kid themselves that they're both exclusive and kind to the poor, or something."

"Anyone can come to the Estates," Freddy intoned. "We are an open community."

"You help write their ad copy?"

"No. Jerry used to say that all the time. He thought it was funny, I suppose."

I considered this. "Or, the Prince's side infiltrated up here a lot longer ago than we're thinking."

"If his father's on the Prince's side, that would make sense," Jack said.

"Not all rich folks have sold their souls for their money," Sexy Cindy mentioned. "Just a lot of them."

We continued on, thankfully meeting no other vehicles. No one other than Bill the Realtor seemed to be out, at least not on or around this tiny stretch of road. We hit the first real street of the Estates and turned off the workman's road. I couldn't speak for the others, but I felt relieved.

We meandered through the humongous and ritzy neighborhood, but we remained the only living things so doing. We were still pretty far from the Little Church, but even if the majority were up there, surely someone other than Bill didn't attend services. "Is this normal for a Sunday morning?"

Jack nodded. "Pretty much. The religious are all in church. The drunks and stoners are sleeping it off. The non-religious are sleeping or prepping to watch whatever sporting event's on TV. Most Saturday night perps are behind bars. And so on."

"Even hookers take Sunday morning off," Sexy Cindy added.

"It is the day of rest," Freddy added.

"Then," Ralph said tensely, "why is that guy not resting?"

I looked where his nose was pointing. Sure enough, there was someone in a copse of trees that stood between two of the lower level estates. He almost looked like a gardener, or a zookeeper, since he was dressed in what looked like a khaki shorts jumpsuit and hiking boots. Only there was no truck or equipment nearby and Ralph and I were the only wild animals in the immediate vicinity.

Jack stopped the car and I got out, Ralph scrambling after me so quickly he sort of fell out of the car. He managed to recover so that he landed on his paws, not his snout, but it was a close thing. I chose to pretend I hadn't seen it, though I did hear Jack chuckling.

We got nearer to the man, whose back was to us. I wasn't sure that he'd heard us arrive, which was sort of odd. Then again, we hadn't shut my door and I could barely hear the S-Class' engine running and I had werewolf hearing. I resolved to find a way to insist on our keeping this car, or getting our own.

We got closer. Whatever this guy was doing, he was intent on it. He also wasn't likely to be good-looking, at least if his backside was any indication. He had skinny legs under a rather hefty body. Light blond hair. I stared at it. The hairstyle had a certain…ancient look to it.

I looked at Ralph out of the corner of my eye. His fur was up. Good.

I cleared my throat loudly and the man spun around. It was nice to be right.

"Nero! My favorite lunatic. What're you up to, big guy?"

🐾 Chapter 49 🐾

Nero's shifty blue eyes did their look frantically for escape thing. Ralph was growling, however, in a way that indicated Nero running would be a bad idea for Nero and a fun idea for Ralph.

Nero was many things, but monumentally stupid wasn't one of them. He gave me what I assumed he thought was a beguiling smile. "Ah, Victoria, isn't it?"

"That's right. Agent Wolfe, Major, Necropolis Enforcement to you, however." He really was dressed like a zookeeper. I found myself wondering why. "Just what are you doing, Nero?"

"Ah, public service," he answered brightly. "Foliage control."

I looked around. "I see no weeds that need whacking."

Ralph's growl went up, but he didn't say anything. I figured he was staying undercover, which, considering where we were, was probably smart.

"Err, ah, well," Nero said, clearly stalling. "I've cleared most of it already."

"Into what?" Nero stood there without an answer and I took a deep breath. A lot of smells mingled together -- exhaust, earth, foliage, garbage, and the like. But one smell stood out. Interestingly, it wasn't the smell of sulfur or Hellfire. I smiled a very unfriendly smile. "You know what I think you're doing, Nero?"

"No. What?" he asked nervously.

"I think you're planting maggots. In fact, I'd guess you're planting all kinds of larvae. Bet they mature quickly, too."

His eyes got more shifty. "No idea what you're talking about."

I said it under my breath, without moving my mouth. "Sic' him."

Ralph lunged. Silently. Well, Ralph was silent. Nero shrieked like a hyena. While Ralph played Bad Werewolf, I considered our situation.

Nero was a ghoul but he looked human, no drippy parts, no distended eyeballs, no stench. I'd always figured it was his payoff for being a royal bastard in every sense of the words. But now I wondered -- Ishtrallum had said Nero was good friends with the warlock who'd spelled The Pleasure Palace. I found myself wondering who this warlock was and if I'd find him nearby, like up at the Little Church.

Once Nero was appropriately roughed up, Ralph tossed him at my feet. Then he went back to where Nero had been and started digging. Nothing beats a werewolf in full dig mode.

I put my foot on Nero's throat. "So, what's my precious puppy digging up, Nero my not-really-a-man?"

"N-nothing."

I pressed a little harder as I heard a car door slam. "Come again?"

"Just something I've planted." Nero looked away from me. Well, as much as he could. "Help me."

"You're kidding, right?" Jack snorted. "I'll help you to a jail cell."

"That creature is tearing up my yard," Nero sputtered. "I demand recompense."

I cleared my throat. "He's fully aware of who, and what, you are, Nero. Nice try, but you're not getting out of this all that easily." Something registered. "*Your yard?*"

"I live here." Nero managed to sound offended and

proprietary, both.

I took my foot off his neck and Jack hauled Nero to his feet. "If it's your property, then you'll be able to enter it with us and prove that it's yours...won't you?" Jack was doing bad cop. Of course, so was I. And, technically, so was Ralph. Well, Nero didn't rate any good cop treatment, really.

Nero got slowly to his feet. "Indeed." He brushed himself off and tottered to the nearest door. The houses on the lower part of the hill were smaller, merely huge enough to fit two normal homes inside them. Nero opened the door and walked in, Jack and I right on his heels.

"This proves nothing," I mentioned. "Anyone can open a door."

"It was unlocked," Nero huffed. "Because I left it unlocked while I was gardening."

"Nice try, not buying it."

"I live here," Nero protested. He pointed to the walls, which were rather covered with Roman, Greco-Roman, and Roman-influenced artworks, some of which stretched the definition of art.

"I can buy that you either helped decorate or you picked a house where the owners are as into Roman history and so-called glories as you are. Not anything beyond that."

Nero sighed. "Fine. Let me get my papers."

He started off towards the back of the house, but Jack grabbed him. "Oh, no you don't. I think I'll accompany you, just to make sure no one broke in while you were gardening." Jack looked at me. "We'd better put the car into the driveway."

"Watch him, he's slippery." As I went outside I heard Nero starting to give a tour of the house. I had a horrible suspicion he was telling at least part of the truth. Freddy and Sexy Cindy were still in the backseat, looking worried. I got in and pulled into what might be Nero's driveway.

"What's going on?" Sexy Cindy asked. "And is Ralph digging to China or something?"

"The guy we roughed up is Nero. He's claiming this is his house. Jack's escorting him to supposedly see the proof. Ralph's digging up whatever nasty stuff Nero was planting. Fairly sure it was maggots, larvae and such."

They both made gagging noises. "Why would anyone do that?" Freddy managed in between retching.

"Flies, mosquitoes, locusts, all sorts of nasty bugs you don't want me to name, they get used by the Prince's minions a lot, because most humans have your reactions to them. The more bugs about, the more freaked and grossed out humans get. Even those whose fight or flight reaction to most bugs is 'stomp 'em' can get freaked by the equivalent of an airplane hangar full of bugs coming towards them."

"So, do Hell bugs mature faster than regular ones?" Sexy Cindy asked thoughtfully as we got out of the car. I took the keys with me. The previous owner hadn't been careful with this baby, and I had an obligation to get it back to them safely. Somewhere in the future.

"Yes. I'd guess we're looking at something that would mature in hours." We went over to Ralph, who seemed about done with the digging. "What has Mommy's precious puppy found?"

He gave me a dirty look, in more ways that one -- his fur was covered with grime and loam. "About what you'd expect. All the usual insects with some specials thrown in. I figure we got here just in time -- another thirty minutes and the first of them would have hatched."

I trotted back to the S-Class and rummaged through the trunk until I found what I needed. Went back and tossed a can each to Freddy and Sexy Cindy. "Spray everything Ralph's dug up and anything that looks like maybe he should have dug it up."

Sexy Cindy looked at the can. "Insect Repellent -- for bugs so tough you'd swear the Devil made them do it." She snorted a laugh and shook her head. "Who names these products?"

I grinned. "Put it this way -- he knew the power of words and hype when he was alive and beings don't change that much over time, not even undead beings. Though he insists that, these days, one's born a whole lot more than every minute."

Freddy laughed. "P.T. Barnum?"

"One and the same, the greatest showman on the face of the Earth." I liked P.T. He was a fun undead to hang around. I'd heard his hype for a long time now, but it never got old to me.

"Will we meet him?" Freddy asked.

"Not likely, not on this case, anyway. He doesn't do field work, he's R&D."

"Research and development?" Sexy Cindy sounded confused. "Why would a circus man do that?"

"He's not just a circus man, or one of the greatest marketing minds around. He's an artist, but with words and images and things, and their effect on humans, demons, and many other beings. He teaches upper level classes at the University sometimes." And I'd taken every one. Okay, I was a Barnum groupie. Was that so wrong?

Jude and I had fought about what he called my

unhealthy fascination with P.T. and I called mild hero worship. It had never bothered Ken. I considered this while we sprayed a goodly portion of what might really be Nero's side yard. Amanda thought it was because Ken was from a time when marketing had already permeated the human experience, and Jude wasn't. I wasn't so sure. I'd always gotten the feeling that Jude was jealous of my attraction to P.T. in a very boyfriend-jealous way. Which was funny. I wasn't attracted to P.T. sexually -- I just loved how his mind worked. And he was an astute student of the human animal and what drove it, and that was something you needed to have a good grasp of if you were going to be any kind of good cop.

While we sprayed Ralph sniffed the rest of the grounds. He came back as we finished up. All three cans were almost out of juice, there was that much to destroy.

"I think this was the only area," Ralph said as he sat on his haunches. "Can't figure out why, though."

I looked around and studied the area. There wasn't much of an obvious reason as I looked at street level. But I happened to look up. I pointed and the others looked the way I directed.

"Huh. Well, I think Nero might have concentrated here because it's such a clear flight path up to the top of the hill."

"And right to the Little Church," Sexy Cindy added.

Ralph was growling and I was close. "Let's go ask Nero some more questions, shall we?"

Chapter 50

We stormed inside the house, to hear Nero finishing up his homeowner's tour. "So, you can see, I've really made this place my own."

Jack looked bored out of his mind, and also frustrated. I raised my eyebrow and he shook his head. "He has the right papers to prove ownership. Could be forged or magically created, I can't tell."

"Well, real homeowner here or not, I'm sure the local Homeowner's Association has a lot to say about the planting of dangerous pests with intent to send them right up to the big house of worship on the hill."

Nero feigned innocence. "I have no idea what you're talking about."

"Oh, I think you do. But, to be fair, we'll take you in for questioning and let some of the beings more adept and dragging information out of suspects have some alone time with you."

Nero looked nervous. "I think you need a warrant."

"If I were arresting you as part of the Prosaic City P.D., yes, I would. Since I'm arresting you as part of Necropolis Enforcement, however, I need nothing more than the fact that I don't like you."

"Fascist," he muttered.

"No, but speaking of which, is Hitler up at the church?"

He tried to control it -- he kept most of his expression neutral. But his eyes opened a bit wider and his body jerked, just a little. "I have no idea."

"You're big on saying you don't have any idea about anything. But Nero, my not-so-favorite ghoul, you're an idea being. So, I'm betting you have a really *good* idea of what's going on. Like who set the fake Hellfire perimeter."

He shook his head. "I'm not saying another word."

I considered our options. Continuing to question Nero could bear fruit, or it could just leave us barking up a very silent tree. I refused to just let him wander off because Yahweh only knew when we'd find him again or what he'd do. But my alternatives weren't all that exciting. Tying him up just meant he'd get free in some way -- I'd seen enough movies and heard enough stories to know that never worked. Taking him up the hill with us would give him a prime opportunity to advise the Forces of Darkness that we were coming, let alone allow him to mess things up in any way he could.

This left taking him the Headquarters. I was all over that possibility, but how was the really big question. Other than the five of us, our entire extended team were in some form of medical rehab, so I couldn't really ask one of them to come on over and cover this. I doubted Jack, Freddy or Sexy Cindy could really find their way back to take Nero in safely, and Nero was a pro at exploiting weaknesses. Which would leave Ralph.

However, Ralph was my only truly trained operative. Sure, Jack was a great cop, but he was a human and we were about to face some serious minions. And I didn't want him to get hurt. Freddy and Sexy Cindy were game and seemed willing, but they had no real training in how to use their undead powers. So, if I sent Ralph away, I was making my meager team even weaker.

I felt out of options. "We need to do something with him before we move on," I said lamely, mostly to fill the silence.

"We could call for a car," Jack suggested.

Ralph snorted. "You don't want humans dealing with this one. Trust me."

I nodded. "Ralph's right."

"Don't you all have some sort of paddy wagon?" Sexy Cindy asked.

Ralph and I looked at each other. "Actually," I said slowly, "we do." It hadn't occurred to me because they didn't really work law enforcement so much as transportation. But they were on day shift duty under normal circumstances and they were always up for anything, and no one was ever able to put one past them -- they'd seen and done enough when they were alive that nothing ever fooled them.

I hit the buttons on my wrist-com for the Tour Bus. "Yo," a man's sexy voice replied. "Vic, baby, what's up?"

"Merc, are you and L.K. available?"

"For you, darling, always."

"I need a perp taken into Headquarters. He's slippery and trouble, and I need it done with some semblance of speed and subtlety."

Merc chuckled. I heard L.K. in the background. "Is it needful circumstances?"

I controlled the sigh. These two did have their little quirks. "Yes, King, it is." I knew what was expected. Fortunately, it was easy in this case. "No lazing on a Sunday afternoon for you two."

They both laughed. "Love working with you, darling," Merc said. "We aiming for your mark?"

"Please. By the way, we're in the Estates.

"I could tell."

"Yes, but here's the thing. It looks surrounded by Hellfire, but it's not real."

"You want us to take your word and risk unlife and limb to cross what could be the most deadly thing out there?"

"Yeah. I figure it'll be a nice flashback for both of you. Not like your human lives were exactly dull and full of boredom."

"You do know how to entice, don't you darling? Be there in two shakes of my tail." Both of them were laughing as Merc signed off.

My wrist-com went dead. Jack cocked his head. "Let me guess -- Elvis is on his way?"

"Not...quite." I went to the front door and waited. True to their reputations, they were as fast as lightning. The Tour Bus flew up the street and came to a screeching halt in front of what might really be Nero's house. I was fairly sure no one had noticed them -- the Tour Bus had a good spell on it. Human's only saw it when they needed to.

The Tour Bus really looked like a tour bus, for some obvious reasons. It was a little longer and wider than normal, but nothing that couldn't drive on a human street without too much notice. Well, as long as no one noticed what was painted on the sides. Merc and L.K. liked their fun, after all.

"Ride with the best Little Devils anywhere," Jack read aloud. "You called in evil demons?"

I snorted. "Hardly. They just have an interesting sense of humor."

Two beings slid out of the Bus. Literally. They were both wraiths now, and they only used doors if they had to. Wraiths are more powerful than ghosts -- they have more of their human abilities with them, and can go solid if necessary. Plus, no icky ectoplasm smell. Of course, with these two, if they had smelled, they'd have found a way to counter it or, more likely, bottled it as the scent to attract the girls *and* boys.

"That's not Elvis," Jack hissed at me as the wraiths solidified, touched ground, and sauntered over.

"Nope."

Merc laughed at the expressions on Jack, Freddy and Sexy Cindy's faces. "You didn't tell them, darling?" He gave me a big hug.

"It's so much more fun to initiate this way."

"How's Fangs doing?" Merc asked, as he let me go and L.K. gave me a hug.

"Maurice is okay. Well, as okay as the rest of our team is."

"There's big trouble going on?" L.K. asked, voice as smooth as single malt scotch.

"Yeah, there is." I gave them the fast highlights, reassured Merc that Maurice was really okay, and stressed that they were here for transportation assistance only.

"Sounds like you might need us to do more than just drive," L.K. said, looking and sounding worried.

"L.K., you guys are the greatest but you're not trained. I'm working with enough non-Enforcement personnel already."

"Why do you call him L.K.?" Jack asked finally. "And not Jim?"

Merc and L.K. grinned. I shrugged. "He really is the Lizard King."

"And I'm not into titles all that much," L.K. added. "But there are some undeads...well, you know...it's easier if they don't know where you are at any given time."

"Groupies hard to shake in unlife, too?" Sexy Cindy asked dryly.

"You know it." L.K. gave her a long, appraising look. "But, your Lizard King is always willing to make an exception for lovely and lonely succubae."

She snorted. "I'll keep it in mind."

"Do." L.K. looked at me. "And, of course, any time you're ready, babe. You have the open invitation."

Jack glared and Ralph growled. I just laughed. "And I appreciate it, too."

Freddy was staring at Merc like he was seeing a ghost. Which, I guess, he sort of was. "That's...you're...this is Freddy Mercury," he choked out finally.

Merc nodded. "In the not-flesh, darling." He cocked his head. "You were a fan?"

Freddy nodded. "The biggest."

"A theology professor who was into Queen?" I wondered if I'd heard everything now, and figured I hadn't.

Freddy shook his head. "The insinuation that rock and roll was the Devil's music always seemed unfounded to me."

Merc and L.K. grinned at each other. "Oh, Satan did have a lot to do with it," Merc said.

"He's a cool dude," L.K. agreed.

Jack cleared his throat. "Anyone here want to help us get Nero into custody? Anyone at all?"

"What's the rush?" Merc asked. "Armageddon has a build, darling. There's still time to avert it."

"Says a dead rock star," Jack muttered.

"Undead," Merc corrected. He stared at Jack for a few long moments. Then he pulled me aside. "Why is he along?"

"He's my human partner. He's handling all of this really well."

"And you're sleeping with him."

"How can you tell?"

He shrugged. "I can tell. Anyway, I don't like him. And I know Jimmy doesn't either." Merc only called L.K. "Jimmy" when he was making the point that he was talking in a very personal way and about personal things.

L.K. joined us. "I agree with Freddy. This one. Not his zombie namesake." And, similarly, if L.K. was calling Merc "Freddy", they were both making it clear that they weren't kidding around. At all.

"What's wrong with him?" I asked a little more defensively than I wanted.

Merc shook his head. "I don't know. But...something's off."

"Like what and how do you mean?"

"He's hiding something," L.K. said. "You know, we spent our human lives around people who were hiding their real intentions."

"Or what they really were," Merc added. "And, the Gods and Monsters know we spent our own time hiding things, too. Darling, I know you like him, I mean, I have working eyes, what's not to drool over, right? But...."

"Something's off," L.K. finished for him. "In fact, it's off enough that we're coming back, once we get rid of your perp."

"Guys, really, you're not trained. And I think we're going up against all the big minions."

"And you're going up against them with someone backing you we both feel is hiding something," Merc said. "It's decided. We'll be back."

"Now," L.K. said briskly. "Who are we taking in?"

How they'd missed Nero I couldn't figure. I sighed

and looked around -- and resisted the urge to curse impressively. "Are you kidding me? Jack! Where in the depths of Hell is Nero?"

We all looked. Sure enough, the little weasel was gone.

Chapter 51

Ralph and I both sniffed the air. "He's heading up the hill," Ralph called as he took off.

"Follow that werewolf!" I shouted.

Jack ran for the S-Class. "The keys are gone!"

Oh, right. I had them. I was about to say so, when Merc grabbed me. "Come on, we'll take the Bus."

L.K. floated into the bus and opened the door for those of us still corporeally challenged. "Our weapons are in the trunk," I said as Merc shoved me in. He rolled his eyes and went to the back of the bus.

The others were behind me so I sort of had to get on board. The Bus was nice. L.K. hadn't had it this plush in his day, but Merc had seen plenty before he left the human plane, and it was all here. They even had a hot tub. Not that I felt now was an appropriate time to try it out.

"Full bar?" Sexy Cindy asked as she looked around and headed for one of the more plush and comfy Captain's chairs. "We get to drink as undeads?"

I coughed. "I do."

"Why don't I?" She was back to defensive.

I shrugged. "Succubae don't...eat or drink."

"Say *what*?"

"Now probably isn't the time," Jack said as the Bus lurched and he fell onto a couch. "Vic, sit down."

I would have, and almost had no choice as Freddy flew past me and, thankfully, landed in another Captain's chair. But Merc wasn't in the Bus, and L.K. was peeling out like he's been a NASCAR driver, not a rock star.

One of the benefits of going from two feet to four feet on a regular basis was that your balance became exceptionally good. I was able to maneuver to the back of the bus without too much issue.

To see the S-Class flying along behind us. Backwards.

As I gaped, Merc floated in next to me.

"How --?"

"We have a towing cable. Not all undeads are without their own transportation, you know." He grinned at my expression while I wondered if I looked as dumb as I felt. "I love the ability to shock anyone in Necropolis Enforcement. It's a good day."

"It's probably not going to stay that way."

He shrugged as we made our way up front. He leaned down when he reached Sexy Cindy. "They tell you that wraiths, ghosts, succubae and our related undead brethren can't eat or drink. They lie, pretty baby...they lie. We don't need to eat, but we sure can still enjoy it -- if properly prepared."

Sexy Cindy shot me a dirty look. "Hey, I just go by what they tell me," I said. They could eat? Really? This particular case was full of fun, new, interesting facts. I found myself wishing I could go to sleep and process even one of them. I moved my mind off how many hours I'd been awake and considered the benefits of tossing some chow down my gullet before I keeled over.

Merc seemed to read my mind. He opened the impressive fridge and tossed me an entire ham. "Enjoy." He handed Sexy Cindy and Freddy something, too, but I was too busy wolfing to pay a lot of attention. "I have nothing a human can eat," he said to Jack. "Sorry." Merc didn't sound sorry, but I chose not to mention it.

"Not a problem," Jack said. "I snagged a snack

while Nero was giving me the full-on home tour. That should be grounds for arrest, right there."

"Huh." Merc looked back at me. "Ralph need a meal?"

"I have no idea, but I'd figure it couldn't hurt." Werewolves needed to eat a lot and even if Ralph had pigged out at the hospital, which I doubted, it had been too long and we'd been too active, him in particular.

Merc nodded and grabbed another ham. "He can probably clean this off before we go in."

"Go in?" I hoped my burp at the end of that short sentence had been discreet enough to be missed.

"Into the Little Church," L.K. called from the driver's seat. "Because that's where we are and Ralph's stopped, but only because they aren't allowing pets."

"Hilarious."

"No, really. There's a sign and everything."

I trotted to the front of the Bus. Sure enough, they had their huge parking lot cordoned off and there were a variety of signs, one of which clearly stated that no pets were allowed.

Merc opened the door and Ralph scrambled in, grabbing the ham in his jaws on the way. Yeah, he was hungry, if how fast he ate it was any indication. He also had strong jaws, possibly stronger than mine, because he crunched through the ham bone like it was a banana.

"He went into the Church," Ralph said as he finished in record time and we gathered back in what, for want of a better term, I considered the Bus' living room. "I figured I'd better wait for you."

"Why was he able to beat you up here?" Ghouls weren't normally considered faster than werewolves.

"No idea, but I'd guess he had warlock help."

Ralph looked and sounded exceptionally irritated. "Just how did he get away? I thought Wagner here was supposed to be watching him."

"He was surrounded by four of us," Jack replied. "Sorry, I guess I assumed your werewolf senses would have noticed when our prisoner took off."

"We don't have time for internal bickering," I interrupted. I didn't want to go back to wondering if Ralph, or anyone else, was a mole and so had somehow let Nero escape. We had too much trouble right in front of us. "We're likely to be facing at least one major minion, probably a whole lot more than one. We need to work together or we're all going to be dusted."

"Good point," Jack said. "What *is* our plan?"

"Call for backup," L.K. said quietly from the driver's seat.

"What? Our team's out, it's just us."

"I don't think we're going to care about that, Vic." L.K.'s voice was measured but tense.

I went back to the front, the others trailing after me. It was a big driver and shotgun area, so we all fit, though it was a bit tight. Jack was on one side of me and Ralph was shoved up against the other. I was about to mention that this was a tad too cozy when Sexy Cindy pointed at what I realized L.K. was already looking at.

"What's going on?" Her voice shook, but then she hadn't spent most of her life performing. At least, not on stage and for large audiences.

Not that I could fault Sexy Cindy for sounding like she was about to lose it. Because I had a feeling fear and horror were the right reactions here.

The suns -- both the one for the human plane and the one for Necropolis -- were different. They were blood red for starters, and it was like they were much closer, because we could see the eruptions and solar flares and the like. It looked like death throes.

A black disc was covering each sun. Normally, you'd think this meant we were in for an eclipse. But one wasn't scheduled for either plane and the discs weren't moons.

I tapped the code into my wrist-com without looking. Some things they trained us to do from the first day on Enforcement payroll, and this was the number one thing.

"All being alert, all being alert. We have the start of Armageddon. Repeat, we have the start of Armageddon."

Chapter 52

I didn't wait for replies. "Let's get everything out of the trunk and get in there."

L.K. opened the door and we piled out. I popped the S-Class' trunk and started handing paraphernalia to the rest of the team. Ralph didn't even argue about the bullet-proof K-9 vest. Too much.

"It hinders me," he muttered as I strapped it around him.

"You want to go to human, then you can wear the other one."

"No, thanks. What's the plan?"

"We storm in and kill anything that looks, smells or acts like minion."

"Doesn't that mean innocent people could get killed?" Jack asked.

"Yeah, it does. Here's a news flash -- if they bring about Armageddon, *all* the innocent people will be dead. You pick."

"There's one positive," Merc said quietly.

"What's that? I'd love a positive." I felt completely out of my depth. Stopping the evil bad guys was my job, on both planes, but stopping Armageddon once it was begun? That wasn't exactly in the Agent's Handbook.

"The suns' light will be blocked. Meaning that we can have vampiric help."

That was a good thing. "Sadly, though, that means any turned vampire they have can show up, too."

"All are called to serve in the great war," L.K. said quietly.

"Yeah, I know, per you, no one gets out of here alive."

"But many have and can still enjoy a vibrant afterlife," Merc said. "If we don't panic, that is."

It was odd getting calming platitudes from one of the gods of rock, but I let any comebacks pass. "I'm not panicking. I'm managing my stress in a commanding manner."

"Wow, you really must have done well on the verbal tests," L.K. said. "Don't worry, babe. It'll all work out. It's not time for everything to end yet."

"Glad you feel so confident." I looked around. Jack had a bulletproof vest on. Sure, it was made for humans and human bullets, but I had to hope it was going to work. The others could go to mist -- I heard Merc giving Sexy Cindy a fast lecture on how -- and Freddy, being a zombie, was reasonably safe as long as they weren't shooting rock salt at him. "Freddy, put on a vest."

He did as asked. "Victoria, if I may, what is your plan?"

"I have no plan other than storming in and shooting things. I don't know what they're doing, but spells of this magnitude can be disrupted by the tiniest things. I'm hoping we can all disrupt in more than a tiny way."

"But, if you're right and we're facing Hitler, then he's going to be thinking in a military fashion." Freddy looked around. "You know...."

I waited, but he didn't add on anything to that. "I know what? Right now, I don't feel all that knowing."

"Tanks."

That was it. Apparently when he was under duress, Freddy went monosyllabic.

"Yes? Tanks? We have the Tour Bus."

"There are all these cars here." Freddy walked

towards the nearest. "And this is the Estates. 'Safe enough to leave your keys in the car.' I wonder...." He pulled on the door handle and the driver's door opened. "Sure enough."

"Wow, people are really easily influenced. And, seriously, did you just memorize their advertising?"

Freddy shook his head. "I told you, Jerry quoted it. Not just these lines, every line about the Estates."

A thought crawled up from the back of my mind. "Merc, L.K."

They came over. "Nice car," Merc said. "We borrowing?"

"Yeah, I think so, credit Freddy with our becoming a tank unit."

"I see lots of big ones," L.K. said. "Several Hummers and similar."

"We'll take those if we can. But I want you both to listen to Freddy recite every bit of Estates advertising propaganda he can remember."

All three of them spoke as one. "Why?"

I headed off for the nearest Hummer. "Because I think they're part of Hitler's spell." And while they weren't warlocks, they were both musicians and undead proof that the right lyrics had magic in them.

Sexy Cindy caught up with me. "You want each of us driving?"

I considered. "If we can, yeah. Ralph needs to ride with someone, though."

"I'll take him with me," she offered.

I almost said no, that I wanted him with Jack. But reality reared its head. Jack was a trained policeman, and Sexy Cindy wasn't. "Sounds good. Ralph!"

He raced over. "You want me to go in first?"

"Bad dog. No, I want you to ride with Cindy."

He glared. "Why is that?"

I opened the Hummer. Nice, keys were in it. How in the world anyone in the Estates kept a car longer than five minutes was beyond me, but I had a suspicion it was because this place was under a heavy spell we'd all missed for far too long. "I want you with Cindy because she's new and I don't want my only trained Enforcer shot down in the first wave."

"You're in charge." Ralph and Cindy trotted off towards another humongous SUV. I hoped she could reach the pedals, but figured if she couldn't, Ralph could do the highly trained pet thing and push them for her.

Jack grabbed me and pulled me into his arms. "Be careful."

I leaned against his shoulder. "I'll do my best."

He kissed me. It was deep and urgent and far more arousing than the situation should have allowed. "You're mine, I'm yours, no one in between -- right?"

"Right."

"Promise me. No matter what happens, we're together forever." He looked worried and possessive and very masculine.

"Well, forever's a long time." I didn't want to mention that if we failed, forever wasn't going to last too long for any of us. And he was a human, meaning that even if we won, his forever and mine weren't necessarily going to mesh.

Jack shook his head. "I don't care. I'll figure out how to last forever, okay? I just want to know that you'll be with me, when I do."

"I will be." I leaned up and kissed him. "I promise."

He hugged me tightly, kissed me one more time,

then headed off for a nearby Suburban.

The others ran for similar vehicles and we started off. It wasn't too hard to maneuver, the parking lot was huge and orderly. As I barreled towards the front of the Little Church worry flashed a fang. What if I was wrong? What if they weren't in here at all? What if I blasted in only to find nothing but nice, churchgoing, normal people?

There are times for prayer. I decided this was one of them. "Yahweh, could I have a sign that I'm doing the right thing?"

I waited, pedal to the metal, for some sort of clue that this wasn't going to be a really bad idea. Just as I hit the front steps and worry that I was completely wrong washed over me, a bolt of lightning hit the doors, blasting them open.

"Thanks," I murmured as I plowed through, the others right behind me.

Chapter 53

The first thing I noticed was that there were no people inside the building. That was nice in that I wasn't going to run some innocent down. What wasn't nice was likely to be the answer to the question of where all the people actually were.

The church wasn't empty, however. There were a variety of beings there. I recognized most of them. I had no idea if being hit by a big Hummer would cause any of the major minions damage, but I was willing to give it the old college try.

I aimed for Hitler. He was unmistakable -- short, military garb, ridiculous little moustache, funky-ugly haircut, overbearing and supercilious attitude. Not only did he look exactly like he had when he'd been running the Nazi Party, but he was in the center of the dais, pretty much on the exact spot where I figured Johnson did his preaching.

Hitler had an eerie glow around him and he was waving his hands about. I was pretty sure he was in the middle of casting a huge spell. I wasn't sure if it was part of the spell already cast or a new one, but decided not to care.

The Hummer rolled over the comfy stadium-type chairs this place had instead of pews. It was a bumpy ride, but I was sort of high on adrenaline, so I didn't notice all that much. I took in the rest of the scene, though, just in case.

Apollyon and Abaddon were flanking Hitler. They looked similar -- huge no-longer-angelic wings, meaning they looked more bat-like than feathered. Their faces were beautiful, but distorted by eons of hatred and evil, so they were both compelling and repulsive at the same time. They stood a good ten feet high, and they glowed an ugly, dark red. Apollyon held a flaming sword while Abaddon had a Hellfired crossbow.

Abaddon took aim, but not towards me. I realized he was shooting towards the car Jack was driving. Well, that wasn't acceptable.

I spun the Hummer so it skidded towards the three minions on the dais. It had the double advantage of clearly causing Hitler to stumble and messing up Abaddon's aim. It had the disadvantage of landing my door right next to Apollyon, who took the opportunity to slice through the metal like it was butter.

Some things are instinctive, and some beings react more instinctively than others. As far as undeads go, you don't get more instinct-heavy than a werewolf. Even daemon cats and hellhounds had more instinctive control, though not much. I was in danger, and I did the thing I knew kept me most unalive. I shifted into wolf form -- and attacked.

Apollyon and I went tumbling, mass of claws, wings, and teeth, snarling up a storm. He gave as good as he got, which was a pity. I didn't feel so great after a few minutes of this, but the positive was he wasn't doing anything to anyone else.

I caught Ralph and Abaddon in a similar roll around and kill each other situation. So, we were fighting the big guys. But there were plenty more here who needed distracting, if killing wasn't going to work.

I landed a really good chomp on Apollyon's neck, and risked a look around. Interestingly, Sexy Cindy and Freddy were attacking Hitler and seemed to be making progress. Merc and L.K. were dealing with some of the other minions hanging around. But I didn't see Jack or the Adversary, nor could I spot Nero. However, what I could see was the fact that I'd been wrong earlier -- there were indeed humans here, they were just floating up against the ceiling. I couldn't tell if they were alive, dead, held in suspended animation, or worse. But I knew without asking that once the spell holding them was broken, they were going to tumble down the four stories and splat onto the floor.

Apollyon used my temporary distraction grab my stomach and start that horrible insides burning thing the fallen liked to do. It was boil like a cabbage or let him toss me off. I picked flying through the air, landed and scrambled to my paws. Apollyon had his sword in hand again, but he was backing away.

I would have congratulated myself on being totally badass, but I knew he'd hurt me more than I'd hurt him. I also spotted Abaddon backing away from Ralph. I risked a look around. Our troops were arriving.

The momentary relief washed away as I looked around some more. The minions were still backing away -- all of them, Hitler included. But they didn't look worried or defeated. They looked smug.

Smug minions is never a good thing. Risking a look upward, I saw a variety of angels covering the floating humans. Okay, so it wasn't that. I looked behind again. Nope, our guys were filling the Little Church right up. So, why the happy looks on our enemies' faces? Something was wrong, and I had to figure it out fast.

A fact reared up. The Adversary was nowhere around. If this was the big battle, then the Adversary was supposed to lead it. If he wasn't with us, then what was really going on?

The base of my tail wanted a word. Just one word. It shared the word and I knew it was right. "It's a trap!"

I bellowed. "All Enforcement personnel clear out!"

Sadly, this didn't have the effect I was hoping for. The minions continued to smirk and my side didn't turn and run. Nothing for it.

I leaped and landed on the podium where the microphone was. "Clear out! That's an order!"

The mic was on and I'd been shouting at the top of my lungs. Anyone who missed that was deaf, because I was loud enough to raise the dead. Some of the Enforcement side started to do as they were told.

The angels, in particular, didn't. I knew they were trying to save the humans. But a thought occurred. "They're an illusion," I broadcast. "All the humans are tucked away in their homes, waiting for whatever automaton orders may be coming. But those aren't real."

Jack made it over to me. "Are you crazy? Retreat? We can stop them."

"It's a trap. We need everyone out."

"How so?" Ralph and the others were with us now.

"Illusion. It's all illusion, like the Hellfire was. It's not the start of Armageddon. It's a trap to get rid of all of us."

I heard a horrible rumbling sound, like the depths of Hell were coming out through the bowels of the Earth. The doors that had been blasted off the front of the church reappeared and slammed shut. I reminded myself that the bad guys knew how to fake a being into thinking they were getting Godly assistance when they really weren't. The windows and glass all went black. I didn't need to ask if they were covered with something we couldn't get through. I heard a great deal of slamming, indicating that any and all exits were now firmly shut.

As I was wondering just what was coming next, a voice I knew well but sure didn't want to spoke up.

"You were always too smart for these creatures."

I turned around. Sure enough, there he was, in all his so-called glory. Twelve feet tall, looking like some sort of cross of every horrible, icky thing in all the planes of existence. Dear old Dad. And, lucky me, there was the Mother of the Ages, standing with him. Family reunion time. I couldn't wait.

🐾 Chapter 54 🐾

The Adversary shifted -- now there was what looked like a man in front of me. It always interested me that, when using human form, the Adversary went for a Big Harp likeness more often than Little. By all accounts, they looked enough alike that it probably didn't matter, but I figured he liked being larger because it was more intimidating.

My mother beamed. "Eudora, time to come home." She took the Adversary's hand like they were normal beings. "Your father's been very patient with you, but you must stop this foolishness."

"He's not my father, and you're not my mother."

She shook her head. "You know that's not true."

The Adversary patted her hand. "Now, dear, you know how stubborn our little girl is."

I managed not to gag. "I am stubborn, but I'm not your little girl. Get out of here, before we destroy you." Hey, I was good with the false bravado.

He laughed. "You and all your personnel are trapped. Easily, I might add." The Adversary leaned closer to me, and I managed to hold my ground. "Did you really think we'd make it this easy for you?"

"Well, you're all none-too-bright, so, yeah, I did." Right now, none-too-bright was running in the family but I figured any stalling I could do would be a help.

I jumped down from the podium and went to human form, during which process I took a quick look around. We had a lot of Enforcement personnel in here, but not all. The injured members of my team weren't around, as far as I could tell. Whether that meant they'd been held at the hospital or if it meant we had more than one mole, I couldn't guess.

Our angels were down from the ceiling and behind me, creating a barrier between the minions and the rest of our troops. Angels were also into the self-sacrifice thing, if it was the only option. I didn't like that it appeared to be the only option.

"So, just what are you hoping to accomplish here?" I figured questions might get answers and any extra time was going to benefit our side more than theirs.

"Extermination of most of Necropolis Enforcement," the Adversary replied like it was obvious. Well, it was, but it never hurt to see if there was more going on.

"That's it? All the pretty pre-Armageddon displays were just to lure us? You're not really bringing about the Apocalypse?"

"Oh, we are." The Adversary let go of my mother's hand and stepped closer to me. "But there are certain…things we…need first." He put his hand out toward me. "Certain beings we wish to…protect."

In human form Big and Little Harp had murdered every sibling I'd had, so I was quite clear that they didn't have a truly paternal bone in their horribly creepy shared body. Ergo, they wanted me for another reason. But I had no clue what that reason might be.

"I'm good here, thanks." I backed up a step, keeping the distance between us so the Adversary couldn't just reach out and grab me. "I chose my side a couple of hundred years ago, remember?"

He shook his head. "It was chosen for you. By that *creature*." He spat the last word.

"Black Wolf wasn't a creature. He was a hero."

"You gave him your fealty, your love. A werewolf! The lowest of all the undead creatures. You became one of them, for no reason other than childish pique."

I heard someone snort behind me. "Werewolves aren't the lowest," I heard Merc say, presumably to Sexy Cindy and Freddie. "Far from it. Wonder what his game is."

Merc had spoken loudly enough to carry, so I knew he'd wanted me to hear it. And he had a good point. Werewolves weren't up to angelic standards, but then, neither were vampires. But we were by far the most adaptable and versatile of all the undeads.

Black Wolf's pack had slowed the Adversary down long enough for me to become a werewolf. There were several of them, yes, but I tried to think -- had any other undeads actually engaged the Adversary in hand-to-hand battle? And even if they had, did it matter? The Adversary could be killed, and had been killed, over and over again. Each Adversary was different, based on the being who took over the position. So, each one had different weaknesses.

Hoping he was listening, I spoke low and without moving my mouth. "Sic him, boy."

Ralph leaped, fangs bared, as I did the same, changing in midair back to werewolf form -- might as well test whether wolf or werewolf did the most damage, after all. We hit at the same time. There was a boiling of evil undead ick and werewolf fur and fangs. But I could tell -- we were hurting the Adversary.

I heard someone who sounded like Jack shouting orders to attack. There was a lot of activity around us, but Ralph and I were pretty busy. I felt someone slamming something against my back.

"Bad girl! Get off your father!" Great, my darling mother was adding in.

"Yo, bitch, get off our girl." I heard a thwack and no one was hitting me any more. As we rolled around I caught a glimpse of Sexy Cindy and my mother in a total girl fight. Happily, Sexy Cindy still had enough street in her to really have the upper hand.

I got the Adversary's neck and chomped down hard. He did the shake and bake thing, but if Slimy hadn't been able to shake me off, Daddy Dearest wasn't going to manage it.

However, Apollyon and Abaddon decided to get involved. One grabbed me and one grabbed Ralph -- both pulled hard. This was almost helpful, in that we both had our jaws locked and they were essentially helping us take chunks out of the Adversary. However, it wasn't good for either one of us to be held by a major minion -- I could feel my skin and insides starting to get hot. Soon they'd be boiling, and it was hard to make that stop once started.

Ralph and I let go at the same time, which sent the Adversary flying backwards. I changed to full wolf, bit and clawed, and managed to get Apollyon to loosen his hold enough that I could scrabble away. I slammed into Abaddon which gave Ralph the opportunity to escape as well.

We fell back, side-by-side, both in full snarling mode. There was plenty of other activity, including what I was pretty sure were some of our witches and warlocks casting counter-spells that seemed to be working, if some of the darkness falling away from the glass ceiling was any indication. So our side wasn't down and out yet. Good.

Hitler wasn't around. Neither were any other minions, other than the Three A's. This was unsettling. I had no idea where they'd gone or what they were doing, but before I could ask anyone for a fast debrief, Abaddon pointed his Hellfired crossbow at me.

"If you will not join us as decreed," Abaddon intoned in that reverberating way the major minions loved to do for any group of beings larger than two, "then you will perish."

I readied myself to jump. I had to time it right, because I didn't want to leap into Apollyon's sword, the Adversary's arms, or into the path of the arrow, and Abaddon had top minion reflexes, meaning he could follow me if I leaped too soon. I also didn't want Ralph or anyone else to get the arrow instead of me.

Of course, what I wanted wasn't always on the menu. As Abaddon twitched, indicating to my canine senses that he was about to fire, and as I readied myself to leap, I heard the last thing I wanted to.

"Vic, look out!" Jack flung himself in front of me, as Abaddon pulled the trigger and Ralph leaped for Abaddon's throat.

Ralph hit and the crossbow went flying. I shifted to human and caught Jack as he went down. The arrow was in his chest.

"Jack, no. You weren't supposed to get in the way." I tried not to cry, but didn't manage it too well.

He gave me a half-smile. "Sorry. Had to protect...my girl," he gasped out. "Guess forever wasn't very long, huh?"

He was dying, I didn't need werewolf senses to tell me that. But for some reason, all my senses were hyper-aware. I could tell the minions had left for whatever reason. The building wasn't a cage any more -- light was coming in and I could hear beings going in and out, carrying wounded, doing cleansing spell, shouting orders here and there. Ralph, Sexy Cindy and the others were gathering around us, but no one was speaking.

"I can make it longer," I whispered. Then I shifted to werewolf form and bit his throat.

🐾 Chapter 55 🐾

As I watched Jack's face go from pain to shock to the pasty-white I knew meant he was dying and being reborn undead, I heard Ken's voice, shouting something.

"It's okay," I murmured to Jack as I pulled the arrow out of his chest. "Just tell me when you're hungry."

Someone's hand landed on my shoulder. "Vic, what did you do?" Ken sounded freaked out beyond belief.

"He was dying. I bit him." That sounded lame, but it was the truth.

"You shouldn't have done that," Ken said. "No one was here to check, to make sure --"

"To make sure the man who sacrificed himself to save me isn't evil?" I snarled. As I looked up at Ken's face I remembered that we had a mole, and there was no guarantee Ken wasn't said turncoat. Maybe he didn't want me turning Jack into a werewolf because that wasn't in the bad guy's plans.

Ken shook his head. "No, Vic. You know better than that."

"Do I?" I clutched Jack to me. "How do I know you're really on the side of good?"

Ken stared at me. "What are you talking about?"

"We have a mole. Someone knew what we were doing and alerted our enemies, kept them several steps ahead of us. How do I know that wasn't you?"

"Don't talk to Ken like that," Ralph said quietly.

I spun on him. "Could be you, too, Ralph."

His lips pulled up over his teeth and he bared his fangs. I'd seen Ralph growl this way before, but it had never been directed towards me. Now, twice in one day, meaning Ralph was seriously angry. "You get one for being upset. But that's it. Before you accuse anyone else who's spent decades working with you, caring about you, and being friends with you of being a spy, you'd better consider all the options, including what it'll be like if we all kick you out of the pack."

Before I was able to come back with any kind of retort, suitable, stupid, soothing or not, Jack jerked in my arms. "I need food," he gasped. "What's happening to me?"

Merc tossed a ham over and Jack grabbed it -- with paws. His transformation was fully complete. I almost asked Merc if the Tour Bus was stocked with unlimited hams, but then decided I had more pressing concerns.

I looked Jack over as he ate. He showed no signs of injury, but then that was common when a being was turned undead. Frankly, it was part of the point -- the eternal cure for what was about to ail you on a permanent basis.

Jack was a pretty good-looking wolf. I noted that he was about Ralph's size, so bigger than me, but that was to be expected. Ralph had a better coat, but that might have more to do with transition than anything else. In wolf form, just as in human, Jack radiated masculinity. I was still definitely willing to be his puppy-mamma, heroic save or not, though the save was a definite turn-on.

"Let's regroup," Freddy suggested. "Everyone's tired, hurt, on edge and frightened. Let's go back to Headquarters and try to figure out what's going on. Without any more recriminations or accusations."

That sounded like a sane idea, and I had just enough self-control left to recognize it as such. "Good plan." I nudged Jack, who was toying with the hambone. "You able to move on?"

"Yeah, I think so." He got to his paws and fell on his face. "I think."

"You're trying to walk like a human, not like a wolf. Four feet. Just think canine thoughts."

"How do I do that?"

"Most of us manage it without a lesson," Ralph muttered.

This was true, but I wasn't in the mood to hear it. "You could help, instead of offering criticisms."

"I wouldn't want to presume," Ralph snapped. "Since I might be trying to lead him straight to Hell."

Sexy Cindy cleared her throat. "Ah, I thought we were going to go with not yelling at each other."

Ralph ruffled his fur, nodded, turned around, and trotted off. Ken was still with us, though he didn't look any more appeased. However, his dominant emotion was written on his face -- worry.

I decided I'd better get myself and the situation under a semblance of control. "Ken, I'm sorry. Let's do what Freddy suggested and get back to Headquarters. You can run any tests there, okay?"

He nodded, but the worry didn't go away. "They aren't definitive, once the change has happened," he said, but under his breath. I chose to pretend I didn't hear it.

"I think it might be a good idea to take as many as possible back in the Tour Bus," L.K. suggested. "We have the wounded loaded in already, but there's plenty of room for more."

"Is all our equipment out of the S-Class?"

"Yes," Merc said. "And loaded into the bus."

"Any sign of Nero or the other minions?"

"None," one of the nearby angels confirmed. "Whatever they wanted, they either got it or we messed them up enough that they're going to have to try again another time."

We headed out of the Little Church. It looked much the worse for wear. I heard the angels discussing what they were going to do with the humans who, as I'd guessed, were all in their homes, acting like they couldn't see or hear anything that was going on outside. Maybe they couldn't.

Our team climbed into the Bus, L.K. shielding Ken from the sun with what looked like a huge rain poncho. Ralph was already in there, curled up between the driver's seat and the passenger's. I decided now wasn't the time to try to sniff and make up. I wasn't sure that I wanted to, anyway.

The Tour Bus was alter-dimensional, meaning it could hold a lot more than it looked like it should. Common enough, but I never got over it. Today, however, I didn't really want to look. Jack collapsed in a heap and I cuddled next to him. He fell asleep before the rest of those hitching a ride were loaded in. I wanted to sleep, but couldn't. I had too many things flying around in my mind, not the least of which was that I'd turned the guy I was in love with into a werewolf.

This was a good news/bad news scenario. Most of it was on the good news side -- extended longevity, ability to actually mate with the intent to create progeny, able to share everything, truly mated for unlife. The bad side has its possibilities, though. Some couldn't successfully make the transition and survive it mentally. Maybe he'd get antsy or curious, now that he was an undead. Maybe he'd want to continue with interspecies dating, meaning that I'd be boring and tossed aside.

I shoved my mind away from these worries and any others that wanted a word. The base of my tail was bugging me, but I ignored it, too. It had been too long since I'd slept and the motion of the Bus and the chummy nearness of all the other beings lulled me to sleep.

As I slipped into slumber, the base of my tail got one question in. Why did the minions leave when victory was likely to be theirs?

I jerked awake, head fuzzy and mouth dry. We were at Headquarters, and the Bus was unloading. From what I gathered, we'd already made the hospital stop. I started to get to my feet when Freddy pushed me back down, gently.

"They're taking you and some others to your homes. So you can sleep in your own beds. We'll attack it all when we're fresh, tonight."

I put my head back down on my paws. "Sounds like a plan."

Chapter 56

Of course, from my perspective, the plan shouldn't have included anyone other than me and Jack being at my place. Freddy, Sexy Cindy, Merc and L.K. tagging along wasn't how I felt the plan should go down.

I'd been too tired to protest too much, though. Jack and I were in my bedroom on the Prosaic City side of the building. I'd been too exhausted to slide over, and I didn't feel up to making sure Jack could handle it right now. The others were on the Necropolis side, so we could see and hear them if we wanted to, and ignore them if we so chose. I so chose.

Jack had managed the transition back to human form without too much trouble, so after some fine "we survived" lovemaking, we were sleeping wrapped around each other.

Along about sunset I woke up. I could have slept longer, but a couple of centuries of training mean an internal alarm clock doesn't shut off just because you've had a rough time the night and half the day before.

My moving roused Jack. He gave me a sleepy smile. "Hey, you."

"Hey yourself. How're you feeling?"

"Different." He kissed my nose. "But good. Better. Stronger."

"You are. You're one of the stronger undeads now." I took a deep breath. "I'm sorry I didn't ask you what you wanted...before I made the decision for you."

Jack shook his head. "This is what I would have picked. What I wanted to be, as soon as I knew you loved me back."

My throat felt tight. "I hope we make it through

everything to make it all worthwhile."

"It's already worthwhile, to me." He sighed, stretched and sat up. "So, brief me. What're my strengths and weaknesses now?"

This was a little sudden, at least in my experience. Most newly formed undeads were confused, like Freddy and Sexy Cindy had been. Then again, Jack had been clear on everything prior to the change, so maybe that was it. "I think we need to figure out the Prince's next steps."

"Sure, but I'd like to know how to defend myself when the time comes, which I'm sure will be sooner, not later. Like, what can kill me now?"

"Not much."

"What's my best form of attack?"

"Uh, depends on what you're fighting."

"Do we really run in a pack? I mean, I haven't seen any werewolves other than you and Ralph. Are there more?"

"Yeah, plenty."

"Where are they? Why aren't they fighting with us?"

Jack's curiosity was unsettling me for some reason. The base of my tail, in particular, was upset. "We're sort of...instinctive. Show up when needed, sort of thing." I hadn't asked this many questions of Black Wolf, but maybe that was just me. Though the base of my tail said it wasn't just me, since I'd seen plenty of werewolves form over the course of time. You woke up with a lot of this knowledge in you -- at least, you were supposed to.

I figured I'd screwed up Jack's transition somehow, which wasn't too much of a surprise. I'd never made another werewolf before. There had never been a need or an older, more experienced werewolf or undead was with me and made the determination. Since he'd joined up and made it through basic training, Ken had made all the transition decisions for our unit. I could understand why he was upset with me -- precedent alone said I'd overstepped my bounds, let alone the situation.

"We need to figure out who the mole is." I realized the base of my tail was what had shoved that statement out, not my conscious mind.

Jack shrugged. "Could be anyone. Probably one of the ones you're closest to. If I were going to bet, I'd put my money on Ken, Ralph or Monty. Though really, it could be any of them."

This didn't make me feel warm and snuggly. "Maybe we don't have a mole." This was wishful thinking. I knew we did, and my tail agreed.

"Oh, I'm sure we do." He stroked my face. "But you can count on me. I've got your back."

"And I've got yours." I couldn't let it go, though. "But, wouldn't we have spotted *something*, if we had a mole?"

"Don't know. I mean, our side has moles in the Prince's ranks, right?"

"I guess. I don't work that side of undercover. Just the human side."

Jack gave me a searching look, like I'd seen him give a perp we knew was lying. "Come on, Vic. I'm on your side. We need to determine who the mole is, you're right. So, does our side have double agents?"

"Yes. But I don't know who any of them are." This was true enough that I could get it past Jack. I hoped.

"So, they have double agents, too. And it should be someone we'd never suspect, right? Or else, they're a pretty crappy double agent."

"I guess."

I didn't want to stay on topic now, but Jack pressed on. "So, maybe it's a like for like thing. Say it's Monty who's the mole. Who would be his counterpart on the Prince's side? Or Ralph's or Ken's?"

I considered this. "I have no idea." I didn't. I wasn't clear on the Prince's real hierarchy. You had your major minions and your lesser minions. But if they were set up like Necropolis Enforcement or not, I didn't know for certain. Nor did it seem remotely relevant.

"Is the Count the right counterpart to the Prince?"

"Not...not really." I rubbed my forehead. "We don't line up like they do, I don't think. Our leaders are the Gods and Monsters."

"You mean the beings who never show up when you need them?"

"What's that supposed to mean?"

Jack snorted in disgust. "Where were the Gods and Monsters today when we needed them? Nowhere around."

"They work through us, mostly."

"Right. Bang up job today."

"We're all still here, and you said you didn't mind being undead."

"I don't. I just think that maybe our side's not listening to the right leaders. Or rather, our leaders aren't taking much of an active interest."

"They do. They're always there when we really need them." I considered mentioning that Yahweh and Usen had saved me when I'd really needed it but refrained.

"Won't matter." Jack got out of bed, stretched again, shifted between human, wolf, and werewolf forms for a bit, then trotted to the bathroom. "Whatever comes, we'll handle it," he called as I heard the shower start.

This was odd behavior on top of odd behavior, for Jack and for a newly turned werewolf. Canines weren't enamored with bathing. We did it because it was expected of us, but a werewolf pack out in the field could and would enthusiastically roll in dung before they'd willingly take a bath. We were animals and animals liked to smell like they should, not like perfumes and soap.

In the time I'd known him, I couldn't recall Ralph ever trotting off to shower after a big battle. I never did it, either. We bathed daily, but because we had to fit in, not because we wanted to. But I could hear Jack, happily humming away, while the smell of soap wafted through this side of my apartment.

The realization that something was wrong and I had no idea of what to do reared up and waved its paw at me. If Black Wolf had still been unalive, I'd have called him for guidance. I'd have done the same with any of his pack. But they were all dead, killed off one by one. It was one of the reasons werewolves didn't run in packs any more. The Prince's side had used that against us, lying in wait for the moment a werewolf strayed even a little bit from their pack, pouncing on him, dusting him when he was all alone.

Ralph felt we should have banded more strongly together. The other undeads didn't. We scattered into different teams, made up of a variety of undeads. It had kept the remaining werewolves alive. But Ralph said we weren't as strong. And part of me knew he was right.

He was angry with me, and he had every right to

be. He could be the mole, and the Gods and Monsters knew enough signs said it was possible. But he was the only one who would understand, immediately, why I was freaked out. I hit his numbers on my wrist-com.

"Yes?" Ralph sounded just this side of sleepy and still on that side of angry.

"I'm sorry. Something's wrong."

"Everything, but what do you mean specifically?"

"Jack's taking a shower." There was dead silence on the other side of my wrist-com. "Ralph? You still there?"

"Are you alone with him?" Ralph's voice was strained.

"Sort of. Cindy, Freddy, Merc and L.K. are on the other side of my apartment. The Necropolis side."

"Get over to them. Now." Ralph wasn't my superior in Enforcement hierarchy and he wasn't my mate or my pack leader. But the tone of his voice told me that now wasn't the time to pull any kind of rank.

I scrambled towards the line separating Prosaic City from Necropolis just as Jack walked out, one towel around his waist, the other drying his hair. "What's up?" He sounded normal. He looked normal. He looked totally drool-worthy, too. But the base of my tail said it didn't care.

I jumped for the other side, but Jack caught me around my waist, spun and tossed me back onto the bed. "What's wrong with you?" he asked, as he climbed into bed with me.

"Nothing." Canines don't lie well as a rule and I was pretty sure I wasn't going to win any awards this time. "Just need to check on the others."

"They can wait." Jack grabbed my wrists and shoved me back onto the bed. "C'mon, Vic." He smiled, a really sexy, enticing smile. "We haven't even tried to do it doggy-style yet."

I wondered if, on another day, I would have found this appealing. Maybe. But today it struck me as totally wrong, and off-putting to the nth degree. "Jack, now isn't a good time."

His eyes narrowed. "As I understand it, werewolves are a pack-like animal. And that means there's a pack leader." He leaned closer to me. "And that pack leader is supposed to be male." He wasn't growling, but only just. "And you promised me -- together forever, no one in between."

"What about Susan?" The words came from somewhere, but not the front of my mind.

Jack grinned. "She's not in between us."

"But you're sleeping with her."

He shrugged. "So what?"

I'd said it in the present tense, not the past. And he hadn't argued. True we'd only become a couple a day or so earlier, but in my experience, you explained past lovers as being past, if only to appease the current lover. And he wasn't even trying to make an excuse.

"Get off me."

He bared his teeth at me. He was still in human form, but I realized he made Ralph's growl look kindly. "You're mine. And I do what I want with what's mine."

I started to fight in earnest. He'd always been bigger, but as an undead, I'd been stronger. But not any more. My struggles were futile. In fact, I could tell he was enjoying them. I wanted to cry, but that wasn't an option. Survive first, cry later.

The shift happened naturally -- I was fighting and I fought best in wolf form. But it didn't work. He still had my paws in an iron grip. I was reluctant to claw his stomach with my hind claws -- what if he was just having a bad reaction to the transformation?

Jack grinned, and it looked feral. "You like it rough?"

I decided, confused or not, he was getting the claws. I raked his stomach, but he transformed to wolf, too, and all I got was fur. "Back off."

"Bad girl."

"I'll give you a bad girl." I lunged up and caught his throat. But he batted my head away with a paw like it was nothing. On the positive side, this meant one of my front paws was free and I raked at his head with it. On the negative side, he'd hit my head hard and I felt it.

"I don't know what's wrong with you," Jack snarled.

"Me? You're the one acting all Call of the Wild." I managed to scramble away and off the bed. Sadly, Jack was between me and the Necropolis slide point. "So what's up with you and Susan the Dispatcher?"

"Come on. Animals aren't monogamous."

"Wolves are."

As Jack lunged across the bed at me and I leaped out of the way, all the angelic warnings coursed through my mind. Ken's worries, too. They'd been worried about Jack's ability to face the Prince because they were picking up something wrong with him. Something I'd either never noticed or ignored.

I focused now, while he played with me. It was play, too. He'd lunge, I'd leap, he'd bat at me, I'd scramble out of the way. He never let me get near enough to the slide point to cross over and he also blocked my path to the door. He was good, I had to give him that. Too good for a brand new undead.

"How did you do it?" I asked as I tried to leap over his head and got batted down onto the bed again.

"Do what?"

"Fool me, fool the others."

He flipped me onto my stomach and pinned me. His muzzle was next to my ear. "It was easy. You wanted a mate so badly. And you had one, right in front of you. That had to be stopped before it could start."

"What are you talking about?" I tried to crawl out from under, but he was using his full weight to hold me. I decided to focus on the more pressing point. "How did you give us away?"

He chuckled. "It was easy. You were so trusting. I could do anything, you weren't paying attention. But get over it. It's time to follow your heart. After all, you're in love with me."

"Not any more."

"You promised. None in between us, forever." His voice was a deep, terrifying growl. "You promised on sanctified ground."

Something slammed into Jack and his weight was off me. I rolled to see Ralph between me and Jack. "She's not her mother, and you're not taking her."

Jack shifted again. Only this time, he wasn't in wolf or werewolf form. And while he looked human, he sure didn't look like himself. He looked just like Little Harp. He smiled, and it was the most evil thing I'd ever seen. "Bet me, dog-boy."

Chapter 57

The Adversary, or at least part of him, was in my bedroom. Inside, point of fact, my until-just-now boyfriend. Meaning I'd slept with the Adversary at least once. Did things get better than this?

Yes, they did, if by "better" I meant "really, horribly worse".

Ralph and Little Harp attacked at the same time. Ralph was all angry, protective werewolf in action, but Little Harp was using Adversary-type skills, including a set of horrific claws I'd only seen on the vamps in major Nosferatu mode. He slashed while Ralph bit and clawed, and they both rolled around my room. Well, until they crashed through the walls. Then they rolled through the living and dining areas, right before they flipped and slid onto the Necropolis side, I assumed to destroy the other half of my living quarters. Not that I was too focused on that.

I tried to get into the fight, but they were flipping around so much it was impossible to be sure I'd bite the right being. Ralph was holding his own, but I didn't think it was going to last, especially since I could see him bleeding from a variety of locations. Sadly, I got the feeling Little Harp wasn't trying too hard. They did like to play with their prey, as I recalled, when they felt they had the time.

And he seemed to have the time. What was a shock, once we were on the other side, was that no one else was there. I knew for a fact Sexy Cindy and the others had gone to sleep over here. So, where were they? I sniffed -- nowhere around. I didn't smell death, so hopefully they'd just wandered off for some strange reason.

The Adversary was playing, but Ralph wasn't looking good. I ran for my weapons room. But I'd already shown Jack where that was, so the Adversary blocked me. By throwing Ralph at me. Showy, but effective. Ralph slammed into me and we both slammed into the wall. Meanwhile, Little Harp sauntered into my weapons room. This was definitely on the "horribly worse" side of things.

He sauntered out carrying what looked like an elephant gun. Well, it *was* an elephant gun, but it was modified into a Duster. Yeah, I was one of the beings entrusted with one. "Nice," he said to me, grinning widely. "All loaded for me, too. What a good girl you are."

We all had something that would dust another undead -- in case one of our own turned to the bad. But, from mildest holy water bullets to the mighty Dusters, we never turned it on each other until that point. Of course, this wasn't really a situation where I could say one of our own had turned against us. Frankly, if what I was seeing was real, and Ralph's blood all over me said it was as real as it got, part of Little Harp's soul had always been in Jack.

I got in front of Ralph. "Get out of here."

Little Harp laughed, then shifted. It was Jack looking at me, holding the gun which he had cocked and aimed right at me. "Come on, Vic. Let me get rid of him. Then we can go off together, just like you always wanted."

"I wanted what I thought you were, not what you really are."

"You're sure?" He cocked his head at me and looked almost boyish. "Maybe I'm exactly what you wanted."

"I didn't want to hook up with one of the Prince's major minions. To set the record straight and all."

He snorted. "Sure you did. You were hot for me from the first moment you saw me. And what's wrong with that? We belong together. You don't fit with him and you never will," he pointed at Ralph with the gun barrel. "He's a loser. Besides, you can't stand him, and you know it."

"He's a better being than you'll ever be."

"Big words. Impressive and heartfelt, I'm sure." Jack sighed. "But let's be realistic. He's not the one for you, now, is he?"

"I think the bastard's trying too hard," Sexy Cindy said as she slammed one of my end tables against the back of Jack's head. "Or however that quote goes. And like I said to her freak mother, get away from our girl."

"Methinks the lady doth protest too much, my dear," Freddy said, as he hit Jack at the knees with my coffee table. "From the Bard. And I agree with both sentiments."

"Shakespeare," Merc added as he swooped in and grabbed Ralph. "I'm sure he had a 'get away from our girl' quote, too."

"Nice to see you guys, where did you come from?" I leaped over the table and grabbed the gun. Sadly, Jack still had it firmly in hand, but at least I had the barrel pointing up and not at any being I cared about.

"We were hiding," L.K. said, as he wrapped at bath sheet around Jack's head and held it there. Jack shook his head wildly, but L.K. held on.

"Where?" I tried to wrench the gun away, but Jack wasn't having any of it. I decided not to complain -- if he had both hands on the gun, he couldn't take the towel off or get L.K.

"Somewhere we'll tell you about when enemy dude isn't right here," Sexy Cindy said. "Now might be a good time to tell you that he wasn't an infrequent visitor to our corner, both before you were his partner and after."

I was well-placed and, by now, beyond angry. I slammed my knee into Jack's groin. Happily, he made the sound men make when they're so slammed. I slammed my other knee into his face as he crumpled to the ground, still holding onto the gun.

"We're officially broken up. I promise. On sanctified or desecrated ground or just totaled apartment building. I'm officially cutting you loose."

"You promised." How he could get that out clearly I didn't want to contemplate.

My doors burst open and four beings swarmed in. Black Angels One and Two looked angrier than I'd ever seen. I really hoped they weren't that angry just at me.

Cain reached us first, grabbed the gun, and wrenched it out of both of our hands. I fell back into Freddy's conveniently waiting arms. L.K. zipped over to us. Merc still had Ralph, who wasn't looking anything close to great, but who was, for all I could tell, still unalive.

Miriam grabbed Jack and spun him towards her. "I warned you."

I couldn't see his face, but I could hear him clearly. He laughed. "You warned a part of me. That part cared. But it's dead. Like you'll be." He shifted again, and instead of Jack or Little Harp or a werewolf, the Adversary was there, all twelve feet of him. He smashed through my ceiling as he leaped into the air, still holding Miriam.

I didn't think and I'm pretty sure Ralph didn't,

either. Instincts took over and we both leaped. I caught one leg, Ralph caught the other. We locked our jaws and held on. Then we went on Mister Adversary's Wild Ride, Magdalena, Cain and Abel right behind us.

We weren't slowing him down. Hampering, maybe, but not slowing. I couldn't see what he was doing, but I could hear, and the sounds were awful. Miriam was one of my heroes, and he was killing her, slowly and with great malice aforethought.

It's risky to change form while you're only holding onto something with your jaws, because the human bite is nothing like the werewolf one. But I needed hands, not paws. I took as deep a breath as I could, relaxed, and did the switch, grabbing his leg as my jaws lost their hold.

It worked. I was still flying through the air attached to the Adversary. I considered my concept of "working" but decided to table it for when my feet were on terra firma. I wrapped my legs around his leg and started to climb up his body.

This gave new meaning to the term "icky" but I gritted my teeth and tried to ignore what I felt moving under his clothes. It wasn't Jack, it was the Adversary. It wasn't someone I'd been in love with, it was my most sworn enemy.

He was either vastly overconfident or Miriam was causing him to have to concentrate. Either way, I made it up to his neck. Then I wrapped my arms around it and squeezed. "Let her go."

He laughed. "If you insist." He opened his hands and Miriam dropped like a stone. I saw Black Angel One catch her. Magdalena was still on our trail. "So brave. All of you. But you can make it stop."

"How's that? By killing you? Good plan." I

squeezed harder.

"No. By accepting your true place. I'll let them all live, if you just acquiesce and come home with me. I promise."

He sounded calm and reasonable. I was exhausted and heartsick and, the moment I thought about it, frightened. Giving up sounded so safe and easy.

The base of my tail wanted a word. "Really? You'll just stop trying to kill all my friends and associates, stop trying to take over all the planes of existence? And all I need to do is say yes to you and go down to the depths of Hell as your baby-mamma?"

"Absolutely."

"Really. Does that offer cover Ken?"

"Yes."

"Jude?"

"Yes."

"How about Ralph?"

I knew what the answer was going to be, before it came. I felt the Adversary flail about, felt the kick connect, heard Ralph's canine whimper of pain, looked around to see him plummeting towards the buildings below. "No. He's dusted. Sorry."

"Then I have nothing to lose, right?"

"Right."

"That's what I thought." I flipped myself into the Adversary's arms. "Let's kiss and make up."

He smiled, and shifted to look like Jack again. "I knew you'd come around."

I wondered just how stupid the major minions really were. I shifted to werewolf form as I bit his neck again. Only this time, I wasn't going to let go.

Chapter 58

Jack, or whatever he was, really hadn't been expecting me to bite him, if his reactions were any indication. He flailed about and I was happy to note he was having trouble flying. How he could fly without wings I didn't know, but now seemed the wrong time to inquire.

"Let go, you stupid bitch!"

"Nuh-uh." That was about all I could reply with that wouldn't cause me to lose my hold. I took the opportunity to rake all four sets of claws against his chest and stomach. I couldn't tell for sure about his body, but I knew the clothes he had on were trashed.

He pried at my jaws. He was strong, but he wasn't able to get me off. I wondered about this. I figured he'd been able to kick Ralph off because he'd been so badly injured. I wasn't really hurt, so he wasn't having the same effect on me.

Of course, I wasn't the only one able to put two and two together. Jack started hitting me, hard. "You want me to really make you hurt?" he snarled. "Let go, or I shred you like I did your pathetic wannabe-mate."

I sank my claws into his flesh, let go of his throat, and grabbed an arm with my jaws. I bit down, hard, and heard the happy sound of bone breaking and Jack screaming in pain. He was going to have to change forms soon, or this one was going to be trashed.

He hit me with the other arm. Okay, I was happy to switch sides. Let go, grabbed the working arm, chomped down again, heard the bone crunch and the scream of pain. So far, so good. But at the same time, so very stupid.

Jack wasn't a moron. He was a great cop. All other

issues aside, he was smart enough to know that he should be defending himself differently, at least changing form. The Adversary, on the other hand, didn't necessarily have all the smarts in the world. But their lack of intelligence was overcompensated for by their innate, total viciousness. Still, were they really this stupid?

He kicked at me. So maybe yes. I could bite his legs, but that was going to move me into a more precarious position than I was already in and I'd have a better chance of success in wolf form -- and I needed to stay in werewolf in order to ensure I didn't lose hold of Jack. I went back for his throat.

"Let go of me, or I'll take you to Hell with me right now."

It seemed an idle threat, considering we were still flying in the air and not heading towards much other than maybe the moon. It was getting chilly, but werewolves don't feel the cold all that much. Fur's a great insulator.

However, I was still a cop, and I wanted some answers. I switched back to human and flipped around onto his back, arm locked around his throat again. "I wonder how you could actually do that."

"You promised yourself to me, on sanctified ground."

"And you're about the most unsanctified thing on any plane of existence, so how would that affect me?"

"Your promise ties you to me -- forever."

"Right. If you're really all that I think you are, you're also my biological father. Can we just say that the gross-out factor is beyond high and then follow that up with a 'no way, José' comeback?"

"You love me."

"No. I was in love with Jack Wagner. I don't know what you've done to him, if you were always a part of him or not, but he's not there any more. Looking like him and being him aren't the same thing."

His body started jerking around, like it was fighting something other than me. The body changed, too, going back and forth into a variety of forms. It was creepy to watch and worse to hold on to, but I didn't let go. It also looked like it was healing itself, which was a real disappointment on a variety of levels.

Jack's face was back, but the body was that of the Adversary's favorite monster from Hell form. The head turned around, so it was facing me. Considering I was on its back, this was nauseating and vile.

Jack's eyes were wide. "Vic -- help me!"

"You're not Jack."

"Yes, I am! What's going on? Why are you doing this to me?"

"I'm not doing anything to you that you don't deserve."

The body was still jerking and writhing, giving all the indications an internal fight of some kind was going on. I felt the claw of doubt run over my spine.

Jack looked more like he always had, albeit terrified. "Help me," he whispered. "Please, help me."

"Tell me how long you've been a part of the Adversary."

"I...I don't know." He closed his eyes as he winced in what sure looked like pain. "Vic, you have to believe me." He opened his eyes and they were really Jack's eyes. "I love you. I always have."

My throat felt tight. "But...you're evil."

"Help me. You're the only one who can save me, I know it."

He looked sincere, and if I didn't look lower than his neck, just like the Jack I'd been partnered with for a year. The guy who was so male that he made everyone else look wimpy by comparison. Maybe he was telling me the truth -- maybe Jack was taken over by the Adversary when I bit him. Maybe he was still in there, and I could save him.

Jack's face disappeared and Little Harp's made the scene. "Come home, you hellion child! Your mother cries for you every night. You belong with us, on the dais with the Prince himself. I, your father, order it."

"Wow, I guess it's because you killed every sibling of mine before they could walk so you've never dealt with a teenager or anyone older. But, seriously, that 'because I said so' thing doesn't work, pretty much ever."

His eyes narrowed. Didn't look a thing like Jack's. The claw of doubt tapped my shoulder. "We will give you the being you want, separate from us, if you return. You shall have him, as his own entity, as yours, for eternity."

"How could you possibly do that?" I tried not to wonder if it would really be Jack, but I couldn't help it. Wolves *were* monogamous, and I'd given myself to him well before we'd actually acknowledged the relationship.

"As we did it before," Little Harp answered, almost kindly. The body moved to match the head, and his arms were around me, but he wasn't trying to hurt me. "We will be father to you, and he will be mate, as you always wanted. After all, don't you long for a true family?" His voice was gentle, soothing.

My head nodded, without my brain's consent. "But...you're evil."

"Evil is in the eyes of the beholder. I'm not evil to your mother. And to those who fight alongside us, I am the leader, the one they turn to for guidance. Is that evil? To care for your people?"

It sounded so reasonable. The claw of doubt was drumming on my head now. But the base of my tail was twitching, and I'd spent a lot more time listening to it. "How can you separate Jack from you?"

Little Harp smiled. "As we separate ourselves. Souls are simple things to divide. And highly overrated."

"Was your soul always inside Jack?" I had to know, one way or the other.

Little Harp nodded. "We studied you. You are our daughter, your mother's daughter. You needed the male of males -- anything less left you feeling incomplete. We created your perfect mate, over time. Put the right humans together at the right time, a nudge here, a shove there. Finally, he arrived, exactly what you needed. Throwing you together was simple."

"Uh, wow." I didn't know what else to say. I wouldn't have credited either Harp with the brains to perform the ultimate genetics experiment.

He smiled and kissed my forehead. Just like a father would. "You are our only living child. We want the best for you, for you to be mated with perfection, so you can enjoy all the planes of existence have to offer."

It all sounded so reasonable. If I didn't think. But I'd never been able to not think, even when it had seemed like I was going to die because of it. The base of my tail asked the question it had asked before, as we were leaving the Little Church. "Why didn't you all finish us at the Estates, when you had the chance?"

Little Harp chuckled. "The work was done. We

want you safely with us, before we destroy the others. You are more important than all of them put together. You are our child."

Something clicked. All the little things, from the first time I'd met my real father until now started to fall into place. And something Jude had said -- that I always made the right decision when it came to good and evil -- surfaced. Jude had said that I made mistakes in my love life just like every other being, but that when it came down to it, I was important because I always made the right choice. And I was the child of the Adversary. And a werewolf.

The Adversary had hunted werewolves for all of my existence. Because of me. No one had ever said it aloud, but I'd known, for all my undead life. I was the reason my undead kind were forced to separate, to live more like other undeads than werewolves. I was the reason we no longer had a true Pack.

And one werewolf out of all of them refused to give in to the fear, refused to hide, even though it made him an outcast within the group. No wonder they wanted me kept away from him. What would have happened if I'd ever actually listened to what Ralph was saying?

I didn't have to guess. I knew. It was why they wanted me with them on the other side. Why they'd gone to the trouble to create Jack. I was the Child of the Adversary, title totally important.

"Can I see Jack again?" I needed to, just to be sure.

Little Harp smiled. "Of course. Whatever you want. You are our child, and we will care for you as you need and deserve." The entire being switched and now I was in Jack's arms. "Vic, are we going to be okay?"

I looked at his face, studied it really. It looked

exactly as it always had. There was no difference. He was still incredibly male, still appealing to me in ways no other male ever had been.

Over the centuries, I'd been many things. But what I'd always been, from the moment Black Wolf brought me to Necropolis, was a cop. And cops knew how easy it was to become just like the perps they spent so much time with. Hang with drug addicts, become an addict.

I stroked Jack's face. "You're my drug, aren't you?"

He gave me a half-smile. "I suppose so."

I leaned up and kissed him. "Jack, thanks for the offer, but I'm going to have to do what all our stupid posters suggest...and just say no."

Then I shoved out of his arms and let myself come down from the high.

Chapter 59

I landed a few seconds later. Because I crashed into Maurice.

"Ooof! Let's work on losing a few pounds, shall we, Vicki darling?"

"Nice catch." I looked around. Amanda and Ken were here, too. Here was, easily, a mile up. I stopped looking down quickly and focused on something sure to keep my mind off going splat -- everything else that was going on. "Ken, I'm so sorry. For everything."

He shook his head. "We picked up that something was wrong, but he was pretty well hidden, Vic. Him suggesting we had infiltrators was pretty ballsy, though."

I sighed. "I'm the one who came up with that."

"Correctly, I must add," Amanda said. "You just didn't look in the right place."

"Clearly." I looked up, where the right place had just been. "Where did he go?"

"Disappeared," Ken snapped. "I'd love to say he was worried about the three of us arriving, but I doubt it."

"So, Kenny briefed us on what was going on, at least what we think was going on." Maurice gave me an arch look. "Mister Yummy was actually the Adversary? As in, you just personified the Elektra Complex?"

"You know, I feel grossed out enough about it. You don't have to add salt to the wound. But, yeah, from what I can tell, there was at least a part of the Adversary's soul mingled in with Jack's. Maybe his entire soul. I'm not sure yet."

Amanda hugged me. This is hard to do while

flying in the air when the huggee is being held by another vampire. But she managed it. "Oh, honey, I'm so sorry. You were so crazy about him."

"Yeah, I was. I was supposed to be." I filled them in fast on what Little Harp had told me. "So, apparently, they've been setting this up since I became an undead."

Ken shook his head, as we started back towards the ground and I did my best to pretend we were already there. "I never got the impression the Harps were that smart."

"That was my thought, too. I don't think they are."

"Then someone else is helping with the hard work of thought processes. Vicki, darling, stop thrashing."

"Trying, trying. So, any ideas of who came up with this plan, and why?" I had some, but I wanted to hear what these three thought first.

"Possibly the Prince himself," Amanda suggested. "Though it seems too...."

"Detail-oriented for him," Maurice finished. "I agree. It's possible, but he's reputed to like minions who can come up with havoc on their own."

"But all the long term plans are the Prince's," Ken protested. "And this is certainly long-term."

"There are other options. Hitler, some of the other major minions. Lucifer." As I said it, I knew I was right. Which sucked in a variety of ways, not that I could mention any of them aloud.

The vampires nodded. "This is his style. Smart, sophisticated and very well hidden." Ken grimaced. "But why execute it through the Adversary?"

I wondered that myself. I had a couple of ideas of why, but one reason stood out the clearest -- because, ultimately, it wouldn't work. But I didn't suggest this aloud. There were only a couple of beings I could talk to about this possibility, both of them hanging at the Salvation Center.

But there was another reason, and it was also just as likely. Probably both reasons were true -- Lucifer would have to have a cover reason that flew in the Depths, after all. "Because I've got a nifty title down in the Depths -- the Child of the Adversary."

"Snazzy as that is, or rather, isn't," Maurice snipped, "what's the point?"

"I think I'm the Adversary's weakness, his Achilles' Heel."

Amanda and Maurice didn't look convinced, but Ken was clearly thinking. "That makes sense," he said slowly. "Every Adversary can be killed. We've killed every one but this one, after all. And we *will* kill him," he added fiercely.

"I agree, but I think I'm going to have to be the one to do it."

"Possibly," Amanda said. "But I'd like to hear more of a reason why, other than blood ties."

Maurice jerked. "But that's it, isn't it? Blood ties. Not necessarily for every Adversary, but certainly for this one. It's all about bringing the family together for Vicki's fab parental units. Why would they care unless there was a survival reason involved?"

"Considering my so-called family's history, they wouldn't. I think they've been after all the werewolves because that's what I was turned into. Either they're more affected by whatever breed of undead I am -- so if I'd become a vampire, they'd have spent the last couple of hundred years hunting vampires -- or because it was werewolves who saved me, or a combination thereof. Bottom line is I think that the undeads with the best chances of killing the Adversary are werewolves."

"That's great, but there's a new wrinkle, then," Amanda said. "You turned Jack into a werewolf, and he's a part of the Adversary. Meaning that they now incorporate all the werewolf skills along with their standard minion abilities."

"We're so screwed," Maurice muttered.

I considered this. "No, I don't think so. At least, not yet. Jack sucked as a werewolf, that's why I got clued in that something was wrong. So either they can't handle the idea, or the additional skills, or, because of already being the Adversary, they aren't really a werewolf. No matter what, it's not taking like it took with me and everyone else."

"Or they're processing it more slowly," Ken said. "And if that's the case, we have to work fast, before they fully incorporate this new aspect into their overall being."

"We have to work fast anyway, since there are other aspects of the overall plan working, active and in place. It's easy to focus on Jack and that part of the plan, but really, we still have a bunch of doppelgängers wandering about, the major minions are still on the human plane, and Nero's gone AWOL again. And that's merely for starters."

"Where do you want to start?" Ken asked as we finally reached the tops of some of the tallest Prosaic City buildings.

"The hospital. I need to talk to Ralph."

There was a distinct, thudding silence. I waited it out.

"Ah, Vicki," Maurice said finally. "Are you sure?"

"Is he dusted?" I made sure I had my cop-voice on. Just the facts, no emotional attachment, no guilt.

"No," Amanda said quickly. "Magdalena was able

to catch him. But...."

"But?" I had a horrible feeling what the "but" was going to be, but I didn't want to guess aloud, just on the off-chance I was wrong.

"But he's unconscious and in critical condition," Ken supplied. Damn. I'd guessed right. "He's about as close to dusted as you can get without actually *being* dust."

"Wonderful." I tried not to focus on the fact that I'd essentially put Ralph into harm's way and kept him there. But it must have showed on my face.

"No." Ken shook his head. "You didn't do this to Ralph. Our enemies did, but you didn't."

"Really? I didn't fall for their perfect man trick? I didn't turn Jack into a werewolf, without asking anyone to verify if he could make the transition well? I didn't help the Adversary set things up to take out Ralph and everyone else?"

Maurice coughed. "Okay, yeah, you did. But not on purpose."

"I'll bet that'll heal Ralph right up."

We hit the ground, and I breathed a heavy sigh of relief. I had to figure it was going to be the only one I so sighed for a while.

Amanda put her arm around my shoulders. "He'll forgive you," she said quietly.

I pulled away. "Maybe he shouldn't."

Ken sighed. "Lord, what fools these undeads be."

Amanda gave me a look I was familiar with -- her "you're an ass but I love you" look. "Come on, idiot-girl." She grabbed me again. "Let's go to the hospital and see just how rotten things are in our personal Denmark."

"Everyone's quoting Shakespeare," I muttered.

"What, did H.P. do some weekend course I missed? Just in case, I have one, too. Hey, nonnie, nonnie."

Amanda laughed. "Glad to see your sense of humor's back."

"Such as it is," Maurice said with a snort.

"Yeah? Let's hear your Bard quote, then."

Maurice gave me a long, slow smile. "Some Cupid kills with arrows, some with traps. Let's go see which it'll be for you, shall we?"

"Um, I fell for the trap, remember?"

Maurice still had that wide, sly smile on his face. "We shall see, Vicki darling. We shall see."

Chapter 60

We reached the hospital, but getting to Ralph's room proved to be a challenge. Due to all the activities we'd been indulging in, admittance rate was still at an all-time high, and we had a lot of beings, both sick and well, to get through.

Monty was just being released as we arrived. He hugged me. "So sorry to hear about what happened."

"Yeah, I suck at the romance."

Rover curled up around me and gave me white worm lovies. I scratched his head and felt a tiny bit better. White worms were great because it was exceedingly rare when they made you feel guilty. Usually they just made you feel needed and appreciated.

"So, Jack had us pretty well infiltrated," Monty said, back to all business. "But it brings up a good point -- how do we know we don't have more double-agents among us?"

I groaned. "I can't handle it. Maybe we do. I think I don't care. I can't spend all my time trying to discover which unlifelong friend of mine is really working for the Prince. Unlife's too short, okay?"

Monty shook his head. "Maybe, but we want to extend it as long as possible." He sighed. "I'll work on it. You just take care of the here and now."

"You were suspect number one, if that helps with your search."

He looked startled, to the point where I thought an arm might fall off, but then he laughed. "You know, that makes sense."

"You saying we should dust you?" Maurice asked.

"No. But it's the right kind of thinking. Position of

authority, person you'd least suspect, and all that."

"Ah, that was Jack, and I least suspected us right into almost losing the War." Something Jack had asked occurred to me. "You know, for sure the Prince's side suspect we have double-agents."

"How so?" Monty shrugged. "I mean, it makes sense, especially since they had an active double-agent within our midst. So, really, why wouldn't they suspect?"

"Why haven't we suspected? Maybe because the agents, whomever they are, are so good. I mean, Jack was excellent. If he hadn't lost it tonight, werewolf-wise, I might never have guessed until it was too late." That it was almost too late for Ralph I did my best to ignore for right now.

Monty looked off into space. "Why do you think they're searching for an agent? If that's what you mean."

"It is. And it's from the questions Jack asked me. He was trying to figure out if our spies were placed like we were. You know, were the spies equal to your rank, the Count's rank, and so on."

Monty and Ken exchanged worried looks. Maurice and Amanda looked blank. "Why would rank matter?" Amanda asked.

"They're trying to determine how deep our mole might be," Monty said.

"Or moles. Jack sure seemed to think we had plenty."

"Which could mean they do, too, or could simply mean they aren't sure about us," Ken said. "But, Vic, you said something just now -- Jack lost it? How do you mean?"

"He acted unlike any werewolf I've ever known

after transition."

"The walking thing?"

"Yeah, but more than that. He was acting...you know, like someone who didn't know how werewolves really were might act."

"Like he'd seen a lot of bad movies?" Amanda asked.

"Yeah, exactly." I considered this. "Which makes no sense, because they have turned werewolves on the Prince's side. All he'd need to do was ask them what their transitions had been like and how to act."

"So either he did that, and ignored it, or he didn't." Now it was Ken's turn to stare off into space. "Speaking as a cop, and not a jilted lover, how smart is Jack?"

"Speaking as myself, who, all things being equal, just did the jilting, smart. He's a good cop. One of the best, many times *the* best. Oh, damn. I have to call the Chief. He has no idea, and that means Jack could be doing Gods and Monsters knows what to the Prosaic City P.D."

Maurice cleared his throat. "The Count may have been down, but he was hardly out. Your human police chief's been warned. He was quite angry -- with Mister Yummy, not you, by the way."

"Well, that's something." Another thought occurred. I was so proud. "Susan."

"What?" Monty was apparently asking for everyone.

"Susan, the day dispatcher. Jack was sleeping with her. And if my family's history is any indication --"

"He's gone off to grab Bride Number Two," Amanda finished for me. "I don't want you to go," she added quickly. "You need to regroup. Maurice and I will take a full squad and see if we can track her down before Jack does."

"Call him the Adversary," Ken said.

"No." I put my hand on his arm. "You really are the best guy anyone could be exes with. But, no. Call him Jack. I need to fight Jack, not the Adversary."

"You sure?" Ken asked. "Because that seems so...harsh."

"But it's reality. My reality's always been harsh." I had to remind myself, Ken was the Undead Ideal, but he was from an era so far removed from mine that sometimes it was like we weren't even talking the same language. "Don't worry. I'll be stronger this way."

"Hell hath no fury like a weregirl scorned," Maurice suggested.

"Canines don't lie much and we don't like those who do. We really hate it when someone close to us has lied, particularly when it's us they've lied to."

"As I said." Maurice rolled his eyes. "So, Amanda and I are off to the races. What are the rest of you going to be doing?"

"Hunting moles," Monty said. "Ken, I'd like your help."

"He was suspect number two."

They both gave me a dirty look. "Anyone else called out as the potential betrayer of the ages?" Monty asked rather more snidely than I felt necessary.

"Ralph, the Count, and Clyde, for starters. By the time we were done, pretty much any being could have been the main suspect. It's easy to get paranoid, especially when there's proof that paranoia is the right way to go. Jack even insinuated that the Gods and Monsters could be in on it."

"The Prince's side would like us to think so, yes."

Monty gently removed Rover from my waist and draped him over his shoulders. "We'll be in touch. Give Ralph our best...you know, when he wakes up."

The four of them gave me the hugs and the standard atta girls, and then I was alone. Well, as alone as it was possible to be in a hospital teeming with personnel I knew. But, I wasn't with any of them. I was a lone wolf. I wondered how Ralph had stood it all these years.

It was easier to maneuver through the hospital this way, though. No one really paid me much notice, and I was able to find Ralph's room in a few minutes. I hated hospitals, but I shoved that aside. I wasn't here for me, I was here for him.

He looked pretty pathetic. His fur was matted with blood and he had an inordinate amount of tubes and wires going into his body. Beeping and blinking machines filled up half the room. He was twitching, which I hoped meant he was dreaming and that there was brain activity. I didn't bother to look at the machines -- I had no clue what any of them did or were trying to tell me, and now wasn't the time to learn.

I grabbed his chart as I pulled the one chair in the room over and sat down. My last hospital visit I'd been in a similar position, only sitting on Jack's lap. How long ago that felt.

Ralph was as bad as everyone had said. The doctor's weren't giving him a rosy recovery outlook. My throat felt tight as the words "all my fault" went across my mind like a repeating electronic banner. I took his paw in my hand.

"I'm so sorry I didn't listen to you. You were right, all along -- about Jack, about what we werewolves should be doing, maybe about everything. I'm sorry I never paid any attention until it was almost too late."

He didn't respond. I'd known he wouldn't, but the disappointment rolled over me anyway. I thought about what Sexy Cindy had said, that she'd love it if a guy like Ralph wanted her. He should want her -- she'd seen him for what he was, a hero.

But, hero or not, Ralph was a werewolf fanatic, and fanatics didn't mate outside their species. Meaning he'd spent all this time hoping I'd wake up and smell the kibble.

Whether he'd wake up, or wake up still even remotely interested in me, was a mystery. I had to ask myself if I could be interested in him. It was hard to say yes or no. I'd called him when I was frightened and he'd come to save me -- *had* saved me. Just like Black Wolf and his pack had come and saved me.

I gave up and let the tears come. I'd closed the door tightly behind me, so hopefully no one was going to hear me bawling my head off. I just hoped I could keep the howling to a minimum.

Not to enough of a minimum, apparently, if the arrival of a nurse I'd seen around but really didn't know was any indication. She was older, plump and sort of motherly, complete with her hair in a bun and her nurse's cap on just so. Just looking at her was calming, which is why I figured she looked and dressed this way.

"Ah," she said as she came in and shut the door behind her. "You must be our poor brave boy's next of kin."

"Sort of." I already knew Ralph had no kin, and with no official pack, he was alone. But I was his superior officer, and that had to count for something. "Is he going to make it?"

She took the chart from me and glanced through it. "Well, it's hard to say, but he's a fighter, so I think he has a good chance." I took a look at her nametag -- Nurse Nancy, P.W., which meant Practicing Witch or Warlock, depending. Good, they made the best medical personnel, and I wanted Ralph to have the best.

"What about his mind and his physical prowess? Will he be back to normal, do you think?"

Apparently this was some sort of hospital code, because Nurse Nancy gave me a conspiratorial wink and patted my shoulder. "Oh, I'm sure he'll be chasing you around the park in no time. Werewolves come out of anesthesia quite frisky, dear, don't you worry. You'll have your mate back good as new, if we have anything to say about it."

I felt my cheeks get hot. "Uh, not quite what I meant."

She giggled. "Oh, don't be embarrassed. It's one of the most natural things, for any species, alive or undead. And most spouses are worried about it, even though they don't want to say so out loud. You're not asking anything wrong or anything every other being whose loved one was injured doesn't ask. Will I get my honey back and will he or she be the same honey? It's an understandable concern."

"You know, I have to ask -- why do you think Ralph and I are…mated?"

She shrugged. "Well, I know I don't really know you two well at all, but you're a werewolf, too."

"Yes."

"And, as I understand it, werewolves are attracted to strength and virility."

"True." I had no idea where Nurse Nancy was going with this.

"Well." She gave me another conspiratorial wink. "Not to insinuate that we've had our way with your boy here, but, ah, well, trust me when I say that he's an impressive specimen. Quite a big boy, best in show, sort of thing."

"I guess. I mean, he's bigger than me in wolf form, but that's to be expected."

Nurse Nancy coughed. "I didn't mean just in body structure, dear. You have quite a virile young wolf here, if I'm any judge."

It took a while, but what she was euphemistically insinuating finally became clear. My cheeks got hotter. I'd never exactly lifted Ralph's tail to take a look, but it made sense that the medical staff had. Nice to know Nurse Nancy was impressed.

She was also still prattling on about Ralph's attributes. "Quite strong, too. Even unconscious he was still fighting -- it took six of us to have a prayer of holding him down until the drugs took effect."

"He's dedicated, yeah."

"Well, understandable. At least if what he was saying was any indication of what happened."

"He'd been talking? That's good, right?"

"Hopefully, yes. He was saying 'get away from her' over and over again." She cocked her head at me. "You look a little worse for wear. You're the 'her', I imagine?"

"Yeah." I was the her. And even unconscious Ralph was trying to protect me. I couldn't help it, the howling started in earnest.

"There, there." Nurse Nancy was patting my head. Normally someone being this wolfy-cutesy would make me want to bite them, but it was definitely her thing, because it had the desired effect. I buried my face in her stomach and sobbed. "It'll be alright, dear, it'll be fine. He's got you to come back for, and he will, I promise."

"Are we on sanctified ground?"

Nurse Nancy pulled away from me and raised my chin with her hand. She looked confused. "Not that I know of, dear. Not desecrated, but only certain areas are sanctified. Do you want an angel or a saint? I don't know that a blessing will help your young wolf, here, but it certainly couldn't hurt."

"No. He'll get better from your and the others' work, I'm sure. I just wanted to check that it was a normal promise."

Nurse Nancy shook her head. "As normal as we can be, which is not at all and completely, at the same time." She patted my shoulder again. "Now, you relax. Visiting hours are almost up, but under the circumstances, I'll let you stay. However, I can't bring another bed in here, so if you need to have a lie-down, there's a waiting area just around the corner, with couches, throw pillows and blankets."

With that she trotted out of the room and left me and my guilt alone with Ralph. I held his paw again and leaned my head on the bed. And thought -- about everything but mostly about Jack.

But it was weird -- my heart hurt, but not like I thought it should. Like Amanda had said, I'd been crazy about Jack, for well over a year. And yet, there was no part of me that wanted him back. The revulsion was too strong -- Jack was part of the Adversary and there would never be a way I'd willingly let him touch me again.

But even so, I thought I should be feeling more bereft. But I wasn't. Some of this had to do with Susan the day dispatcher. It had been clear she and Jack were an active item. Even if he hadn't been a part of the Adversary, I'd want to rip his parts off for the infidelity.

The sex had been great, but the memory of what he'd tried to do right before Ralph had arrived was a total turn off. Playing was one thing -- but Jack hadn't been playing. He'd been, as I thought about it, just like I'd read my real fathers had been.

My whole body shuddered. I'd fallen in love with Jack's exterior and now that I'd been exposed to the interior I was done, turned off like a light switch. It had never happened before, but if there was ever a time to recover fast from a bad relationship, now was it.

I considered whether part of my speedy emotional recovery was because Ralph was here and I was finally willing to look at him as an option, should he pull through. Possibly. But why was I open to Ralph now? Just because he'd been incredibly heroic and brave and had saved me from the most horrifying experience of my unlife? Well, those were pretty good reasons to be impressed, as I thought about it.

Ralph was a dork, yes, but he was a brave, loyal dork. And regardless of what he'd look like as a human -- should I ever find out -- that had to beat handsome, manly, evil hot guy. At least if a weregirl wanted a mate she could count on. Should said potential dorky mate pull through, of course.

My heart was hurting again, but I realized it was because I was afraid Ralph might dust and then I'd never get the chance to see how short I'd sold him for all these years. I tried not to think about all the times I'd let the exasperation with his loving, loyal interest show in my expression or voice.

Sadly, my personal electronic scroll ensured all of them played merrily through my mind. I'd been a bitch, and not in the canine sense, and if Ralph woke up and never wanted to speak to me again, he had more than every right.

But what was I going to do or say if he woke up the same Ralph who I'd known for centuries?

"You know, if you make it through, I'd probably be open to a date. Maybe even going steady. You know, if you can even look at me after all of this."

He didn't wake up or even twitch. So, the sounds of a loved one's voice idea either was a crock or I wasn't in the loved ones category any more. I gave it even odds for either option.

I heaved a heavy canine sigh and settled in to watch Ralph be unconscious. My love life -- truly, was there a better one in all the planes of existence?

Chapter 61

A loud beeping jarred me awake. I hadn't realized I'd fallen asleep -- I'd been so out I hadn't dreamed.

I looked around. The monitors and machines were going crazy. Ralph was still breathing, so I controlled the impulse to do CPR. But I had no idea of what to do.

I ran for the door just as a passel of medical personnel raced into the room. The door managed to miss slamming into my face, but only because I had great reflexes. We did the "this way, no that way" dance a bit, which would have made me laugh under different circumstances. Right now, though, any time I was moving and the staff were moving with me was time they weren't getting to Ralph.

I gave up and leaped over his bed and back to my chair. Sometimes that gets a whistle of admiration or round of applause. Today it got me a nod of relief.

The doctors and nurses swarmed over Ralph to the point I was shoved into the far corner of the room. Nurse Nancy bustled in shortly after and motioned to me. I went to her reluctantly.

She took my arm and led me out to the hall. "They need you out of the room, dear."

"But, I want to know what's going on." It didn't come out as a whine, but it was a near thing.

Nurse Nancy shook her head. "Come along." She led me to the waiting room she'd described. It was rather cozy, all things considered, with a variety of chairs and couches, as well as the pillows and blankets as advertised. "You wait here, dear. We'll send someone for you once the doctors are through."

"Ralph's going to be okay, right?"

She gave me a small smile. "I'm sure."

"Will someone come and tell me when it's okay for me to go back and stay with Ralph?"

"Yes, dear, I'll make a note on his chart." She patted my arm then bustled off and I was alone.

I had no idea what time it was, but I could say for sure that my pseudo-nap hadn't done me too many favors. I figured I could pace and worry or sleep. I grabbed a pillow and a couple of blankets, made a nest on one of the couches, contemplated what would be the most comfortable in this situation and switched to wolf form, curled up, and went to sleep.

Well, I tried. Intermittent sleep is better than nothing, and that's what I was getting. I was alone in the waiting room, but I could hear medical personnel running here and there, doing their jobs. Sadly, Ralph wasn't the only one in this wing and there was a lot of ruckus for a variety of beings.

There was another little undeads tour group who came by and though they tried to be quiet, twenty youngsters "whispering" was enough to rouse someone deaf, let alone someone with my hearing. I played dead dog, but it still required waking up and going back to sleep.

And so it went. If I fell asleep and no one in the hospital managed to wake me, then my wrist-com was going off with updates. Updates I was too fuzzy to do anything with. The exhaustion and heartache had caught fully up to me and I was a basket case. The best I got was that Ken was in charge but wanted me back on the case, however the Count wanted me recuperated, and nothing was happening, but Monty felt it was the calm before the next storm.

I listened to these updates, grunted or growled, depending, and then flopped back down to sleep.

Somewhere around dawn Nurse Nancy brought me some food, shared she was going off duty, and reassured me that Ralph was still alive. I was still relegated to the waiting room, however. I scarfed the food and did the flop back onto the paws thing.

I was on my back, in the first deep sleep I'd managed, paws in the air, when I felt someone watching me. I was pretty sure I'd been snoring -- per Jude and Ken both, I snored up a storm in what everyone who wasn't canine called the "dead cockroach" sleeping position.

Police training combined with werewolf senses meant I evaluated the situation in the room quickly, eyes still closed. There was definitely no feeling of danger, but I was also not alone. I cracked an eyelid.

Upside down, the man standing there looked okay. Tall, long dirty-blond hair, medical scrubs. Wasn't a doctor I knew, but then again, I did my best not to be here much.

It was clear he knew I was awake, because he looked amused. I did the flip and roll thing, which flipped me onto the floor. He helped me up and I figured it was time to go to human form, since I'd embarrassed myself enough in wolf form.

"You okay?" He sounded concerned but still amused.

"I think so. Are you one of Ralph's doctors?" Right-side up, he was pretty cute. Not too bulky but extremely sinewy, big brown eyes, nice smile. He wasn't Jack, but then again, hopefully that meant he wasn't also carrying around evil incarnate in his soul. I considered that maybe I should spend more time cruising the medical personnel, then reminded myself that I was here for Ralph, not to pick up one of the people trying to save his unlife.

His eyes widened and he shook his head. "I'm a patient. Just wanted to get out of the room for a minute." He let go of me and sat on one of the couches. "Sorry, I'm not supposed to be standing for too long right now."

I considered sitting next to him -- he was in the middle of his couch, arms stretched out on the back of it, one leg crossed over the other. He looked good in this position, but picking up on one of Ralph's fellow patients didn't say "I care about you and I'm sorry" any more than making goo-goo eyes at the medical staff did. I checked the clock. It shared that it was six o'clock, but since it was an old-fashioned dial clock, there was no a.m. or p.m. and I was far too out of it still to be able to offer a good guess. "Is it day or night?"

"Night, I think." He had a nice voice, deeper than you'd expect from just looking at him. I reminded myself that I was not looking. Sort of.

"Good, then I didn't sleep for twenty-four hours straight." Not that I couldn't have used it. I sat back down on my nest and tried not to notice the drool marks on the pillow. I had to figure I'd been quite the sight, particularly if you were looking for a good laugh. "So, what're you in for?"

"Bad...accident." He cocked his head at me. "Why are you here?"

My throat felt tight. "A...friend of mine got hurt and I just...I wanted to make sure he was going to be okay."

"Ah. That's nice of you." He sounded a little disappointed.

"I guess."

His eyebrow raised. "You guess?"

"It's my fault he's in here." I heaved a big sigh, which I hoped meant I wasn't going to start crying again. "I screwed up, big time, and he paid the price for it."

"You're Enforcement," he said with a shrug. "It happens."

I didn't ask how he knew. It wasn't the first time someone had recognized me even though I didn't know them well or at all. Besides, I'd been out, so for all I knew he'd just asked someone who the weirdo was sleeping in the waiting room like it was a kennel.

"It shouldn't have happened. If I'd been paying attention, really paying attention, it wouldn't have happened."

"How is that?" He didn't sound accusatory or even salaciously interested. He sounded genuine.

Put it down to hunger, exhaustion, heartache, or guilt, but I opened my mouth and the whole story poured out. He nodded, asked the right questions at the right time, and pretty soon he had the whole thing. "So, now Ralph's at death's door and I've given the Adversary all he needs to destroy us."

"You couldn't have known," he said gently. "Besides, you were being set up by the best."

"That helps Ralph exactly how?"

He gave me a long look. "You know, he's Enforcement, too. He knew the risks. And it sounds like you think he's in love with you. Any male who isn't willing to die to protect his female really isn't worth keeping around."

I couldn't hold his gaze. Rehashing it all hadn't made me feel better -- it had confirmed that I'd been blithely clueless. "I fell for it, by falling for Jack. So I've been stupid for at least a year, and the Gods and

Monsters know what he managed to do while I was mooning over him."

He chuckled. "From what it sounds like, Jack was a sleeper."

I looked up. "A sleeper?"

"Sure. An agent programmed and put into place. He doesn't know he's an agent until he's triggered. Then, once he is, he reverts to the programming. In some cases, sleepers can have moments when the programming takes over and their conscious mind doesn't know it. I could go on, but there've been a lot of movies about things like this."

"But there's no way to know."

"Sure there is. The angels didn't know what was wrong with him, just that something was. That says sleeper to me. He bothered Ken and plenty of others, heck, he even bothered Sexy Cindy, as you call her." He grinned. "Not the most subtle of street names. But no one could put their paw onto what was wrong with him. Again, that says sleeper to me. If Martin and Black Angels One and Two couldn't spot what was wrong with Jack, you certainly couldn't have known, you don't have the psychic skills."

There was something wrong with what he'd said, but I couldn't put my paw on it. "I suppose. But that doesn't help Ralph."

"You in love with him?"

It was so straightforward I was almost taken aback. "I don't know."

"But you think you should be, because he's in love with you?" He seemed intent with this question. I wasn't sure if it indicated general or specific interest and figured all the recent emotional trauma with Jack and confusion about Ralph had me so turned around that I probably wouldn't be able to tell, anyway.

"Sort of. But that's not really it. I feel like I've never given him a chance and maybe that was part of the overall plan, too, you know? Maybe if we hadn't stopped running in packs, things would be different between me and Ralph."

"Maybe, maybe not. Maybe you were supposed to come around to it this way."

"Maybe Ralph won't want to speak to me ever again and this entire conversation will be moot." I didn't add that maybe Ralph was going to die, which would make the conversation even more pointless and a lot more painful.

"So you think he's going to decide that you're not worth it, just because he got hurt?" He sounded annoyed. Great.

"I don't know. I mean, I'd understand if he did. Wouldn't you?"

"No. Wolves are monogamous. That includes when they make mistakes." He stood up. "I think you should stop worrying and just relax."

I rolled my eyes as I stood up, too. "Thanks for the advice." I was about to add something sarcastic when a nurse raced in. Like Nurse Nancy, I'd seen her around but didn't really know her.

She gasped in what sure sounded like relief. "*There* you are!" She grabbed my waiting room buddy's arm. "You need to get back into bed, excellent recovery or not."

He pulled gently out of her grasp. "I'll get back there myself, I promise."

She gave an exasperated grunt. "Your kind drive me crazy," she muttered. "Fine. I'll tell the doctors and your superior officers." Interesting. I didn't know him, so he couldn't be Enforcement. I tried to think if we had Special Ops in the vicinity and couldn't come up with any activity I knew about.

"Is Ralph going to be okay?" I asked before she could leave the room. "Ralph Rogers?"

The nurse gave me a look that said I was really weird. "Yes. Obviously. Though he needs to rest."

"Excuse me? What do you mean 'obviously'?"

She shook her head. "Special Agent Rogers, the doctors want you back in bed, pronto." With that she stomped out.

And I stared, with my mouth open.

He grinned. "Surprise."

Chapter 62

I stood there, still staring, as shock ran through my entire body. "Who are you?" I knew, but some things you wanted to hear live and confirmed.

He laughed. "You heard her. Vic, relax. It's okay."

"You…you…." I got a hold of myself. "You *jerk!*" He looked taken aback. I stepped closer and poked my finger into his chest for emphasis. "You sat there, listening to me tell the story that you already knew about, listening to me wax rhapsodic about you, and you never said a thing." I was growling. "I ought to put you right back into that hospital bed."

"The doctors would be happy if you did," he said easily. "I thought you'd recognize my voice."

"You don't sound like you do in wolf or werewolf form, you unutterable jackass! None of us do! And I've never seen you in human form, ever. Name someone in all of Necropolis Enforcement who *has.*"

Ralph shrugged. "The Count. And, before he died, Black Wolf."

My jaw was back to hanging open. It didn't help that I also had tears in my eyes.

Ralph closed my mouth gently. "I'm Special Ops, Vic. I have been for almost double the time you've been undead. But for the last two hundred and some years, I've had one assignment and one assignment only."

"What was that?" My voice was a whisper. Did I know anything about anyone?

"Protecting the one being likely to be able to stop this time's Adversary. Protecting you." He shook his head. "I had the freedom to do that job in any way I saw fit. And I saw fit to do it like Black Wolf told me to -- as a wolf, not a human."

I felt my bottom lip start to tremble. "Why all the werewolf rights stuff, then?"

He smiled. "You're right. I'm a werewolf fanatic, Ralph Rogers, werewolf with a cause. I want our kind allowed to do what we do best. I want us no longer afraid to be seen as werewolves." He sighed. "Unfortunately, I'm still me. As you accurately described me, kind of a dork."

"Kind of a dork who just managed not to tell me who I was pouring my heart out to for like an hour?" I was working hard to hold onto the anger. It seemed so much better than letting the tears out. Memory waved and reminded me of the last part of our conversation. "And you had the *nerve* to ask me if I was in love with you, and you aren't clear why I'm upset?"

He growled and it sent a different kind of shock up and down my spine. I'd never heard Ralph growl like this before. It wasn't threatening -- it was sexy, deep-seated sexy, the kind of growl that made my butt start moving in that tail-wagging way.

I opened my mouth to try to say something, he grabbed me by my upper arms, pulled me to him, and kissed me, still growling. I tried to resist it, but in about two seconds I'd melted against him while his kiss and growl both got deeper. I managed to keep my cool, if by that I mean I didn't rip his clothes off. I just pawed at him like I was trying to climb up his body. I was proud -- I kept both feet on the ground. Well, one foot, anyway.

The possibility of our consummating the relationship right here and now was increasing in likelihood when I heard someone give an exasperated sigh. "Mister Rogers, this is not the way the doctors want you resting." I decided I really didn't like this nurse. She'd sounded a lot nicer when she'd first found him in here.

Ralph ended our kiss slowly, giving me some time to sort of get myself under control. I only whined a little. "Coming."

Well, not quite yet, but it'd been close. "When does Nurse Nancy come back on duty?" The base of my tail wanted a quick word, and that word was "mister", as in, why had she called Ralph that this time, when she'd used his title before?

The nurse gave me a dirty look. "No idea. Why?" I examined her. No nametag. But she'd had on one before, I just hadn't bothered to look at her name.

"I like her better than you." I looked closely at her. Eyes were just a little wrong. Everything was just a tiny bit different from when she'd been in here only minutes before. "I like her a lot better than you, as a matter of fact." I didn't question the instinct that said to hit her, I just went with it.

My fist slammed into her face and she went flying. I switched to werewolf form as she hit the wall and also changed -- into a being with huge bat-wings.

I got my jaws on her throat while I heard Ralph shouting that we had a loose fallen angel. I hoped he was using an intercom of some kind and wasn't going to get involved, because it didn't take genius to guess she was here to kill him, not me.

Angels are hard to kill. Fallen ones are even harder. But she'd waited a little too long and I wasn't in nearly the bad emotional or physical shape I'd been in hours, even minutes, before. I was still in a form of shock from everything that had happened, but I'd fought the Adversary one-on-one recently and one fallen angel chick wasn't a real challenge after that.

Plus, I'd spent many an hour up at the University Library, going through every edition of "How to Dust Dangerous Minions" written by a variety of heroes over the ages. There were a lot of chapters on how to deal with fallen angels and they all agreed on one thing -- strip the wings from the body first, sever the head from the body second. Do it right and you wouldn't need step three.

Did my flip around to the back while still keeping her neck in my jaws maneuver. Used my claws to rake at her wings. Ignored her clawing me back. We were in a hospital, after all. If I needed to get fixed up after this I wouldn't have far to go.

I heard the sound of running feet and a variety of beings raced into the room. I was a little preoccupied, but I did spot Sexy Cindy and Freddy in the group. She had a spray can which she aimed and emptied right into the fallen angel's face.

How Evil Fairy Repellent would be useful in this situation I had no idea, but it seemed to stun my opponent enough for me to get the upper claw. I wrenched my head and heard her neck snap. Good, but not good enough, and her wings were still attached, though much worse for wear.

"Vic, jump now!" Ralph shouted in a voice that didn't really brook argument.

And I didn't argue. I leaped off, up and over. I felt something swish by my tail as I flipped. I saw Merc swing an ax and cut off the fallen angel's wings while L.K. did the same with her head. Apparently others had read up on fallen angel destruction. I got the distinct feeling these two were over bus driving as their main pursuit.

I didn't stick the landing, but instead gracefully

slammed right into Ralph. I was afraid I'd hurt him, but he didn't seem too rocked by it. I switched back to human as he helped me up. "Nice one. Thanks for the save." He kept his arms around me. I didn't mention it. And my arms were around his waist purely in the interest of not falling over.

"I kind of owed you." I didn't know what else to say. There were a lot of other beings in the room and I wasn't sure if that one kiss had been just to see what it was like before he trotted off into the sunset.

"Is that why you kissed me?" he asked softly. I wasn't prepared to swear to anything, but he looked like he was trying to act casual and brave. But his eyes were sad and disappointed.

"Well, *you* kissed *me*." Hey, it was true. "But that's not why I kissed you back."

He swallowed. "Why did you?"

I heard a dramatic sigh before I could answer. "Because she's finally seen what you look like on two legs." I looked over my shoulder to see Maurice saunter into the room. He shook his head. "I told you to go human a century ago, Ralphie. But did you listen?" He looked around. "What a mess. I hate to interrupt, but we do have a situation."

"You're not interrupting," Ralph said, sounding very disappointed.

Maurice rolled his eyes. "She thinks you're hot, stop acting hangdog."

I looked back and forth between them. "I thought you two didn't like each other."

Ralph shrugged. "It was easier to deal with you that way."

"I beg your pardon?"

Maurice sighed again. "Ralphie didn't want you

compromised, Vicster. However, not exactly being a wolf of the world, he somehow felt that you thinking we couldn't stand each other was a good way to protect you." He shook his head. "The things I've had to put up with over the decades. Specifically the whining. No being whines quite like a werewolf in love."

"Are you Special Ops, too?" I was prepared for Maurice to say yes. Maybe the entire team was Special Ops. Maybe all of Necropolis Enforcement was there as an illusion for me, the clueless idiot.

Maurice snorted. "Hardly. I just found Ralphie a little…secretive and checked him out carefully, a long time ago."

"He thought I was hiding that I was gay," Ralph said flatly.

"He's not," Maurice reassured, though if the kiss had been any indicator, I didn't need the confirmation. "However, what he *is* is Minion Target Number One. As I see you realized."

"Why are they trying to kill Ralph now?"

This time everyone in the room gave me the "really?" look. "I don't know," Sexy Cindy said, sarcasm overly evident. "Maybe it's because the dude's finally gotten you to look at him as more than an annoyance?" I couldn't argue. Ralph's arms were still around me and I hadn't exactly let go of him, either.

"Could we have maybe one minute alone?" Ralph asked. "Perhaps while everyone else cleans up the dead lesser minion?"

"Not lesser," Merc said quietly. "I think we just offed Enepsigos."

The room was quiet. She'd been very powerful, not up to the Three A's level, but close. "Uh, yay team."

"Thanks, Vic," L.K. said with a morose chuckle.

"You know what this means?"

"We're really popular?"

"There's a convergence point open," Maurice said. "We'll advise the Count while you two get your situation taken care of." I opened my mouth but he put his hand up. "It wasn't a guess. I'm here because there's a convergence point open. Three guesses which one and the first two don't count. Beings are advised. Trust me when I say you two getting your one minute of requested alone time is probably a good use of time and leave it at that." He spun on his heel and flounced out.

The others followed him, taking the dead body and severed wings and head with them.

Ralph sighed. "Back in action."

"Not you. You need to rest and get well."

He stroked my hair and the side of my face. "I am well. And I'm also not letting you face all of this without me."

I thought about all the grandstanding he'd done with me over the years. Not grandstanding, though, not really. He'd spent all this time trying to protect me, because it was his job and because he'd fallen in love with that job.

"I know this is hard for you," Ralph said softly, still stroking my hair. "And with what just happened with Wagner," he snarled the name, "I'm sure you're confused and not really ready for a relationship with anyone, let alone me." He closed his eyes. "I just want to know if, after this is over, you think you might still be open to a date, or even going steady."

"You heard me?"

He opened his eyes. "Yeah. I heard you talking -- to someone else and to me. I couldn't answer, even though I wanted to. So I had to struggle to get to you. According to the doctors, if I hadn't woken up when I did I'd have dusted." Ralph gave me a half-smile. "You know what they say about hearing the voice of someone you --" He stopped talking and smiling and looked down. "Well, you know." He let go of me and headed for the door.

"You really are a dork, you know."

Ralph's shoulders slumped. "Yeah, I know."

"I mean, you have the girl all ready to burst into tears and tell you how sorry she is that she was an unobservant idiot and how much she wants you to hold her and do that growl thing again, let alone that kiss thing again. And instead of taking advantage of the moment, you decide to trot off. Did you date at *all* before I met you?"

He spun around. "Not really, no."

"It shows." He stood there, looking very unsure and also, I was happy to realize, really cute. Like a big puppy who wasn't sure if he was going to get swatted or loved on. Clearly, I was going to have to help. "Ralph, this is the part where you kiss me again."

He brightened up. "Really?"

I couldn't help it -- I laughed. "Come closer and find out."

Chapter 63

Our incredibly hot make-out session was interrupted by Sexy Cindy. "Maurice says to stop slobbering on each other because we need you two, now. Exact quote, by the way. If it were me, I'd let you two go at it."

Ralph and I separated. "Fine, fine. But Ralph has to stay here."

She shook her head. "Nope. Maurice got him cleared. The doctors want him under observation, so he has to stay in a full team, no solo work. Otherwise, good to go."

"Our kind heals fast," Ralph reminded me.

"True. I just don't want you to get hurt again." My voice was back to almost-whining.

Ralph hugged me tightly. "We'll be fine. A pack together can never be defeated."

I didn't make any sarcastic comment and I wondered at myself. His outlook, while still a little militant, made sense now. And I felt safer next to him.

Normally I'd have been in a funk over what had happened with Jack and hesitant about getting involved with Ralph for a variety of justifiable reasons. But I'd made the fastest mating switch of my entire existence, thanks to Jack actually being evil incarnate, and I still wasn't having any problems with it. And if it would make the horrific ick factor about having been intimate with what was at least a part of my biological father fade away sooner as opposed to later, so much the better.

"You got a big pack, if they don't all have to have four legs," Sexy Cindy said. She gave me a wry grin. "Told you he was gonna be worth it."

"You did. Good insight. Who's with us besides you?"

"Freddy, Merc, L.K., pretty much everyone else from earlier." She gave me a long look, then stuck her head out the door. "Boys!" Freddy, Merc and L.K. arrived. "You three take Ralph back to Maurice. We girls'll be along as soon as we clean up a little."

No one argued. Either Sexy Cindy was really gaining some on-the-job authority, or I looked like hell.

The males trooped out. "Okay, how bad do I look?"

Sexy Cindy shook her head. "You look okay. I mean, brush your hair and straighten your clothes, but otherwise, you're fine. You and Ralph seem all loved up. You sure you're okay?"

I considered lying, but Amanda wasn't here and I needed someone to talk to. Besides, I probably wouldn't fool Sexy Cindy either. "I think I am, but let's be honest, I'm not totally sure. I've been thinking about it a lot. I feel completely out of love with Jack and more than grossed-out by the whole experience. I wanted to give Ralph a chance, even before I saw him in human form, and it feels natural and right to be with him like this. But, Adversary or not, beyond-gross familial relationship or not, I was so in love with Jack...."

"What you thought was Jack."

"Ralph thinks he was a sleeper. He's probably right. But that means I didn't just fall in love with Jack's exterior, I had to have fallen in love with at least a part of *him*. So, the part I fell in love with was likely more Jack than Adversary." I considered Jack without Adversary parts. "Of course, he was screwing Susan the day dispatcher, and as far as I can tell, planned to keep on doing it even while professing undying love to me."

She snorted. "Could be a good reason why you're not losing it."

I shook my head. "Maybe, but still, even though he wasn't cheating on me with another being, Jude did have a mistress -- saving the planes of existence. But when I broke up with him I couldn't consider dating for close to a decade. It was easier with Ken."

"You were in love with Jude, and you weren't in love with Ken." Statement, not question.

"Yeah, I suppose. But I thought I was in love with Ken."

"Why didn't it work for you?"

I thought about it. "He was too perfect. He never minded that I wasn't as perfect as he was, but I felt...inadequate, I guess."

She chuckled. "He told me you dumped him and he was really crushed because he couldn't figure out what he'd done wrong. He went out of his way to be perfect, from what he said."

"Thanks, 'cause I don't feel bad enough."

"Oh, he's over it. He realized you two weren't really going to work out, and he's relieved you're still close friends. Jude wasn't perfect, was he?"

I controlled the snort. "No. He's awesome, but not perfect. He'd be the first one to tell you that, too."

"Flaws are interesting. Ken's realizing that, I think."

"How so?"

She giggled. "He told me he's hemoglobin-intolerant."

Ken had bad reactions to drinking blood? Who knew? Well, Sexy Cindy, apparently. A thought waved its tail. "Are you two becoming an item?"

She shrugged. "Maybe, if we all survive this. He

feels real bad for messing me and Freddy up, undead-wise, so he's spent a lot of time apologizing. More to me than to Freddy."

I looked at her carefully. "You like Freddy, too, don't you?"

"Yeah. He always treated me like I was more than a whore, you know?"

"Because you always were more than a whore."

"But I didn't know that." She looked down. "This is gonna sound stupid, I think. But thank you."

"Uh, for what?"

She looked up. "For also seeing me as more than a whore."

I shook my head. "Everyone gets a fresh start, once they undie."

"Girl, you knew me as a human, okay? Maybe Ken and the others, they look at me clean. But you're a cop, and I was a street hooker, and you knew me that way for a good long time. But you still listened to me and let me back you up, and I don't think any other being would have done that."

"Well, we'll never know. But for what it's worth, if I'd known how smart you were back when you were a living human, I'd have dragged you off the streets and into some sort of hooker-rehab."

"I'd have fought it," she said flatly. Then she grinned. "But not any more. I like being a sorta-cop."

"You're good at it, so I'm relieved you're not wishing you were safely tucked away at the University."

"Nah, I like kicking butt and taking names."

"It's addictive, isn't it? So, before we hug and sing 'We Are the Undead World', you want to give me your thoughts about my twisted love life, just in case I've missed something? Like that I'm *not* handling it well and will fall apart at the worst possible time?"

"Sure." She laughed. "If we ignore the whole 'he's really the Adversary' thing and your suspicions about him sleeping around -- which he was, but you didn't know that when it mattered -- Jack was too perfect. He was almost like Ken, only Ken's got real flaws, he just knows how to hide them well. But Jack was made to be perfect for you, and that made him actually the wrong guy."

"Somewhere there was logic in that explanation, but I've missed it."

She shook her head. "Girl, you're gonna have to trust me. Maurice thinks if you'd seen Ralph in human form years ago you two would already be married."

"Married seems a little fast and extreme." Only, in a way, it didn't. I considered checking myself for fever.

"Right. As if you're determined to be single forever? Face it, you saw the dude without fur and started drooling. No argument there, either. He's hot."

"Jack was more handsome." Jack was more everything. I didn't care any more, but facts were facts.

"Maybe. Ralph's a lot more…real."

And per Nurse Nancy, well-endowed. And Ralph not only was a great kisser, but not even Jack had done that growl thing. My breathing got heavier just thinking about the growl-thing.

"So you don't think I'm rebounding, or rebounding stupidly or dangerously?"

"Nope. I think you're doing so good because Jack was wrong for you and Ralph is right. But I think the bad guys are gonna try to play Jack against Ralph, maybe even against Ken and Jude, to get you."

"Wonderful."

We did a fast straighten of the room, just to show willing and pretend we hadn't been spending time on girl talk. I managed to make myself look somewhat presentable, then we caught up with the others.

Ralph was there, flanked by Maurice, Amanda and Ken. I relaxed a little and it was a shock -- I hadn't realized I'd been worried about his safety, but clearly I had. I looked around -- Ken and I were still the highest ranking officers. Unless, of course, Ralph ranked higher, which was a real possibility.

"What're your orders, Vic?" Ralph asked, as if he was reading my mind. I wondered if he was. It wasn't really a werewolf trait, but instincts were so strong in our race that he might just be reading my smell.

It dawned on me that he was still in human form. "You're going to go out without paws on?"

"The doctors want me remaining in human form for a while." He sounded evasive and I decided to have the rest of this particular conversation in private.

"Okay. I'd like fast, high-level updates. What've we got?"

Ken pulled out a list. It looked like a long list. Lucky us. He sighed. "Maybe you want to sit down."

Chapter 64

I chose to lean against a nearby wall. "Can't wait."

"No," Ken agreed. "We can't."

He took a deep breath but before he could say anything I remembered something. Something important. Something important that I'd left behind. "Oh, no. The bag!" I didn't wait. I turned wolf, turned tail, and ran, as fast as I could.

Wolves can run fast to begin with, but werewolves are faster. I left the shouting far behind me in short order. However, I wasn't alone.

"What are you doing?" Ralph was panting a little, but he was right next to me.

"What are *you* doing? You weren't supposed to change, per the doctors."

"You're not supposed to act insane and then race off without warning or backup."

"Whatever." I hadn't seen that memo.

"What are we doing and why?"

"I'm going after the stuff we took from Cotton's pawn shop. The things that Tomio left and Jack selected. I just hope we're not too late." I sped up. Jack might have forgotten them, too, what with all that had been going on, but if it had dawned on me, then it was likely to have dawned on him. So the only thing our side had going for it was that he might not have realized where the bag of stuff had ended up.

As we ran like Hell was on our tails, I filled Ralph in on what was in said bag. "Wonderful," he growled as we reached the OLOC. "So Gods and Monsters knows what is in the hands of the Prince's minions."

"Not yet. I hope." We raced alongside the moving sidewalk -- we were going faster than it could ever hope to move. Just before we reached the doorway I changed back to human. Ralph followed suit. Only, in his case, it was more like birthday suit. "Whoa!" I didn't know whether to look or not. But, you know, I looked. I mean, it was there, on full display. Full, impressive display.

"Whoa what?" It was cute, he was confused.

"You never told me you went commando. Back to wolf! Back to wolf!" I couldn't help it, I wasn't looking at his face. I was looking at his naked body. All of it, and then specifically one part of it.

"What? Why?"

"Ralph, the special werewolf suits, that you're not wearing? The ones that change with us so we're never butt-naked if we go human...that you're not wearing!"

I managed to wrench my eyes up. He was turning bright red. "They itch," he muttered.

"Poor baby. Back to wolf!"

"Sorry."

I snorted. "Trust me. You have *nothing* to apologize for. However, any straight women or gay men who see you like this will ensure that you're not spending any time fighting evil tonight, okay?" Nurse Nancy had *not* overstated Ralph's endowment. I was managing not to drool only because time was truly of the essence. Okay, maybe a little drool.

He shifted and I could breathe somewhat freely again. "Sorry." He sounded ready to kill himself.

"Ah, Ralph? Let's just say that next time you should listen to Maurice and let it go at that. I'm not repulsed or horrified. But we're in the middle of a situation, so now isn't the time for me to realize the fantasies are true and all. Let's get this handled, then get back to Enforcement Headquarters and get you some appropriate clothing."

"I didn't mean to flash you."

"Ralph, really. Apologize to me later. Like, after you go to human again but before you put on the special suit." My mind raced off and suggested Ralph change in my bedroom. I wrenched it back to the present. "Right now, though, we have to hurry."

I took off, Ralph next to me, rounded the corner to the parking lot and, to my relief, the unmarked sedan was there, seeming unmolested. I took a careful look around. If we were being watched, I couldn't tell.

"Sniff for bombs or whatever."

"Why me?" Ralph asked. "You can sniff, too, you know."

"Yeah, but you're all set up for it. Be Mommy's precious puppy and act like a K-9 cop."

"Why?"

"Because there are humans around and I don't know if we're being watched."

Ralph gave me a grumbling growl but trotted over and started sniffing. He wagged the "all clear" and I opened the driver's door. To my total lack of surprise, the keys weren't in the ignition. "Bite me."

"Happily, but I thought we were waiting for a better time."

"Ralph, you have hidden depths."

"Supposedly. Where's what we're looking for?"

"I'll get it. I was hoping to take this car with us, though."

"Why?"

I didn't have a great answer. Sentimental value. Prosaic City P.D. property. I didn't want Jack to get it. "I don't want Jack to get it."

"Remind me to run if we break up. Uh, are we

actually dating?"

"You are so cute. To think I've missed it all these years. I don't know, do that growl-thing again." He did. Didn't change a thing that he was in wolf form while doing it. I was ready to go, in any form requested. "Yeah, if we live through this, we're dating."

I popped the trunk and got out of the car. Ralph trotted around back with me. "You know, the growl-thing, as you call it, is part of the overall werewolf mating ritual and dates back to the first known werewolves --"

"Ralph, honey, did Maurice suggest this topic as the way to go in the 'getting to know you on an intimate level' chit-chat category?"

"No. He said to shut up."

"Listen to Maurice. He is your friend." I breathed a sigh of relief. The bag was right where I'd stuffed it. I pulled it out and took a quick look. Bunch of scrolls, whacked out pseudo-guitar, a book, a knife, bag of marbles, an ancient record player complete with vinyl only a desperate DJ could love? Check. Hideous little statue that still made me shudder? Double check. "It's all here." And someone needed to help me figure out what this stuff was for and why it was important. "Can you hotwire a car?"

"Yeah, but I have to go to human form to do it."

"Okay. Make it so." I went back to the driver's door and held it open.

"What part of I'll be naked didn't you catch?"

"None of it. I'll cover you, so to speak. Sure, I'll be staring at you the entire time, but I promise, I won't let anyone else see." I was kind of jealous that way.

"How would you manage that?"

"Big bag, I'll hover so I don't miss anything, and so

on. Hurry up, I want to miss the minions, if you know what I mean."

"I thought you said humans were around."

He had a point. "Okay. In boy!"

Ralph glared at me, but jumped into the car. "Now what?"

"Hunker down, do the change, hotwire the car. Really, are you sure you're Special Ops?" I got another glare as he did as requested. I got in, put the bag on the seat between us, and closed the door. "You know, you have a great butt."

"I'd be flattered if you were telling me this when I didn't have my face right by where everyone's feet have been."

"Why's that?"

"I can still smell him." The way he said "him" -- snarling and with fangs clearly bared -- I knew who he meant.

I sniffed. "I can too, but it's faint." I sniffed again. The scent was getting stronger. "Ralph, hurry up."

"I am, but why?"

"You're not smelling him from the car." I looked around but I couldn't spot where Jack was. However, the scent of him -- him mingled with the Adversary -- was getting stronger.

This being a police vehicle, it didn't have power windows. While Ralph did the slowest hotwire ever, I made sure they were all rolled up and I locked the doors. This was absolutely no protection against anything determined to get us, let alone a major minion, but, like hiding under the covers, it made me feel better.

Right when I was going to suggest running like crazy the car caught. I flipped it into reverse so fast

Ralph's head slammed into my lap. "Go to wolf form."
It was all I could do to keep both hands on the wheel.
That growl-thing was worth its sound in gold. Plus he
had cool hair. And a truly awesome butt. But I needed
my eyes on the road.

Ralph grumbled as our tires screeched and I got us
out of there. I looked in the rearview mirror and saw a
big SUV pull around the corner just before I turned a
different corner. "I think they saw us."

"I hope they didn't see me naked."

"Don't whine to me. You're the one who's gone
commando all these centuries."

"It's not funny." He nudged the bag with a paw.
"What are these things?"

"No idea. At all. But we're going to go where I
hope someone can figure them out."

"Enforcement Headquarters?"

"Despite your needing an official, itchy, werewolf
uniform, no. I don't think we'll find who we need
there."

"Sanctuary Center?"

"Much as I'd like the comfort of seeing Jude, no. I
think we're going to be there soon enough. No, we
need those beings who live to figure things out."

Ralph heaved the big canine sigh. "And we
couldn't get there by going through Necropolis?"

"No. I think we need to get there through the
Estates."

"Vic, that's crazy. The minions are running the
Estates. Us sliding to the University from there means
any one of them could get these things from us. You
know, whatever these things are."

I hit my wrist-com. "Monty."

"Here Vic. What's up? Where are you and Ralph?

Why did you run off like a rabid dog?"

"Only the canine side of the undead house gets to make the dog-jokes in times of great stress and danger, Monty."

"Sorry. What's going on?"

"I need Dirt Corps, in a very real and very immediate way."

Monty and Ralph spoke together. "Why?"

"Because we're going to war."

Chapter 65

"You're kidding," Monty said. He sounded like he wasn't totally sure, either way.

"Sort of yes, sort of no. I really want the other side to *think* we're going to war, how about that?"

"And you talk about me grandstanding," Ralph muttered.

"Thanks to Sexy Cindy and your impressiveness from the other day, I now think of it as you being heroic and brave and all that."

"I'll take it."

"I would," Monty agreed. "But, Vic, while Dirt Corps always lies ready, do you think the minions are going to believe we're going to war if they show up with you?"

"I think the minions are very clear on the idea of 'cannon fodder'. Let them raise their evil dead to stop our good guys, okay? Seriously, I have a plan."

"Not that I know what it is," Ralph mentioned.

"I need to run this by the Count."

"Monty, we don't have time. The Count loves how I think on my paws. Just do it, okay? I need Dirt Corps to go to the Estates. They're cover for us to get to the University."

"Why don't you just go through Necropolis?"

"You know, I asked that, too," Ralph said. "I still don't know why, and I'm in the car with her. All things considered, could you send some kind of backup? I'm not feeling confident we're going to survive the drive, let alone any kind of fight."

"You wound me."

"No, I realize why Wagner always drove." Ralph yelped. "I think we're supposed to avoid hitting things like fire hydrants."

"I didn't hit it."

"Only by the grace of the Gods and Monsters."

"I think I liked you better when you just made sad puppy eyes at me."

"I'll keep it in mind."

Monty coughed. "Are we through? Can I go now? Or do I have to listen to you two catch up on two centuries worth of romantic banter?"

"And here I always thought you had romance in your soul."

"Vic, if you want to go ancient lich, I'm your being. However, I have an army to raise and all that jazz."

"Fine, fine. Keep in touch." My wrist-com went quiet. "We're being followed, you know. That's why I'm taking a circuitous route."

"You mean that's why you're flinging us around corners in a pattern that makes no sense to any being, alive or undead?"

"I really liked you better when you were completely undercover and pining. You talked smack a lot less."

"This from the queen of smack talk."

"Flattery will get you everywhere."

"Really? Hasn't worked for two hundred years."

"Bitter much?"

"No. Honestly, I'm worried."

"I have a plan."

"Vic, so do they. I promise you that. And their plan centers on you. On the plus side, they don't want you dusted."

"On the not plus side, they want you dusted with extreme prejudice." My stomach clenched. "Ralph, really, why? I mean, why do they want you specifically dead? Is it that you're the only werewolf left who refused to bow down to the fear?"

"Some of it's that, I'm sure. But I was listening, even while I was getting beaten up. They're really afraid of you mating."

"Then why didn't they try to dust Jude or Ken?"

"Mating," he said patiently. "As in having a litter, puppies, babies, offspring, propagation of the species. Am I getting through?"

"Yeah, yeah. Again, why no dusting of Jude and Ken?"

Ralph sighed. "I have to keep reminding myself that you never got the full werewolf indoctrination and also remind myself that you never listened to a word I said before tonight. While we can make a werewolf any time we want with our bite, werewolves can only reproduce genetically with another werewolf. And we have to be in wolf form to impregnate."

"Oh." I truly learned something new every day. Recently every hour. It was a good thing I was a being open to learning. "So, they don't want me mating with you?"

He coughed. "I think so. Might be with any werewolf, though."

"You're the only werewolf I know well enough to consider mating with." I thought about this. It was true. "Ralph? Why haven't I ever considered dating another werewolf? We have plenty around. And, by that token, why don't we have more werewolves working with us? We have plenty in Enforcement, but they never team with us. You're the only werewolf I've worked with in at least a century, maybe more."

Ralph was quiet for a few long moments. "The party line is that we need to have a variety of beings in teams. And it does make sense. I think we fight well in mixed teams."

"But?"

He sighed. "But a werewolf pack is unstoppable, and that's not just rhetoric. The Adversary couldn't claim you because Black Wolf and his pack arrived in time. Before you were made undead, that was what we werewolves did for the most part -- we wandered in packs to protect the newly formed undeads, save beings from being murdered or dusted by the Prince's minions, and so on."

"So, werewolves were the guerilla fighters."

"Yeah, we were. Most of us were in Special Ops. Black Wolf was one of the highest ranking officers in Special Ops. You joined Necropolis Enforcement, got your training, and then, if you were good enough, you moved up and over to Special Ops."

"I'm not in Special Ops." I tried not to sound disappointed.

"You're too important."

He said it like it was obvious. It was to me now, because of what had just happened, but the way Ralph said it, it was clear that it wasn't a new idea to him. "What am I supposed to do? I mean my overall role in the grand scheme?"

"I have no idea. I wish I did. No one knows, really. But the Adversary wanted you too badly, and you stood up against him when it looked like your only option was to die horrifically. You have no idea how rare that is in any being, let alone a human with no training. To stand against ultimate evil and choose your God even though horrible death awaits you otherwise. It's why more than just Yahweh watch over you."

This was news. "I know Usen was there, because of

Black Wolf. Is that what you mean?"

"I mean you're special to all the Gods and Monsters and they all watch over you to some degree. Why do you think Jude took such an interest in you? He knew you were special. I think he started out like I did -- staying close to protect you."

"I suppose." I let the obvious statements slide -- Jude and I would always be more than friends and have to avoid each other for eternity because of it. I hoped it wasn't going to turn out that way with Ralph. I also didn't want to talk about how two beings who were supposed to protect me had fallen in love with me, and vice versa, as I thought about it. I wasn't sure if I was in love with Ralph, but lust was by now a total given and realistically, the thought of him being dusted made me want to throw up in the same way the thought of Jude being dusted did. "Was Ken also on Guard Victoria duty?"

"No. Not that I know of, anyway." Ralph sighed. "He'll be a good replacement for the Count, but he still has years to go."

"Let's hope he gets them. Because I'm sure the Count is right after you on the minion's hit list."

"Most likely. Face it, they want all of Necropolis Enforcement neutralized."

"And yet, they had their best opportunity at the Little Church and they didn't take it." I was heading us on a fascinating tour of Prosaic City. Sadly, our pursuers weren't losing us. Trailing, yes, but not getting lost. Some days you just couldn't get rid of a tail.

"Right. Meaning they need something else before they're sure of victory."

I looked at the bag on the seat. "They need what

we're carrying."

Ralph nosed through the bag. He jerked back, growling -- and not the sexy let's-go-my-puppy-mamma growling, either.

"What is it?"

"No idea what's important about the other stuff," Ralph said, still growling. "But that figurine is the worst kind of bad news."

"The little statue? Yeah, it gave me the creeps every time I looked at it."

"It should. It's a representation of Adlet. I think it's *the* representation of Adlet."

"What is it with the Prince and minion names beginning with 'A'? Couldn't the supreme evil being get attached to any other letters?"

Ralph sighed. I got the impression our new relationship was going to involve a lot of sighing on his part. "Did you take any classes on undead history? Any at all?"

"I took the fun ones. And the ones that dealt with killing off minions. The Count said my scores were so good that I didn't have to take any courses I didn't want to in order to get onto Enforcement."

"Must be nice to be everyone's favorite."

"It doesn't suck. But that statue thing does. Who's Adlet?"

"Every species, living or undead, has its originators, and the good and bad sides always exist."

"Right. That's in the orientation class, Ralph. Everyone takes that one."

"But I have no proof you ever paid attention. Adlet was the eldest son of the first werewolves. He turned to the Prince before he was ten, but he married and mated before anyone realized it. Supposedly some of Adlet's blood runs in the veins of every werewolf. Which is technically true, since we all have the blood of the originals in us, and their blood created Adlet."

"I saw that statue. We don't look a thing like that." It looked like an inverted creature with a lot of its insides on the outside, loaded with claws and fangs. On my worst fur day, I didn't look like that.

"We don't, but the werewolves in Hell do. You just haven't seen too many."

"Have you?"

"A few. Our kind doesn't seem to survive well in the Depths. No idea why."

"Let's hope whatever the reason for that is, that it affects Jack."

Ralph jerked. "He was trying to mate with you." He was back to angry growling.

"I call that rape, Ralph. You know, me saying 'no' and him trying anyway? What you saved me from? I wasn't mating, I was trying to escape."

"I know. But the position he had you in, what he was saying, you were both in wolf form -- he must have been about to start when I showed up." Ralph sounded angrier than I'd ever heard. "He'd have raped and impregnated you. That's what they were waiting for, what they still want." His voice was shaking. I risked a fast look. His whole body was shaking -- from rage, I was pretty sure, at least based on his expression.

I reached out and stroked his head. "It's okay. You saved me, he didn't get what they wanted. And he never will."

"I'll dust before I let him touch you again."

My throat was tight. "I know. But...Ralph?"

"Yeah?"

"I don't want you to dust." I swallowed. "I don't

want you to leave me. Every werewolf I've ever cared about has...dusted." I managed to keep the tears from falling. "Because of me."

"No. Because of the Prince. Never let someone give you that guilt, Vic, not even me. Especially not me. I swore over two hundred years ago that I'd never let the Prince's side take you from us, and I meant it."

I wanted to stop the car and cuddle more than anything else. But we had more than one big SUV following us, we'd given Monty what I hoped was enough time, and we were too near to the Estates to try to confuse our followers any more.

Instead, I focused back on the job. "What did you mean by the statue being the representation of Adlet, heavy emphasis on 'the'?"

"You think that ring of fire's real Hellfire this time?" Ralph asked, a little nervously.

"No idea. Into living dangerously right now."

"I'm not big on going out in a blaze of glory, just for the record. Job description aside, I'm sort of hoping for the vast ancient age, surrounded by sobbing loved ones exit."

"Noted. Look at this option as wildly romantic and just go with it." We plowed through, no problems. Nice to know the illusion was still going on. Probably more than one illusion, I reminded myself.

"I don't find death romantic. Again for the record."

"Again, it's noted. My question?"

He sighed. Yeah, I was going to need to get used to hearing that. "Adlet was defeated centuries ago by Black Wolf and some of our more powerful witches and warlocks. Per the legends and Black Wolf himself, he and the others bound Adlet's spirit and turned it into a totem. It was lost in one of the big battles from centuries ago, before you were born, let alone undied."

"Well, someone found it." Interestingly, the SUVs weren't following us. It looked more like they were creating a road block. To keep what beings out was the question. But not the question of the moment.

"I'd like to know who."

"Tomio's the one who pawned it over to Cotton, for whatever that's worth. I'd like to know why."

"Oh, I know why." Again, Ralph was all matter-of-fact. I wondered if what he really wanted to do was lecture at the University and he was just making do by lecturing to me. Probably. My taste in men ran to the intellectual side of the house.

"Want to share?"

"You don't want to share your plan, I don't want to share the why. Equality."

"Let's try it this way. Until such time as someone higher up the chain of command shares with me that you rank higher, this is your impatient superior officer asking, Lieutenant Rogers."

"It's low to pull rank."

"It's also effective."

"Fine. The why is to destroy us, all werewolves, permanently. And this totem's the most effective way to do it."

Chapter 66

"Huh." I didn't know what else to say. But memory waved a paw. "You know, Cotton had all these things appraised. By Benny the Fence."

"Who's nowhere around here," Ralph mentioned.

Another memory reared its head. "Why was Bill Bennett, our dog-loving realtor, the only human not affected by whatever spell Hitler and the Three A's had cast over all the Estates?"

Ralph was quiet while I drove through the neighborhood. No one was out and about. It was night, but no lights were on.

"He didn't smell undead," Ralph said finally.

"Benny the Fence isn't an undead. He's a human who can see into the realms and who's managed to stay sane."

"Wouldn't he have looked and smelled like Benny the Fence to us? If that's what you're insinuating, I mean."

"Maybe. Maybe not. Nero's got a warlock pal. Who's to say Benny doesn't have a lot of them?"

There was one house with lights on. I pulled into the driveway and honked the horn. This was an instinct move and I didn't argue with it.

"What are you doing?"

"Either asking one of the bad guys to take a drive with us or saving the only sort of good guy still here."

Bill Bennett came out of his house cautiously. I'd known in my gut it was his but it was always nice to be right. "Yes?"

I rolled the window down a crack. "Hey, we met earlier, Sunday morning. I was in a better car. You petted my dog."

"Oh, the lady with the Russian wolfhound. Right."
He didn't get closer.

No time like the present to go for broke. "Benny,
you want out of this mess, or at least a ride with the
beings likely to protect you?"

He jerked and looked around, but not at me. He
stared at the car. "You a cop?"

"Detective Wolfe, Prosaic City P.D. Night Beat." I
paused. "And, to reassure, Agent Wolfe, Major,
Necropolis Enforcement."

He ran for the car and I just managed to unlock the
door before he flung it open and himself into the
backset. "By all the Gods and Monsters, get us out of
here!"

"Benny, welcome to the party, so to speak. Want to
fill us in on what's going on?"

"Yeah. But who's the dog?"

"Wolf," Ralph snapped. "I'm a wolf. A werewolf.
You work with us all the time and you can't recognize a
werewolf?"

"This is Ralph, he's with Enforcement, too. Now,
happy intros done, what's going on, from your
perspective?" I pulled out and considered. We had the
guy who could actually tell us what these things were.
Did I want to try to slide to the University, or did I
want to go with the more exciting choice?

"Something big. I don't know what."

"Why were you jogging on Sunday when everyone
else was mind-controlled to stay at home?"

"I have a spell blocker, pretty powerful one. Good
friend cast it on me. I didn't even realize there was
something going on until I got back and saw what had
happened to the Little Church."

"Is your good friend's name Hitler?"

"No!" Benny sounded shocked and outraged. "I may be a fence, but I don't consort with the major minions! Sure, I have to take merchandise from lesser minions, but they're just regular folks trying to make a living."

"Nice cover you have," Ralph snapped.

"I'm a realtor by day, fence by night. If you two are looking for a cozy love nest, I can fix you up, special deal for my friends in Necropolis Enforcement."

"Uh huh, I'm sure."

"No, really. You drove past it on the way up to my place. It's on the market, cheap."

Ralph and I exchanged a look, I turned the car around, and drove to Nero's place. "This it?"

"Yeah."

"No 'for sale' sign."

"This is the Estates. We don't do 'for sale' signs. That's what realtors are for."

"Who's living in it right now?"

Benny sighed. "Nero. I know, I know, he's bad news. But houses without tenants don't sell. Even if said tenants decorate hideously."

"What about Ishtrallum?"

"Oh, he doesn't know. His house is higher up on the hill. Besides, he's not home a lot. His business keeps him busy twenty-four-seven sometimes. And he'd be unhappy if he knew I'd let Nero stay in the house. You know how it is, the boss doesn't like the employee to look like he's doing as well or better."

"Currently I like Ishtrallum a lot more than Nero."

Benny snorted. "Who doesn't? But Nero had the money and all beings need shelter and the chance to earn a living."

"Nice," Ralph said with a growl. "But that doesn't

tell us who cast that spell on you."

"Or why you faked us out the other day."

"I didn't. I don't spend my time looking at the Enforcement duty rosters. You were a hot babe with a great-looking dog and an expensive car. Pardon me for giving it a shot on the personal and professional level."

"I knew you were petting me to butter her up," Ralph muttered.

"Actually, no. I really love dogs." I looked at him in the rearview mirror. He shrugged. "What can I say? I'm a normal guy with abnormal vision. It's a tough life sometimes, but it's never boring. Terrifying, yes, but not boring."

I sniffed. No lying. Fear, but he was right to be afraid, and I didn't pick up that the fear was directed towards us. One last question. "Why don't I recognize you? And why didn't you recognize me? I've been in your place before, the fence side of your house, I mean."

Benny leaned forward and examined me. "Years ago, right?"

"Yeah."

"Okay. Well, for me, I also have a spell that alters how I look when I'm fencing. It keeps me safer that way, and also means no human clientele will realize I'm also their realtor. For your part, it was at least a decade ago and you weren't the officer in charge. This Sunday you weren't in a place I'd ever associate with Enforcement, and you weren't talking about police business."

It made sense. I looked at Ralph out of the corner of my eye. "What do you think?"

Ralph sighed. "He's telling the truth."

"Of course I am!"

"Benny, that's a rarity for us right now. But, since you seem to be on the side of right, we have some things in the bag on the front seat that Cotton Mather said you appraised."

"Probably. I'm considered the top appraiser on at least three planes of existence."

"Super duper. Take a look-see and tell us what, exactly and in specific detail, we're carrying."

We were still in front of Nero's house. Well, the house Nero was claiming was his. I drummed my fingers on the steering wheel.

"Vic, why are we still here, burning time and gas, but not road?"

"I'm not sure where to go now."

"I thought you wanted to get to the University."

"I might." I looked over my shoulder at Benny who was rummaging through the bag, grunting, whistling, and muttering. "But if we have a reliable source -- and we think that we do -- we don't really need to go."

"What about getting these items into some sort of safe place?" Ralph asked. "I don't want them falling back into minion hands."

"You got that right," Benny said. "Good lord, and I mean that to cover all the options, but there's a lot of Armageddon in here." He looked at both of us. "And some nasty things for werewolves, too. You two are at risk just being in the same vicinity as this idol."

"Idol, totem, statue -- no matter what you call it, it's still worse than butt-ugly."

"It's also incredibly dangerous," Benny said. He shook his head. "I told Cotton to lock this away."

"Shocker alert, he didn't. However, at least it's in our possession now."

"It needs to be destroyed," Ralph snapped.

"No, no, no!" Benny seemed freaked by the idea. "You want to destroy all your race?"

"No, but you yourself said that thing could do it." Ralph growled. "What do you suggest we do with it?"

"It needs to be contained," Benny said, with forced patience clearly showing. "If you destroy it, it'll pull out all the were in the wolf, so to speak. You'll all lose your abilities to switch forms and be stuck in whatever form you happen to be in when the idol is destroyed."

Ralph and I exchanged another look. "You always stay in wolf, I'm usually in human."

He nodded. "No way to mate, ever." He growled again. "I loathe these beings."

"It gets better," Benny said. "Without the power from this idol, werewolves as a race would start weakening. Oh, not immediately, but over time."

"I thought it was evil."

"It is." Benny sighed. "Think about it."

"I mean, I thought whatshisname was contained and all that, and that he was the evil one."

"Adlet," Ralph said shortly. "I told you, what, five minutes ago?"

"Longer than that, but whatever."

"He *is* contained," Benny said. "However, this was a being who wanted all the werewolves under his control or dead. Legend has it that as he was overthrown he passed a curse, that if he was fully destroyed, he'd take the rest of the werewolves with him."

"That must be why Black Wolf chose a totem instead of complete annihilation."

"Most likely." Benny sighed. "We need to get this thing locked away where no minion can ever touch it. Same with most of these items. Singly they're horrific enough. Put together they could end everything tonight."

"What's with the bag of marbles?"

"Representation of every inhabited world in the known planes of existence. Destroy the marble --"

"Destroy the world. Got it."

"Right. Miss Wolfe, we need to get to someplace safe."

"There is no place safe, really. And call me Victoria or whatever nickname from that you like." I thought about this. There really wasn't a safe haven. It was going to come down to us protecting a big bag full of life-as-we-know-it ending items in whatever way we could. "They blocked us in here, but didn't follow. Why?"

"Who?" Benny asked.

"The minions trailing us," Ralph answered. "And I'd guess because they either knew where we were going and planned to meet us there, or there's something worse up here waiting for us."

I hit my wrist-com. "Monty, where's Dirt Corps, exactly?"

"Waiting for your signal to attack. No idea what they should be attacking, by the way."

"Me either. Makes it more fun. I'd like Dirt Corps to swarm randomly all over the Estates, then head to the convergence chasm, preferably leading as many minions away from the Estates as possible."

"Why?" This was asked by all three males within my hearing.

"Because I'd like us to be as alone as possible for a while."

"Is now really the time for you and Ralph to make that relationship commitment?"

"I hope not," Benny interjected. "Because I'm not in the mood to watch and I don't know who could be in the mood to actively participate at this precise time."

"You have company?" Monty asked.

"Benny the Fence. You okay with that?"

"Yes, always checked out as clean."

"I should hope so!" Benny sounded offended.

"Benny, I think we mentioned that we've had an eventful few days, filled with chaos, complicity and betrayal?"

"Fine, fine," he huffed. "But I still want to know why you're trying to send what sounded like protection and backup away from us."

"Because I want to get up close and personal with my God. Or at least, some of his representatives."

Chapter 67

Dirt Corps did as requested. As a variety of undeads swarmed all over the Estates, I had Benny open Nero's garage door so I could store our car. Then the three of us and our bag of evil goodies went into the house.

Ralph and I did a fast check for Nero or any other unsavory beings. We found nothing, literally.

"I think you're going to have to find another transient tenant," I said to Benny as we looked at the last room, a room as devoid of Nero's trappings as all the others were. He'd cleaned out his stuff and he'd done it fast.

"He must have come back here, after the incident at the Little Church," Ralph suggested.

"Maybe. Maybe he came here during the incident. He's a being big on creating havoc but he's also good at getting out of his own messes relatively unscathed."

"He must have used one big truck," Benny said. "He had a ton of junk last time I was here to check on things."

"It was all here the other day." Whenever that was. Oh, right. "Sunday."

"It's Tuesday night now. Plenty of time. Unless you all were watching the house."

I sighed. "No. We were watching other things."

Ralph leaned against me. "Stop it."

I stroked his head. "Okay. I'll try, anyway."

"You two actually want to be alone?" Benny asked. "I was serious, I'm not in the mood to watch."

"Yes, we'd love to be alone. Sadly, we've got that whole trying to avoid Armageddon thing going, so we'll hold it." Nero had left the larger furniture, so I could sit down on a couch. Ralph hopped up next to me and I leaned against him.

"I can't speak for your partner, but I'd like to have some idea of if I'm going to survive the night or not." Benny didn't sound like he was joking.

Neither Ralph nor I corrected Benny on the partner statement. "Okay, first, I need to call a couple of beings." And I needed to come up with a full plan. I had a sorta plan, but not a real one. Something was missing. I knew what was going on and roughly how it had been done, I was sure of it, but I needed one more piece of information -- I just didn't know what it was or how to find it.

Ralph groaned. "You do this all the time. You hate sharing."

"True." My wrist-com went live. "Merc, you there?"

"Right here, darling. What's shaking?"

"The worlds. Did Freddy ever get time to tell you and L.K. what the Estates advertising slogans were?"

"He did, and we've gone over them. You were right, they're a spell for sure. We aren't positive, but the goal seems to be to lull the human residents into a sort of stupor."

"That makes sense. Any analysis of who created it?"

"P.T.'s working on it. His first guess is Hitler, but he stressed that he wasn't sure by any means. Could just be someone imitating his style."

"Super. Can you and L.K. meet me at the Salvation Center? I think we're going to need beings who can counter spells."

"I'll bring along some support, then. Any suggestions?"

"Surprise me. Just make sure they're powerful."

"The Bard's been complaining that no one ever lets him do active service. Want him along?"

"Sure. If we don't do it right, we're all dusted or minions anyway."

"Love your sunny outlook, darling. Over but hardly out."

Ralph and Benny didn't look happy. "Why aren't you pulling in trained witches and warlocks for this?" Ralph didn't sound happy, either.

I rubbed my forehead. "You know as well as I do that the Count already has all of them working on counter spells. The few who showed up for the pre-Armageddon party are either hurt or back with the rest of their counterparts. They're our last line of defense, so I'm not going to ask any of them to go to the front lines if I can help it."

"Why Merc and L.K. then? Or Will?"

"Because Merc and L.K. are already deeply and willingly involved and both of them are really clear on the power of words. And we might as well have the best of the best with us, too, especially if he's antsy to get into the action."

"The Bard's more of a lover and talker than a fighter," Benny offered.

"Well, I'm hoping to have him focused on the talking side while the rest of us take on the fighting portions." I tapped my wrist-com again. "Agent W-W-One-Eight-One-Niner."

"Agent Wolfe, the formality, it's almost heart-stopping."

"Missed you, too, Count. Are Black Angels One and Two ready for action?"

"Yes, and impatient for it, as well."

"Good. Have them meet me up at the Little Church of the Country as soon as they can fly by."

"Any other directions?"

"Tell them to listen intently. They'll know what to do when."

"Does your love of mystery drive Agent Rogers mad with desire or merely to distraction?"

"Both. Count, I have no idea what she's doing, just for the record."

"Agent Wolfe keeps us all on our toes, doesn't she? Anything else before I rush to comply with your demands?"

"Yeah. Please call the Chief and tell him I need a lot of black and whites standing ready. If I'm right, we're going to need the police escort."

"And if you're wrong?"

"Really, how often am I wrong?" Ralph started choking. "I mean about things like this?" Ralph was up to gagging. He even rolled on his back, paws waving in the air. "Must dash, I need to put Ralph out of his misery."

"Thank you for making eternity go by so quickly, Agent Wolfe."

I rammed my elbow into Ralph's side. "You're not funny."

He righted himself, doing that canine grin thing that looks so cute. "You were hilarious. 'How often am I wrong?' Wow. I'm sorry only Benny and the Count got to hear that one."

"You know, this kind of attitude doesn't get you past a hearty handshake."

Ralph put up his paw. "I'll risk it."

I ignored the paw, stood up, and took a look outside. I could see the last vestiges of Dirt Corps heading back down the hill. There were SUV's following them, more than I'd seen following us, so hopefully my subterfuge had worked. "Let's get back into the car. Ralph, think you can hotwire it faster this time?"

"No," he said flatly. "I'm not hotwiring it at all."

I stared at him. "Oh. Right." I looked to Benny. "Know how to hotwire an unmarked police car?"

"If I say yes will I be arrested?"

"Only if you say yes and then can't actually do it."

"Then, let's go with 'we'll see'."

We went back to the garage. I opened the door and listened.

"Sounds like pursuit is going away from us," Ralph said softly.

"I agree. Turn your ears up, though."

We both strained. "It's faint," Ralph said finally. "But I think you're right -- there are beings of some kind up at the Little Church. But why?"

The car started and we piled in. "See, this is why I don't like to explain until we're moving." And because I still wasn't sure. But cops never admit when they're not sure, it's bad for the longevity. "There was a bigger why that I've been trying to solve."

"What was that? I thought we'd figured out the Adversary's plans."

"I think we have. But the bigger why is simply this -- how did the Three A's get past Jude? He's one of the strongest angels in existence, and he's on the convergence chasm solely to keep them out. So, why didn't he even know they were around?"

"You think he's a traitor?" The way Ralph asked, he wanted to hear me say "no".

"No." It was nice to see Ralph and Benny both

relax. "I think there was a powerful spell put in place that blocked Jude's abilities."

"Come on," Benny said. "You're talking Judas, right? And that means his best friend, too, since they work together more often than not." Ralph and I both turned and looked at him over our shoulders. "What? I told you I had a good friend who's pretty powerful. So he let some things slip out of school. So what? As has been amply stated, I'm on your side."

"Who is your good buddy the warlock? You never told us."

Benny sighed. "You just talked to him."

"The Count? He's not a warlock!"

"No." Benny grinned. "You forget -- liches are dead spell-casters."

"Monty? Monty's your buddy?" I looked at Ralph. "Every hour, it's new information. Am I the most uninformed being in all of Enforcement?"

Ralph shook his head. "Didn't occur me, either." He eyed Benny. "But I've also never seen any lich cast a spell…in over four hundred years."

"You mean you don't know that they're casting them," Benny said. "Look, kids, liches are powerful. But the ones on our side are smart enough to lay low." He patted our shoulders. "You want me to tell you about the others?"

"What others? And why do you know so much more about the undead than we do?"

He shrugged. "Watch the road. I'm in real estate and I'm a fence. It pays to do your research in both cases. So, I researched. And by the others, I mean those undeads who have additional talents, more than their undead race would insinuate."

I groaned. "Okay, this is information for another

time, unless it helps us now."

"Well, you already talked to one of them, if I'm not mistaken."

I thought about it. "Merc and L.K. are also warlocks? As well as wraiths?"

"Let's say they're continuing to cast the same kinds of spells as undeads as they did as living rock stars, and leave it at that. The Bard, too."

Ralph heaved the big canine sigh. "Are we the only undeads who don't do all the fancy spell-casting?"

"Oh, any being can learn it," Benny said cheerfully. "You just have to have an open mind and a willingness to experiment."

"You a spell-caster, too?" Why not? Maybe everyone did it other than me and Ralph. It'd been that kind of week.

Benny snorted. "Hardly. But, as I said, if you want to be a good fence, you need to know what's coming through, what it does, what it's worth, who needs it, and who should be kept away from it."

"You know," I said to Ralph, "when this all started, I felt pretty competent."

"I know what you mean."

"So, you think someone cast a spell on Judas?"

"Benny, call him Jude, okay? It's easier." It also kept newer undeads of certain religious persuasions from attacking him before they understood just what his role in Yahweh's grand scheme had been. "But, yeah, I think so."

"I don't buy it," Ralph said. "Jude's too powerful not to notice."

"Agreed, over a long period of time. Only, I don't think it required a lot of time. A lot of effort, probably, but not time. It's like when Nero escaped when we were here before. Everyone else was focused elsewhere, he slipped off quietly, by the time we caught on, he was long enough gone you couldn't catch him."

"Of course, Wagner let Nero get away." Ralph wasn't trying to hide the snide.

"I'm sure. Now. But however it was done, my guess is that Jude was blocked just long enough to cast the spells that blocked him and let Abaddon in. Then blocked again when Slimy showed up, dragging Apollyon and the Adversary along with him. That's all it would take. Jude's focused on keeping them out. Once they're in, it's our job to spot and stop them."

"And we're doing *so* well."

"Why the sad dog face? We're alive, we're together, we have the bag of badness, and Benny the Know-It-All Fence. I think we're doing pretty well."

"Here's hoping that can-do attitude helps us when it matters," Benny muttered.

"No worries. We're about to find out."

Chapter 68

We reached the parking lot for the Little Church. It wasn't blocked, but it wasn't empty, either. There were a few nicer cars parked near the entrance. I pulled in next to what I was pretty sure was the S-Class we'd lifted. It was nice to have a semblance of confirmation that I was on the right scent.

We got out of the car, Benny clutching the bag of evil goodies. "What do I do if someone attacks me for this?" he whispered.

"Scream like a banshee, run like a werewolf, hold onto it like a miser."

"You're such a help and a comfort."

"I do my best for all citizens of Prosaic City and Necropolis."

Ralph sniffed. "How about for citizens of other cities and, I think, countries?" He sniffed again. "And these cars were at the cemetery the other day, at least some of them were."

More confirmation. No conclusion, but at least confirmation. "Well, let's just say that I think they're going to be relieved to see us and leave it at that." Honesty forced an addendum. "Or else they're going to all try to kill us. But, you know, either way, we're ready."

"We are?" Ralph didn't sound convinced.

"Yes. We have everything we need right here." I hoped.

We entered the Little Church quietly. It didn't look like anything had happened. "It was practically destroyed when I saw it Sunday," Benny whispered in my ear.

"Some spells work faster than others," I whispered

back.

What the church wasn't was empty. It was hardly filled to capacity, but there were at least a couple dozen people here. Which fit with the number of cars in the parking lot.

"Most of these were at the cemetery the other day, for that funeral," Ralph said, sniffing up a storm.

"Isn't that Reverend 'Jeremiah' Johnson?" Benny asked, nodding towards the good-looking man in the center of the group. "He must be sick about what's gone on in his church."

The base of my tail started to vibrate. "Benny, is he a good man or a charlatan?"

"Actually, he's a good one. I know, hard to believe. But he *does* believe and he wants to help people. Very decent. Pity about his son."

The base of my tail shared that it loved Benny and wanted to keep him around forever. "I know how they did it."

"How who did what?" Ralph asked.

I didn't answer. I was too busy looking for a minion. Of any kind. Only, none were in evidence. I considered the possibility that this was a trap -- the possibility was high. Then again, we didn't have a lot else to work with. Because if I didn't get the beings responsible for the spell that had blocked Jude onto our side, pronto, we were probably going to lose.

There were two distinct groups of people in this church -- those who clearly spent their lives preaching the Word in one way or another and what I was about a hundred percent sure were our favorite group of deaders' nearest and reasonably dearest. They were divided, with the Right Reverend and his wife literally bridging the gap.

The humans were involved in what seemed like an animated conversation on both sides, but they noticed us, finally. A man dressed in what I was pretty sure were African ceremonial religious robes nudged Reverend Johnson and he gave us his attention. No toothy smile, though. None of the humans looked happy.

"Can we help you?" Johnson asked.

I strode forward, Ralph trotting next to me, Benny scurrying behind. "Detective Wolfe, Prosaic City P.D. I'd like to ask you some questions."

The humans all looked at each other. Clearly, questions were not on tonight's church social agenda. "What about?" Johnson asked. "And why do you have a...dog...in here?"

"K9 unit. He's trained to sniff out drugs, bombs and illegal immigrants." Ralph started sniffing all the attendees. "Good boy. So, Anthony Tomio, how many of you know him? Oh, and protestations that you've never heard the name will be met by some nasty police brutality."

"Brutality?" Johnson asked.

"I believe in truth in advertising. Now, show of hands, how many here know or have at least met Tomio?" I ensured my voice didn't sound kindly and Ralph put on the low-level growl that all canines can do that shares said canine is considering the benefits of going Cujo.

Led by the few kids in attendance, all those in the relatives crowd raised their hands, some quite slowly. Seeing this caused a goodly portion of the religious leaders' paws to go into the air, the Right Reverend and his wife included. With typical group behavior, finally all arms were raised. Minus one.

The one individual who didn't raise a limb was small and mousy-looking, dressed like an old-fashioned Anglican minister. "I'm afraid I don't know who you're referring to," he said nervously as I gave him the full benefit of my attention.

This time I didn't even need to give an under-the-breath command. Ralph was on him faster than a starving dog on a week-dead possum. The little guy shrieked and the humans started to make a fuss.

"Humans -- back off!" I barked, literally. I was louder that way.

The "little man" changed fast. He was still little, but a lot more powerful. I heard one of the women shriek. "He looks like Adolph Hitler!"

Ralph and Hitler boiled around each other. Ralph was doing serious damage, but Hitler was talking, and that wasn't good. I desperately wanted to get in there and help kick evil warlock butt, but I didn't think it was wise to leave Benny and the special bag unprotected.

Happily for all, Black Angels One and Two deigned to take an interest. There was a flurry of wings and then Ralph jumped back and out of the fray. He scrambled back to me and Benny. "That was gross. He tastes awful. Worse than the Adversary."

We both gagged. "I didn't think that was possible."

"Are they winning?" Benny asked nervously.

I turned back and watched them rend Hitler limb from limb. I heard him begging for mercy. Miriam laughed, a very harsh, terrifying laugh. The humans huddled closer together, both groups mingling out of fear.

"Why are they being so...horrible to him?" one of them asked.

Magdalena looked over her shoulder. "Lord, forgive them, for they know not what they do." Then she went back to the task at hand.

Ralph went to the woman who'd asked. "He actually *is* Adolph Hitler. And before they were angels, before they had a place in the pantheon of the religions of this world, they were Jews. Think about it." He looked around. "Anyone else with a stupid question?" There was a pleasant silence, if you didn't count the sounds Hitler was making.

Dusting a powerful minion isn't the same as dusting your average baddie on the street. As with fallen angels, warlocks require specific steps. We'd rarely had the time in the past. Yet Black Angels One and Two were well into the process and no other major minion, or even a minor minion, was on hand to try to stop them.

I went to Johnson. "Why did they decide to sacrifice him to us?"

Johnson looked blank. "I'm sorry?"

"The missing bodies," Miriam called. I really did idolize them, but they weren't the most communicative operatives out there.

However, I had most of my puzzle pieces put together and that one fit in nicely into one of the holes in the big picture. "As Ralph said, the being our best teams are destroying there is really Adolph Hitler. He's been the highest level warlock on the Prince's team since he died on the Earth Realm. The Prince is evil incarnate. You're all about to help bring Armageddon about, though I'll wager you either think you're stopping it or about to ascend in the Rapture. Which is it?"

Johnson shook his head. "We were warned that

evil demons would come and try to ruin God's plan."

"Right. They did. And you're working with them. You did some kind of prayer that blocked our agents and allowed some of the most evil of the Prince's minions onto this plane. And you did it at least twice. I want to know what that spell was."

Everyone was silent. Lots of foot shuffling and eye contact avoidance. Okay, it'd been a long week. "Fine. Ralph, Benny, we dust them all."

"What?" Johnson looked horrified. "You can't just kill us!"

"Can and will. If the Prince's side wins, we're all dusted or evil minions anyway. And despite the fact the bad guys showed you your loved ones, they're dead and they're not ascending to heaven, nor joining us on the undead realm."

"I don't believe you," Johnson said calmly. "The Devil has an attractive face and tells beguiling lies."

"That's nice. I'm not Satan. He's a cool guy. Not evil, just doing his job for Yahweh. That's your god's real name, by the way. I'd imagine he'd like you to cooperate. But here's the deal -- my soul belongs to him, and I'm charged with the destruction of any who would destroy all the planes of existence. You stand in the way of the safety of billions of souls, in this and a variety of other realms. So, good of the many versus good of the few. You pick."

"Don't bother talking to him." I turned to see Sexy Cindy and Freddy coming up behind us. "Dude doesn't see what's right in front of him." She went up to Johnson's wife. "But she does, don't you? You know why you didn't see your loser son, when they faked that resurrection?"

Mrs. Johnson shook her head. "They said...they

said you were dead. I asked after you because you'd always...been so kind."

"I am dead. I'm an undead, and damned proud of it. So's Freddy. Know why we're here and the others aren't? It's 'cause we had good souls. You know your son could never resurrect on the side of good, so you didn't question. But I saw him dusted, and it wasn't by our side, either."

Mrs. Johnson shook her head. "He just wanted to make us proud."

"No. He just wanted to hurt you."

The Johnsons both looked at me. "How can you say that?" Johnson asked.

"I'm a cop, you idiot. I've seen plenty like your son. And I had the rare privilege of talking to him, ad nauseum. He wants you two to rot in Hell. He helped set it up so that you would, too. If you don't help us now, no matter how good the rest of your lives have been, you'll have caused the destruction of all that's decent, and Yahweh and the other Gods and Monsters will ensure you burn in the Depths for eternity."

"Gerald, this...young lady was always decent to me when I visited Jerry." Mrs. Johnson touched Sexy Cindy's shoulder than looked at Freddy. "You were always polite and never begged."

"This is a compliment from the rich," Benny whispered to me. I realized I was growling.

I cleared my throat. "So, you're happily joined up with Adolf Hitler? I mean, really? How long have you been listening to him?"

"Months," Mrs. Johnson answered. "Mister Tomio introduced us. Said he was working with Jerry and the others to try to rehabilitate them."

"Why are you telling them anything?" Johnson

hissed. "They're evil!"

"No, they're not." Mrs. Johnson managed a weak smile. "I've seen you, your kind, well, kinds...all my life. Not as much when I was young, but when we moved here, all the time."

Interesting. "Are you crazy?"

She laughed. "No. I prayed to God for guidance. And...He showed me the way."

"What way was that?" I felt it was going to pay to ensure she was dealing with one of the Gods and Monsters, not the Prince.

Mrs. Johnson opened her mouth and then stood there, staring. We all turned to see what she was looking at. Martin, as it turned out, wings on full.

He gave us all a gentle, twinkling smile. "Helen, my dear, how delightful to see you, albeit under some quite awful conditions."

Mrs. Johnson's jaw snapped shut and she pointed to Martin. "He came to me. Before, I mean."

Martin did some extra twinkling. "I did indeed. Yahweh does like to provide the personal touch when it's truly necessary." He winked at me. "Now, let's finish off our easiest major minion kill of this century."

"It's either a trap, or they're really unhappy with his performance."

"I'd go with the latter, Victoria," Martin tossed over his shoulder as he went to help Black Angels One and Two finish off Hitler in fine, albeit rather horrific, style. Holy water does just terrible things to a major minion, especially when said minion has to swallow it.

Ralph cocked his head. "If it's punishment, then who made that decision? The Three A's are all powerful, but I've never heard of any of them being given the authority to destroy one of their peers."

This was quite true. Additionally, the humans --
religious leaders from all over the world -- had been
manipulated by Hitler for weeks. Undoubtedly more so
once Slimy had come through. Meaning they'd likely
been praying up a storm in their minds. Meaning that
any being could have come through. And I was pretty
certain which one had just joined the party.

"They aren't the ones who made the decision." I
looked at Johnson. "I want the spell, what you're all
calling a prayer, and I want it now. We have a
command performance you're making us late for."

Chapter 69

Fortunately, Martin felt it was acceptable to use the old angel influence to clear the heads of all the humans. This saved considerable time, though the angst level remained high. Nothing like finding out you've been helping the ultimate evil to put a damper on the moods of those who do religion as their life and livelihood.

We got the prayer out of them. It was well set-up, mentioning evil names all over the place, purportedly to send them away. Only it was sending them away from their normal planes of existence and inviting them to this one, while at the same time creating this aura of holiness around them. I was impressed.

"The Prince and company must have been more than extremely displeased with good ol' Hitler's performance, because that is one massively good spell, spoken as a non-practitioner."

Martin nodded. "We found the rest of the doppelgängers. All destroyed by angelic forces. Easily, I must admit."

"All subordinates of Hitler's?" I asked while Black Angels One and Two swept up Hitler's dust into a container of holy water. Tidy and smart.

"Yes. On the plus column, I believe we've finally destroyed what's left of the Third Reich."

"Better late than never." I was touchy about human wars. Because we weren't allowed in them. "Anyway, Martin, this is Benny the Fence, or, as they know him here, Bill Bennett, realtor. The bag he's clutching is filled with nastiness. Ergo, once we leave, I'd like to ensure that Benny remains in the most alert and nasty protective custody known to man, beast or undead."

"I'd like to mention that the nasty shouldn't be

focused on me," Benny added.

"Right. Benny good. All others bad."

"What are we going to do with the humans?" Ralph asked as Black Angel Two flanked Benny with the same expressions they used when they flanked Martin.

"That's why I asked for all the black and whites. We're taking them with us."

"Are you serious?" Ralph actually yelped.

"Do I look like I'm funning around?" I motioned to Johnson and, as she was insisting we call her, Helen. "We're going to leave our unmarked police car here, mostly because we don't have the keys and we're all tired of hotwiring it. I'm going to take a wild guess and ask if you had your car stolen the other day, only to find it in the church parking lot."

They both nodded. "You took it?" Johnson asked.

"All in the line of duty. We're taking it again. I just want to make a quick call, and then we're all piling into the luxury mobile. I'm driving." Johnson opened his mouth and I put up the hand. "It's not optional."

"I wish it was," Ralph muttered.

"Can I drive with Martin?" Benny asked. "Or really, anybody else?"

"Actually, no. The angels can fly. You and the bag I want up close and personal. You're coming with us. Trust me, there's plenty of room in that car."

"It was covered with animal fur," Johnson mentioned. "Does the city reimburse for auto detailing?"

I gave him a long look, turned into werewolf form, then wolf, then back to human. "Wanna ask again?"

"Not at all. I love animals!" Johnson seemed to realize his faux pas, possibly due to Ralph's growling.

"I mean undeads. Whatever you people are!"

"Beings. Beings with souls, just like you. Now that that's all cleared up and Hitler's ashes are all cleaned up, let's get moving."

Black Angel One ensured the rest of the humans got into their respective cars while I threw the P.D. a bone and checked in. "Darlene, how goes it?"

"Detective Wolfe! You're alive."

"Yes." Well, in that sense. "What have you got for me?"

"Every available squad car is waiting at the south entrance to the Estates. The Chief says he hopes you know what you're doing."

"Not as much as I do."

"Sorry about Detective Wagner." She sounded sympathetic but also a little angry.

"Ah, just what did you hear?"

"Variety of rumors. I'm sure the more lurid one is the closest to reality."

"Possibly."

I heard the radio band click and all the background noises disappear. "We're secured now, Detective Wolfe. The story around the precinct is that Wagner wooed you, suggested a polygamous relationship, and when you said no, he ran off with Susan from day dispatch."

"Wow, in a nutshell, accurate. In that very high-level, doesn't really get to the gist way, I mean."

"Per the Chief, Wagner tried to lure you to the Prince's side and if we're able to dust him, good, though chances are that you'll beat us to it."

"How long have you known?"

Darlene chuckled. "Oh, a while. I got it out of the Chief."

"How?" In my experience, no one got anything out of the Chief he didn't want to let out.

She cleared her throat. "Let's just say I see him in the off hours and let it go at that. For now, at any rate. From what we've heard, your time would be better spent stopping the forces of evil from destroying all the realms of existence."

"Succinctly put. Please advise the black and whites that I have about twenty cars, luxury through to POS. I want funeral procession, but the fastest funeral procession ever, and I don't want any of the civilian vehicles other than mine allowed out of police protection. Someone tries to make a break, shoot out the tires and handcuff anyone in the car, children included." I heard Cain sharing these instructions with the humans.

"How will the officers know which car is yours and so allowed to drive erratically and fly in the face of all the traffic laws?"

Geez, it wasn't like I was that bad a driver. "I'll be in a black S-Class. They'll recognize it, it was recently stolen and recovered."

"We do admire your style and dedication to the suggestion, versus the letter, of the rules and regulations, Detective Wolfe."

"I unlive to serve, and so forth. Oh, and Darlene?"

"Yes?"

"In case…well, we don't actually make it? I just wanted to say it's been a pleasure bantering with you all this time and, having just had the opportunity to compare you to the day shift, there is no dispatcher anywhere that's your equal. And I thought that before I hated Susan on a variety of personal levels, too."

"I appreciate the kudos, Detective. Same to you, in

that sense. I'll pass your thoughts along to the Chief, however I'd like to mention that we'd all prefer it if you succeeded. Just saying, and all."

"Thanks, Darlene. I needed that little bit extra pressure to turn into a diamond."

"Good. They're pretty much indestructible. Go with that." The radio went dead. I heard another click, and the standard background bands were live again.

I clicked to All-Band. "Guys and gals of the Night Beat, this is Detective Wolfe. We're all about to go hunting very bad things. I'd like you all to remember why you're on this particular shift in this particular town. I'd also like to remind you that what we do tonight will affect everyone we know and care about."

I took a deep breath and continued. "So, let's win one for the home team and all that jazz. Sure, most won't appreciate it and they'll whine about our destroying a little property or shooting some very bad things dead without reading them the shortest version of their rights. But in the long run, we don't do this for the congratulations or the adulation -- thankfully, right? No, we do it because we're cops. So, let's go do what we do best -- protect and serve...and kick bad guy butt." I hung up and went to the S-Class.

The Johnsons were in the backseat with Ralph in between them. Benny had shotgun. He gave me a weak look. "We drew lots. I lost."

"Good grief! I do not drive that badly!"

"You have my harness on, right?" Ralph asked Helen.

"Yes. We have a big dog and this keeps him nice and safe." She patted his head, then yanked her hand back. "Sorry."

"I'll let it slide." Ralph looked at Johnson.

"Seriously, buckle up. You'll be happy for it in about thirty seconds. You might want to close your eyes, too."

"How are the…angels protecting Mister Bennett if they aren't in the car with us?" Johnson asked as he put his seat belt on.

"They fly overhead, and we're all being watched over. Routine."

"I think that means they can save us before the car crash," Benny said.

"Ha ha, I am *so* not amused." I checked to make sure everyone else was ready to roll. "Which car are Freddy and Sexy Cindy in?"

"They went with Bobby's wife and kids. Since they know them. I think most of the alleyway relations are in that car. She's got a huge, extra-long Suburban, so they all fit as near as I could tell."

"Always nice to be with folks you're comfortable with during a high-speed chase. I hope someone's kicked Cindy's ex in the balls, though." I revved up the S-Class and ensured we squealed out of the parking lot. Hearing Johnson's gasp of horror was worth it. Not that he seemed a bad guy, even without Benny's endorsement. He was just a little on the stuffed shirt side for me.

We barreled down and out of the Estates, the other cars keeping up nicely. Hit the street and were joined by our police escort. There were a lot of cars on Night Beat. Night shifts were always more active in any city, and in Prosaic City it paid to have a car every half-mile. And they were all here.

They'd taken the wise precaution of clearing the fastest path to what was fast becoming my least favorite block in the entire city. Lights were flashing, but no sirens were going, which was a relief. Police sirens are hard on werewolf ears, and a whole fleet of them blaring creates the kind of pain that makes you dust yourself to get away from it.

"Do you have a plan, beyond running the major minions over with our mighty cars?" Ralph asked.

"I seriously liked you better all mopey and mooning. Yes, I have a plan." Sort of.

"Would you like to share said plan?" Johnson asked as we hit a bump and sailed through the air.

"Nice shocks on this baby. And, Johnson, you I've never liked, so really, button it unless you have something helpful to add."

"This is just like those movies with the chase scenes," Benny offered as we skidded around some corners. "Only we're inside the car. I think it's better if you're in the movie theater."

"You know, I could have left you huddling in your house, surrounded by the Servants of Evil. But no, I rescued you." Another bump, another flight, another reasonably comfortable landing.

"True. I didn't really have time to think it through, of course."

"You and the rest of us, Benny."

Helen cleared her throat. "Um, are you going to share your plan, Detective Wolfe?"

"Victoria. Or whatever nickname, and so forth. We're about to face the Big Evil Ones, you can feel free to be informal." I felt the rest of the car's occupants waiting. "I want to keep this car for future Necropolis Enforcement and Prosaic City P.D. undercover work."

"That's your plan?" Ralph barked.

"If you'd let me and Helen out here, and Mister Bennett as well, without crashing the car or killing us, I'll happily sign it over to you."

"Johnson, I heard you were Mister Personality from the pulpit. Why so negative now?" Did a fast rearview check -- all cars flying along behind us still. So, clearly, I wasn't driving so dangerously that the others, including Bobby's wife, in a Suburban loaded up with at least a dozen beings, couldn't keep up.

"Shutting up back here," Johnson said. "Carry on not telling us what you're planning."

We rounded another corner and once both right wheels were back on the ground I got a clear look ahead of us. Maurice hadn't been kidding. The convergence chasm was out of control. It was at least four times bigger than when we'd been here last and it glowed.

"That looks pretty," Helen said cheerfully.

"That's how Hell gets here."

"Oh. Then, that looks pretty evil." Helen seemed reasonably unfazed.

I did another fast rearview check. She seemed relaxed. "You seem to be handling this rather better than anyone else, other than myself."

She shrugged. "It's so nice to be able to say, 'see that?' and have someone else honestly say 'yes'."

Johnson reached across Ralph and took her hand. "You could have told me, you know. You didn't have to bear the burden alone."

"You had more than you needed already. And once Jerry went...bad, there didn't seem to be a point to mention your wife was sort of crazy only not really."

"I honestly hate to interrupt this, and I hope you two get to continue in a little while, but we're pretty much at the Evil Zone. Ready for my plan?"

"Yes!" Chorused by all four of them. Cool. I truly wished I had one, they were so eager for it.

I saw our troops. Interestingly, they were spread out on the side of the block that The Pleasure Palace, Killjoy's, and the Sanctuary Center were on. The Three A's were opposite them. Jack was there, separate from the Adversary. I didn't see any other major minions, but there were more fallen angels than I thought good for our health. They were all in the big parking lot.

I considered my meager options. Well, why not? We had a lot of cars to park, after all.

Chapter 70

"Vic, what are you doing?" Ralph asked as I aimed the S-Class at Jack. Pointedly at Jack.

"Parking. It's the good driver thing to do."

"That's your plan? Parking?" Ralph was barking. I was pretty sure sighing and the non-sexy growling weren't too far behind.

"Only part of it. Once we park, we're going to cut off their escape and attack from the rear."

"Their escape is into the chasm."

"We'll see."

Jack smirked and waved in that "come and get me" way and I pushed the pedal down hard. Yep, there was a little more the S-Class could give me. It leaped forward, a little faster than Jack had been expecting. We slammed into him and he went flying over the car.

I didn't pause. I knew he wasn't dead. Probably wasn't even hurt. However, I'd still enjoyed it.

The Adversary jumped in front of us. Ploughed through Dear Old Dad, too. He chose to cling to the car and bellow. "Hellion child! Have you come to join us?"

"Meet my father, one of the big baddies. We're estranged."

"Good for you," Johnson said.

I put the car into a spin which took a variety of fallen angels by surprise. Some jumped or flew out of the way, but there were a few satisfying bumps before we finally came to a halt.

The rest of our entourage followed our lead. I was particularly impressed with Bobby's wife. She aimed right for Apollyon and did a spin at the same time. I was pretty sure she wiped out at least one fallen from the weight of the loaded Suburban alone.

We waited until all our cars were parked, or at least close enough for government work. "Johnson, you're going to need to pray, but in a specific manner. No naming bad guy names, including the Devil or Satan or Lucifer. Especially not Lucifer. You need to pray for the Gods and Monsters to save us, do you understand?"

"No, not at all. However, I'm clear that, per Martin Luther, Father of the Reformation and Angel Superior, I'm to do what you say, period. What do I say, other than that?"

"Nothing. I want you and all the other religious types to say that phrase, and that phrase only. 'May the Gods and Monsters save us.' Got it?"

"Yes. Anything else?"

I turned and looked right at him. "Yes. Remember this -- when it comes down to it, it's just your soul against the Prince. You can't save anyone else if you aren't saved yourself. You, more than many others, know this. You need to remember it now. You've been used, so you've been tainted. They'll try to take you again. And no one can save you but you. Yahweh helps those who help themselves."

He nodded. "Got it." Johnson leaned over Ralph and kissed Helen. "You'll help with the others?"

"Of course." Helen released Ralph's harness. "We'll be fine, Gerald."

"Ralph, guard Benny. Benny, guard Ralph. You're both going to be targets, big time."

Ralph put his head next to mine. "You be careful. You're more of a target than I am now."

I nuzzled my face into his fur. "No worries. Just look at it as my side of the family being a bunch of back mountain wacko polygamists with scary religious views. I escaped the compound, they're unhappy about my career and romance choices, the arranged shotgun wedding didn't work out, and now I'm trying to run off with a long-haired militant."

He barked a laugh. "It's scary how accurate that assessment is."

"Any other suggestions?" Benny asked.

"No. But I do need one thing out of the bag of wonder." I took the bag and rummaged through it. "If I touch the totem, will that harm me or anyone else?"

"No, at least as far as I know." Benny sounded worried. "Let me stress that I don't know for sure."

I wrapped my hand around Adlet's image. It felt as icky as it looked. "Well, what's unlife without a little risk? Everyone ready?" Nods all around. "Great. Then let's go rock the baddest guys in the baddest part of town." I couldn't help it, I started humming "Bad, Bad Leroy Brown".

We all got out of the car. The rest of the civilian humans did the same. The Night Beat cops were already in typical standoff positions.

I stepped away from the car. Ralph and Benny, holding tight to the bag, flanked me, with Sexy Cindy and Freddy flanking them. "You guys aren't supposed to go to the front lines with me."

Sexy Cindy snorted. "Girl, as if. We came in with you, we go out with you." She put her hand on Ralph's head. "Like your dude says, a pack together can never be defeated."

"What she said." Benny smiled. "We survived the car ride. Clearly the Gods and Monsters are on our side."

"Hilarious. Freddy, Ralph, any comments?"

"Once more unto the breach, dear friends," Freddy said.

"Watch each other's backs, fight for right, and bite your enemy where it counts." Ralph looked up at me with the doggy grin on. "That was Black Wolf's favorite."

"Then it's good enough for me."

The Three A's were back in formation. I checked out their minion support aside from Jack again. It was still light. A little too light, all things considered. But that confirmed which being I was pretty sure was waiting to make an impressive entrance now that we were here to see it.

I thanked the Gods and Monsters I'd had Jude put the block in my mind. I also hoped Jude was monitoring my thoughts. The glow from the convergence chasm was so bright I could barely see the other side of the street, but after a little squinting and scanning I could just see him, in front of the Sanctuary Center.

But Jude wasn't who I was here to see. The Three A's and Jack weren't either. I took a deep breath and we sauntered over. "Yo, boys, how goes it in Evil Land?" I asked as we walked past them.

"You dare," Abaddon hissed.

"Yeah, I do. Because, when it comes down to it, it's me against the Prince." The glow from the chasm got brighter. I grinned. "Or, in this case, it's me against the Morning Star."

On cue, he rose up, like he was on a rotating platform, though I knew he wasn't standing on anything but air. The light radiated from him like he truly was a star fallen to Earth. Then he faced me and I saw Lucifer for the first time.

Unlike the other fallen angels, Lucifer was still beautiful to look at. I wondered how he both maintained that and wasn't an object of massive suspicion because of it in the Depths. He was, I had to admit, the most beautiful angel I'd ever seen.

He nodded to me. "Victoria." Nice voice. Seductive.

"Lucifer. Nice of you to join the party."

"My presence was...required." His eyes narrowed as he looked at the Three A's.

"Yeah, well, I'd like to suggest you take your flunkies and go back to the Depths. We've dusted Hitler and his cronies, so you're down a few, but you're a go-getter, and I know you'll find more. Just not here, and not now."

"That is not in our plan, Victoria, I'm sorry."

"Pity. It's in mine. Oh, want to hear the rest of my plan?"

"She's willing to tell the beings representing ultimate evil but not her partners?" Benny whispered to Ralph.

"Vic has her own style," Ralph replied in kind. "It's the kind of style that gives you ulcers, but it's a style, nonetheless."

The Three A's, Jack and my darling mother flanked Lucifer. They were all glaring at me. Lucifer wasn't. He was looking at me like I was an interesting creature, so far below him that concern wasn't an issue. He inclined his head. "Please."

"We're going to send you all back to the Depths of Hell, without any destruction of the planes of existence, without Armageddon...and without me."

He smiled. "We'll see."

The Adversary and Jack both moved towards me, in lock step, which was beyond nauseatingly freaky. But Lucifer put his hand up. "You've already failed me."

"Minor setback," Jack snarled.

"Utter failure," Lucifer replied. "I note who she's standing with. Let me emphasize the word 'with'."

Abaddon aimed his Hellfire bow at Ralph. "Not for long."

Lucifer sighed, reached out, and wrenched the bow from Abaddon's hands. "You and your partner have also failed." He looked around at the others. "In fact, I see nothing but failure as I look at all of you. A perfect plan, approved by the Prince himself, and yet you all managed to destroy it." He looked back to me. "I'm sure you're as disappointed in them as I am."

"Totally." I had no idea where Lucifer was going with this. For all I knew, he'd snapped and was on the other side of crazy. But playing along until an opening presented itself was something I'd learned to do a long time ago. "So, since the plan's all wrecked, why don't you all trundle along to plot another, better takeover bid, and we call it a night?"

"No, it cannot be that easy. You destroyed our warlock."

"You left him there as punishment and you know it."

Lucifer smiled slowly. "True. He assured us all was in readiness, that nothing had been left to chance." He pointed to Jack. "That you would do whatever he asked." Lucifer shrugged. "Clearly Hitler was wrong. He and his direct reports have failed the Prince constantly over the years. They will be no loss to his Great Army."

"You're not raising the Army of the Damned tonight, or any other night."

"What will you offer me in return if we do not?"

This was a good question. Pity I didn't have a good answer.

🐾 Chapter 71 🐾

I knew Lucifer had a plan, and that he expected me to figure out what it was so I could conveniently foil it and he could retreat with the rest of the minions. This whole thing had been his plan, after all. Set in motion centuries before, effective and terrifying, yet created to fail without blame resting on Lucifer himself.

I was pretty sure the Prince wasn't going to be appeased with the loss of the Three A's or Lucifer. I was willing to dust them -- well, the Three A's, Jack and my mother. My concern about what I'd do when face-to-face with Lucifer was coming true -- I didn't want to destroy him, I just wanted him to leave and take all the creeps with him.

"We want what he holds," the Adversary said, pointing to Benny.

"No can do, Pops, sorry."

"You will refer to me as Father."

"I'll refer to you as dust. I don't respect you and never will." I remembered what was in my hand. I looked at the Adversary and Jack. They were moving in unison, but they weren't joined. "It backfired."

"What?" Lucifer asked pleasantly.

"The plan to have me turn Jack into a werewolf." I thought about it. "Because of me. Because I won't join the Prince."

Jack snorted. "Why would you matter that much?"

"Oh, please. This from the guy created to be my own personal will-o'-the-wisp to lure me to the Depths of Hell? Clearly I'm important." I held up the totem of Adlet. "And I think this is why."

Apollyon made a sound of disgust. "That is your destruction, not ours."

"Not you and your partner's, no. But I think it's causing some problems for the Adversary. Werewolves are your weakness, aren't they, Daddy-o?"

"Hardly." The Adversary changed to resemble Big Harp. "You have no understanding, no vision."

"I also don't have a part of me infected with something deadly to me." I looked at Jack. "You're going to be destroyed. Not by me, but by your own, well, being. Because it can't join you in any more, but still feels the effects of your...infection."

"That's not true. Vic, you love being dramatic. There's nothing wrong with me. I'm stronger, faster, better."

"Yeah, uh huh. Show me how you walk as a wolf."

He growled. It was good, but it wasn't as good as his had been before. "Drop and do me, bitch."

Ralph growled, and his truly was frightening. I put my hand on him and did the low talking with no lips moving thing. "Down, boy. Sit, stay. You jump, you engage right now, they win."

Jack smirked. "We win anyway." So he had the werewolf hearing. Pity, but not the end of the world. I hoped.

"I don't think so." I shifted to wolf form. It was hard, but I could keep a hold of the statue in my paw. "Feel free to destroy this now."

My mother hissed. "You evil, wanton girl!"

"Oh, don't start with me." I looked to Lucifer. "See, here's the thing. I think that, if I attack them now, holding this, they die. I think if I don't attack them and they just go back into the Depths, they die. And I don't think the Prince wants to lose this particular Adversary, does he?"

Lucifer inclined his head. "This Adversary is

particularly…effective, yes."

"Yeah. So, while we're all here, first lines of defense all ready to go, let me point out a couple of things."

"Please do."

"First off, we have you surrounded. I know, I know, you're the all-powerful baddies and such. But we have a lot of soldiers, undead and human. Sure, some of them might turn, but not most. And some of them will die or dust, but not all of them, and you'll lose minions for sure, after having lost plenty already. Plus we have more firepower than you might be aware of." I sincerely hoped.

"Perhaps." Lucifer smiled. "Any other points?"

"Yep. We have all the people who Hitler conned into doing that nifty prayer that wasn't really a prayer back on our side. But, they were so effective, we have them praying for us."

"Really? What are they praying for?"

"You'll find out." I sincerely hoped. "Last point. I have this beyond-butt-ugly statue thing of Adlet and I'm not afraid to use it. If the rumors are true, it's not going to create any issues for me in the short term and who knows about the long term?"

"It will destroy your race," Lucifer said calmly.

"Worse than you all, the Adversary in particular, are already trying to?"

Lucifer shrugged. "Good point. But still…to be the destroyer of your race. Are you willing to bear that burden?"

I looked straight at him, right in his eyes. "If that's what it takes to keep the Prince in the Depths and the planes of existence as they should be, then by all the Gods and Monsters -- yes."

Lucifer nodded slowly. "Then…do what you must.

What you feel is right."

Jude said I always knew what to do in these situations. But I had no idea. The base of my tail wanted a word, however, and the word was "Susan". I broke eye contact with Lucifer and looked around. "Jack, where's your girlfriend?"

He grinned. "She was a lot more adaptable than you."

"You bit her?"

"Of course." He nodded towards my mother. "And joined her in. We like it better that way."

I looked and sure enough my mother shifted and there was a blonde chick who looked vaguely familiar standing there, smirking and looking like she'd won the Baby Daddy fight. She also, I realized without a lot of shock, resembled my mother. And they were both named Susan. How sweet. I managed to hold off on the gagging, but it was hard.

However, this brought up an interesting point. My mother had never, as far as I'd known, shared her soul. Which meant either she'd changed her mind now, always a possibility, or she and Susan were somehow sharing a body. This was also possible. Good undeads almost never tried this. It had been done, but only in the most extreme of emergencies, and you'd really better like the being you were sharing with, because if you co-joined too long, it was permanent. It was a safe bet Susan and my mother had been co-joined long enough for this to last for eternity. Or until I dusted them.

"So, you're infected, and you infected your host, your mate, and your host's mate. Wow, nice job, Jack." It was. I wasn't something the Jack Wagner I'd fallen in love with would have done, but it was clear I'd fallen in love with either the little part of him that was still good or I'd been fooled by the best. The base of my tail was betting on the latter.

But it also brought up an interesting situation. The Adversary was clearly having issues with the werewolf parts. And two beings sharing one body, and then sometimes wanting to be a werewolf, too, was more strain than I figured either my mother's mind or Susan's were prepared for.

So, if I left them alone and did nothing, they'd self-destruct over time. However, I was learning how Lucifer thought, and there was no way he would have planned that in as a possibility -- it wouldn't fly with the Prince and Lucifer had to make sure whatever he did had all the signs of working. I needed to figure out what my undercover counterpart expected me to do and actually do it. And fast.

I looked at the totem of Adlet in my hand. It was still hideous, but it looked different. I got the distinct feeling Adlet was not only truly trapped within it but also completely aware. So, what we were calling a statue or totem or whatever was really something else -- a cage.

Before I could do anything meaningful, I heard chanting. The humans were all repeating the prayer I'd given Johnson, police included. But there was sound from the other side of the street, where our forces were waiting. I strained.

"Double, double toil and trouble, fire burn, and caldron bubble." They were repeating it, over and over, just like the beings praying were. Clearly the Bard had taken charge.

I looked down. The convergence chasm was acting funny, and considering it was already off the scales in terms of normalcy, this was worth noting. It looked, I had to admit, like it was bubbling.

"Your team's into cheerleading," Jack said. "Not going to help."

I looked back and forth between him and my so-called parents. "Double, double. You've doubled yourselves up. Been a lot of toil and trouble. The fire burns below as the cauldron bubbles." Benny was right -- there were a lot more beings casting spells than I'd realized. Anyone could do it. Even me.

I shifted back to human form. "Vic, what are you doing?" Ralph sounded worried. I figured my next move wouldn't reassure.

I threw the statue of Adlet right towards Jack's head.

Chapter 72

The natural human and demon reaction when a projectile is heading towards them is to duck or catch it. Since most undeads had been human or demon, that instinct remained.

The natural werewolf reaction is to catch it in your mouth.

Experienced werewolves either ducked or turned into a form that could catch. But Jack wasn't experienced.

He also wasn't very good at reacting now. If we hadn't been in the Ultimate Undead Standoff, it would have been pretty comical to watch his body fight with itself. And because he didn't know whether he had hands or paws, he caught it in his mouth.

"Good boy!"

Jack managed to turn into human form and spat Adlet's totem into his hands. "How stupid are you?"

"I'm wondering that myself," I heard Benny mutter behind me.

"Adlet, got a deal for you!"

"He's dead," Jack said, derision clear.

"Adlet, there are four werewolves who just don't know what to do with themselves. They're all connected to the one who bit you -- and they're also all connected to the being who caged you, Black Wolf. I wonder -- if you drew their powers, could you break free of your bonds?"

"Vic, seriously, what are you doing?" Ralph hissed.

What I was doing now was praying. To Yahweh, to Usen, to all the Gods and Monsters. Because I could see Adlet's totem -- and it was moving on its own.

The totem wrenched out of Jack's hand and floated

in the air, high above Jack's head. "Destroy it!" Lucifer thundered.

It was small, and the minions were quite large, but I'd judged Adlet right -- he wanted the chance to get out of his cage.

There was another positive, of course. All the minions, major and minor, were now trying to catch or hit a small object that was, as near as I could tell, having fun being close to impossible *to* hit or catch.

I focused all my mental energy on one thought. Surely at least one of our angels was monitoring me, right? Jude, at least, should be. I also said it aloud, in that no-lips-moving undertone way, to save time. "Attack all but Lucifer now. Leave him to me."

Ralph lunged silently at Jack. I didn't think she heard me, but Sexy Cindy followed Ralph's lead and took the chick combo of my mother and Susan. Freddy, showing real guts or real insanity, or both, joined the fray and slammed into the Adversary. Abaddon and Apollyon looked like they were going to get a free ride, but then Dirt Corps arrived, Monty in the lead. They swarmed over the Three A's.

That was the frontal attack. The rear attack was everybody else.

Adlet was still bounding around in his cage, making things confusing and hard for the minions. Lucifer had given them a direct command, and that meant it was their prime objective. To make sure Lucifer couldn't give them another, smarter objective, I turned to werewolf form and jumped him.

I knocked him down -- a feint on his part I was sure, because he felt strong, stronger than the Adversary. We rolled around on the ground, but I didn't bite. We were in a rather intimate position when he reared up and locked eyes with mine. *Make it real. Try to kill me. I must try to kill you. Or we both die, and everything else with us.* He'd said it in my head, in a way I was pretty sure no other angel could have heard.

I reminded myself that, in the grand scheme of things, Lucifer was technically my superior officer. So, I chose to follow two centuries of training and do what the boss-man said. I lunged up and bit his throat. Hard.

As we flailed around, this time, fighting much harder and more realistically, I did get a glimpse of the rest of the activity. Mostly because Lucifer kicked me off him and it's easy to take in the scene when you're airborne.

Ralph and Jack were still going at it, though it looked like Ralph had the upper paw. I hoped this meant Adlet was taking my suggestion and draining the werewolf out of Jack. Sexy Cindy was beating the crap out of my mother, then Susan, then my mother. They kept changing on her, but they didn't seem clear on the fact that no regular white chick has a prayer against a really pissed off street hooker.

Hansel finished off a fallen angel and leaped onto Jack to give Ralph an assist. Gretel did the same and joined Sexy Cindy. Ken, Amanda and Maurice focused on the Adversary. The three of them were in full Nosferatu mode, and doing some damage. I really hoped this meant Adlet was doing the draining thing on not just Jack but the rest of my "extended family".

There was a risk Adlet would try to drain me, too. But, as with any other choice, if it saved all the planes of existence, I'd find a way to deal with it later. I was the only other being at risk, though -- Black Wolf's were-line had been wiped out with the exception of me. And if it was going to go on, I didn't want that to happen through the Prince's minions.

I landed back on Lucifer -- because he conveniently rolled in the way so I hit him, not street -- and had to turn my attention back to survival. He hadn't been joking -- he was fighting for real. I got onto his back and tried to shred his wings.

The chanting was still going on -- the humans weren't getting into the physical fighting, other than some of the cops, and clearly some of our troops were spending their time keeping the Bard's spell going.

A shriek worthy of any banshee cut through the air. But it had come from my mother. She dropped to the ground, moaning and rolling. I noted that the totem of Adlet was bigger. Not by a lot, but enough to notice.

It made sense, he'd drained the werewolf out of the newest and weakest option. Hopefully that meant Jack was next, because this had caused him to fight back harder than ever. Ralph went flying into the convergence chasm.

I didn't hesitate. I leaped off of Lucifer and raced over. Ralph had caught the lip of the chasm with his paws, but paws weren't great for holding onto something like this. I flung myself in a horizontal position and just managed to get my hands around his front legs as his grip slipped.

This was good, as Ralph wasn't plummeting into the Depths. It was bad, however, because I wasn't stronger or heavier than him, and we were now inching towards the Depths anyway.

"There's nothing for me to get a toehold on," Ralph panted. "Let go."

"No way."

"Vic, let go!" This was snarled.

Didn't work. "Nice try, but still no."

"Oh, don't worry," Jack said. I felt his feet straddle me. "I'll make her let go, how about that?"

"How about I show you what I do to guys who screw over my ex?" It wasn't Ken's voice, it was Jude's.

I managed to look over my shoulder to see Jude, wings on full. He grabbed Jack's head and yanked him backwards. This was nice, but Ralph and I were still sliding towards imminent doom.

"Vic, let me go."

"No. I can keep this up for hours. No."

I felt two hands grab my left ankle, then two more grab my right. "On three," Amanda shouted. "One, two, three!"

My legs wanted to come out of their sockets, but we flew backwards. Literally. We were in the air -- in an awkward position, but still, in the air. My right side was higher and steadier than my left. I risked a look. Sexy Cindy has the left side and while she was giving it her all, she still wasn't all that adept at flying.

"Drop us on Lucifer!"

They let go. Conveniently, we were right above him. I wasn't sure if they'd just been listening or lost their holds at the right time, but I didn't have time to question.

Lucifer flipped us both off, but we landed on the ground. On our paws. Apparently cats weren't the only beings that could land on their feet when it mattered.

I took a look around. We were doing some serious damage to the fallen angels and other lesser minions fighting. I noted Ishtrallum -- he was standing behind Merc and L.K., chanting. The same thing the others on our side were chanting. I looked carefully -- there were a lot of minor minions doing the same, hiding behind our side and lending a helping hand, claw, paw, talon, or vocal chord.

Jude had Jack and was doing some seriously nasty things to him. The totem of Adlet was hovering over them, twirling. I saw a dark mist drain from Jack into the totem. Adlet grew larger, Jack dropped like a stone. Jude was about to deliver what I knew was a deathblow when Jack disappeared.

I knew he wasn't destroyed. The Adversary was still fighting and grew a little larger as well, now that Jack was back within it.

But it didn't help. The totem of Adlet sailed over the Adversary's head, spinning even faster. Dirt Corps and a variety of beings were in full on attack and occupying all the Adversary's focus. A larger dark mist sailed from the Adversary to the totem. Adlet was now about the size of the Maltese Falcon, though nowhere near as pretty.

Lucifer grabbed me. "Adlet! Come drain her and break free!"

Chapter 73

The totem of Adlet moved towards us. "Adlet," I shouted. "Remember that deal? I never mentioned what you needed to do for me to give you the great idea."

The totem hovered in front of me. It was definitely malleable because it shrugged what I charitably thought were its shoulders.

"Here's the thing. The Adversary? It's vulnerable to werewolves. That's why you could drain them all so easily." I talked fast. Who knew how long I had? "Think about it. You could destroy the Adversary and take his place. You know how the Prince works. You kill it, you can take its place."

Adlet cocked his statue-head at me.

"Seriously, what are you waiting for? You don't need me to break those bonds. You need the real power that's sitting within the head of the Prince's Army of the Damned."

Adlet looked at Lucifer.

"No, not him. Really, he's like the Prime Minister or something. The Adversary's where your kind of power is. Besides, if you destroy the Adversary, the rest of the werewolves will have to follow you, right? We won't have a choice. So, why not hurry up and kill two minions with one bottle of holy water? Or whatever the evil undead equivalent is."

"I forbid you to do this," Lucifer said imperiously.

Adlet was big enough that I could see his eyes narrow. He also bared his fangs. Clearly, this wasn't the right thing to say to the being who the Prince's side had left locked up in a tiny statue for hundreds of years.

Adlet nodded to me and flew straight at the Adversary. Dear Old Dad saw him coming, reached out, and yanked the Mom and Susan combo to him. They melded into one being. I gagged. Adlet sailed into them and was also absorbed.

The internal struggle started immediately. The Adversary was jerking and flinging itself all over the place, flailing and hitting out at anything.

"Retreat!" Jude shouted, and our side disengaged, fast.

Which was a good thing, since the Adversary hit Abaddon and Apollyon at the same time. Now the Three A's were going at it, since the two fallen angels were still trying to follow Lucifer's orders and destroy Adlet.

"Let me go, withdraw the rest of your troops, or I'll give the order to attack again. Only this time, we'll focus all our energy on you."

Lucifer threw me to Jude, who caught me easily. "So be it. It's not over. We *will* meet again."

"Looking forward to it."

Lucifer's eyes locked with mine again. *Thank you.* Then he opened his mouth. Sound came out, but nothing like I'd ever heard before. It was loud, but not painful, and not in a language I understood.

The minions did, though. To a one they disengaged and flung themselves into the convergence chasm. Lucifer spread his wings and opened his arms. He tackled the Three A's and they all tumbled into the chasm as well.

Lightning flashed down from the sky, hitting all parts of the chasm. Our side scrambled to get away, though Jude and I didn't. The ground rumbled as the lightning struck and this time the sound was deafening.

I and all the other animal-based undeads covered our ears but it still hurt.

And then, just like that, the chasm was gone. Along with all the minions, other than those already living on the human plane.

"Well done." The voice came from the heavens. I'd only heard it a few times, in my mind, mostly.

Those beings who recognized the voice knelt or bowed their heads, and yanked those who didn't recognize the voice into similar positions. Jude and I didn't bow. We knew it wasn't expected.

"Thanks, Yahweh. To protect and serve and all that."

Lightning went around me, but it didn't hurt. It was Yahweh's way of hugging. He didn't manifest in a physical body as a rule. But that was fine. I thought of him as lightning anyway, even though he was much more than that.

Then the lighting was gone, just like the chasm and the minions, and we were left standing on a street in the bad part of town. Just us, all of Prosaic City's Night Beat cops, a handful of other humans, and hundreds of undeads.

"What's your cleanup plan?" I asked Jude.

"The usual. Memory wipes for the human side, as appropriate. Strong lectures for those who need to retain the memories. Subtle 'thanks for helping and here's the spell you were supposedly under' messages to the minor minions who like the status quo enough to have risked their unlives to help us tonight."

"Routine."

Jude kissed my forehead. "You were all anyone could have hoped for and more." He sighed. "They'll be back, you know. Either Adlet will win or the

Adversary will. Or they'll combine."

"They can't combine. That's why the plan worked, all the way along. Because I'm the Child of the Adversary and a werewolf, my kind is poison to the Adversary. That's why they want me with them in the Depths, to break that weakness. But it'll never happen."

He smiled. "I know." Jude looked over my shoulder. "He's not as jealous as your latest ex, but he's not as cool about it as he's going to pretend to be."

"Ralph?"

"Yeah, your mate."

"Am I making a mistake? I mean, undoubtedly not on the same level as the mistake with Jack, but still, I'd like some kind of clue. I think I deserve it."

Jude chuckled. "While I'm not a prophet, he does rub off the more you're around him."

"So Magdalena and Miriam said."

"I think, out of all your choices, this is the one most likely to be right for you. I wouldn't expect it to be all smooth sailing, mind you, but I give it very good odds for success."

"I'll take it." I leaned up and kissed his cheek. "Thank you."

"I won't be at the Sanctuary Center any more."

I shook my head. "You can be. You can let me know where you are, too. I can handle it now."

"You're sure?" He looked hopeful.

"Yeah, I am. It doesn't...hurt...to see you any more. Besides, Ken shouldn't be the only ex I go whining to when I have a relationship problem."

"Oh, good. Can't wait. Maybe I'll still hide." Jude grinned. "He's getting really impatient, and since patience is truly one of his virtues, I'd suggest you trot on over and reassure your mate that you're still a monogamous wolf, and that I'm not the being you're doing monogamy with any more."

I kissed his cheek again and did as he said. I wasn't stupid. Ralph was sitting on his haunches, and he had the worried and annoyed expression going. I figured I was going to see that a lot, too. "You okay?"

"Never better. I think we have another hospital overload situation, but I don't think anyone on our side dusted."

"Glad those prayers worked."

The rest of our team gathered around us. I saw a variety of undeads and some humans being loaded into the available vehicles, heading for the hospitals without a doubt.

"I saw Bobby and the others," Sexy Cindy said. "When all that lightning was going on. Because they tried to help us, they were forgiven. At least as far as I could tell."

Freddy nodded. "They'd been resurrected to fight, but you wouldn't have spotted them, Victoria, because they were focused on the humans. But they wouldn't attack, and in fact tried to keep the fallen angels away from their families."

"Even the hookers were protecting their pimp," Sexy Cindy said. "Go figure."

"Whatever works." My wrist-com went live. "Yes?"

"Agent Wolfe, how goes it?"

"I think we won, Count. At least for right now."

"Excellent news."

There was something in the tone of his voice. "And that's excellent news because?"

"Your police chief asked me to pass this along. We have a situation in Prosaic City's religious quarter. Seems small and human-created, but one never knows, does one?"

I took a deep breath. "All available personnel who aren't badly injured will head on out, Count."

"Not necessary. I understand the Reverend Johnson has donated his car to the Prosaic City undercover unit. I'd suggest just a small team until events are known."

"Gotcha. Over and out." I looked around. "Who's up for it?"

Sexy Cindy, Freddy, and Benny, still holding tight to the bag, all raised their hands. Ralph put up his paw.

"I think our vamps need some medical attention," Sexy Cindy shared.

"Amanda and Ken do, though they're waiting until they get all the humans taken care of," Maurice said, landing behind Freddy. "But I'm in perfect shape. Fallen angels, ha! They're not so tough."

"Good to know. You'll do aerial support?"

"Vicki, I live to serve."

I shrugged. "Then, let's roll out and do what we do best."

"Drive in a terrifying manner?" Benny asked.

"Avert the end of the worlds?" Ralph suggested.

"Bring order out of chaos?" Freddy offered.

Sexy Cindy snorted. "Dudes, we kick icky butt and take unpronounceable names."

I smiled. "Isn't she the greatest? And, she's right. Per the boss, duty shift's not over. So, let's head out to protect and serve.

Chapter 74

I was running, but not too fast. I didn't want to get away, after all. But not too slowly, either -- I didn't get to frolic in wolf form all that often that I wanted it to end immediately.

After a few more minutes Ralph landed on my back and we rolled around. There was a lot of foliage, and the smells were nice, all earthy and natural. We were playing, wrestling, nipping, that sort of thing. Nothing too rough, nothing remotely threatening.

He rolled me onto my stomach. "Give up?" he growled in my ear. The sexy-growl. The one that made me pant for all the right reasons.

"Mmmm, maybe." I stretched out and Ralph rolled onto his back next to me.

"It's nice to be here, instead of the park."

"Yeah. Benny really needs this place tenanted and I can't complain about the size of the yard or the privacy." I nuzzled his ear. "Think we can afford it?"

"Well, I'm never living where you had sex with Wagner, and I think we've removed all traces of Nero here. Besides, the Estates were affected badly by the last big attack. The Count thinks it might be a good idea for us to base out of here. So, yeah, I think we should see about affording it."

"The neighbors are nice. Not nosy."

"And we have a personal relationship with the Reverend, too." Ralph snorted. "Though I like Helen a lot more."

"Oh, Jeremiah Johnson's not so bad, once you get past the stuffed-shirtedness."

"Yeah. I have to admit that the itchy werewolf suit bothers me a lot more than Johnson does. And I hate having to spend at least half my existence now in human form."

"Not my fault I needed a new partner on Night Beat."

"Explain how you ended up with three of them, then?"

"Well, Sexy Cindy's a natural, and until Freddy shows that gray zombie look, he's invaluable. Covers us for the three different undeads rule even while on Prosaic City P.D. business. Besides, you're job is to protect me, so I don't know why you're complaining."

"The suit itches, remember?"

I nudged him. "But you're not wearing the suit now."

Ralph changed to human and grinned at me. "True enough."

I rolled onto my back as I went to human, too. "Not trying for puppies today?" I was almost disappointed. Ralph had introduced me to a lot of new things, including that there was nothing better than having sex with another werewolf, in all three forms.

He stroked my hair. "Not today. Well, not this moment. How about that?"

I was already familiar with his stamina. "Not a problem." The afternoon was young, after all, and we didn't go on duty again for another night. Ralph rolled on top of me and I sighed. "Does unlife get any better than this?"

Ralph kissed me. "Not that I've found in over four centuries."

"Makes eternity seem too short."

He grinned. "I'll do my best to make all parts of it last forever."

There was an old saying, and I'd found it was true -

- once you went werewolf, you never went back. I was a weregirl in love and it finally felt right. What the next nights would bring I didn't know, but I figured unlife was a journey, not a destination. And come what may, I was going to enjoy the ride -- in the donated S-Class, with my mate and our pack along for the wild ride. Unlife truly didn't get any better than this.

🐾 Acknowledgements 🐾

Many thanks, oohs and aahs to Lisa Dovichi, Mary Fiore, Cherry Weiner, and Veronica Cook for their usual above and beyond. Thanks also to Helen King, and authors Marsheila Rockwell, Kris Tualla, Amber Scott, and Jordan Summers, for tons of help and support.

Much love to my family for encouraging me to always go for it in everything I do, but especially in my writing career.

Last but not least, a big thanks to my fans around the world who've been asking (for quite a while now) when I'd tackle the undead. This one's for all of you.

🐾 About the Author 🐾

Gini Koch lives in Hell's Orientation Area (aka Phoenix, AZ), works her butt off (sadly, not literally) by day, and writes by night with the rest of the beautiful people. In addition to the Necropolis Enforcement Files series, she writes the fast, fresh and funny Alien/Katherine "Kitty" Katt series for DAW Books and the Martian Alliance Chronicles series for Musa Publishing.

As G.J. Koch she writes the Alexander Outland series for Night Shade Books. She also writes under a variety of other pen names (including Anita Ensal, Jemma Chase, A.E. Stanton, and J.C. Koch), listens to rock music 24/7, and is a proud comics geek-girl willing to discuss at any time why Wolverine is the best superhero ever (even if Deadpool does get all the best lines). She speaks frequently on what it takes to become a successful author and other aspects of writing and the publishing business.

Reach Gini

Her website - **www.ginikoch.com**
The Blah, Blah, Blah Blog -
http://ginikoch.blogspot.com/
Twitter - @GiniKoch
Facebook - facebook.com/Gini.Koch
Facebook Fan Page -
http://www.facebook.com/pages/Hairspray-and-Rock-n-Roll-Kicking-Evil-Alien-Butt-since-2010-GINI-KOCH/247377348018
Official Fan Site, Alien Collective Virtual HQ -
http://aliencollectivehq.com/

Made in the USA
Lexington, KY
25 September 2012